THE LAST TO KNOW

LISA M. CARETTI

This is a work of fiction. Names, characters, places, and incidents either are a product of the author's imagination or are used fictitiously, and any resemblance to actual persons, living or dead, business establishments, events, or locales is entirely coincidental.

ISBN: 1517528127
ISBN 13: 9781517528126
Library of Congress Control Number: 2015921168
CreateSpace Independent Publishing Platform
North Charleston, South Carolina

Acknowledgements

I wish to thank Richard J. Caretti II for his exceptional proofreading skills.

I would like to express my sincere gratitude to Judy Doughty, Heidi Johnson, and Tanya Nieschulz who provided support, read, edited and offered encouragement.

I beg forgiveness of all those who have been with me over the course of the years and whose names I have failed to mention.

In memory of Michael Christian Wells

"Men hate those to whom they have to lie."

-Victor Hugo, 1802-1885

Prologue

She was an ancient nuisance. An interfering old bat that they should have dealt with years ago.

Pleased with himself, he attempted to stuff her thick, wrinkled body into a battered trunk he was fortunate enough to have stumbled upon while exploring the forgotten treasures of her attic.

He considered his next step carefully as he wiped at the sweat that had begun to drip freely from his brow onto his shirt sleeve and let out an exasperated sigh.

Perhaps if he would have thought this out a little further in advance he might have devised a more suitable plan, but whatever. The deed was done. He killed her and he would simply have to deal with it. The others will thank him.

At least now, for once, he could reminisce through his old stomping grounds at his leisure and not have to worry about her tiresome meddling and unending interfering.

The peace and quiet would be a welcomed luxury.

He sucked in an oppressive, dusty hot breath and held it in for a moment in appreciation before slowly lowering his eyes back down to the blob at his feet.

She was gone but still within the window of passing that he actually considered playing the game with her.

For old times' sake he told himself.

But she was old and nasty with thick yellow toenails, so in the end decided against it. He had to use his time wisely plus it would hardly be the same without the others.

He tapped his foot loudly on the attic's bare wooden planks while he plotted. Her oversized remains would have to fit in that chest one way or another, even if things got a little messy.

He wondered how much time would pass before anyone would even notice she was missing.

"The wicked are always surprised to find that the good can be clever."

-Luc de Clapiers de Vauvenargues, 1715-1794

Chapter 1

The very first thought that occurred to Bretta Berryman as she stepped through the weathered front door of the decaying old manor was how much her husband would hate a place like this. The second consideration that pulsated to her brain was how completely happy that made her. Both reflections brought a smile to her lovely face.

Well, he was the one who insisted that they pack up everything they own and leave their friends, family, and all that they held dear behind. He certainly has had his way enough over the years Bretta thought bitterly to herself as she forced herself to tune back into the real estate agent's canned enthusiastic speech.

Wanda Bee, Chester's top selling real estate agent, or so proclaimed the Chester Realty website anyway, was now leading her out of the massive parlor towards the back of the house to view the kitchen, her high heels clicking noisily on the aged and scarred wooden floors. The stagnant air of a house that has been closed up and empty far too long overcame them as Bretta looked wistfully at the tall dining room windows and wondered why in the world the agent had not thought to open at least one of them in preparation for the showing.

When they at last reached their destination, Wanda moved to the side so her client could take a good, long look.

The linoleum was beyond worn out, missing in some spots and what little was left was darn right ugly. The walls, which had once been painted an awful shade of sickly green, were now peeling and discolored from years of cooking.

The cabinets might have at one time been attractive. They appeared to be of decent quality and were in noticeable need of a paint job, new hardware, and to have all the critters living inside relocated. Two of the cupboards on either side of the sink hung at an awkward angle, giving the illusion they were suspended in space.

As it turned out, the kitchen was the nicest room.

The house was indeed a "real fixer- upper," just as Wanda Bee had promised over the phone. She requested that the agent wait back while she gave herself a tour of the rest of the house and found it to be old, filthy, and essentially falling apart.

Bretta finished her assessment with the upstairs floor and went in search of Wanda Bee to inform her she was ready to leave. She found the plump, bee-hive haired agent in the dining room studying her notes and punching in numbers on a calculator which, if she had to guess, would contain the commission on one of the houses Ms. Bee had told her about. Both houses, she was positive were a hundred times nicer than this archaic eyesore and most likely five times the price. She lifted her head to offer Bretta a knowing smile as she wandered into the room.

"Who lived here last?" Bretta inquired, curious now after moving through each gloomy, vacant room. This had once been someone's home. A family resided here no doubt, perhaps filling it with many children, laughter, pets, and big Sunday dinners.

"Old lady Barrett was the last person to live here, and then some family before that. It's a real shame it sat unoccupied, well not counting the mice and bats of course, for all these years. It's probably haunted. Have you seen enough dear?" With an air of confidence, she smiled and began to shove her papers and planner into her tattered briefcase.

"Yes, I have." Bretta took in a deep, gratifying breath and choked slightly on flying dust mites. The house was so utterly different than anything she had ever lived in and yet she was strangely fascinated with it. With one more glance around the tired old room, she made her decision.

"I'll take it."

Chapter 2

It took a full minute for her words to register in Wanda Bee's brain and when it did, she witnessed the agent's face change from a look of disbelief to pure panic.

Her lower jaw dropped down and she allowed it to hang open for several seconds before noisily clamping it back together.

"Dear, I like you so I'm going to be honest with you." She lowered her voice as if someone might be hiding in the closet and catch her telling the truth. "This rambling old Victorian is really nothing more than a bunch of loose boards that rattle when the wind blows. Come winter, the entire house will most likely collapse. There are roofing and electrical problems to boot. Do yourself a big favor and keep looking."

"I appreciate the warning, but I'll take it just the same."

"Well, I am sure you will want to have your husband come take a look at Huddelstone before you make your final decision dear."

Bretta gave her a questioning look. "Huddelstone?" She had never heard the irritating agent refer to the old house by a name before.

"The Huddelstones were the original owners of the house. The mansion was once considered rather grand in its day. Should we set up an appointment now for your husband to come and see it? I could call him."

Bretta shrugged her shoulders. "He can certainly come and see it if he would like." Good luck trying to get a hold of him she thought somewhat despondently. She had tried calling her husband several times yesterday morning to say that his family arrived safe and sound, but could only reach his voicemail.

Tiny bubbles of excitement were unexpectedly erupting in her belly, catching her off guard. How long has it been since she has felt anything other than anger or anxiety?

Plans were rapidly starting to take shape in her creative mind. The house needed work but it was not about to blow away with the next big gust of wind like her agent had forewarned. She and the kids could continue to stay in the motor home while their new house was being renovated. It would be an adventure for them all. They could park it right in the backyard where they would be able to observe the progress and perhaps even help. After all, it wouldn't be like they were living in a pop up tent. Who would ever think that beast of a vehicle she had been so dead set against John buying would turn out to be such a handy haven?

Bretta was eager to leave and get back to the girls. She started making her way to Wanda's car, hopeful the agent would take the hint and follow her.

Exasperated, the agent tried a different approach. "Mrs. Berryman, I think you should at least look at the other two listings. Really, they are spectacular showpieces that are in move- in condition." She lowered her voice for effect while yanking at her waistband. "And, they are much better suited for a woman of your social standing in the community."

"No, thank you." Bretta stated firmly as she proceeded to open the passenger side door. "I'm looking forward to this project; it's exactly what I need."

She turned her head to gaze out at the small town called Chester that she was suddenly looking forward to calling home. "I've had the stunning showpiece, now I am ready for something different."

A few minutes later, Wanda stopped the car in front of a newer, large red-brick colonial with a circular driveway and professionally manicured landscaping. It looked identical to all the other gorgeous homes on the block with the only difference being a large for sale sign bearing Wanda Bee's cheesy picture stuck in the middle of the lawn.

"Well, since we were in the neighborhood, I thought you might want to take a peek at one of the other homes for sale." The agent dropped her voice again as she took another tug at her waistband. "You know dear, your husband may not be as passionate about Huddelstone as you are."

"Thank you for the tour Ms. Bee, however I do need to get back to the girls now. I have numerous arrangements to make and I am eager to get started."

Wanda attempted to stifle a frustrated sigh. "Well then, let me know when your husband arrives in town. After he sees the house, I'll get the papers ready for him to sign."

Bretta turned and gave Wanda Bee her full attention. The look in her eye made Wanda sit a bit straighter. "Please have the papers ready by tomorrow morning Ms. Bee. *I* am your client and the only one you need to be concerned with."

"Well in fact, both husband and wife will need to have their signatures on the sale papers. The house will belong to the both of you."

"The house will be in my name only. It is my money, my house." She surprised herself with that decision, but as soon as she said the words she knew it felt right. It probably wasn't wise to have yelled it though. She did not need her personal business aired out like the laundry for the entire town of Chester to see or make an enemy before she even had a chance to make a friend. She heard how small towns were. But she needed the agent to understand who was in charge. She gave wide eyed Wanda a sweet smile and tried to sound cheerful. "What time can I expect you tomorrow?" She asked as they pulled up in front of their campsite.

She was eager to show her daughters Huddelstone. She liked calling the old house on the hill by its name and intended to learn more about the family that once made it their home. The town library was sure to have something of interest and she looked forward to stopping in while the house was being renovated.

It had never entered her mind to make Huddelstone exclusively her own, but once the agent had indicated John's permission was needed, something in her snapped. She knew she wanted to do this by herself, even though there would be hell to pay when he found out.

Bretta quickly said her good-byes, slammed the car door shut, and took off running over to the girls. She did not want to risk Wanda giving her biased opinion. Sure the house was unquestionably not what they were used to. But they were not spoiled, pampered little girls. Bretta had seen to that.

Tears pooled in the corner of her eyes and clouded her vision as she watched her daughters play. Iris and Ivy were happy. It made her sad to realize just how long it has been since the girls were this carefree.

Even though she was against the move at first, she could indisputably see now it was the best thing for all of them. Amazingly, it had not been as difficult as she thought it would be to use their summer vacation to uproot the girls from their school, friends, childhood home, and relatives.

Iris and Ivy had wanted to move. After all that ugly scandal, who could blame them?

Bretta had been raised on the motto to face your problems, not run from them. But she was not about to make the children pay for the sins of their parents. Besides, she wasn't in truth running away from all of her troubles.

Part of the dilemma would be joining them in about a month. But at least she had four weeks and a plan.

Chapter 3

It was that stagnant time of early dawn where nothing had yet begun to stir. The birds had not yet started their morning song nor had the sun found its way to light the sky.

A masculine voice bellowed abruptly out of the darkness, jarring Bretta from her slumber and was quickly followed by loud pounding and men shouting.

The workers were back, early and punctual as promised.

She leaped out of bed and quickly threw on a pair of well-worn jean shorts and her favorite "*Life is good*" tee shirt that for some reason always pissed John off when he saw her in it.

The edges of her mouth formed a small smile as she tried to recall the last time she had been this enthusiastic about anything. To top it off, she felt marvelous. After the last couple of years of hell, that in itself was amazing.

Each morning she would eagerly awake to start laboring on her new home and happily collapse in bed with exhaustion at night. Somewhere in between those hours, she would squeeze in laundry, cleaning, and cooking. Suddenly she had the energy for everything she wanted to accomplish and the confusion, nausea, and headaches that had plagued her for the past two years simply vanished.

They would stop and greet their new neighbors or introduce themselves to those they had not yet met. Almost daily they would visit with the Muncy sisters; two unconventional but delightful ladies that lived across the street and whose spectacular gardens Bretta greatly admired.

They were finding their new town to be warm and welcoming.

She had arrived prepared to hate the small town of Chester simply because John had suggested they move here. In fact, he was pretty insistent on it. Even though he himself had never been to this exact town, he was positive this would be the ideal spot for his family to live.

The plan had been for Bretta and the girls to arrive in Chester first to scope out the various houses for sale and get a feel for the town.

But the more Bretta saw of this charming little town, the more puzzled she became.

This was the exact last place on earth she would think John would want to live. Small towns were not exactly his idea of fun. He was more of a big city, out on the town kind of guy. She understood when he said he wanted to get away from all the publicity and his former colleagues, but if that were true, what was taking him so long to get here?

She had called John the first night Wanda had given her the tour and told him she had found the perfect house that both she and the girls loved and causally mentioned it needed a little remodeling. She neglected to mention that they were practically rebuilding a home that had been scheduled for demolition in the upcoming year.

Well, she did not feel too bad about that. There had been a few things her husband had failed to mention to her in the past few years as well.

Bretta sprinted up the back door steps leading into the kitchen. It still looked very much the same as it had that first day she saw it with Wanda Bee, but her imagination had already begun to transform the dismal room into the kitchen of her dreams. This morning she brought with her a pencil and paper and rapidly began to jot down ideas as well as a list of appliances she wanted. She, along with the entire crew, had spent the week clearing out the house. All the treasures that she discovered and wanted to have cleaned and repaired were relocated to the barn. Anything remaining went into a large rented dumpster out in the front yard. It did not feel right, sorting and discarding the contents that came with the house, even if the house now belonged to her. Wanda Bee had confirmed that no one wanted this old junk and she should just burn it all in a giant bonfire out back, but she could not help but be mindful of the fact that a family once lived here so she tried to preserve what she could.

A new roof was added, the walls were patched and repaired, and everything was brought up to code with the electricity and the gas to make it livable. Now they were taking it room by room, starting first with the kitchen and bedrooms.

The plumbing had several major issues, but that was one of the specialties of Cal Denham whom she was assured could tackle any problem she had. He owned Denham's Plumbing and had spent an entire two weeks at the house wrestling with her old pipes. He promised he would come on back to work in the kitchen when they were ready for him.

Since all her other recommendations had been right on, she went to Wanda again for the names of a couple of companies who did this type of renovating work. The agent simply said "Spencer's. He's the best and anyone worth their salt will be already working for him."

The owner of the company himself, Marc Spencer, agreed to meet her at the house. He said he knew the house all right and admitted he was more than surprised to hear someone had actually purchased it. He had a deep, masculine voice and Bretta had formed a picture in her head of him having a large pot belly with a chewed up cigar dangling out of the corner of his mouth.

When Marc Spencer stepped out of his green pickup truck she was unsure at first who he was. But as soon as he spoke, she immediately recognized the distinctive sound.

His voice was smooth and smoky and could easy have belonged to a radio personality. Actually, with his good looks, more like a movie star. He was tall with big shoulders, well defined muscles and exceedingly handsome. The brilliance of the morning's sun shone on him like a spot light, picking up the paler shades of summer blonde in his hair and as he moved closer, she took note of his startling blue eyes which quickly reminded her of the ocean.

"And what are you so happy about this morning?" That same voice interrupted her thoughts and returned her to the present. She snapped her head up from her sketches, slightly flustered but still smiling.

"I'm just excited to get started on the kitchen." It was a true statement, even though he caught her daydreaming like a schoolgirl. Her face felt hot and she was sure her cheeks where crimson. But she wasn't lying; she was full of enthusiasm to start her new project. Late last night she went online and began her research on the latest state of the art appliances that she wanted to fill her kitchen. She spent two hours alone simply on the breath taking Garland six burner gas range with a raised griddle and broiler that she will soon be calling her own.

She glanced down at her notepad, finished writing something and then handed it to him. "I was thinking of something like this. I have some pictures I pulled from Pinterest as well that we could pull some concepts from."

Marc appeared to study the drawings carefully. "Ok. We can do this." He broke his gaze away and fixed it on the enclosed back porch off the back of the house. "I think we should tear down that inside wall and make this all one big room. That would extend the kitchen out another twelve feet. It could be the dining area. With all those windows, you'd have a nice view of the yard."

She loved the idea and dashed over to the porch to look out at her backyard. She would plant a magnificent herb garden and tons of flowers that would all be in view while dining. Her mind raced with one creative idea after another and she went back to her notebook to jot them down before she forgot any of them.

"I take it you like the suggestion?" He was grinning, obviously enjoying her eagerness.

"I love it!" She almost went over to hug him, but she did not want to scare away the only worker in town. She was not sure if he was married or not. For some reason, they talked about numerous things, but the topic of spouses for either one never came up. He knew of course that she had two daughters as they were in and out all day. He might have heard in town that she had a husband that would be moving here soon. Wanda Bee looked like the type to tell all she knew and then some.

Just thinking of John made her stomach tie up in little nauseating knots. He called last night and told her it would be at least another month before he could join them. She was so happy with the news; she almost did a back flip across the lawn. She was not ready to deal with him yet.

Aware that Marc was watching her face, she tried to look happy again.

"Well, I am going to take out the cabinets today and put them in the barn. Did you want to paint them and pick out the new hardware?"

The offer delighted her. "Yes, I do! I'll have the girls help me. I've already chosen the colors I want to use so I will run out and pick up the paint and the other supplies I need. But first I am going to make the girls breakfast. Did you eat?"

He looked taken aback. "I had coffee."

"How about some pancakes?" She had promised the girls blueberry pancakes for breakfast and was simply pleased they both for once agreed on the same thing.

"Sure, that would be great. Hey, you know it's not too late for you to get new cabinets in here. Save you a lot of work."

She was quick to respond. "No. I'm looking forward to doing this project. Plus, the entire kitchen will be redone. It's important to me to keep something from the original owners so I can feel they are still a part of this house. I'm not a spoiled city girl afraid of a little hard work you know." She stuck her hands on her hips and waited for his reply, as if he might challenge her.

She had marched up mere inches to the face she was growing so comfortable with. He had his own particular scent; outdoor fresh and crisp-clean, that she had come to know and enjoy. His fragrance, like the man himself was now becoming an important, integral part of her new home.

"No, I never thought you were Bretta. I'll take them down now for you." He looked like he wanted to say something else, but offered a weak smile instead.

Happy she got her way, she glowed. "Thank you! I'll run and start breakfast then."

"Hey before you go, I'm having my buddy Lou stop on over to look at that fireplace in the parlor. I assume you want all the fireplaces in working order?"

"You mean the ones in the dining room and the one in the reception hall?"

Marc glanced up from the notes he had been jotting down. "Yeah, those and I'm pretty sure you have one in just about every bedroom as well."

"What?" She screeched in delight and inspected the wall in front of her for a fireplace. She has been busy true, but she would have remembered seeing fireplaces in every room. She adored fireplaces.

"Lou can tell you for sure, but most likely someone had them covered up. I know there is one for sure in your bedroom."

"Oh, I've always wanted a fireplace in my bedroom!" She could already picture herself snuggled up in a rocking chair on a cold winter's night, reading a book. Maybe she would learn to knit.

"Ok, well before you get too excited, you should know there are some major issues with the parlor fireplace. First of all, it's sinking into the floor below. The marble mantle is cracked in spots and when I went to go clean it out a bit to see what we're dealing with, the entire firebox floor crashed to basement."

"But the fireplace is the focal point of that room!" She practically bought the house because of that fireplace.

"Don't panic; let's just wait for Lou to get out here and take a look. He does this thing for a living. "

"All right then…I'll go and get breakfast started. Oh, one other thing I thought of last night when I was leafing through some magazines. Can we turn bedroom number four into a second floor laundry room? I would like it to include a work space for folding and sorting, plenty of cabinets for storage and a recessed ironing board that we can pull down when needed and then simply fold back up when we are finished. "

"Well…yeah, we can do that. We still have the walls open in the living room directly below that room, so we can add the gas line, hot and cold water lines and drainage lines." He said more to himself as he was writing something down on his clipboard and then glanced back up at her. "Do you think you will be making any more improvements? He asked cautiously.

"Maybe I should do another walk through." She said as she ran out of the room and called out over her shoulder. "I will right after breakfast."

Marc nodded. "I think that's a good idea."

Marc began the process of taking the cabinets off the walls and moving them out to the barn. He had finished up with the last one when he heard the slightest of sound behind him.

"Mr. Spencer?" He turned to see a young girl with straight, long blonde hair and inquisitive green eyes watching him. "Are you supposed to be getting rid of mom's cupboards?"

He grinned down at the petite inspector standing in front of him, her arms crossed tightly over her chest. "Yes, Ivy. I moved them to the barn where your mom is going to fix them up. Then I promise to put them back." He was able to keep the girls names straight right from the beginning because Ivy had blonde hair and Iris had black. So he just thought of Ivory for Ivy. Both had been in and out of the house since he started working here, but Iris soon lost interest and became more concerned with her new friends down the street. Ivy however, came by daily to pepper him with questions.

She gave him a look like he was feeding her a line. "Well, mom said to come and eat, but you better wash your hands first."

He held up his dirty hands and faked surprise. "These aren't too bad; I can wait at least 'til supper."

Ivy put her hands on her hips and tapped her foot.

"Okay, Okay, I'll clean up now and be right out."

When he reached the backyard he saw a picnic table straight out of a Better Homes and Gardens magazine. It was tastefully set with a red and white checkered tablecloth and matching napkins, a towering fresh fruit bowl as the centerpiece and a steaming basket of muffins.

Bretta was stepping out of the motor home with a platter of sausage and pancakes and smiled brightly when she saw him.

"Hey Marc, hope you're hungry. Have a seat."

"Wow, this sure beats Dolly's." Or anything his girlfriend Carol could come up with even if her mother and both her sisters pitched in to help.

"Mom, did you know Mr. Spencer took out all your cupboards from the kitchen and stashed them in the barn?" Ivy quizzed.

Iris rolled her eyes and Bretta shook her head and sighed. Both accustomed to Ivy's reporting practice they paid her no attention.

"If you're going to be telling on me all the time Ivy, maybe you should call me Marc. It would make things easier."

She studied him for a brief moment and then shook her head. "I'll call you Mr. Marc." She took her seat across from Iris and began to fill her plate.

Marc laughed, took a seat and reached for a muffin. It smelled like cinnamon and was loaded with raisins and walnuts. Bretta set a cup of steaming coffee in front of him as he took a bite of what he would swear was the best tasting muffin he had ever had in his life.

Something was really wrong here.

The kids were great. Bretta was an intelligent, beautiful woman and it would appear she really knows her way around a kitchen. So what in the hell was taking her husband so long to get here?

Iris broke some kind of speed eating record and announced she was off to her new best friend Molly's house down the street. Ivy took a little longer as she thoroughly examined each and every morsel, drilling her mother on freshness and expiration dates and food preparation. Once the meal finally passed inspection, she finished and left to visit Molly's younger sister, Hannah.

He observed Bretta taking it all in stride. She had a pleasant relationship with her daughters and truly seemed to enjoy them, but at times he caught a glimpse of guarded sadness and he wondered what the true story was.

"You know Marc, there was another idea I had for the house. I was going to wait until the rest of the house was completed, but it wouldn't hurt to share my plans for the attic with you now." She picked up her sketch pad from the bench next to her and laid it on the table in front of him.

"The attic?" The coffee cup that was half way up to his mouth went back down so fast, dark brown liquid splashed out over the rim.

"Yes. I want to make it a studio so I can set up shop here and get back to work." She had only toyed with the idea last night, jotting down ideas and sketches until she finally got sleepy. But the more she thought about it while flipping pancakes this morning, the more she liked the idea.

Marc was dumbstruck. She never mentioned anything about working before or the attic.

"A studio for what?"

"I'm a fashion designer. I freelance for different labels, but mostly I design for my mother's stores. I'll be able to work from here and send them my designs." She put it in the simplest terms while he continued to study her sketches.

He nodded his head slightly then handed her back her drawings. "Let me think on this a day or two. I need to get up there first and take a look around. And Bretta, if you're going to be making any other changes or additions to the house, now would be a good time to tell me."

"I believe I will stop with the attic." She laughed and began clearing the table as Marc simply shook his head and stood up, obviously intending to help. "Oh no, I'd rather have you building my new kitchen than washing dishes."

"All right then, I'll get back to work. The painter will finish early this morning. You can start moving your things in the bedrooms later today. I'll have the guys move any of the heavy stuff for you."

"Weeeel! Doesn't this look cozy?" A grating noise boomed loudly from the rear of the RV.

Marc ignored the uninvited guest, picked back up his coffee and drained it in one steady gulp before replying. "Good morning, Ms. Bee. What brings you out of your hive so early in the morning?"

She patted her hair and then made a show of checking her watch. "Hello, Marc. Taking a break already? Good morning, Mrs. Berryman. I see Mr. Berryman still hasn't been able to join his family. Poor man, working so hard." Her eyes traveled around the table and grew wide when they landed on the basket of muffins. "My, don't those look yummy?"

"Good morning, Ms. Bee. Please, help yourself." Bretta picked up the basket and dropped it in front of the pesky agent as she continued to clear the table.

"Well if you'll excuse me ladies, I need to get back to work. Thanks for the pancakes Mrs. Berryman." He took off in a slow sprint as Bretta escaped into the RV with a load of dirty dishes. She looked longingly over at the driver's seat, tempted to jump behind the wheel and drive off, leaving Wanda behind at the picnic table in a cloud of dust. When she came back out to collect more dishes, she found Wanda with a muffin filled mouth and two eyebrows elevated so high, they connected at the center. She looked like a silly cartoon character. Upon seeing Bretta return, she quickly borrowed a coffee cup to wash down her muffin so she could talk.

"It looks like you and Marc are getting along rather well." She kept her eyebrows raised as she spoke and Bretta wondered how long she was physically capable of holding them in that position.

"We are. Thank you for referring him to me. He and his men are excellent workers and I am incredibly pleased." She continued clearing the table as swiftly as possible so she could get to the hardware store and at least get a start on the cabinets. She also needed to get away from Wanda; the woman was giving her a nervous twitch. She excused herself as she made another trip inside and went to the sink to wash whatever dishes were not disposable. Wanda's galling voice unexpectedly spoke directly in her left ear, causing her to yelp in surprise.

"This is some fancy camper!" Wanda dragged out the word *some* as if she were about to burst into song while she gave herself a tour, poking her head in every door and cabinet she could find including the refrigerator. "I never knew the walls could slide in and out on these things! It certainly does give you some space. If I were you, I would forget about that dilapidated old house and live here."

Here we go again. "Well, it was good to see you again Ms. Bee." The lie rolled easily off her tongue. "I'd like to visit longer, but I have a few errands I need to do."

Wanda continued on as if she had not spoken. "I'm just surprised at all the sudden interest in Huddelstone. For years, no one ever gave it a second thought. Now this week alone I've received two phone enquiries and an email."

Bretta hesitated as she reached for her keys. "Someone else was interested in buying it?" If Wanda Bee had thought *anyone* would buy Huddelstone, she would have tripled the price. Something wasn't right.

"They wanted information on the house, yes." She took her still raised eyebrows and narrowed them skillfully to one accusing point. "But I'd say they were much more interested in you."

Chapter 4

In all honesty, Marc would have enjoyed staying for a little while longer and having another cup of coffee with Bretta, but he knew better than to sit and play chit-chat with the county's most notorious busy body.

Since Wanda Bee essentially had no life of her own, she made it her mission to ruin everyone else's. The miserable bitch could craft a story out of dust and he had no intention of getting wrapped up in one of her tales again. If you lived in or around Chester, starring as one of the lead characters in one of Wanda's cunning work of fiction was just like death.

It was something everyone got to take a turn at eventually.

He did not care much what Wanda Bee broadcasted about him but she would without a doubt take down a couple of innocent bystanders with her. He hated all the drama it created and all the time and energy it would waste. He was one of the fortunate people that truly enjoyed his job and he worked hard at it.

His big, powerful hands pried away the last remaining shelf in the kitchen while he contemplated what he would do with the back porch.

He just happened to be full of ideas for the Berryman's new home because the reality of the situation was that Marc's eye had been on Huddelstone for as long back as he could remember. He had mentally planned the renovations and repairs that would transform the crumbling old mansion into a masterpiece. Ideas and diagrams were jotted down on scrap paper and scattered all throughout his den. Sketches, which included plans to turn the barn into *his* office and work space, plastered the walls of his office. It was one of those projects he was going to take on once he finished the work on his own house and had a little spare time.

His entire staff and crew knew Huddelstone had been his dream which he was sure was the reason why no one was questioning why he was doing most of the work himself and overseeing every detail.

He never considered what he would do with the all that space in the attic. Probably nothing. The house was big enough for him and of course the barn was to be his dream workshop. He groaned out loud as he grasped precisely how much he would miss that aspiration.

He recalled how stunned he was when Bretta first had called and said she was the new owner of Huddelstone. Hell, he hadn't even known the place was on the market or he would have bought it himself. He was going along at his own pace and figured he had all the time in the world because no one in their right mind would want it.

At first he wasn't even sure that he could renovate the old house that he had considered his own for as long as he could remember so he agreed to meet Bretta under the pretense of telling her the place was an unsafe dump that ought to be demolished. But after meeting her, he realized she understood all that but wanted the house anyway, apparently as badly as he did. So, he decided then to restore Huddelstone as if it was his own.

He recalled envisioning her to be a frumpy farm girl who moved from one small bad town to the next for some reason. But when he stepped out of his truck that first day and he saw Bretta Berryman standing on the porch, he felt a stern kick in the gut. *Whoa* was the only lucid thought his brain could muster up.

She was no farm girl that was for sure. Standing before him barefoot in her designer blue jeans and snug fitting t-shirt it was obvious; city gals were different. They talked different and even smelled different and he decided right then and there, against his better judgment to take on this project even though he knew his heart would surely take a walloping.

Then there was this annoying curiosity that he found hard to own up to. This fine smelling oddity would now be living and breathing within the walls of his treasure and he accepted that he had to be there to see it firsthand.

Chapter 5

The quiet solitude of the old barn allowed Bretta to work alone and uninterrupted for hours at a time. Ivy and Iris were still out having fun with their friends, allowing her a decent stretch of time to scrape and sand the cabinets and to reflect. She had changed her mind about asking her daughters to help. There were plenty of other tasks she and the girls could do together; today she did not feel the need for company.

The barn reminded her despondently of her studio in New York. The one that, along with her life, she gave up before moving here. Of course it was not that the barn looked or smelled anything like her old work space. It was the other similarities that gave her a bittersweet smile. The treasured solitude. The busy work with your hands while your mind traveled far away or worked out the day's existing problem.

Today, she could not help but to wonder who had been asking Wanda Bee about her. She lightly traced the scar on her forehead as she did so often when she was contemplating a difficult matter. Most likely a reporter had tracked her down. Her dream had been to simply blend in with the other towns people if that was possible and prayed that the media would someday lose interest in her. Eventually she knew that they would. Some other idiot was bound to screw up more than her husband but until then, she did not think she could tolerate being chased around again or her children spied upon.

Scraping off layers of paint that had been piled on over the decades wasn't nearly as much fun as she imagined it would be and she had the weirdest sensation that she was being watched. Too much alone time especially in an old barn was bound to do funny things to your imagination. It did not take long before her back and shoulders began to scream in objection. She tossed the putty knife down on the work table and stretched her arms up high over her head and then bent over in a forward fold.

She felt whole and happy and laughed out loud when she got a glimpse of her fingernails. Once perfectly and professionally polished, they were now ragged and torn and truly she could care less. The one luxury she genuinely did miss though was her bathtub. Her body was begging for a good, long soak once her bathroom was completed and she was extremely glad she splurged on the large Jacuzzi style tub.

She was bent at the waist, fingertips touching her toes and her backside facing the barn door when someone spoke behind her.

"That looks interesting. Is that one of those yoga exercises?"

Bretta yelped in surprise and nearly fell over trying to straighten up too fast. It was exasperating the way she never seemed to hear him approach. "Marc! You scared the daylights out of me."

"Sorry about that." Though he looked anything but and did his best to hide a grin.

Marc was still standing in the door with an odd look on his face. He was probably getting tired as well. "I was going to go in the RV and make some lemonade. I'll bring you out some in a few minutes."

"Thanks that would be nice. Hey, Cal is working on your bathroom right now and should be finishing up by tonight."

This time she scared him when she shrieked in delight. "I can't tell you how I have been fantasizing about that tub! Will it be in working order by tonight?" God, she hoped so. Frantically she tried to recall what box her bubble bath was in.

Marc enjoyed her enthusiasm. "I'm not positive, so don't go hunting for your rubber ducky just yet."

She had to laugh because he was not that far off from the truth. "Ok, I'll run and make us some lemonade." She was out the barn door when Marc called her back.

"Hey, wait a sec." He pulled something out of his t-shirt pocket and handed it over. "One of my men found this old photo when we were working on the parlor. I thought you might like to have it."

Two young boys, about eight or nine sat on the porch steps of Huddelstone and smiled brightly for the camera. It looked to have been taken in the early sixties and Bretta was delighted to have a piece of the homes history.

"I would love to have any other pictures or really anything that you stumble upon that belonged to the former owners." She studied the photo a little longer. "Maybe these are brothers that used to live here."

"Well, I am pretty sure that is Tony Barratt on the right. I don't recognize the other boy. I know Tony was an only child, so the other boy could be a friend or someone vacationing for the summer."

Bretta was drawn to the images for a reason she could not explain. The unidentified boy seemed to be looking straight at her, making her feel uneasy. Although he was smiling, there was something discontented and ominous about the child. There was also something incredibly familiar about him.

"What's wrong?"

She spoke without looking up. "The boy on the left...I believe I know that face."

Chapter 6

The music was playing again.

Soft, exquisite notes that did their best to appease and entertain had begun floating through the air not long after she took over ownership of the old manor and today they were performing another concert solely for her.

At first the music frightened her and she spent a great deal of time trying to trace its source, silently praying it was not coming from her once troubled mind.

She had searched everywhere for a radio, speakers, wires or even a music box, anything that would offer an explanation, but soon it became apparent that the unusual but familiar harmony played only for her.

Wisely she avoided mentioning her private recitals to anyone else. No one needed to know she was having a bit of trouble again. Today the sound rang out gently but clearly as she sat in her bedroom and thought about the little boy in the picture.

It might have been a good idea to have left Marc with a little more of an explanation other than blurting out she recognized the little boy's face and then bolting out of the barn.

Sane people did not do that.

Maybe she could smooth things over later by saying he resembled a boy she once knew that use to torture her which was not that far off from the truth.

But the unfortunate fact was she did know that face. The question was, what in the hell was it doing in an old photograph in her new dream house?

⅄

Wanda Bee was a first rate busy body. Not only was she a gifted eaves-dropper, but a crafty, greedy and often underestimated, self-proclaimed pest.

She had witnessed Bretta coming out of the library across the street for the second time that week and had to wonder what the devil that woman was up to. No one could be *that* interested in the history on that run down piece of crap for God's sake, she thought to herself. Especially when there still had to be so much work left to do to make it even fit for human habitation. She simply showed her that rotten house to send her high- tailing it to the only other two prime pieces of real estate available in Chester. It was a solid plan that had always worked before. Who in their right mind would want to live in that rat infested eye-sore?

Besides, it didn't matter how much research the little nitwit did, she would never uncover what had once existed within the walls of Huddelstone. Few knew its malicious and immoral secrets and those that did, would never tell.

This woman had her own skeletons and Wanda was determined to reveal them.

It was the reporter in her and she simply could not stop herself. It was in fact her true calling and she often felt like an imposter at times by living the life of a real estate agent.

Snooping, digging and then spilling her guts was the job she was born to do and this business of selling houses was suffocating and restraining her almost as much as the stupid contraption she wore around her middle.

However, in a small town like Chester it did not pay the bills and quite frankly, it was boring. Like her Aunt had replied after first hearing of Wanda's career choice, being a reporter in a hick town like Chester was like being the world's tallest midget. It simply wasn't that big a deal.

Sure she could supplement her reporter's income by uncovering tiny bits of scandal here and there for which people would begrudgingly pay her not to repeat, but that was hardly enough to generate a living. She knew to get to the big bucks she would have to move to the city which she bitterly thought was impossible.

She was tied to Chester forever.

This time Wanda had spotted Bretta while driving down Main Street and could wait no longer. She pulled over, threw the car in park and yanked her laptop off the passenger seat. Her fingers began their magic, flying across the keyboard as she happily dragged up all the dirt she could find on their new resident.

For each new client, it was her strict protocol to first open a file and download every article and scrap of information she could find and then second, Google them to death and anyone connected to them. Huddelstone sold so fast though, she never needed to look past the first clipping.

Or so she had thought.

⅄

By the time Bretta made her way back home, her body was begging for a hot bath and a handful of Advil. Muscles that she was not aware existed either ached or grumbled loudly in some way from her morning's work in the barn and then later in the day pouring over books in the library. Silently she said a little prayer that Cal and his people had worked their plumbing magic today but as she turned her car onto Hollyhock Lane she felt her spirits fizzle.

Her expensive, shiny-new special order Jacuzzi tub was parked out on the front lawn instead of her new bathroom.

She climbed out of the car and went over to have a better look at the Victorian Claw foot tub with Whirlpool Jets she had custom ordered. It was simply gorgeous but as tempting as it was to go ahead and fill it out here on the front yard with hot water and jump in, she appreciated that it wouldn't make such a great impression with her new neighbors.

Emotionally drained, she felt the stress of the past year catching up to her and she knew that a major source of her anxiety was one way or another related to her spouse.

She had allowed herself to get talked into giving him another chance for the sake of the children but she was beginning to suspect even they could see right through him.

Only this morning she had promised her mother she would take better care of herself after she gently reminded her about how ill she had been last year. Even though they had often worked side by side together in the city, they had longer, more meaningful talks now that they lived farther apart. Her father's death early in her childhood shaped a tight bond between mother and daughter even though they were polar opposites. Now her mother had begun a campaign of calling every other day to check on her and although she felt fine, she knew her mother was right. She needed to be kind to herself.

"Bad day?" A male voice spoke directly behind her.

An unladylike sound escaped her mouth and she spun around to find Marc behind her, smiling.

"Bad year. And must you always scare me to death?" Why was he always so darn happy?

"Sorry. On both counts." He replied still grinning. "Maybe I should wear a bell."

"Well at least clear your throat or something. And I was rather hoping this would be in my bathroom and in working order by tonight."

"It will be. Cal's on his way back over now. His wife had called him home for supper." He assured with another one of those smiles and then glanced up at the house.

"Well, I think your husband will be pleased with the amount of progress we've made here so far. Will he be coming to see the house soon?"

Now her head really begged for Advil or perhaps something a little stronger. An IV drip of Morphine would be nice. Thankfully the subject of her ever absent spouse did not arise too often but she guessed it was only natural to wonder where in the world her husband might be after all this time. She of course wondered the same thing but was not complaining. His absence was apparently good for her health.

"I'm not sure. He's pretty busy with work right now." She did her best to sound causal and prayed that he would either change the subject or be suddenly called away on some type of handyman emergency.

"I heard he's a dentist. Is he planning on opening an office here in Chester?" He wedged his hands in his front jean pockets while he seemed to ponder the issue of her phantom husband.

Oh, she was certain he heard plenty over flapjacks at Dottie's Diner and what he probably wanted to know but was too polite to ask was; shouldn't he have already secured a location for his new office before they made a big move like this?

"He actually owns a chain of dental offices. I believe he is looking at opening one in the shopping mall over in Walton Park and the town just past that one."

Marc let out a low whistle. "That's rather ambitious."

That was one way to word it. "Yeah, well John likes to have power and money, and he always did know how to attain them both." She thought of something else her husband was fond of and felt that familiar sting of betrayal and jealousy.

"Sounds like you don't approve."

"He doesn't require my approval. He was born with a business plan and as soon as he finished dental school, he started taking business courses. He first opened a charming little dentist office in a trendy neighborhood. It immediately flourished as planned which allowed him to continue on with his strategy which was to open smaller versions in shopping malls. Each location is exquisitely decorated and offers a sample array of spa treatments to be done while you wait and during your dental work. It was an instant hit and soon after *Berrybrite Dental* opened their doors for business, it became a successful franchise." She felt her face flush at her mini commercial, she had heard it and said it so many times, it came out naturally. What she hadn't planned on was spitting it out with such venom.

Marc raised his eyebrows most likely at the obvious tone of bitterness in her speech but refrained from commenting. When the cell phone clipped to his belt rang, he glanced down at the caller id, made a slight face, and silenced it.

"Did you go shopping?" He asked, glancing in the direction of her car.

"What?" She was back to staring at an empty bathtub. "Yes, I did."

He quickly made his way to her car and started to unload it. Her jaw dropped open.

No one ever helps her unload anything unless she screams her head off for someone to come and give her a hand. John was never around to help with shopping, loading or unloading because he had a real job. Since she drew pictures of dresses for a living, her work never counted and she was expected to do everything. Amazing how the country air makes your head clearer.

When she was at last able to close her mandible and speak again, she decided to ask the question that has been on her mind all day.

"Marc, why didn't someone tell me Huddelstone was once a funeral home?"

⅄

After thirty long minutes of sitting in her car trying to extract the mystery on Chester's newest citizen, Wanda's bottom half of her body turned painfully numb. The combination of the pantyhose and her girdle were cutting off the blood flow to her lower extremities. Carefully she started the car, put it into drive and promptly sped home where she could free herself in private.

It may be foolish to some to inflict torture upon her own body like this but her Aunt Madelyn had raised her well. No woman should be seen in public with her fanny or other parts for that matter jiggling in the wind. Oh, her Aunt Maddie had plenty of other rules as well, like waving around a perfumed hanky and wearing fancy hats to church, but she had to let a few of those slide. For starters, she was not about to flutter around a scented snot rag in a client's face and second, she hated hats. They smashed down her hair something awful.

The instant Wanda stepped through her front door she kicked off her sweaty shoes, yanked down her skirt and unzipped her girdle; unleashing the demon that had a hold of her waist. The relief was instant and in her opinion, better than sex. At least from what she could remember since it has been longer than Christ walked the earth that any action has come her way. She reached down for her favorite gray sweat pants that she had left in a ball by the front door and quickly climbed into them. Now that she was comfy, she was ready to do some serious prying.

Sorry Mrs. Berryman, but your secrets are no longer your own.

Chapter 7

Cal Denham and his men were as good as their word and by ten o'clock that evening, Bretta was blissfully filling her new tub with hot, steaming fragrant water. The bathroom was like having her own private spa, Bretta thought to herself happily as she admired the room's astonishing transformation. She planned for this space to be her private retreat and aimed for as many luxuries as she could think of such as heated towel racks, a separate standing shower stall with a rainfall shower head in antique brass to match the other fixtures, and a restored fireplace. A vintage walnut mantel that she was ecstatic to have discovered while antique hunting matched handsomely with the trim and dressing table and the ugly light fixture in the ceiling was switched out with an exquisite chandler.

It had been less than thrilling however to discover that her new home had once been a funeral home. She tried to convince the rational side of her brain that it did not matter, but no luck.

It did bother her. Not enough to send her packing and running out the front door, but her plans for having a home movie theater in the basement were definitely put on hold.

Marc had told her now that she mentioned it; he did recall talk about it when he was younger. He had assumed it was just kids sharing ghost stories, that kind of thing. He hadn't even thought about that in years.

Wanda Bee surely must not know about this little morsel of history or Bretta was certain she would have thrown it into her pot of horrors along with all her other horrendous predictions. She had already warned her that old homes like this would indisputably be haunted and that the Pied Piper himself could appear to help her rid the attic of the multitude of rats and mice that have declared Huddelstone as their own but she guaranteed they would be back. And even if she hired every electrician in town to fix up all that faulty wiring the house would still, in all probability, burn to the ground.

Bretta herself had visited the library a half a dozen times and was somewhat surprised it did not pop up in some article or reference to the house.

But according to Rose Delaney, the owner of the charming antique store on Main Street that she had stopped at this morning, the house had indeed been used as a funeral parlor for a brief period in time. Huddelstone was once a true gem and Rose said she was delighted that it had a new homeowner to bring it back to its original glory.

She didn't think her daughters would be pleased about this development either. The thought of embalming bodies in the basement shot an icy chill down her spine as she peeled off her clothes and slipped into the warm, welcoming tub, allowing her eyes to close. It had taken some effort, but she had located the box that contained her precious collection of bubble bath, salts, and soaps and now she was neck deep in a peaceful blend of patchouli scented bubbles.

Suddenly, her eyes flew back open as her hands gripped the edges of the tub's slippery surface.

What made her assume they embalmed bodies in the basement? She allowed her prior conversation with Rose to float in her mind and could not recall her saying anything about the details of funeral operations or what room they took place in. She had only been in the basement on two occasions; maybe tomorrow she should take another look.

It was silly to allow this uneasy sensation to ruin her bath, what she needed was to relax and forced in deep, calming breaths learned from years of yoga and three different therapists. Obsessing over small, insignificant details was not helpful or healthy, she reminded herself. She stared at the purple candle in front of her until her eyes began to cross and finally after about five minutes of no blinking she felt tranquility return.

The shrill sound of the telephone ringing force her relaxed limbs to tense painfully. She grabbed it on the second ring, pleased that she at least remembered to bring the cordless in the bathroom with her. Next time she would at least turn the ringer off.

Maybe it was Marc calling to see how she was enjoying her new tub. Instantly she felt foolish for thinking a rather intimate thought about her handyman while sitting naked in a bathtub. Seriously, what was wrong with her? Evidently it was time to start socializing with other adults if she is already daydreaming about the hired help.

"Hey, just checking in." Not the handyman. The deep, familiar voice infiltrated the line and filler her with trepidation. He sounded distant and as usual, preoccupied. Like he was reading the days mail while watching the evening news.

The bath water grew tepid. Even the temperature in the room appeared to have dropped a degree or two and her serenity was replaced with a peculiar and uncomfortable humming sensation.

"How's everything at the office?" She drew her knees in tightly to her chest and gave herself a hug. There were several offices actually, but she happened to know John was spending most of his time these days at the Canal Street location. The same building that housed the very young, beautiful, and not that bright dental assistant named Kimber.

"Busy. Still wrapping things up, but I thought I would come up sometime next week to take a look at this house you picked out. What'd you say the name of it was again?"

"Huddelstone. ."

"Well text me the address." He cut into her sentence before she could elaborate further. "I'm sure I can find it. I'll let you know next week what day I'm looking at."

She hesitated briefly. "I think you'll find it easy enough. I believe you've been to this house before."

"What? To this Huddelstone?" He sounded rushed, ready to end the call most likely so he could get back to something more worthy of his time. Like Kimber.

"Yes."

He exhaled loudly to make his point. "Well Bretta, that would be impossible since I never have even been to the town of Chester before."

"Someone you know then use to live here John. I found a picture of you as a child here in this house."

"Really Bretta, I don't have time for this. It's probably some kid that looks like me. Hell, you didn't even know me as a kid and you think that what, from glancing at an old photo album once at my mother's house you can remember what I looked like?" He blew out a deep, aggravated breath. "Get a hobby Bretta or Christ, go back to work for all I care, but find something constructive to do with your time. I gotta go." He slammed the phone down to solidify his annoyance.

"Liar, Liar." It felt therapeutic to finally say the worlds out loud. She sat motionless in the now barely lukewarm water and stared at her chipped magenta toenail polish.

Once upon a time his words would have stung; his hanging up would have been crushing. It always felt so personal. Her hand would have automatically reached out to ring him back and apologize.

She was conscious of the fact she no longer cared what he thought of her, perhaps because she thought so very little of him.

All respect for him as a man and a husband had been lost last year after his outrageous behavior and this much needed distance between them has given her a renewed perspective. She was ready to discover what her husband was really up to and one by one, she was pulling out his secrets for analysis and evaluation. She wanted to know what was going on.

Absence does not always make the heart grow fonder.

Sometimes it simply makes you wiser.

Chapter 8

Baked French Toast Soufflé filled the RV with a warm, sweet cinnamon smell and both girls squealed with delight when they saw their favorite breakfast casserole on the table.

Once the girls were seated, she knew she had to speak quickly before the girls dashed down the street to see their friends. She was thrilled her daughters found friends so fast but she regretted their swift mealtime together was getting shorter and shorter.

"Girls, I found out some rather interesting history on this house." Bretta turned to her daughters to show them her happy, excited face while continuing to fix their plates. The girls in return exchanged a slightly worried look.

"Families would use their front parlor as a place friends and family could come and pay their respects to the deceased. That's what the original owners of this house did and then I believe a generation or two after that the house was actually used as a funeral home for the public for just a short time. "

"That's gross." Iris had her nose scrunched up but kept up pace with her eating. Her friends must be waiting on the porch. Ivy, however, was watching her mother with suspicion and uncertainty.

"Anyway, I just thought you would want to know that." Of course she considered not telling them. But secrets have a way of coming out anyway and she has learned that by being open and up front in the first place saves you some grief later on down the road. She paused and tried to look cheerful.

"Also, your father called last night. He is going to try and come for a visit next week."

Iris raised her eyebrows with fake indifference. "What's the rush? We've only been here a month." She was an intelligent girl and wise beyond her years, but she was also still a child, hurt by her father's lack of attention.

Ivy wanted the facts. "What date will he arrive?"

"He was not sure honey. He said he would call when he knew his schedule. I do know he loves the both of you." That she did believe. He just was not so great at being a father, husband or a human being for that matter.

Ivy was not going to let her off so easy. It was her way of working things out. "How long will he be staying?" Her fingers tapped loudly on the table as she cross examined her mother.

"Honestly honey, I do not know. But I promise to get the precise facts the next time he calls." She leaned across the table and kissed her daughter's forehead.

"You know mom, it has been peaceful without dad here." Iris spoke up tentatively.

She could not argue with that. Life was peaceful without John and all the tension he carried around with him. She searched Ivy's eyes to see if she would defend her father but she stayed quiet.

The three worked as a team to speed up the cleanup process and the chore was done quickly. The girls went in search of their friends; Bretta went to face the basement.

As soon as she reached the bottom step, Bretta recognized her movie theater vision was way off. It was a dreadfully old, damp, depressing, and smelly basement and she did not think there was anything Marc and his men could build to make her want to spend any amount of time down here. Besides, the ceiling was way too low and if they added a drop ceiling to that they would all have to crawl around on their hands and knees.

She walked unhurriedly around the small basement, her arms crossed protectively over her chest to keep warm. No embalming apparatuses so far. Not that she had a clue what embalming tools and equipment looked like, but she only wanted to find regular, old basement stuff. The average crap people leave behind over the years and not evidence that her home was once used as a place that would groom and prep dead bodies to be put out on display.

She was more than grateful Marc said he could turn that spare bedroom upstairs into her dream laundry room so she would not have to come down to this dungeon every day.

Her curiosity had been satisfied and she felt better, but decided she would spend the least amount of time possible in the lower half of her home and only use it for storage. As she moved towards the stairs, she found she almost missed the door flush along the wall, under the stairs. Wanda Bee had mentioned something about a cellar in the basement. Extra storage space for all her canned goods wasn't a bad idea. She could handle a quick trip down the stairs from time to time.

The cellar door refused to budge without a few vigorous tugs and a couple of minor swear words. When it finally gave way, Bretta stepped aside and extended the door fully open. The air that swept past her was cool, musty and laced with a putrid, unidentifiable stench. She waited a second to let the odors dissipate before reaching in the darkness for a pull cord like the ones she had discovered in the upstairs closets. Her first attempt put her hand in contact with more than a few cob webs, making her want to screech in disgust which she bravely resisted. She was not about to have Marc and his men come charging down to rescue her from a few spiders. She kept up her hunt and at last was rewarded with a cord that miraculously when tugged, produced light from an ancient, grimy bulb.

Rows of dusty shelves held the evidence that this was indeed once the family pantry. Canning jars, a large stock pot, bowls, and other cooking utensils were scattered amongst the shelves and covered in a thick coat of dust. Somehow it made her feel sad to see someone's prized preserves or canned tomatoes left behind and forgotten about, their contents now unrecognizable. A few of the jars had shattered open long ago, it's filling now spoiled and rotten which would account for the disagreeable odor.

The storeroom most likely came with mice which in her book, rate far worse than spiders. They were such small and potentially harmless creatures, yet they undoubtedly bothered her and she could say for certain that if one ran across her foot right now she would have to holler.

Pleased with her new pantry she turned to leave when she was struck with the sensation that something in the room was not quite right. She allowed her eyes to scan the small space one more time slowly until she found what it was that was troubling her.

To the far left and under the last shelf were two wooden doors that were joined in the center with a padlock.

There would be no sleep tonight until she had a glimpse inside so she could see for herself what would most likely be an empty cabinet full of dead bugs and spider webs. But still, she had to look. She took the stairs two at a time in search for Marc's wire cutters and was half way back down the stairs when it occurred to her that the lock looked fairly new in comparison to such an old house.

In one swift motion she cut the padlock to expose a hefty, beat-up old trunk inside. It was the same type of luggage people used to travel with years ago on long voyages. Vaguely she recalled seeing a trunk similar to this one while browsing at Rose's antique store the other day. Considering the way she and the girls pack for a trip she was grateful they did not have to lug a colossal thing like that to the airport

No wonder this one was left behind. There was no way it could be sold as something valuable or even useful. Besides it being remarkably beat-up, it was also stained with a dark black substance down the front and sides.

It was not locked, but that same dark substance had cemented the lid closed. She stepped back and gave it a hefty kick. This would also be a good clue as to any dwellers in the chest. If she heard scurrying, she would run like the wind.

On the third kick and what was about to be her final, and the lid started to give.

A certain thrill exploded through her and she wondered what else lay undiscovered here in this moldy old basement. She had always enjoyed rummaging through estate sales and snooping through other people's abandoned and forgotten possessions. It was like a treasure hunt to her and even though she essentially didn't collect antiques, she had a few pieces that meant a lot to her. The attic was her next stop; hopefully the previous owners left a little something of interest behind.

She dragged the trunk closer to the light and perceived it to be heavier than she would have guessed. Perhaps it wasn't empty after all. This was fun. Maybe it was filled with antique dishes or silver.

The cover released an angry screech as it was raised and when Bretta leaned in to get a better view, she let out a scream so deafening, Marc and his men did indeed come running.

Unfortunately, so did the visitor that had been watching Bretta.

Chapter 9

Her petrifying shriek echoed off the pantry's damp walls and sent her in a clammy sprint that landed her abruptly in the center of Marc's solid chest.

He grabbed a hold of her shoulders in an effort to slow her down. "Whoa, what happened? Did a family of mice jump out and scare you?"

Now that she was still, she felt irrational and slightly silly. What she had found concealed in her cellar could not harm her. In fact as the reality of the situation was sinking in, so was a profound sadness. It had caught her so off guard it shook her very soul.

Suddenly a veil of doubt clouded her mind. At least that is what she thought she saw. What if she was wrong?

"You'd better go take a look Marc. Down in the cellar." Panic swelled her throat, making it difficult to swallow. She had only looked once. She should have taken a deep breath, went back into the cellar and opened the trunk again before calling for anyone. Thank goodness she did not say out loud what she thought she saw. Marc merely raised his eyebrows and went down the stairs.

She had not been well last year and she had no desire to broadcast that bit of news to all her new neighbors. People are more forgiving of that sort of thing in a big city but here in a small town you would be forever labeled as crazy. Even her own husband was not cutting her any slack.

She pressed her back firmly against the cold, hard brick-stairwell while she waited for Marc. As the seconds ticked by, she became aware of heavy footsteps gradually making their way across the floor above her, coming to a stop at the foot of the stairs. Most likely one of the workers heard her scream, but it was odd that whoever it was would not come down to see what was wrong.

Someone was waiting silently upstairs, just around the corner. She was sure of it.

She often sensed things in her mind that her eyes did not see. She had a strong sense of intuition that unfortunately she did not always follow.

However there was a time last year when her mind started playing tricks on her and it became unclear of what was her internal voice and what was her imagination.

Marc approached her from behind and rested his hand on her shoulder, startling her slightly. "Well, you definitely still have mice."

Her hand flew to cover her mouth. "Oh, God not again." Her barely audible words sung out like a weak plea for help, her knees went fluid.

Everything had been going so good; the new house, all the renovations and her garden plans. Her stomach constricted painfully and she felt a fierce surge of panic take hold of her body. She tried hard to think of what to do next.

Marc started making his way up the stairs. "Let's go and call Stan."

"Stan?" Bretta's voice was faintly more than a whisper as she struggled to keep it together.

"Stan's the Sheriff."

"The Sheriff?"

"Well, yes. Don't you think we should let him know there's a trunk full of bones in your basement?"

He was watching her now with an odd expression. She remembered this look well. It was the one people gave you when they questioned your sanity. She thought quickly and came to a decision. There was no way she would allow this to happen again.

Bretta's eyes quickly darted up the stairs towards the heavy footsteps that proceeded to move further away before bringing them back to focus on Marc's concerned face. He did not seem to notice the sound. She sped through her own mental self-help check list and did her best to look normal.

"Of course we should, that simply shook me up a bit. Lead the way."

The sheriff arrived in less than twenty minutes and if he was shocked by the fact that half of the residents of Chester were now standing on Bretta's front lawn he did not show it.

Marc made it to the police cruiser in three giant strides and stuck his head in the window to speak to the sheriff. From her front porch view it appeared that the men were close friends. The sheriff said something into his radio, climbed out of the vehicle and the two men walked up the front path together.

Sheriff Stan Meyers was tall, well built with muscular arms that were straining the sleeves of his tan uniform. He was also amazingly gorgeous. He swiftly ran a large hand through his thick black hair that she guessed was more out of habit than of any sort of vanity given the fact that he didn't seem to care that it didn't fall neatly back into place. The slight graying around the temples gave him a serious bearing, but the smile he was offering made him instantly appear approachable.

"Bretta Berryman, this is the Sheriff and my buddy, Stan Meyers." Marc made the introductions and as she moved forward to greet him, she felt the Sheriffs intense scrutiny somewhat soften.

"Nice to finally meet you, Mrs. Berryman. I heard Chester had a new family, although I must admit I had to ask twice when they said what house you were moving in." He glanced back at the house like he still couldn't believe it. "You have two daughters?" He inquired but she had the feeling he knew exactly who came in and out of his town. She was also oddly aware of the Sherriff in a way that a woman notices a man.

"Yes, Ivy and Iris. I requested that they stay down at their friends for a while." She smiled at the mention of her children and felt such relief that they were not with her when she opened that trunk.

He took a hard look at the front of the house and nodded. "It's coming around. Marc here knows what he's doing, that's for sure. Ok, let's go have a look." He held the screen door open and waved Marc and Bretta through before turning back to the crowd.

"Go on back home to your families now. I promise you'll hear all about this later. Just give us some working room. Go on now." He motioned to an officer that just arrived on the scene to take over. It was a harmless enough crowd that knew after all if they dropped by Dolly's later on for some of her famous blueberry-peach cobbler, they would indeed get the full story.

The sheriff walked in the house and allowed the screen door to slam boisterously against its frame a few times as a final signal to disperse.

Sheriff Meyers peered inside the chest carefully without touching anything, using the tip of his pen to gently move a piece of fabric to the side. He spoke without looking up. "Did Marc here tell you we've been buddies since the first grade?" He shook his head and sighed, continuing to poke delicately through the chest with his Paper Mate.

"Got into more trouble with this one here than I care to remember. Folks around here were pretty surprised I ended up at the academy instead of prison. But I figured I knew enough about breaking the law and can usually recognize when someone is feeding me a line of BS, so police work seemed like a natural fit."

The words that were dancing around her brain slipped through her lips before she could stop them. "I know a thing or two about liars."

Sheriff Meyers raised an eyebrow. "Yeah? Well, that's a handy skill to have." He straightened up when he heard someone coming down the stairs. "That should be Kuster with crime lab. They are going to take some pictures and samples so let's go upstairs to give them some space."

A tall, lanky, balding man with an enormous smile bounced down the stairs and went directly to Bretta. "Hello Mrs. Berryman, I'm Deputy Kuster. Kevin. Good to meet you. How do you like living here in Chester so far?" His smile faded fast and he patted her arm. "Well, I suppose this put a damper on things. Let me get to work here and then we can get this out of here for you ok?"

Since there was not much she could say, she shook her head in agreement and watched the pleasant deputy go to work. She liked him instantly. He appeared competent and proficient, his hands moved with practiced ease. Within seconds his hands were gloved, his black evidence kit open and he had begun taking pictures of everything in and around the chest. She noted how vigilantly and precisely he took things out of the kit and then replaced them. She had to believe he did not get too many opportunities around here to carry out this sort of work but one would never know it by observing him.

As if reading her thoughts, he turned back and said softly; "I use to work in one of those big cities before I came here." He gave her a wink and went back to work.

One of the techs scraped some of the black muck from the side of the chest into a glass bottle, labeled it and followed the same procedure with a separate bottle for the stain on the floor.

She understood then what the reddish-brown substance was and felt a sincere sadness for whoever was dumped in that chest. Could it be possible someone was murdered right here in her own basement? Deputy Kuster glanced her way and sadly shrugged his shoulders.

It was almost as if this was left here for her to find because why wouldn't the person who did this do a better job of hiding the remains? It was foolish to think that her biggest fear had been that she might cross paths with a mouse.

"I heard an elderly lady lived here last." She recalled Wanda saying it had been vacant for a few years. Suddenly, she felt sick over her decision to purchase this house and for the first time, wondered if she made a mistake. Not only did she relocate her daughters to a house that was once a funeral home, but apparently the last resident was a murderer.

A deep and penetrating chill bristled down Bretta's spine as she wondered how long this poor soul had been waiting to be discovered.

"A nice little old lady by the name of Irma Barrett. Her son moved her out to live with him in the desert a few years back. The house has been empty ever since." Deputy Kuster spoke as he gathered up his gear.

The techs had transferred the chest into a large plastic bag and were getting ready to move it upstairs, Deputy Kuster picked back up his camera and slid its strap around his neck.

"We're going to take a look around the rest of the basement now." Kuster was stretching a fresh pair of latex gloves over his long, thin fingers as one of the other officers came out of the cellar holding up two mason jars, motioning for Kuster to come over.

The Sheriff spoke directly to Marc. "I take it you have been through every room and closet throughout the house?"

Marc nodded. "Yeah, we gutted the place. Not the attic though. No one has been up there yet."

"Kuster, stay and finish up down here. I'll take one of the techs and go on up to the attic to have a look around."

Wanda had warned her that there was nothing in her attic but dust, bats and mice, so she had wisely stayed away. She planned to have Marc clean it out before her first visit. "I haven't been up there yet myself, but I had the movers put a couple of boxes of my stuff up there."

"Ok, why don't you come on up with us then to identify your possession?"

The long forgotten space greeted them with hot, idle air and a deep stillness. Thousands of minute dust mites danced in a single beam of light that shone down brightly from the window peak.

Time had stood still up in the crest of her new home and there were indeed treasures left behind for her to discover. At first glance, without really concentrating on anything in particular, the items scattered around the floor appeared to be well kept and from a different era.

In fact, Bretta thought to herself there was a lot of *stuff* up here. Nice stuff. She had to wonder if Wanda had deliberately lied to her or simply did not bother to look for herself, never thinking that the city girl from New York would want to make Huddelstone her new home.

Warily, she stepped lightly around the room with her hands secured away nicely in her pockets, reminding them not to touch. A small Tiffany table lamp sat on the floor partially hidden behind a pile of exquisite hand-made quilts that had her questioning how anyone could leave such a gem behind. Even from a distance and covered in dust Bretta was aware of its exceptional quality.

Perhaps Irma Barrett was not in her right mind when her son took her to live with him, because it appeared she left behind what would have been women's most treasured possessions.

"Maybe her son was supposed to return and pack these things up and forgot or he never even came up to the attic." Absent-mindedly, she spoke her thoughts out loud. When she turned around, all three men were looking at her strangely.

"Well these aren't my things." She pointed to the boxes and then to the lamp. "So, I was wondering how you move your mother out of her home and get away with leaving all this behind." She waved her arms around. "She must be suffering from dementia, because there is no way a woman is going to forget about all this stuff. " She continued to wander around, taking it all in, unaware that they were still staring at her. The men had just started to go back to doing their own thing when she spoke again.

"You know, these are not even attic things." She was on her knees examining a box that held a teapot, cups, and different cans of tea. Bretta tucked her hair back behind her ear as she reached into the carton and pulled out a teacup and then held it up for closer inspection, forgetting her promise not to touch. Before she knew it, she was elbow deep in tea accessories.

After a few seconds of silence and exchanging glances, the Sheriff spoke up.

"What do you mean by that Mrs. Berryman?"

"These things look like they would have been her show pieces; they would be out on display or in a curio cabinet." She turned slowly around the room and allowed her gaze to rest on another one of the boxes. "And some of these things appear to be every day, household items."

Sheriff Stan took a walk around the room and began to see something other than knick knacks. They were all things that would have had some meaning to a woman and he had to agree that these tossed aside pictures and vases could very well represent Irma's life. One of her friends should be able to verify that for them. He regarded the carton at his right foot; it did look as if someone dumped in the contents of a kitchen cupboard and tossed it upstairs.

Did the old women have these items put up here for storage because she thought she would be returning or did someone pack for her? After considering a couple different scenarios he gave the box a light shove with his foot and what he found underneath led him to believe Irma did little of her own packing.

"Jim," Stan called over to the other officer "Bring your kit on over here."

Hidden under the box of what Bretta would guess was Irma's favorite tea set was the now familiar looking rust stain.

Chapter 10

It was easy enough for Stan to find the two closest acquaintances Irma had still living in Chester and ask them to take a look at some of her things.

Alice and Athena Muncy were sisters that lived directly across the street from Huddelstone and he guessed they would be only too happy to help.

The Sheriff made his way across the street and up the red brick pathway that led to the Muncy's front porch. Simply stepping on the grounds of the Muncy property gave the sensation of being transported back in time. Their Victorian landscaping and gardens both in the front and in back of the house were a meticulous showpiece and the pride of the neighborhood.

Before his booted foot had a chance to make contact with the bottom porch step, the wooden door opened wide and Alice Muncy appeared with a tall, frosted glass of ice tea in her dainty hand, a thin slice of lemon and a spring of mint balanced perfectly on its rim.

"Hello Sheriff." Alice called out in a little girl like, sing-song voice. "We have been waiting for you to stop in and pay us a visit. Don't my Forget Me Not's look lovely this year? They represent true love you know." The petite older woman batted her eyelashes dramatically a few times and then waited patiently for a compliment.

He reached out to gladly accept the tea when a sharp voice bellowed in his right ear.

"Oh for God's sake Alice! He's not here for a date! Good afternoon Sheriff Meyers. I see you had some commotion over at Huddelstone yesterday. Why don't you come on in and get out of the sun?"

"Thank you, Athena." He followed behind Athena as she marched up the stairs, pausing before Alice who stood in the doorway, looking like a scolded schoolgirl. "Alice, your flowers are spectacular this year. It's a pleasure to simply take a drive down your street." He took a sip of the ice tea and offered her one of his heart stopping smiles that he didn't realize caused half of the women in Chester to fall in love with him. "And thank you for the tea."

Alice beamed like a school girl as her sister shook her head in disgust. "You are very welcome." She smoothed down the hem of her trademark flower dress and slid into the house.

For as long as Stan could remember, the youngest and smaller built of the two sisters wore some type of peculiar floral dress. He wondered if she made them herself. Athena, if he recalled correctly usually chose a simple and somewhat masculine approach to her wardrobe of pants and a plain button down top which fit her personality perfectly.

He went over to the coffee table and helped himself to a homemade oatmeal cookie from an elegant silver serving tray. Adjacent to that sat a crystal bowl of raspberries, an assortment of finger sandwiches, and a dish of mixed nuts.

They were expecting someone for a visit, that was for sure.

"Did you ladies figure I would want to chat with all the neighbors or did you have something special to tell me?" He looked from one to the other as he spoke and smiled easily. They reminded him of the two elderly sisters on the television show The Waltons.

Athena dropped down hard in the chair next to the fireplace. "We assumed you would want to talk to us being that we are two nosy old ladies that have lived here forever. If you wanted history on Huddelstone or the gossip on who was coming and going, you would ask us. Obviously we have nothing newsworthy to report though or we would have called you."

"I appreciate that Athena." He said leaning forward to sample one of the tiny sandwiches.

"So, was that Irma stuffed in that trunk?" Athena inquired, ignoring her sister's loud gasp.

"We haven't positively identified the remains yet."

Alice sat with her back against the afternoon sun as bright rays streamed in past the heavy, parted drapes. Her hands were folded on her lap and a content smile on her face.

Athena leaned forward, picked up a plate and piled it high with a heaping helping of everything on the table. "Eating like a bird" was for the birds as far as she was concered. She was proud of her healthy appetite and liked to show it off.

"Well, I have been waiting to tell you something." Alice spoke up abruptly and with more authority than characteristic. She reached forward, gently picked up a plate and began to leisurely fill it. Her fine boned hand paused by each dish as she precisely made her selections, so different from her sister's reckless approach. She took great care in her choices, seemingly unaware of the time that was passing.

Stan put his own plate back down on the table and shot Athena a questioning glance; she appeared as completely caught off guard at her sister's announcement as he was.

Athena sat straighter, her bottom jaw dropping lower and as the seconds dragged into minutes Stan sensed Athena's mounting frustration at her still silent sister.

He held up his hand for Athena to wait. He did not need her scolding Alice and scaring her.

"Something you wanted to tell me Alice?" His smooth and tender tone conveyed that she need not rush.

She took her time nibbling at each of her samplings, swallowed, picked up her napkin, and wiped the corners of her mouth four times all the while pretending she did not know that her languorous performance had her sister ready to jump out of her chair.

"Alice…" Athena warned.

"Déjà vu." Alice whispered softly.

"I beg your pardon?" Stan leaned forward in his chair.

"Speak up for God's sake! You know I'm half deaf." Athena snarled.

"Déjà vu," Alice repeated only marginally louder. "From the French term meaning *already seen*."

"Thanks Alice, we didn't know what déjà vu means." Athena said sarcastically.

"There is a man watching Huddelstone, shadowing Ms. Bretta since that is what he is really after. He could be a reporter who found her, because she does have secrets you know. But I don't think so. It's more personal than that. He is sinister and evil and he has his own personal connection to that house that goes way back."

"How do you know this Alice, did you see someone watching the house?" He inquired quickly, before her sister could jump in.

"No, but I know evil has been around."

It wasn't a secret around these parts that Alice had a way of knowing things. It was weird and he wouldn't necessarily say he believed in that type of thing but there were a couple of times in his career that a professional physic played a role in closing a case.

Athena rolled her eyes. "Well how's that a case of déjà vu?"

"Because death always reminds you of death. Murder reminds you of murder. I was slightly concerned when I saw that nice little family moving in but I thought it was ok now. But then I recognized I was wrong. The evil in that house goes way back. If you don't do something Sheriff, Bretta will be next."

Later that afternoon, Bretta considered calling John to tell him about the skeletal remains she found but for some reason her hand was unwilling to dial his number. First of all, that meant she actually had to speak to him and second, she did not have any real information from the police yet anyway. He would just make light of the matter by saying old houses are bound to come with a few skeletons in their closets and laugh at his own joke.

Then there was a chance he wouldn't even believe her.

So today she was only going to focus on getting her house in order. Marc had helped her move the furniture from the barn into the living room and later she would decide where she wanted a few of her favorite paintings hung.

She gave her word she would not try her hand at hanging the pictures herself when she noticed the pained expression on his face when she had causally mentioned her plans to throw them up on the wall later when she had everything in place.

She knew she would feel more in harmony with the house if she had a few of her own possessions from her previous home on display. Vigilantly she had selected and with care packed only the items that had significant sentimental meaning or gave her immense pleasure. Some had been received as gifts from special friends or family members and the rest she had chosen herself. She wanted to fill her new home with reflections of herself and once again she wondered how John would even fit in to this picture.

John's absence, she began to see, was truly a gift. She needed this breathing space to rediscover who she was and what she wanted out of her life. One thing was becoming exceedingly clear to her; the longer they were apart, the less she missed him or needed him and the better she felt physically as well as emotionally.

Bretta went over in her head once again why she had agreed to giving their broken marriage another chance: the kids, all their years together, and the pressure from his mother. She never even liked his mother, so why that should have been a factor she could not begin to explain. More proof she simply was not right last year.

All these thoughts swarmed her brain as she unpacked a box of memories from her former life and started placing the items on the fireplace mantel in the entranceway which now thanks to Lou, was in perfect working order. At the bottom of the box there were numerous framed photos of the girls when they were little in beautiful matching dresses, some that she designed and made herself.

The sound of the doorbell broke her trance causing her to drop the frame she was holding.

Sheriff Meyers filled her doorframe with a Muncy sister on either side of him. She had totally forgotten he said he was bringing them by to look at the things in the attic. They each wore a strange expression making Bretta wonder if they came bearing bad news or she had dirt on her face.

"Is everything ok?" The Sheriff asked with genuine concern that for some reason, she found touching.

Athena took charge as usual. "Of course she's not all ok! It's bad enough she has to live here all alone, waiting for that ever absent husband of hers to finally show up, but now she finds a trunk of bones in her basement." Her eyes dropped down to the cracked family photo Bretta had retrieved from the floor and was now clutching in her hand.

She hadn't been aware until then that she had been crying and felt embarrassment creep up her neck.

"She is not crying over her husband or the unpleasant surprise in the basement. She was just gazing on back at what might have been." Alice took Bretta's hands and held it tightly in her own, her touch warm and reassuring. "We'll plant some Lily of the Valley out front for the return of happiness to this house."

Bretta wiped her eyes. "Thank you Alice, that's a lovely idea."

Alice hesitated briefly and took her eyes around the room, taking in a reassuring deep breath. "It has been a long time since I have been in this house. Well, should we head upstairs?"

It only took seconds once they all assembled in the attic for the ladies to concur that the items were indeed Irma's most precious possessions. Athena made a tsk-tsk sound as she inspected the items.

Both ladies came to a halt by the ugly blemish on the bare wood floor and gaped down in unison. Alice was under strict instructions not to repeat her forewarning of the stranger to Bretta while the Sheriff was still investigating, but you could clearly see she had a strained expression on her face trying to hold it in.

"Well, thank you Alice and Athena for your help." Stan did not want Alice dwelling on the stain. "We still have not been able to track down her son. Can either of you recall who his friends were from around here? " It was a long shot, but he had to start somewhere.

Athena scowled. "That boy left town the day he turned eighteen and broke his mother's heart, that's what he did. He was pretty much a loner anyway; he never did have many friends."

Alice unexpectedly sprung to life. "Remember the summer people? There was a boy that came visiting each year. His mother rented one of the Wickedwinds cabins by the lake. Later when the boy became a teenager and his mother remarried, he came by himself and stayed with Irma and Anthony."

The Sheriff appeared as impressed as Bretta was. Her sister was looking at her like she suddenly sprouted fangs and a tail.

"How many of those Ginkgo Biloba's are you taking?" Athena peered into her sister's eyes for signs of distress or the onset of a seizure. "Yesterday you forgot to wear your under-panties and last week you left for the store without shoes."

Alice shrugged her shoulders innocently.

"Well, since your memory is on a roll, do you recall the boy's name?" Athena jumped in before the Sheriff could stop her.

"Johnny. I'm sorry but I cannot think of the last name. I am not sure if I ever knew it, but I'll think about it in the garden today."

After everyone left, Bretta went to her bedroom and slowly opened her nightstand drawer. Under a thick stack of books she idyllically had high hopes to at least start reading this summer, was the photo Marc had found.

At least now she knew how her husband spent the summers of his youth.

Chapter 11

A few years had somehow managed to slip by since he had last been anywhere near the old house on the hill and as he made his way up the grassy slope, an innate chill of anticipation trekked slowly down his spine.

It felt strangely refreshing to be home again. Better than he imagined it would be to return to the sleepy, ever boring town of Chester and even though it was a moonless night, the stranger could find his way around well enough. What details his eyes could not decipher his memory could easily provide.

Many late nights and endless summer days had been spent on the other side of those old walls he reminisced and if he closed his eyes, he knew he would hear their cries. There was an intense longing to resume the game again but he knew it was doubtful he would play alone.

He really wished the old house was empty. As much as he enjoyed watching the pretty new homeowner with her young offspring settle in, he was starting to get anxious.

He needed to get inside and back to what was familiar.

He could be incredibly stealth-like if he so desired. They could be in the same room together, sharing the exact air, and she would never be the wiser. She would never even know he was there.

After all, silence was the name of the game.

⅄

Today's strategy was to start on the outside of the house. Bretta threw back the covers and allowed herself the small pleasures of slowly getting out of bed and a little stretching before the launch of a hard-working day. Turning thirty eight this past year was a kicker. The laugh lines around her eyes were more pronounced which she found comical since she hadn't much to laugh at the past few years. After a fast shower, she headed to the RV where she found the girls racing through a bowl of cereal and ready to dash out the door to join their awaiting friends.

"Good morning girls." Bretta smiled brightly. They both in unison replied cheery greetings with their mouths full.

"Gee, it would be something if you moved this fast when you knew I was waiting for you."

Ivy finished first. "Done!" She ran to the sink with her bowl and spoon. "That's cuz we know you will wait for us mom." She ran over and gave her mom a loud kiss on the cheek before running out the door. Iris followed her sister's lead and gave her mom a quick peck as well before running out the door.

The workers, who were busy pounding away in the kitchen of the house, had called out to her that morning that they would be all finished with the house in one week. She allowed herself to laugh as they have been promising her that for the last month. However, today when she glanced around, it did indeed look close to completion. Now all she had left to concentrate on was the exterior she thought headed outside to the backyard.

The sun was clear and bright, the breeze languid, perfect for sitting outside.

Her plan was for the garden and grounds to match the Victorian era as closely as possible. The local librarian was especially helpful in lending her the right books on Victorian gardening and of course she was fortunate enough to have exceptional experts residing across the street.

Athena and Alice Mundy considered her lawn an eyesore and were already giving her unsolicited guidance for improvements. Not that she minded the suggestions, they were all useful and Bretta was becoming especially fond of her new neighbors.

She brought her sketch pad and pencils over to the picnic table and began to craft her vision. Having lived in the city for the better part of her life,

Bretta was unsure which flowers and plants were suitable for shade and which did better in direct sunlight. Without actually selecting the plants, she knew she wanted lots of color, a brick or cobblestone path that trailed through the gardens and a large sundial as the focal point. She glanced over to the area of the yard that received the most sunlight and decided that would be the ideal spot for her herb garden.

It delighted and somewhat astounded her to find this project as stimulating as designing fashion. That same inner hum began to resonate deep within her that she always experienced when she got lost in a creative project.

"Drawing flowers now instead of dresses Bretta? Is this some new type of therapy?" A masculine voice, thick with disfavor, spoke directly behind her.

The blood seamed to temporarily cease to flow through her veins. Deeply engrossed in her imaginary garden, Bretta never sensed his approach. She should have, the birds in the trees suddenly stopped their song and the wind kicked it up a notch. Even the air felt slightly cooler.

She took her time before looking up. "John, what a surprise. You didn't tell me you were arriving today."

He removed his sunglasses and stared down into her eyes. "I didn't know I needed an appointment." His right eyebrow rounded disapprovingly at her. "This *is* my house Bretta." He put the sunglasses back on and shoved his hands into the pockets of yet another new Armani suit and took in his surroundings.

Now was not the time to call him on a technicality, but the fact was this was not his house. A small tremor of fear formed in the depths of her stomach because when he found out, he would not be pleased. Memories of John's irritation with her when she made a mistake or forgot something flooded her subconscious and she appreciated just how much she has enjoyed his absence.

"Where are the girls?" He glanced down at her sketches while he spoke, his right hand continuously toying with the loose change in his pocket.

She kept her tone neutral. "Ivy and Iris are with their friends down the street. Would you like me to go get them?" John was one person she could read easily, but then he made his thoughts so obvious. He was refraining from lecturing about how she allowed the kids to run wild while she sat around and drew pictures of daisies.

"If you are sure they are fine, let them visit with their friends a little longer then. First show me my house." He proceeded to walk towards the house assuming she would follow.

It was at that moment she knew what she needed to do. She had only been putting off the inevitable. This was *her* house that was being designed according to her vision and it was filled with peace and tranquility. The very instant John set foot onto the grounds, she felt that shift.

Bretta had turned to speak to him when she became aware that he had stopped moving and his eyes were fixated on something across the street.

Slowly she turned to follow his fierce glare to find it locked with Alice Muncy. Today the eccentric elder wore a large straw hat with fresh red tulips sprouting from the top and grasped a rake in her right hand. Her friend stood motionless to return John's intense stare.

"Who's the fruitcake?" He said irritably. "And what the hell is she looking at?"

"That's our neighbor, Alice Muncy." Bretta said softly. "And I would say she is looking at you."

"Daddy!" Iris ran up and wrapped her arms around her father's waist.

He broke his stare with Alice and beamed down at his daughter, clearly happy to see her.

"How are you, beautiful?"

"Fine. I want to show you my room. How long are you staying?"

Bretta was curious about this as well.

"A few days. Let's go take a look at the house."

When he glanced back across the street, his strange new neighbor was gone.

⅄

Bretta's eyes flew open wide to meet the darkness as her brain went to work to match the sound to its source.

She lay unmoving, trying to understand what had jarred her out of a peaceful and medicated sleep. With John in the house, sleep had been hard to come by without a little pharmaceutical help. She refused to be led down the road of insomnia again and took something at the first sign of sleeplessness. The pills allow her to fall asleep, but not so deeply she would not be able to hear the children if they needed her.

A muffled crash directly above her bed jolted her out of bed and had her staring wide eyed at the ceiling.

She was slowly becoming accustomed to the many sounds of living out in the country. This did not sound like an animal on the roof or a tree branch scratching against the window in the wind.

She found the living room where John had been sleeping vacant, its recently refinished hardwood floors felt like a frozen pond under her bare feet. She had been relieved last night when John announced he wanted to stay up and catch the late show and would probably crash on the couch. She had to admit she was becoming used to and enjoyed sleeping alone.

Now she stood with her hands on her hips and strained her ear to catch the faint sound above her and wondered where John had run off to.

A subdued shuffling sound made its way across the floor boards over her head and it took only a second for her brain to clear out the fog.

What in the hell was he doing up in her attic in the middle of the night?

There was only one way to find out. If she marched up the stairs and demanded an explanation he would only fabricate a story.

She made her way up the narrow stairway as silent as possible, attempting to synchronize her steps to the soft thuds above. When she reached the top stair, she held back in the dense shadows and quietly studied her husband.

John held a lantern type light high in his hand which cast an eerie glow over the boxes and left behind his ghoulish silhouette. Evidently he did not want her to know what he was up to or he would have chosen daylight to his snooping. He opened each box he came upon, carefully checked its contents before closing it and moving it aside.

When he came to the quilts he froze. Tenderly, as if picking up a newborn, he lifted up the blanket on top of the pile and hugged it tightly to his chest before pressing it to his nose. He inhaled deeply several times before muttering words Bretta could not make out. After several long minutes he sighed dramatically and then proceeded to fold the quilt back up, taking care that the corners came together perfectly and then tenderly placed it back in its box.

"How long do you intend to stand there spying on me Bretta?"

The baritone voice that bellowed out of the darkness made her jump but to her credit not shriek and the murky corner of the stairwell hid her panic.

"Just long enough to figure out what it is you're up to John."

He held the lantern up high to his face and she could not help but to feel dread, even though it was her own husband. Her spouse. His index finger beckoned her closer as he mouthed the words *come here.*

Sprinting back down the stairs felt like a good idea, so was running him over with her car, but it was probably best to stick with reality. Sure he could be a callous, insensitive asshole and a stinking cheat, all issues they were supposed to be working on. But there was never physical abuse that would account for the sudden fear now crawling up her backside.

Gradually she made her way forward until she was mere inches from his face.

"You've gotten awfully brave living out here in the sticks Bretta. Too bad you didn't have more of a spine a few years ago; things might have turned out different." He set the light to rest on one of the boxes and reached over to the quilt he had been examining earlier. After carefully unfolding it, he spread it out on the wooden attic floor like they were about to have a picnic, patting the spot next to him for her to have a seat.

"There, isn't this nice?"

Surely he did not expect an answer to that, but since he was in a chatty mood and the kids were not around, perhaps now would be a good time to tell him she wanted a divorce. His off-handed compliment on her courageousness encouraged her.

"What were you looking for John?"

Looking bored, he allowed his eyes to wander around the perimeter of blackness that caged them in. "I couldn't sleep so I thought I would check out the attic; see if the former owners left behind anything valuable."

There it was. Proficient and skillful liars never venture far from the truth.

"Were you hoping Irma or Tony Barrett left something behind for you?"

"Are you losing it again Bretta?" He appeared amused. "I can only assume these creatures you mention are the former owners of this house, or are they new little playmates you have spawned in your crazy head to keep you company?"

"You know who they are. Tony Barrett was someone you made friends with when you spent your summers here as a boy, Irma Barrett was his mother. Alice also said you would stay with the Barrett's after your mother remarried and you came to Chester alone."

His face was expressionless and difficult to read. "Alice is that screwball from across the street?"

She answered with a slight nod of the head.

"Well, it's nice you've found a friend here in Nutville Bretta. The two of you seem to have a lot in common. However, I hate to shatter this blissful delusion you have fashioned for yourself. I have never been to this town before today; I do not know the people that use to live here."

John's palm shot out in front of Bretta's face, silencing her protests.

"Randomly, I selected the small town of Chester thinking it would be the perfect location for my family and healing for you. Realizing of course that part of your trouble came from my lack of discretion and bad judgment, I wanted to help make amends and give us all a fresh start." He raked his hands through his perpetually neat hair, causing a rare disturbance. "You are sliding back down through the rabbit's hole again and I don't have time for this! I have my own hands extremely full at work and now I see I have to worry about the girls here in your care."

Bretta jumped to her feet fast with fury.

"You bastard! You're the one with the record!" She brought up the unspeakable, but there was no turning back. "You're the disturbed one. Now you're trying to make me feel like I'm unbalanced and a bad mother. It won't work John! I feel better than ever. You're hiding something and I *will* find out what it is. In the meantime, I think it is best if you leave."

He remained quiet and for a moment she feared she had gone too far. Although she refused to be bullied by him, perhaps now was not the best moment to lay it all on the line.

"All this fresh air appears to have temporally altered your perception, but don't be fooled Bretta. You're not well, only you can't see it. You never could." He stood up and his lips parted slightly as if he were about to speak. The sour smell of Grant's Blended Scotch, his preferred brand, filled the space between them and made her queasy.

"I am doing fine. I've never felt better." A slight exaggeration if you take into account some the recent occurrences and the fact that she now felt like vomiting.

"You may think you have recovered, that you are normal. But don't be deceived." He smiled brightly and for the first time since his arrival in her new home, looked genuinely happy. "You know what they say about crazy people, Bretta?" He jeered, not bothering to wait for a response. "They're always the last to know."

Chapter 12

If this were a cartoon strip, Wanda Bee would have a swarm of bees blissfully buzzing around her head. The dirt she had spent two days uncovering proved not only to be tantalizing and unscrupulous, it would also pay extremely well.

John Berryman had been a very naughty man.

Who was to say she could not dabble with her favored career path now and then? It had been such a long time that she treated herself to this particular rush that she felt exhilarated.

Today her girdle felt even tighter than usual and she raced across town to temporally offer herself relief before a vital organ ruptured. Her new daily habit of two sticky buns from Sonny's bakery appeared to be making her midsection a tad thicker. She would have to yell at the baker next time she saw him for making them so darn fattening.

She had an appointment later in the day to show a home to a gentleman from New York and had at least a few hours' worth of preparation before their scheduled meeting time.

Suddenly Chester was the hot new relocation spot for yuppies and she didn't think the big draw was Sonny's sticky buns.

Wanda entered her house through her side door and immediately dropped the tattered manila folder down on the kitchen table to quickly exit out of everything from the waist down except her underwear.

She gave herself a mental ass kicking for underselling Huddelstone. It never occurred to her that someone would actually want to buy that dilapidated piece of shit.

She plopped down at the kitchen table to devour everything she could about her new client so when it was time to meet face to face, all his dirty secrets could easily roll off her tongue. That was one thing she learned early on is that everyone has bones in their cubby if you simply dig deep enough.

Perhaps if all went well, she would finally be able to free herself from the clutches of Chester.

⅄

Breakfast in the Berryman's RV the next morning consisted of Bretta's blueberry pancakes only this time her husband was present at the tiny table. He joined in the conversation, laughed with the girls, and carried on as if he had not been absent at every meal for the last two months.

She noticed Ivy watching her intently as she methodically cut up and chewed her pancakes. Last week her daughter had declared, after much study and research on her part, that she was a vegetarian and presented her mother with a list of expectable substitutions, meal ideas, and an online video that she wanted the entire family to watch together. Accompanying the list was a short essay on why she had chosen to become a vegetarian, the many health benefits of such a diet and what her mother's role would be in this new lifestyle.

Bretta responded that she needed a few days to process all the information and promised to get back to her. She wasn't against the idea and had to admit the essay was well written and factual, however her daughter was a little too dictatorial.

She recalled that meatless sausage links were one of the suggested items which were notably absent from today's breakfast table and Ivy was probably annoyed with her.

Bretta's stomach was not in the mood for pancakes or anything else as long as John was around but she put on her best spurious smile and when she couldn't take it anymore said she needed to check on something she had been working on in the barn and dashed out the door.

She was grateful to get back to the old wooden chair she had been refinishing. Her hand automatically reached for the sandpaper and went to work while taking in deep breaths.

She wanted to scream at John to get out of *her* house only she was afraid to tell him that she was the sole owner. It was something else he would only use against her, another unstable decision on her part.

You are not well Bretta, only you can't see it.

The sandpaper fell from her fingers and her hands covered her face to stifle her anguish.

"God, how can you be crazy and not know?" She cried into her hands as she allowed the terror of her worst fear to flow through her. She can't lose her children; it simply was not an option.

"You're not crazy, who said you were?" A familiar voice spoke from the barn door.

She was almost getting used to him sneaking up behind her and scaring her, but this time she was more mortified than frightened.

Bretta turned her back to Marc and dried her eyes the best she could on her hands before turning back to face him.

"Good morning Marc. You're here early today." She tried to smile.

"What's wrong Bretta?"

She had not talked much about John. Only a few comments slipped out of her mouth in the past without checking in with her intellect first and they had not been favorable. Until she understood what she wanted in life and her marriage, she thought it was best to keep quiet about that part of her life.

"My husband showed up yesterday, we had a disagreement." She gave it her best 'you know how it is' voice and shrugged her shoulders. Bending over she picked back up the sandpaper to give her hands something to do.

"There's nothing wrong with you, don't let anyone try to convince you otherwise."

"You don't know John. He can cause a lot of trouble for me if he wants to." The minute the words left her mouth she felt regret. Marc was her handyman, not her therapist.

"Why would a husband want to cause trouble for his wife?" He inhaled deeply and put his hands in his pockets, something she noticed he did often when he was thinking about something. "Are you afraid of him Bretta?"

Her eyes grew wide. She had said a lot of things, but she had not mentioned fear. Her apprehension of her spouse was growing stronger each day and evidently it was showing on her face. Suddenly, the need was great to share a small part of her life and unload the burden of carrying so many secrets only she was not sure where to begin.

"He wants me out of the way by claiming I am an unbalanced and an unfit mother." Her voice came out in strangled whisper. "Yes, I am afraid."

Disbelief and surprise widened his eyes when he saw that she was serious.

"You're a sensational mother and there is nothing wrong with your sanity. What's he after?" Marc shook his head. "Because if he simply wants custody of the kids that makes no sense. He only just arrived after you all have lived here for over a month."

"I don't know exactly. I think he just wants me out of the picture totally."

"Knock-knock." The voice from the barn door took them both by surprise and they glanced over to find the Sheriff standing in the opening, watching them curiously. It was obvious from the look on his face he had been standing there long enough to hear their conversation.

Marc walked over to shake his friend's hand. "What brings you out this early?"

"Marc. Morning Mrs. Berryman."

"Good morning Sheriff." The pit of her stomach abruptly turned to acid; she knew he wasn't stopping by to see how she was settling in.

"I wanted you to hear it first before Wanda Bee came around. She has been making a pest of herself over at the station and I imagine she will show up sooner than later to torment you. You probably didn't know this, but she used to be a reporter."

Bretta was speechless. She was not so much shocked over Wanda's previous career choice than by fate. The profession definitely fitted the insufferable woman even more so than selling houses. She couldn't believe that the very thing she was running from she invited unwillingly into their lives.

"No, I didn't realize that." There was no doubt then that Wanda Bee knew all about her and the past she had been hoping to leave behind. "Did you identify the remains yet?"

"Yes. They were the remains of Irma Barrett. We have been trying to locate her son to notify him." The Sheriff rolled a rock around the dirt floor of the barn with his foot while he seemed to be trying to find a way to ask her something.

"Did you ever meet Mrs. Barrett, Mrs. Berryman?" The Sheriff now looked directly into her eyes while he waited for her reply.

She was momentarily caught off guard by the bizarre question. How could she ever meet the woman, she only moved her a couple of months ago? "No, Sheriff. I never meet her."

He nodded his head a couple of times. "How about her son, Anthony? He goes by Tony. Does that ring any bells?"

Several bells going off in her head right now, all of them loud and alarming.

"Sheriff, we only just moved here a short time ago. Before that, I had never even heard of the town of Chester or of the Barrett family."

Sheriff Stan magically produced a small plastic baggie his shirt pocket and held it up for her to see.

"I understand that you design clothes for a living." Stan asked a question she was sure he already knew the answer to.

"Yes, I do." Surely he wasn't expecting some type of analysis based on a tattered scrap of fabric. The lab that they sent the remains to for identification would be able to give more useful specifics than she could.

"It appears Irma was an admirer of your work."

Bretta was perplexed. He handed over the bag to her to have a look.

Once in her hand, she comprehended it was a photograph of a label. She did not need to remove it from the bag to see it was *Bluebell*, one of her own private labels.

It might as well be stamped with *Bretta Berryman*, because the two were one and the same.

While it was not impossible that one of her designs found its way into the closet of Irma Barrett, it was extremely unlikely. This particular label was sold only to specialty boutiques. Her mind was swiftly trying to think of some explanation while at the same time praying that John would not come in the barn.

"That's quite a coincidence, Bretta, you moving into this old house and finding Irma's remains dressed in something you designed." She was aware his expression remained calm and friendly, and that he had switched to using her first name.

She would have to agree. She would also need to see more than the tag to know what exactly she was wearing. Some things that were sold to boutiques were made in very small quantities which would make this even stranger.

"Dear God, Bretta, now what have you done?" John's accusing voice ricocheted boisterously off the high ceiling beams of the barn and filled the space like surround sound. "Do not say another word until we consult with an attorney first!" John bulldozed his way across the room and stood next to his wife.

She flashed him an irritated look and moved aside quickly before he could put his arm around her.

"I do not need an attorney for God's sake! I haven't done anything!" Infuriation filled her entire being and she resisted the urge to lash out and do something that may result in the officers removing her in handcuffs.

He ignored his wife as if she were one of the children and stepped in front of her. "My wife has been going through a rather difficult time this past year. Perhaps you should start from the beginning and tell me everything." He turned his head back to Bretta. "Dear, why don't you go up to the house and rest?"

She clenched down so hard on her teeth she thought her back molars might crumble. Why couldn't that have been John's bones that she found in that chest?

He was the crazy one if he thought she would leave this barn so he could tell the sheriff she was unstable and he was planning to remove the children so she could have a *rest*.

"Mr. Berryman, I assume?" The Sheriff inquired of the newcomer.

"Yes." He shook hands with the sheriff and then with Marc. "Dr. John Berryman."

Bretta gave an exaggerated eye roll. It was immature of her she knew, but it always unnerved her so that he insisted on introducing himself as *doctor* and with such gusto. He's a damn dentist, not a brain surgeon.

"Nice car." Bretta heard Stan say to her spouse, referring to his obnoxious, red, midlife crises now parked in her driveway.

"When the lab releases the entire garment, I'll bring it by for you to take a look at Bretta. Perhaps you will be able to give us a little history on where it came from."

"Sure, I'll be glad to take a look at it." She was relieved he was not asking the *doctor* here to elaborate on her mental condition; instead he seemed to be eager to end the discussion and be on his way. She felt the sheriffs watchful eye upon her and knew his eagerness to leave had something to do with the verity that he had learned about Bretta and her difficult year.

Her spirits sank so low they reached the floor. Chester's welcome mat of peace, tranquility, and anonymity that had first welcomed her was now being yanked out from under her feet, leaving her off balance.

Between Wanda Bee and the sheriff snooping in her past and bones appearing in her basement garbed in one of her designs, soon she would be able to sell tickets at her front door.

Chapter 13

Wanda Bee floored her silver Lincoln MKS up the spectacular circular driveway of one of the newer, pricey homes she was at last finally able to show and threw it into park. Being a reporter may be her true calling, but real estate did offer her a different sort of a thrill all its own, not to mention it paid the bills.

Today it appeared that the heavens were smiling down upon her as she was able to weave the two careers nicely together into one fat payday.

Exhilaration traveled throughout her entire being, reminding her that she had forgotten to empty her bladder prior to leaving her house. She only hoped she did not have the urge to sneeze before she was able to get to the powder room.

She did a modified jog up the paved pathway to the house she was about to show, feeling remarkably pleased with herself that she timed her arrival twenty minutes before her client. Her long, hot pink fingernails pressed in the four digit code into the lock box which instantly offered up a key for entry.

She liked hearing the sound of her three inch heels as they tapped loudly on the ceramic tile and echoed throughout the vacant home. Quickly she detoured to the large oak table to dump her heavy briefcase and spread out her ammunition. Part of her success she knew was attributed to the fact that she always arrived prepared.

But what she saw upon entering the kitchen built to delight any cook stopped her dead in her tracks. Her sharp mind worked swiftly to process the unexpected.

Seated at the highly polished, black granite work station was a distinguished looking gentleman with his own briefcase open, its contents spread out in front of him which she noticed, included a not extremely flattering 5x7 shot of herself at last year's Pumpkin Festival.

Well, shit.

This wasn't how it was supposed to go. Could her client possibly have come to blackmail her?

She elevated her brows as her eyes went to work, rapidly scanning over the documents he had artfully arranged on the table.

If that's the case, he has no idea who he is messing with. Aunt Madelyn taught her a thing or two more than waving lace hankies and wearing fancy hats. When it came to manipulating, extortion, or other slightly illegal indiscretions, she was one of the best.

We'll just see who has the bigger gun here she thought as she hauled her own hefty briefcase up on the counter and let it crash loudly for effect.

"Hello, Wanda. Please have a seat." He stood, offering her a big, artificially whitened smile and slid out a chair for her.

Then he took out his gun.

It was clear that he did have the bigger gun here since she did not technically own one, but maybe after he saw what she packed in her briefcase it would not matter.

"Well, well, well," Wanda said as recognition kicked in, her eyes inspecting his custom tailored suit, silk Hermes tie and the expensive Montblanc pen peeking out of his suit breast pocket. "Look what the cat dragged back to town."

"I'm flattered you remember me." He waved his gun again, indicating she should have a seat.

"How could I forget? You always did have such a big *gun*?" She glanced at the weapon and then his crotch as she slid down into a kitchen chair.

Her client laughed. "You don't need to worry about my *gun* today, Wanda my dear." Slowly he walked behind her, allowing his hands to press firmly down on her shoulders as he bought his mouth close to her ear and whispered; "Because today I will be using my bare hands."

She could not think of a single thing that her Aunt would have advised that would help her out of this mess other than if she would have kept her frickin knees together in the first place, she could be home enjoying another damn sticky bun.

Chapter 14

The finished kitchen was fast becoming one of her favorite rooms in the house Bretta thought happily to herself as she plucked the ingredients down from the pantry shelves for their night's dinner and tossed them into a red wicker basket. She was delighted with her new pantry. It was spacious and thoughtfully designed to make prepping for a meal a joy. On her way back out to the kitchen she noticed that several bags of snacks she had purchased only days before were now gone. She would have to speak to the girls about that. No wonder they could never finish their supper.

She felt compelled to create more elaborate, sit down dinners most nights now and enjoyed experimenting with recipes from her stack of previously neglected cookbooks that she had collected over the years or try one of the hundred or so she had pinned on her Pinterest board. Once everything was under control in the kitchen, she made her way out through the side door to stroll around the grounds to start her yard work.

John abruptly fled after having been called away on some dental emergency and seemed to forget that at least for now anyway, that his children needed to be rescued from the clutches of their crazy mother.

Although the girls were a little disappointed at their father's early departure, she was deeply relieved to have him out of her hair. The fact that he worked so much always served her well. His absence in her life gave birth to her creativity. The more he was away, the more she felt free to explore her other areas of interest.

Marc had another job scheduled before he could start her office/workshop in the attic since that was not part of the original plans, so he was not around these days either. She found herself thinking of him often during the day while she worked alone, her mind replaying conversations they had had and it finally occurred to her that what she was missing in her life most was the company of other adults.

When she was designing, she worked alone, choosing to be as isolated as possible. But when her work was finished, she had always looked forward to bringing it in to her mother's office to visit her and the other employees. She never thought she would miss sitting around chatting about who wore what to the Oscars or where everyone was going to dine that evening, but strangely she did.

This morning however she was being blessed with a rare visit from her daughters who both agreed to help tackle the project of developing her landscaping sketches into reality.

The girls didn't seem to mind digging in the earth with their little shovels and dropping in alternating white and magenta Geraniums, the perfect annual for an area that would receive lots of sun.

Since she had read that color had ruled the Victorian Garden, she searched for a variety of wild colors and large plants. She added several enormous Boston Ferns to her porch that now dangled down stylishly and had Marc hang a white wooden swing which completed the picture and the feel she had been striving for. The only thing missing now were hypnotic sounds of wind chimes. Maybe she could take a look online later to see what she could find.

Bretta stood barefoot on the cool grass; her arms folded on her chest and admired the front of her house, extremely pleased with how her vision had taken shape thus far. At least everything with the house was coming together how she envisioned it would.

"Mom, Ms. Alice is coming over. Maybe I should help her cross the street." Iris expressed her concern as she started to move quickly in the direction of her neighbor.

She could see why Iris was worried; her neighbor looked like she was wearing a large flower pot on her head. Today's hat resembled a sombrero and was three times larger than her usual flair. Bright pink and purple flowers sprung from every direction and the wide, floppy brim practically touched her shoulders. She wondered if Alice had created it herself and as the older women got a little closer, Bretta could tell there was an assortment of colorful plastic flora along with fresh that she must have plucked a few from her garden on the way over. Her hands were full of a variety of gardening tools and a bright yellow canvas tote bag was slung over her shoulder.

Alice allowed the tools to drop to the earth, placed her bag down gently, and then lifted the brim of her hat up so she could see.

"Well, thank you to whoever helped me. I can't see a thing with this hat." She offered a big smile and looked around. "Oh, look how lovely everything is!"

"That was Iris that helped you, Alice." Bretta went up and gave her a hug. "Maybe you should wait until you cross the street to put your hat on." She gave her a tight squeeze. "We have missed you around here, where have you been hiding?"

"I was waiting for your husband to leave." She said without hesitation. "I brought some snacks for us!" She pointed to her canvas bag.

One of the things Bretta loved most about Alice was her simple honesty.

As Bretta happily glanced down at the snack bag, she caught sight of the Sheriff's vehicle making its way down the street.

"This won't be good news." Alice stated sadly.

Bretta announced to the girls their child labor hour was up and they were free to go and both ran off hastily in different directions before their mother had a chance to change her mind.

Sheriff Stan Meyers nodded and said good afternoon to both ladies and after a few moments of exchanging pleasantries, a large clear plastic bag materialized in his left hand. Already she understood what was inside the bag and her tired brain worked feverishly to come up with some possible answer, something other than, *this can't be happening.*

"Let's go inside Bretta, I want to show you something." Stan spoke gently. "Alice can come with you if you like."

Once inside he got right to the point. He presented Bretta with the bag as if it were a gift and said nothing.

Wordlessly, she took the bag from his hands and held it flat. The room took on a chilly, empty feel as she stared down at the dress.

It was tattered, old and stained, but of course she remembered the fabric. Tiny Iris's everywhere. She had fallen in love with the pattern the second she saw it at an antique store in Maine and purchased the bolt of cloth to make a dress for her daughter Iris and even one for her favorite doll. To keep things fair between the girls, as she always did, she hunted the stores until she found a pattern with Ivy and did the same for her other daughter.

Her eyes focused back on the women's garment in her hand. She never made one in an adult size dress before out of this pattern, she was sure of it. Her knees began to feel a bit weak as she concentrated on keeping her hands steady.

"Sheriff, where did this dress come from?" her voice came out softly with a slight quiver.

"This is the dress that Irma Barrett's was wearing when we found her." His voice was even toned and non-threatening, but still a shot of alarm bolted through her.

She thought of her Bluebell label the Sheriff had shown the other day and wondered what in the hell he was talking about.

"You showed me my Bluebell label the other day in the barn. You said it came from the dress Irma was wearing. I never made dress out of this fabric for an adult, only for my daughter Iris and her doll." She deliberately kept her voice calm and steady; at least she thought she was. Stan Meyers was looking at her oddly and Alice gently reached over and rested her hand on her arm as if to settle her down.

Without a word, he unzipped the garment bag and unfolded the collar.

Directly below the empty spot were Bluebell label had been removed was another label.

Bretta's hand shook as she pulled the dress closer for inspection.

Made exclusively for Irma.

A strange sound moved past her lips as the room suddenly grew smaller.

"Mrs. Berryman, did you design this?" Sheriff Stan interrogated patiently and gently.

"No." Her head continued to spin as she thought about how impossible it was for this dress to have her label on it. "I had purchased fabric like this to make a dress for my daughter and her doll, but I never made a dress like that in an adult size." Even through the bag she could see this dress would have required an enormous amount of fabric. "I didn't even have that much material left to work with after making Iris's and her doll's dress."

Even to her own ears, her words sounded unbelievable and illogical.

She shows up in town, adamant about buying an old, run down, condemned house where she happens to find bones clothed in a frock bearing her label and a unique fabric she admits to have used for her daughter and her doll.

Out of his pocket, the Sheriff quietly produced another baggie. Bretta was afraid to look but when the sheriff moved it in her direction, it was clear she would have to.

The second baggie was the original Bluebell label that had been taken out of the collar of the garment.

Could she have made this dress for Irma and not remember?

Her hand flew to her mouth to cover a cry of anguish. The very second John got wind of this it would be over. He would take the kids, her house and her life.

Alice was speaking in soothing tones while the Sheriff tried to figure out what to do with her.

Stan's cell phone rang and he excused himself to take the call. He stepped back slightly and spoke quietly. He ended his call and looked solemnly at the ladies before speaking.

"Ladies, I'm needed on another call." He paused for a second. "You will hear it soon enough anyway, news like this spreads faster than a wildfire around here; Wanda Bee has been found dead."

Chapter 15

Alice and Bretta wordlessly made their way back out of the house and onto the front porch swing. Neither one felt much like digging in the dirt at the moment.

"Wanda was a pesky thing, but I didn't want her dead." Alice said unhappily.

"How does something like this happen in a small town like Chester?" Bretta was still trying to shake off the sense of disbelief. The Sheriff had been right about how fast the news would travel. He was barely gone five minutes when Athena sprinted across her front lawn to tell them she heard Wanda had been murdered then continued to make her way down the street to spread the word to the local shut-in's. "How ironic that one of the reasons my husband wanted us to move to Chester was to get away from the all the crime and since we have arrived, I have found a corpse in my cellar and our realtor has been murdered."

"That was not why he wanted you to move here dear." Alice said as she lifted her legs out straight in front of her and examined her feet, pointing and flexing her toes as if she were trying out a new pair of shoes.

It had become one of those well told lies that she had started to believe for herself. The rehearsed story that she gave everyone for abruptly packing up and leaving her big life behind could now roll easily off her tongue and until now, no one ever questioned it except for her mother.

"It would be good for you to talk about all that, you've kept it to yourself for too long and it's unhealthy." Bretta took a moment to carefully look at her new friend. What a contradiction she was. She had to be in her eighties but most of the time acted young and silly. She wore strange, old lady dresses but her hair remained shiny and free of grey.

Today she was witnessing a more mature side of Alice than she typically saw she thought as her new friend wrapped her arm around her shoulder and pulled her close.

It was evident the older woman had a gift and she suddenly felt embarrassed that she might be aware of things that even her own mother did not know. There were things she did not talk about or think about and yet she suspected that her neighbor already knew. "You needn't be ashamed now, there's nothing wrong with you. You were a good wife and always an excellent mother." Alice said as she used her legs to start a slow, gentle back and forth movement of the swing.

It was odd, but today she did feel like talking. "My husband was charged with behaving inappropriately with a few of his female patients at work. There was only one young woman that brought up charges against him, but she later dropped them. The police were convinced that there were several others but they never came forward. Two of his patients that the police wanted to question disappeared. I think he silenced them up with hush money because they both vanished and we never heard from them again. I know the police suspect he had something to do with that as well but they could never prove it. I was so deeply humiliated both personally and professionally and the girls were tormented at school that I readily agreed to move. Friends that they have known since kindergarten were being told to stay away from our house by their parents. Not long after that, I started to have some strange heath issues, both mentally and physically." She breathed in deeply, filling her lungs with the fresh country air and once again marveled at how good she felt now. "The change of scenery was truly good for me because I feel better than ever since I moved here."

They sat in silence, allowing the rhythmic sway of the swing to soothe them.

"I've always said there is something magical about the air in Chester." Alice said with a big smile. "I think it's all my flowers." She tilted her head down to show off the entire bouquet. "Go ahead, take one."

"You might be right about that Alice." She reached out and plucked a yellow rose off of her friend's hat and sniffed it. "I always have that fear that one of those other victims will end up coming forward and start the scandal all over again."

Alice put a hand up to her head and tugged out a flower for herself. "There is no need to worry about that. They won't be coming back." She brushed the side of her check lightly with the soft petals. "I wonder why busy body Wanda was killed. She probably discovered something she shouldn't have." Alice braced her feet firmly against the porch which ended the soothing rocking motion and caused the swing to come to an abrupt stop. Her head turned until she could look into Bretta's eyes. "I bet it was about you."

⅄

Being the sheriff of a small town meant that you could do things a little different than in a big city. Sure there were rules and regulations, but he could stretch or ignore most of them if needed. That was one of the reasons he came back home. He had trouble with rules.

Stan lugged his own briefcase along with Wanda's through the front door of his house and plopped them down on his living room floor. Wanda Bee's briefcase weighed as much as two bowling balls. It was astonishing to him that she could tote the thing all over town wearing those hooker high heels she favored. Apparently, she had about as much faith in confiding in computers as she did other people and preferred the old fashion method of writing it all down.

Tonight he could sift through everything in the comfort of his living room, catch a bit of the game and sip on a cold beer while he tried to figure out what and the hell Wanda had been up to.

The most challenging part was going to be coming up with someone in this town who didn't have a reason for wanting her dead and knowing Wanda, she most likely didn't keep her dirty work within city limits.

The first file he came across pertained to the house she was found murdered in. It contained all the usual specs on the home; three bathrooms, four bedrooms and one fireplace. It also revealed a prudent and methodical background check on the current owners. That was a bit odd, but then this was Wanda we were dealing with. There was another file for a house down the street with again the complete shakedown on the current owners, only this one had the goods on the potential buyer as well. In fact, there was a run down on every client that had viewed the house.

It was odd that there was not a file on the potential buyer of the house. He dug through the contents of the briefcase again in case he had over looked it and came up empty leaving him to assume that her client left with their own file. Looks like Wanda finally blackmailed the wrong person.

He put the file aside for a moment and stuck his hand back into Wanda's briefcase to pry out another. Her traveling file cabinet was crammed so tight with folders it was impossible to see what she had. Turning the case upside down, he let the insides fall out where they may, creating a colossal mess. He gave himself a few minutes to read each carefully printed label before choosing a file at random.

"Son of a gun." Stan shook his head in disbelief as he opened the file and began to read. "I should have had that woman working for me."

⅄

The stranger gripped his hands vehemently on the steering wheel of his automobile and for a moment, fantasized it was the pretty woman's neck.

His brief fascination with her had now turned to frustration. Why was she always home? Didn't women like to be out shopping and doing endless, unimportant errands that gave one the illusion of being busy?

He drove slowly past the Huddelstone manor and saw her wasting away the day on a porch swing next to a familiar looking old lady wearing an enormous, hideous hat. It was his third trip around the block and neither one so much as glanced his way. So much for the Neighborhood Watch sign that had threatened to tattle on him when he had turned his vehicle onto Hollyhock Lane.

It was tempting to simply park the car a few houses down, cut through the neighbor's yard and walk in through her back door. He could hear their yacking from his car and he knew they would never hear him, but once they came inside he would be trapped like a rat in the attic until they eventually left the house or went to bed for the night.

He hadn't moved back to this wretched town to reunite with his crazy freaking family he was now forced to live with or to spend his days driving in circles that was for sure.

He came for a purpose.

To relive, revisit, maybe even revive his past in the grand old manor he once spent so much time at. To silence the nightmares or perhaps feed them, either way he would be a hell of a lot happier than hanging out in this state of purgatory.

The game most likely would not be the same unless the others joined in, after all this wasn't like solitaire. Or who knows? He massaged his scalp with his fingertips while he considered what he would do once he was back in.

Killing never bothered him. He understood he was supposed to feel remorse or at the very least, guilt over taking another's life. But there was nothing. Not a stinking sentiment or a single regret.

It was only a game after all.

An activity he could not partake in anymore because no one had fucking bothered to tell him that someone had moved into his house he thought as a swift eruption of anger blasted through his veins.

He forced in a deep breath and held it before slowly releasing it, focusing on happy thoughts the way he had been taught in therapy and felt only marginally better. At least he didn't throw the car into park and race across the lawn to snap the pretty woman's neck the way he wanted to.

Instead he maneuvered his "borrowed" car leisurely around the block and parked it in front of a depressing red brick house and firmly pressed his head against the steering wheel until it hurt, waiting for divine inspiration.

When it finally came, the corners of his lips turned up into what some would call a frightening smile.

What mother bear wouldn't come running out of her den when she learned her cubs were in danger?

Chapter 16

The pasta had just been tossed into the salted, boiling water when Ivy and Iris came running into the kitchen.

"Mother, there has been a murder." Ivy declared calmly. "Ms. Bee has been killed." Without so much as taking a breath in between, she sped through all the facts before her sister could get a word in.

"However, I don't think we need to be alarmed that a serial killer is on the loose in Chester. Most likely this is the result of Ms. Bee sticking her nose in where it didn't belong."

"Ivy!" Bretta hastily snatched the spoon out of her famous spaghetti sauce she was stirring and dropped it on the counter. Obviously Ivy had been listening in on some adult conversation somewhere in town today.

"Girls, go wash your hands. Supper will be ready in five minutes. We will talk about what happened then."

She had not counted on the Chester grapevine stretching as far as the children. Apparently, it had no limits on who it reached or what it repeated.

Bretta began filling plates from the steaming serving bowls she had placed in the center of the table and frowned. The sauce looked naked without the thick Italian sausage links resting on top.

"Yes, it is true that Ms. Bee is dead. However, we do not know all the facts yet. Let's not jump to any conclusions." She was about to say that they did not know for sure if Wanda had been murdered, but she knew how ridiculous that would sound, even to young ears. Wanda's body had been discovered in a vacant house with a bullet hole in the middle of her forehead. It hardly looked like an accident at this point.

Ivy rolled her eyes. "Mother, there is no need to try and shelter us. Ms. Bee probably just tried to blackmail the wrong person. Did you know she used to be a reporter?"

"Ivy!" Bretta dropped her fork. "Where were you today that you heard all this?" Who in their right mind would say all this, true or not, in front of a child?

"I went with Hannah to the beauty parlor for a haircut. The ladies in there know *everything.* Can I get my haircut there?"

Hell would freeze over before she let those old hags anywhere near Ivy's long gorgeous hair.

"We will discuss a haircut later. What the *ladies* in the salon were doing today Ivy was gossiping and it was wrong. They do not have any real knowledge about what happened other than that Ms. Bee is dead. Therefore the rest is speculation. Please do not repeat what you have heard today with anyone else. Alright?"

Ivy shook her head and reluctantly agreed, smart enough to understand that this was a topic her mother clearly did not wish to pursue, then went on to focus on her spaghetti.

"You know mom, you might try adding the meatless Italian sausage for more flavor." Ivy suggested.

"Thank you, Ivy. I'll keep that in mind."

Pleased with her mother for accommodating her new eating habits, Ivy smiled and continued on with her meal.

"Perhaps you girls would have more of an appetite if you didn't go through a weeks' worth of snacks in two days."

"What snacks?" Ivy's eyes lit up at the mention of possible junk food. She may be on a no meat kick but she wasn't exactly craving fruits and vegetables.

"The ones that are now missing from the pantry." She let it go for now and directed her focus on Iris who was playing with her food.

"Iris, you're very quiet tonight. I realize your sister does not allow you to say much, but are you okay honey?"

Iris's eyes were glued on her dinner plate. She twirled the long noodles around her fork several times before stopping and looking up at her mother. The older and more mild mannered of the two sisters appeared unusually somber.

"I think we do need to be scared mom. I think he's coming after us next."

⅄

Sheriff Stan Meyers sat quietly at the desk in his office and stared down at the three chosen files he had borrowed from the Wanda Bee collection.

The documents read like a special edition of The National Enquirer and he wrestled with his conscious as he ventured into the private lives of the Berryman's. The only difference between what he was reading and the trashy gossip papers that are sold at the checkout stands was that Wanda's records all appeared to be true.

He had started double checking Wanda's files first thing in the morning on the Sheriff's Department official computer and discovered everything she had to be accurate, extensive, and intrusive.

After his initial encounter with John Berryman in the barn that day, he had run a check to see if he had any prior's.

Upon first setting eyes on Bretta's spouse, he had an instant disinclination for him. He found him to be both arrogant and condescending. After he opened his mouth he added asshole to the list. However, that did not make him a felon and when Kuster's background check on him came up clean, Berryman was crossed off the list.

He should have kept digging. That or borrowed Wanda's briefcase earlier.

Stan sat back in his chair and slowly ran his fingers over the two day growth on his chin. He would prefer to have the discussion in person with Dr. Berryman to hear his version of what happened between the doctor and his hygienist and how it came to be that she did not press any charges.

Knowing Wanda, she would have gotten around to meeting with Dr. Berryman sooner or later to share what she had learned.

He scratched out a note for Kuster to run a check on Patrick Howard; Wanda's client and the man most likely the last person to see her alive and tossed it over on his desk.

Stan stood up from his desk, stretched, and grabbed his car keys which had been thrown casually on Bretta's file. The file that he had pushed to the side and had not wanted to read.

It made him feel dirty looking at something that should be private. There was no criminal past, simply a scope into her personal life and one more reason to dislike her husband.

He recalled the first time he saw her, standing in front of Huddelstone, waiting for him to walk up the path to her front door. Bretta Berryman was like a gentle breeze of fresh air to the weary old town of Chester. What he learned today did not change that.

It was time to make his way over to Wanda's house to uncover what secrets could not be crammed into her briefcase. But first there was his own unpleasant business that needed his attention. His head pounded as he sifted through the stacks of folders until he found it.

He nearly breathed a sigh of relief when he saw it but knew he was not out of the woods yet. At least for now it was safely gripped in his own hands he thought as he carried it with him out the door and slid into his airless police cruiser. Quickly he cranked up the air to the coldest setting and felt some of the moisture on his skin begin to evaporate. Summer was winding down but it was still hotter than hell. He knew a few weeks into a Northern Michigan winter he would be missing a day like this, but right about now he was getting a little sick of the overbearing heat.

He looked back down at the ragged manilas Wanda dragged around town. Computer printouts, newspaper articles, and private investigator reports; all ready to destroy someone's life at the drop of a hat.

It was amazing she wasn't killed sooner.

Chapter 17

Betty Grimes will proudly tell anyone that will listen that she has been a dispatcher with the Chester County Sheriff's department for over twenty years. A title that sounded a lot more exciting than it was considering the department only took in approximately ten calls a day and none of them life threatening.

Therefore the other more mundane office tasks that the under-budgeted department could not afford to hire personnel for fell on her shoulders. Duties such as secretarial, janitorial, and informational over time all became part of her day.

Since the town of Chester and the office itself was fairly small, all her assignments no matter how darn hard she tried to drag them out, never took more than twenty minutes to complete. There was at no time a flood of locals or tourists at her front door requesting information or a stack of anything to file, so basically by two o'clock p.m. each day; she was completely and utterly bored.

This sometimes forced her to occupy her time with busy-work that was not in her job description, although she tried to weave it in under filing and dusting.

Casually armed with a can of Pledge in one hand and a feather duster sticking out of her back pocket, Betty worked her way to Sheriff Stan's office. That duster could be in her hand and working faster than an outlaw pulling out his gun in the Old West if she so much as heard a sound.

The trick was not to get so absorbed in your snooping that you missed the sound of a car pulling up or the click of the door knob.

To make it look like she did indeed do her maid duties, she ran to the bathroom and grabbed the container of Clorox wipes from under the sink. Last week Sally Hiller, the departments miserable, smart mouthed and only female officer had the nerve to ask what in fact she did all day.

The next morning Betty added something extra to Sally's coffee. A splash of bleach or a drop of the cleaning product she was forced to preform slave duties with would have been poetic, but not worth all the fuss it would cause if she were to get caught so she settled for coughing up a little something special and blending it with her French Vanilla creamer. She found it so amusing that she was considering making it a daily ritual.

She swiftly ran a wipe over most of the surface area and cleaned up spot on the floor. She was a dispatcher, not a housekeeper for Christ's sake. On the way out of the bathroom, she caught a glimpse of herself in the mirror and allowed a moment to admire her own reflection.

She beamed as she marveled at her massive breasts that have grown along with her bottom each year. Her annual five pound gain in her opinion only added to her allure. Men loved big butts. She smoothed down her long jet black hair that hasn't been cut since the nineties. Men also loved long hair. Quickly she grabbed the files that she thought would be the most interesting and ran to the copier. There was one way to get her blood pumping, Betty thought and that was to wave personal, private, and privileged information under her nose.

Her only regret was that she no longer had her dear friend Wanda to share, well and to sell, her new found knowledge with.

She tossed the duster and Pledge back in the broom closet and brought her reading material to her desk, the pages still warm from the copier and began to learn all about one of Chester's newest families.

She made a loud clucking noise with her tongue and shook her head with revulsion as she became engrossed with the life of John Berryman. She would have to watch herself around that one. Automatically her chin tilted down to do a quick cleavage check. No sense in teasing the man.

Her eyes stayed firmly entrenched on the file in front of her while her right hand instinctively found its way to the top right drawer of her desk and sought out a snack size bag of barbeque potato chips.

Well now, this little tidbit of news certainly grabbed her by surprise. The woman had seemed so pleasant and normal when she dropped in to ask for directions. She stuffed a handful of chips in her mouth and wiped the greasy orange residue on her pants while reflecting how unsafe of a town Chester was becoming.

Things were bad enough with a murderer running around, but now the town had one more concern.

Bretta Berryman was a lunatic.

⅄

One by one he watched them play, the two little sisters by the bay. The stranger put his hand over his mouth to cover up the bubble of emotion that crept up his throat and threatened to escape his lips. It wouldn't do to give away his hiding spot yet.

He had felt quite amused when he had first spotted the girl's bicycles and he perceived that they were a good distance from their home, much too far for them to make it back on foot. A brilliant plan promptly began to form in his exceptional mind.

While the young women were frolicking in the water, he coolly approached their bikes that they had so carelessly abandoned up on a hill in the tall grass. His head shook back and forth in repugnance at the lack of care for their possessions.

Only one had bothered to use her kick stand and both bikes were in desperate need of a good cleaning and waxing. He took the one with the kick stand first, lifting it as if it were no heavier than a twig, and with his gloved hand, placed it in his roomy back seat. The second bike went in the trunk.

He smiled at his own kindness. He could have thrown both bikes in there together, but he didn't want to be the one to scratch up and dent the frames. The little wenches had already done a fine job of that on their own.

As he drove down the hill his grin grew even wider as he considered how delightful it would have been to have thrown the girls in the trunk along with the bike.

However that would end up being a lot more work for him in the long run. He remembered that dead bodies in trunks got awfully messy.

Chapter 18

Bretta did not have to weed too many flower beds in her day and was astonished to find the chore so pleasurable. The morning easily slipped into afternoon before she even thought of the time.

The girls must be having fun on their bike ride to be gone so long. Wincing as she came to a standing position, she felt tremendous gratitude to Alice for her gift of a bright pink foam knee mat. Being a city girl, as the Mundy sisters often referred to her, she didn't own all the gardening gadgets she noticed her neighbors had. She didn't even know what half of them were used for although she was coming to find most of them awfully handy.

She backed up to the edge of her lawn and took a good long look at the front of her house. She was proud. Not bad for a city girl, not bad at all. She knew it was silly, but she wanted everything finished and looking perfect before her mother came for her first visit. Her mother informed her last night she misses her daughter and grandchildren immensely and plans on arriving next week, ready or not.

The ringing of the telephone snapped her back to the present and Bretta ran for the cordless phone she had left on the porch steps next to her cellphone. It was strange that she even thought to bring the house phone out with her. When friends or family needed to reach her they always called on her mobile.

Vaguely it registered with her that the caller ID showed the number as restricted. Not that it mattered, she would answer it anyway. Thankfully, the telemarketers have not found her yet and the news media finally lost interest.

"Hello?" Bretta's voice came out a bit winded and she smiled into the phone.

"Hello to you, Mrs. Berryman." The male voice spoke at a slow, warped speed.

The sun's warmth instantly abandoned her back and instinctively she suspected that something was dreadfully wrong.

"Who is this?" She tried to match his composure as she gripped the phone tighter.

"Do you know where your children are?" The caller let out a strange chortle to express his amusement. "I've really always wanted to say that, you know, after the old TV commercial?"

"What have you done to my girls?" Her voice came out in a forced whisper. It could simply be a prank call, but her gut put her on alarm and panic was quickly taking over. She knew she needed to pay attention to what he was saying.

"Such cute girls you have. They were having a little trouble with their bikes."

"Please, where are my girls?" She pleaded with her caller.

"Little girls love to play; I think I saw them by the bay."

The call ended and she tried to think fast what to do.

"Bretta, what's wrong?" The deep, masculine voice that spoke unexpectedly from behind made her jump and spin around.

Marc was standing in front of her looking concerned. It did not matter that he startled her again, she was extremely glad to see him.

"Marc..." The phone was still clutched in her hand as she began whimper. These were her babies and she could not think of what to do first.

"Who was that on the phone? Tell me what they said so I can help you." He spoke in soft, comforting tones that kept her from screaming.

"A man has the girls." Willing herself to be calm, she understood running around hysterical would not help her daughters. She thought of the small bottle of pills in her nightstand drawer. John's voice suddenly roared in her head telling her she was not well and she almost sank to her knees.

"The man on the phone said he has Ivy and Iris?" Marc prodded when she stopped speaking.

"Do you know where your children are? That's what he asked me." Her eyes flooded with tears. "Then he said what cute girls I have and something about them having trouble with their bikes. They had gone out for a bike ride this morning."

"Do you know where they were headed?"

What had they said as they rushed out the door? Her brain was racing through words and images when abruptly it stopped at something the caller said.

"He said some type of rhyme. Hurry…we have to find them." She covered her face with her hands.

"I need to know what he said." His voice remained calm and even. "Close your eyes a second and tell me what he said."

Remarkably, it only took a couple of seconds and it came to her. "Little girls like to play. I think I saw them by the bay. That's what he said. Then he hung up."

"Ok, good. Call the Sheriff's office and tell them what happened. I just saw Stan drive down Main, so tell Betty to have him call me on my cell when she talks to him."

Bretta nodded then noticed the phone was still clenched in her hands. She started pressing the appropriate keys with shaking hands while she gathered her thoughts.

Marc sprinted into the yard towards the barn. "I'm going to grab a few things then I'll meet you in the truck." He called out over his shoulder. "We're going to look for the girls. Don't tell Betty that though. I'll tell Stan myself when he calls."

The Sheriff's department answered on the second ring and Bretta rapidly gave the details of her terrifying phone call and the instructions from Marc. She was ready to hang up and get in the truck when she became aware that the dispatcher had not said anything.

"Hello?" Fearing after all that they had been disconnected and she would have to call back and tell this story again, wasting valuable time.

"Mrs. Berryman, are you *feeling* okay?"

She knew this tone very well. The town's dispatcher was questioning her mental stability, but what she did not know was why.

"Did you hear me? A man has my girls!" Now she had to worry about not sounding crazy when she wanted to scream at the insensitive dispatcher to help her find her children. "A man called and said something about my cute girls and that they were having trouble with their bikes. He said he saw them by the bay. He made a rhyme out of it."

"A rhyme?" Betty mocked.

"Yes, he did. That's all he said." She was not going to waste precious time arguing with this woman.

"I'm hanging up now. Be sure the Sheriff contacts Marc on his cell phone."

Bretta ran to Marc's truck where he waited with the engine running. She climbed in and he speed off before she had a chance to put her seatbelt on.

"I know a few spots by the bay they may have stopped, we can check there first." He tilted his wrist to look at his sports watch. "It's just a little after 1:00 now; we have lots of daylight left." He offered her an encouraging smile as he gently reached out and took her hand for a moment. His touch was light and presence reassuring; she could not imagine having to endure this on her own.

"Should you call your husband?"

"No." Bretta turned her head and gazed out the passenger window. "I can't let him know I've lost the children."

Chapter 19

Betty swiftly snatched another bag of chips from her desk drawer. All the excitement from her last call left her ravenous. She used her teeth to help tear open the bag and dove in.

"What a nut bag!" She might have faked indifference on the phone but nothing could be further from the truth. There has not been anything this enthralling to come across her phone lines since Harriet Hanson beat her no good loser husband into a coma last year and then dragged his sorry unconscious ass unto the middle of highway 75 and left him there to die. Betty had reluctantly sent a scout car to pick him up before he was flattened by a semi, but only because she knew she would be fired if she didn't.

Thank God she did take the time be so inquisitive because none of the officers around here bother to tell her a thing. They should be thanking her for her efforts. As a direct result of her own investigative work, it eliminated the need to dispatch an officer every time a lunatic calls in requesting help for their make believe emergencies.

She opened ding bat's file again and paused briefly to wipe her hands on a napkin. Simply because Wanda was out of the game didn't mean it was over for her and it wouldn't be smart to get grease stains all over everything, she needed to be professional.

Betty skimmed over the pages quickly until she came across what she was looking for.

"Ah-hh" came out in a forceful spray of spit and chips. "I knew it! We got ourselves one of those certifiable nutcases from the city!"

Betty's beady little eyes opened wide at the last statement and wondered exactly what kind of family had moved into her peaceful little town.

⅄

The first spot Marc checked showed no indication of recent of visitors and the bike trails that he remembered as a kid were long overgrown with tall grass and weeds. He doubted the girls would have chosen this location for an adventure, but he stopped the car just in case and got out.

"I know of another site." He assured as he started the engine, threw it into drive and kept his eyes on the road ahead. "It's about fifteen minutes away."

"Is the Sheriff on his way?" Bretta asked hopefully.

Marc checked his watch and then put his eyes back on the road in front of him. "I haven't heard from him." He tapped the dashboard with his fingers a few times and then retrieved the phone from his shirt pocket, dialing quickly.

"Hey Marc, how's it going?"

"Nothing so far. First we checked out that little bay off to the left when you first come into to town and now were going to stop by the old Lampher homestead, by the water. Do you want to meet us there?"

There was a brief pause.

"I just hung up with Betty. She said the Berryman's girls have been gone a while on a bike ride and the mom was getting worried. I was going to send Kevin to run out and look for them."

Marc never liked Betty. In fact he thought she was a lazy, overpaid busy body. However, he always tried to cut her some slack because she clearly did not have much else going for her in life and she must be good at her job to have kept it all these years.

Today however, all bets were off.

"A man called Bretta and said he saw the girls by the bay." He knew Bretta was listening to every word and he could fill in the pieces later. "He suggested she had better go look for them."

"Really?" He paused briefly. "I'll meet you at the Lampher site."

⅄

Betty located the Sheriff on his car radio, eager to deliver her important message.

"Sheriff, I've got a call for you from a Dr. Mioaki from the crime lab you sent those bones to. I tried to get him to give me the information or just fax it on over, but he insists on speaking to you directly."

"Give him my cell number immediately and tell him I am standing by for his call." She noticed his words came out more as a stern command than his usual friendly suggestions. "And Betty, I want to have a word with you when I get back."

"Okay…" Momentarily taken aback, she mumbled an okay into the phone.

"Well!" She spoke out loud in case someone should have overheard the conversation. "Wonder what crawled up his booty today?" She knew her co-workers were waiting for the day to see her get in trouble. Most were jealous that she was smart enough to get the good job while they have to wait around for a call to separate morons head locked in a drunken brawl or extract a cat out of a tree.

The top drawer of her desk refused to budge, but on the second hard tug it flew open easily and she began to search for the candy bar Scotch taped underneath. Last week when she returned from lunch she noticed her supply had been tampered with. She had no problem with sharing, but when you take without asking it's called stealing.

What the hell? Her hand feverishly explored under the desks rough exterior while sitting up straight, trying not to appear obvious. She was sure it was the top drawer, but just in case she felt under each one until finally she had no choice but to get down on all fours and search.

"Loose something Betty?" Sally called out from over the front of her desk, a wry smile glued on her face and a stack of files in her hand.

Betty froze, waited a moment and then slowly heaved herself back into her chair, her face a dangerous shade of purple from the excursion.

"No, just dropped something."

"Oh." She started to walk away and then hesitated. "Well, if you're looking for that Nestle Crunch bar you had taped under your drawer…" she paused long enough to watch Betty's eyes darken over with fury. "It is on the floor behind your chair."

Chapter 20

Stan fiercely pinched the bridge of his nose while waiting for the Chief Medical Examiner to return his call.

Chester was quickly beginning to resemble one of those "made for Television murder mysteries" his mother always watched and he could not help but notice it started about the time the Berryman family moved to town.

"Sheriff Meyers here." He barked into the phone as if it was somehow responsible for the sudden surge in his stress load.

"Good afternoon to you Sheriff, Dr. Mioaki calling. You are well?"

"Good afternoon Doctor. I am well, thank you." He smiled into the phone and allowed himself to ease back into the seat. They had spoken a few times now regarding the Huddelstone case and he found the man to be both entertaining as well as brilliant.

"I do not like the woman who answers your phone. She reminds me of a vulture that speaks."

He had to laugh at the accurate description.

"I need to have a talk with her." Stan admitted.

Finished with small talk, Dr. Mioaki was eager to get down to business. "I called in a Forensic Anthropologist to look at your bones even though body has been identified. I do a good job already, but this is her specialty so I figure I might learn something. I didn't. But whatever, your report is done. They are all accounted for; no one kept one for a souvenir. Female, late seventies to early eighties with severe arthritis in her hip and knees especially. Looks like a hand saw did the work. I will have full details in my written report which will be available by the end of the day."

"You can tell she had arthritis from looking at just the bones?"

"Yes."

"How?" He finally enquired when it became apparent that the doctor wasn't going to elaborate. He had already had a basic knowledge understanding that bones were a lot like a tree trunk in that it could often offer ones age but he was looking for details, pieces of information that no matter how random might be helpful later.

"With osteoarthritis the cartilage in the joints wears away, so the bones then rub together and become damaged."

Stan released a breath of disappointment that filled his entire car.

He was hoping that what, this funny Asian forensic doctor would put back together old lady Barrett like Humpty Dumpty and tell him who killed her and why?

"Also, the substance that was taken off the chest and the floor did come back as blood. Most likely hers, A positive."

"Yeah, ok..." Stan interrupted. He already knew this from matching the DNA.

"Did you run tests? I don't think so. Be quiet and let me finish. The blood had mixture of formaldehyde and some traces of arsenic in it. There was evidence of arsenic on her bones too, just a small amount."

Now he was speechless. *Formaldehyde and arsenic*? What did that mean?

"Formaldehyde as in someone was trying to preserve her and arsenic as in she was first poisoned?"

"Unlikely with such trace amounts. Long time ago, arsenic was used for embalming, but not anymore. Too unsafe. Could be someone has old chemicals. Can you make a trip here? I want you to come and take a look."

"Take a look?" He was still trying to wrap his brain around the arsenic and formaldehyde. He must have missed part of the conversation.

"I take many pictures, but I want you to come and take a look."

"Alone at last." The stranger said softly to himself as he thoughtfully went around to each treasure. Vigilantly he selected an item, held it carefully then turned it around several times in his hands before gently placing it back down.

He truly missed being able to come and go as he pleased. Sneaking in like a common thief felt so undignified.

It would be difficult for anyone watching him to say if the artifacts covered in an inch of dust brought him great pleasure or intense pain for the look upon his face remained impartial.

He knew her remains were no longer there. *Someone* he had heard had relocated them to the cellar a few years ago. He had been outraged when he first learned the news, taking several days to recover.

He thought it was exceptionally rude to have messed with his handy work. If someone wanted to kill the old lady and put her in the cellar then they should have thought to have done so. Plus, if they were going to go through all the trouble of moving her, why didn't they bury her with the others out back?

He knew it was one of the gang that had moved her. Just because they were all grown up now doesn't mean they don't miss the game.

Many warm and agreeable summer afternoons were spent in this very space and he permitted the pleasant memories to fill his brain as he stood motionless near the window, taking care that one of the old oddities from across the street would not see him.

It was meant for him to live in this house and now having made this lofty decision, he became filled with a certain satisfaction that made him feel an easy contentment he hasn't known for a long time.

These possessions should all belong to him and it angered him further to see them stuffed away and forgotten, just like the new homeowner's dirty past. Each piece should be proudly set out on display downstairs as they once were. The mahogany silverware chest. The lead crystal candlestick holders and Irma's finest tea set complete with a cart.

Now why in the hell wouldn't those fools use a tea set?

He squeezed his eyes shut and there he was, having tea with Irma.

"Sorry little family, but it's time you found someplace else to live."

Chapter 21

She felt vaguely conscious of Marc who sped through the back roads of Chester that she never knew existed, the sharp turns and hills playing havoc on her stomach. He had been on the phone since they left her house though she was unsure if it was all one long call or several. His voice though weaving in and out of her thoughts was soothing and steady, even if he was not speaking directly to her.

She glowered once again at her watch; it was almost five PM. The minutes were flying into hours now with no sign of her little girls and panic began to fill every fiber of her body.

What if the sun sets and they are still out there? What if they are lost in the woods and they keep going deeper into the thick trees and they never find them? The caller's voice replayed in her head and the worst imaginable tried to seep into her mind. If she allowed that, her sanity would certainly be dragged away again.

Most wives would have immediately called their husband. But he was not her partner, her better half and she knew she could not count on him. He would only blame her and God forbid, might even tell the police she had something to do with their disappearance.

Suddenly she realized that Marc had been speaking to her. "Stan had left a message earlier on my cell. He is asking for your sketch book Bretta and anything else that would show your designs."

This time she rolled the window down all the way now, stuck her head out and retched.

⅄

The stranger let out a small snort of indignation as he exited Huddelstone. This was undoubtedly a new twist for him.

He was being watched.

Oh, he could feel it and someone as sensitive as he would certainly know for sure. He felt a thrill of delight at this unforeseen game and only wished he had more time to participate.

It was doubtful it was simply one of those meddlesome old busy bodies that live across the street or the macho brute from around the block; both would have made their presence known by now.

Someone was waiting to see what he found.

Well, they can wait all they want. Finders keepers, losers are well…often brutally murdered.

Slightly he shook his head and held back a cynical grin. Even under stress he was witty.

Irma had been right; he did have a splendid sense of humor.

Chapter 22

If her insides were not twisted with fright, she knew her cheeks would have burned with mortification. She took the tissue from Marc's outstretched hand and wordlessly wiped her mouth, wishing she could rinse out the bitter and unpleasant taste.

She did not want to talk about the Sheriff's request for her sketches and she certainly did not want to chat about getting sick over the side of his truck.

The only thing she wanted right now was to see her daughters come walking up the path in front of them. Marc parked his truck so it faced a clearing in the trees and then both exited the vehicle.

"Mom? What you doing here?"

Bretta spun around so fast a wave of dizziness almost took her down. She saw them in the distance, she was sure of it. Oh God, she hoped this was for real and not a trick from her mind. Quickly she checked Marc's face for validation and with relief so rewarding, she started to cry.

Not the tender tear drops that glide gently down your face that she would have preferred to do in front of others, but the gut wrenching sobs for which she had no control over.

"What's wrong mom?" Iris sounded frightened and both were instantly at her side.

"What have you done to her?" Ivy glared fiercely at Marc, but kept her hand on her mother's back.

Marc chuckled and ignored Ivy's accusation. "Are you girls ok?"

They looked up at him strangely. Iris being the oldest chimed in. "Were fine. Clearly mother's not though."

"I'm fine girls; I've just been worried about the two of you. You lost your bikes?"

The sisters exchanged nervous glances with each other before Iris finally spoke up.

"What makes you think that?" Iris looked intently down at the dirt and kicked a pebble around with her sandal.

Bretta had to laugh. Here she had been terrified for her daughter's lives and not only had they not been aware of the drama taking place, they were up to their old tricks.

"A little birdie called me and told me." She wrapped both girls in her arms and hugged them tightly. She made the quick decision to wait to tell them the details until they returned home. The sheriff would want to speak to all of them anyway.

As they made the turn onto Hollyhock lane, they saw the Sheriff was sitting on their porch, two familiar bikes in front of him.

Ivy and Iris jumped out of the truck and ran up the walk way.

"Our bikes! You found them!" They squealed in delight.

The sheriff smiled at the girls and waited for Bretta to approach him before speaking.

"Hello girls. Are these your bikes?"

Anxiously they looked down at the bikes, afraid they were both in trouble.

"Yes, they are." Ivy spoke up. "Where did you find them?"

"They were at the corner." A friendly male voice spoke up behind her and she turned to find deputy Kuster's smiling face. He gave them a fast wink.

"Shall we step inside then ladies? I think we have a few things to go over." The Sheriff held the door open and the group paraded in.

Ladies? Bretta looked nervously around for him and spotted him back in his truck, talking on his phone. She would have preferred him in here if not for comfort, then for validation.

She couldn't very well stand there in the door wall and insist upon waiting for her handyman, so she walked through to join her girls on the couch who had been seated by the happy deputy.

Wedging her way down between her two girls, she gave them what she hoped was a reassuring smile and then rested her head back on the cushion and allowed her heavy eyelids to close. Tonight's bath would be tremendously hot and exceptionally lengthy if she made it until then.

"Hey, that's a nice tea set mom. When did you get that?" Ivy's voice knocked softly in her left ear.

Ivy's words rolled around her head like a dull thunder until the internal noise finally forced her lids apart.

"Tea set?" She followed their gazes past the reception hall and into the dining room and spotted a stunning mahogany tea cart ready for service.

Slowly she arose from the couch and walked into the dining room, aware that Kuster's concerned eyes were upon her. She remembered noticing a cart similar to this one up in the attic and to her utter astonishment someone had even taken the liberty to set out cups, saucers, a pot of tea which was still hot and a bouquet of fresh flowers that looked to have come from her back yard.

"Wow Mom!" Ivy exclaimed. "This is so cool, thank you!" Clearly thinking the tea party was for her and her sister.

Irritably she rubbed her temples as they began to pulsate and willed herself to think without trying to be too obvious about the fact that something was about to rupture in her head.

When was the last time she was even in this room? She did a fast retract of her actions early in the morning and recalled she had been outside all morning working in the front yard and had walked out through the kitchen to the barn for the tools.

What in the hell should she tell the officers? Strange men calling her on the phone, bikes disappearing and then reappearing and now it appears someone has broken in to have a tea party in her living room. Her face visibly cringed as she recalled the remains in the cellar wearing one of her own designs.

Surely John took great pains to be sure the charming Sheriff and grinning deputy knew about her past little problem.

"You okay, Mrs. Berryman?" Deputy Kuster stood beside her and touched her elbow reassuringly as he carefully studied the tea set.

"Yes, I..."

"Someone's ready for a tea party." Deputy Kuster smiled slightly, letting go of her arm. He squatted down on the floor in front of the display to get a closer look. "Did you move this down from the attic?" He stood up and looked knowingly into Bretta's eyes.

Bretta's eyes enlarged with alarm and she took a moment to think before she replied. This was not the first time she had the sense that the pleasant deputy could pick up pieces of her thoughts, so she thought twice before saying something that was untrue.

"No, I didn't." She had briefly entertained the idea of fabricating a story that she found the set up stairs and put it on display, but trying to explain why three of the cups were filled would not make her seem less crazy.

Kuster remained cheerful and wrote something down in his little note pad.

The sheriff offered Bretta a kind smile. "Mrs. Berryman, why don't you go back and have a seat with the girls so we can go over a few things?"

"Sure, and please call me Bretta." She went and sat between the girls again who were now getting restless and confused.

The sheriff lowered himself to the ottoman in directly in front of the couch while his deputy continued to poke around the room and then eventually left through the front door.

"Let's start at the beginning with the phone call please. Tell me everything that happened." He smiled gently at her daughters that were already uneasy. "Do you want the girls to stay for this Bretta?"

She shook her head yes. "Yes, they need to be aware of what is going on so they can be alert." Suddenly the girls stopped fidgeting and were quiet.

"Where were you and what were you doing when the phone rang?" His tone was reassuring and gentle.

"It was around noon and I was working in the front yard when the house phone rang. It was a man's voice I didn't recognize asking me if I knew where my children were." She recited the rest of the conversation to the best of her memory while the handsome sheriff took it all in, occasionally interjecting questions. His manner was easy going and comforting and Bretta felt herself relaxing.

"Did he say children or did he ask for the girls by name?"

"He said children. He didn't use their names."

He smiled easily at the girls. "What places did you explore today?"

Ivy was fast to cut off her sister. "We only made it to one place, but we were there all day. It had water, bike trails and a forest, it was extremely cool. But when we went to leave, our bikes were gone." She used as much facial expression as she possibly could to tell her story.

"That's right." Iris chimed in. "We were sure we left them by the water, but then thought maybe we got turned around a little, so we searched everywhere. Then we started to get a bad feeling like someone took them. We didn't know what else to do, so we started walking, and then we saw mom."

Sheriff Stan tapped his pen on his foot a couple of times and finally after an eternity of silence he spoke up.

"I don't think your caller was after your daughters, Mrs. Berryman."

Bretta was not convinced and had to wonder how much training did a small town cop actually have anyway?

"I think he wanted you out of the house so he could get in."

Chapter 23

At last the girls were asleep and the evening was her own.

The dark house had filled with its usual nighttime noises that she still could not quite identify but had come to expect. Tonight her bedroom window was open, allowing in the delightful summer sounds and cooler air to leisurely filter in.

Bretta sunk down into her rocking chair in front of the newly uncovered hearth and covered herself with a light throw. After a few seconds her tired eyes closed and she thought about her day. It had been painful to see Sheriff Stan leave with her sketch book. She used it like a diary, often jotting down words or ideas next to her drawings.

Now she felt like a first class fool because she not only drew out a couple of new fall designs, she also created something snazzy for Stan the Sherriff to wear. Out of curiosity, she wanted to see what he would look like in a black cashmere turtleneck and tweed sports coat. Her bold commentaries and suggestions were scribbled alongside in what she hoped was illegible cursive. For fun she wanted to see Marc in something other than jeans and a t-shirt and she knew he made his debut in the book as well. The sheriff was certainly going to wonder why she was dressing up the men of Chester like Ken dolls.

Her marriage though bizarre and unpleasant, was not officially over and it wasn't right that she daydream over other men. She knew the reason for her procrastination and it certainly wasn't laziness or her delicate mental state.

Stirring the pot with John meant she could lose everything. He had threatened to take the children by declaring her an unfit mother, an endangerment to herself and others. Who knows whatever lies he would fabricate? She only knew for sure that if she served him with divorce papers, he would do exactly as he promised. So, trapped in her fear, she has done nothing.

Divorce.

She allowed the word to cascade through her thoughts like a falling piece of silk as if she had never considered it before.

Instead of simply being afraid and sitting in limbo, she should at least find out what she was up against. Before the house is completed and before she takes on another new project she needed to call her attorney.

Her sketch book had most likely been confiscated to see if she had designed any other dresses for Irma or something similar to the one her remains were found in. She was as confused about the dress as they were.

The dress. The tea set on display in her living room.

Did someone want to scare her or make her imagine she was crazy again or was she having trouble again and simply did not realize it? But who would want to go through all that trouble and why?

John would enjoy terrifying her just for sport and he certainly knew how. He had after all claimed he wanted to take the kids away, but his threat did not ring true. He barely saw his children and honestly, with his own past she would have to be both crazy and homicidal for a judge to rule in his favor.

The sudden shrill of the telephone jarred her away from her thoughts and she instinctively grabbed the noisy device before it woke the girls.

"Hello?" A familiar coldness rapidly filled the room. Think of the devil.

"Forgive me for not staying for tea. Next time though." A deep, unfamiliar voice came across the line instead.

"Who is this?" Panic surged through her veins like a hot shot of adrenaline, but a voice in her head cautioned her not to hang up.

"You've done a magnificent job with the house. Lace curtains would look better though." He let out an exasperated sigh. "City folks always think they need to match the comforter with the drapes. I've heard they don't care much about matching their own carpet to the drapes. However, I did see the other night that yours match just fine. Neatly trimmed and no dye job for you I see." He let out a laugh. "But that's a different subject all together now isn't it?"

Bretta flew fast out of the chair, her feet becoming entangled in the ends of the crocheted afghan that fell to her feet. With her eyes remained fixated on the windows, she allowed her left hand to reach out and yank the lamp cord out of the wall leaving her in a veil of darkness. She wondered if his eyes were upon her now, watching her. The intense pounding of her heart inside her chest became intensely loud and faintly painful as she slowly stood up, taking the phone with her.

She put the phone back to her ear but said nothing.

"You've turned off the lights. I can take a hint. You're tired. We'll talk another time then."

Bretta gasped loudly as she got to her feet.

"Your daughter's are lovely by the way, when I saw them frolic and play."

"Stay away from my girls you bastard! Do you hear me?" Her hands started shaking.

"Relax, that's not really my thing." His mellow voice was now laced with amusement. "I must go now, but I'll be in touch."

"Wait…"

"Three for tea. Just you, me and …" He sang it like the two for tea song and then disconnected the call.

Bretta threw the phone back down on floor and crossed her arms tightly around her chest. Her eyes had adjusted to the night and were trained on the window, straining to see if she could make out a face behind the screen. Quickly she pulled herself out of a terrified trance and ran to check the rest of the house.

She dashed from window to door, inspecting locks and pulling down blinds. When she approached the backdoor, she half expected a hand to fly through the glass window and grab her.

Maneuvering her way through the dark house, she found the girls safely tucked away in their beds and repeated the drill with their windows.

Safely back in her rocking chair with the butcher knife she snagged from a kitchen drawer in one hand and the phone in the other, she had something completely new to consider.

Now there were two men in her life she was afraid of.

Chapter 24

Everything does appear better in the light of day; her mother had been right about that one. That still didn't stop Bretta from texting Marc requesting him to come and install new locks on all the doors and windows when he had a chance. Some of the locks appeared to be the home's original and were flimsy, rusty or non- existent which was not reassuring.

After getting that business out of the way, she quickly assembled a breakfast casserole by cubing several slices of thick white crusty bread and mixed it with eggs, some red peppers for color, mushrooms, and a pinch of dry mustard and lots of extra sharp cheddar cheese and stuck it in the oven. She had added veggie sausage that she hoped would please Ivy and not ruin the casserole and before long, the kitchen started to fill with a mouthwatering aroma. Bretta was setting a pitcher of orange juice on the table when a loud knock on the back door almost caused her to have a sea of orange all over her pretty table.

It was barely seven o'clock in the morning and she was not expecting company, but daylight offers an illusion of safety. She exhaled a sigh of relief anyway when she found Marc's smiling face on the other side of the door. Her own features lit up as she quickly undid the lock and noted how deeply relieved she felt at his presence.

"Good morning, something sure smells wonderful." He set his tool kit down against the wall and took the pencil out from behind his ear while searching his pocket for a notepad.

"Breakfast casserole, you're just in time." She went over to one of her newly refinished cabinets that she simply could not stop admiring for a plate and quickly made a place for him at the table.

"So, what happened here last night?" His smile was replaced with concern and his hands were in his pockets while he waited.

Uneasiness suddenly consumed her and she took a step back. There was no way he could have known something happened last night, she was sure her voice gave away nothing on the phone. She kept last night's adventure to herself because it was yet another episode that could not be proved, another card stacked against her.

She put on her perplexed face and went about putting green and red grapes into a bowl. "What do you mean?"

"Let's hear it Bretta. I already know someone was outside your bedroom window last night; did he try to get in? Did you call Stan?"

She froze and the grape bowl she was carrying to the table began to slip through her fingers which thankfully Marc retrieved from her hands before it smashed to the floor.

"How do you know that?" She felt instantly guilty that her words sounded more like an accusation than a question.

A look of hurt flashed in his eyes and he waited a second before speaking. "You sent me a text at 5:00am that you need all new locks on your windows and doors and inquired about installing an alarm system. I took a walk around your house before I came to the door. There were a couple footprints and some smashed plants under your bedroom window. I don't need to call in Sherlock Holmes to piece this together for me."

She retrieved the bowl of grapes from him and put them on the table. "Yes, that is what happened." Minus a few other details.

"And you didn't bother with the truth because you didn't think I'd believe you, correct? I might even think you were crazy."

Her mouth dropped open at his bluntness and she stopped setting the table.

She was saved by the stampede of Ivy and Iris as they came bursting into the kitchen full of life, the oven timer simultaneously dinging with the girls entrance.

"Good morning mom, Mr. Marc." Ivy said with polite awareness.

"Are you two having a fight?"

"Ivy!" Iris was forever overcome with embarrassment from her sister's bluntness. "Mom, the timer went off."

Bretta smiled at the girls. "Good morning girls. No, we are not having a fight. We were having a discussion." Ivy rolled her eyes to show she wasn't buying it. "Sit down everyone. Breakfast is ready."

No one needed to be told twice, especially Marc who pulled Iris's seat out for her and was not in his own seat for more than a second before he started passing dishes around.

It was hard to be anything but cheerful in her fabulous new kitchen. The butter cream cabinets against the Tuscan yellow walls made the room warm and inviting. She had been hopeful that under all the old linoleum there were hardwood floors waiting to be rediscovered, however when they removed the floor they only found tile even uglier than what they started with. Slate gray ceramic tiles were put in its place which nicely complimented the black granite counters.

Almost everything in the kitchen was brand new or least new to her; she decided she did not want anything from their former apartment kitchen. Some of the wall hangings and accessories were from the antique store in town and Bretta loved how it pulled the look together. The wall next to the stove was still bare and in need of something. Maybe later today she could stop back at that store and see if they had anything new.

Iris's questioning snapped her out of her mental decorating and back to the breakfast table.

She smiled at her daughter. "Yes, Iris?"

"I said who was that man outside our house last night and what did he want?"

Bretta's smile froze. Certainly if her daughters knew a man had been lurking around the house after dark they would have mentioned it before now.

She put on a perplexed look and fiddled with her juice. "Someone was outside our house last night?"

Iris rolled her eyes. "Yes, mother. A man was outside your window talking to you. Then he went across the street to the Muncy sisters."

This time Marc spoke up. "Did he go to the side of their house?"

"No," Iris casually shook her head. "He went up to their front porch. They must have known him, because they let him right in."

Marc waited until the girls had finished eating and left the kitchen before he mentioned her visitor again.

"Tell me exactly what happened last night. Please don't leave anything out." His voice was firm, but she could hear the undertone of concern. She might as well let him have the whole story.

She watched his expression change from concern to fury when she described the phone call.

"Was Stan already here?"

Bretta looked beyond him to the clock on the kitchen wall, as if she was expecting the Sheriff to show up at her door at any moment.

"Bretta?" Marc put the pen down he was using to take notes. "You did call him, didn't you?"

There was no point lying to him, he wasn't going to let the topic rest.

"I needed to be sure it really happened first."

Chapter 25

All morgues smell the same. They pretty much even look the same so Sheriff Stan Meyers had no trouble finding Dr. Mioaki's office which was located precisely four doors down on the right at the end of a long and dismal hallway. A uniform sign on the entrance reflected his name in bold, black letters. Someone had stuck on a yellow happy face sticker and drew the eyes slanted which seemed slightly inappropriate given the fact this was after all, the city morgue.

Sheriff Meyers rapped on the door twice with no answer when a woman in a white lab coat carrying a large stack of files marched by and glared at him. Wordlessly she let herself into the office at the end of the hall and closed her door loudly.

Stan turned to leave and was about to give himself a tour of the building when he heard the sound of someone running.

"Hello! Hello!" A short and balding Asian man came to an abrupt halt before him. Bending his severely winded frame at the waist, he rested his hands on his knees.

He lifted his head and smiled cheerfully at Stan while he fought to catch his breath. "So sorry to keep you waiting. I was with one of my patients and thought it rude to leave in the middle of their examination."

He stood up straight, still puffing a bit, and produced a sizeable key ring which looked like it held a key to every building on the block. Stan had to wonder what possible use he would have for all those keys since most rooms appeared accessible only by an electronic key card.

Dr. Mioaki quickly unlocked his office door and with a slight bow and a wave, signaled his guest to enter. Once inside, the doctor locked the door again and moved rapidly around the small room with his keys clinking.

"Have a seat." The quirky little man muttered while he went from file cabinet to desk drawer unlocking and relocking as he went along using his handy dandy keys. He seemed to be searching for something and fascinating as it was to watch him, Stan pulled his eyes away to examine the doctor's office.

His work place was neat and sparsely decorated with some type of bamboo plant on one bookshelf and a mini rock fountain on top of his file cabinet.

"Here we go!" Dr. Mioaki announced with great zest and a hand wave, indicating he was finished with his busywork.

Stan's eye grew wide. He knew he was in a morgue, but from the ebullient way the doctor called his attention, he half expected to find lunch laid out for him.

Instead, spread out on the desk before Stan was several photographs of a dead woman during an autopsy. The doctor stepped back, nodded and waited.

Clearly he was supposed to know something about the photos offered to him but for starters, he did not know who he was looking at and why.

Irma Barrett's bones were sent to him in a box. These were photos of a corpse.

Doctor Mioaki reached in front of him and selected the photo of a close up shot of an arm with a clenched fist and handed to him.

Even though they were nowhere near the autopsy suite, his nostrils filled with the strong stench of formaldehyde and death and his stomach began to protest.

Wanda Bee's case was still unsolved with little to no leads. He has logged countless hours digging through her gossip collection and several sleepless nights which were now apparently catching up with him. However he was certain Dr. Mioaki said it was Irma Barrett's case he wanted to discuss when he phoned. Maybe he thought since I was in the neighborhood, they would have a chat about both.

It was not a clear head shot, but it was definitely Wanda.

The doctor thrust another photo at him and Stan sensed the doctor's impatience. Perhaps if he just verbalized what was on his mind instead of playing this strange game of Asian charades they would both be happier.

The next picture was of the same hand, pried and held open. Resting in its palm was a scrap of paper with the numbers 07181968 printed in black ink.

"This piece of paper was found clenched in Wanda's hand?" Shit, couldn't he simply have told him this over the phone? It would have spared him a two hour car trip and exposure to these horrid odors. This was starting to feel like a bad episode of Quincy.

The Doctor nodded; noticeably delighted his slow student was finally catching on.

"Come with me." With a flurry of activity, the little man relocked everything in his path and ushered him out the door and had them both scurrying down the hall with in three seconds.

Before Stan could object, he was being gowned by an assistant and he knew he was going to have to enter the autopsy suite.

"Son of a bitch." He mumbled under his mask. This better be good. He thought he had made it clear on the phone without sounding too wimpy, that he preferred to look at photos rather than view an actual autopsy. He made up something about an allergy to the chemicals they use which was not far from the truth considering how he felt anytime he stepped a foot near the morgue.

He dutifully trailed behind the doctor into a brightly lit room and held back shouting *yes* when he noticed a skeleton on the table instead of a corpse.

Bones were better.

"Your men did not find a saw or any kind of tools at the crime scene?" Dr. Mioaki probed as he walked with purpose over to Irma where all her pieces were now magically arranged back together.

"No, we didn't miss anything. Why do I have to wear a mask for bones?" His brain was trying to search for a reason, but he was one of those people that found it hard to think when his breathing was restricted. It felt like he was suffocating. He tried snorkeling once on vacation in Mexico and nearly had a panic attack in a foot and a half of water.

"You don't. I just like them." Dr. Mioaki pulled a light close down to the lower left femur and stepped aside so Stan could look.

Stan yanked his mask down around his neck and leaned forward to have a look. He felt out-of-sorts enough around this quirky little man without having to deal with a limited oxygen flow. He did his best to play nice and tried hard to guess why in the hell they were both staring at Irma's leg bone.

As if sensing his frustration, the doctor thrust a magnifying glass in his hand and as Stan glared back at him, he saw the doctor was holding Wanda's autopsy pictures.

Suddenly he knew.

He still could have told him this over the phone, but the trying man was right.

He would want to see this for himself.

Carefully he examined Irma's bones and then reached out with his right hand for Wanda's picture.

The numbers matched perfectly.

"The numbers were more or less dug in the bones with a sharp metal object postmortem."

What could these two women even have remotely in common other than they were from the same small town?

"Wanda was killed by a gunshot. Do we know the cause of death for Irma Barrett yet?"

"Ms. Bee died from manual strangulation. She was shot, but someone choked her first. I don't know about bones yet."

"You've had Wanda's body for over two weeks now. Why am I just hearing about all this now?"

Dr. Mioaki shrugged his shoulders. "I was not on this case originally. I was on vacation with my mother. We went on a Caribbean Cruise. When Ms. Barrett came in and I saw they were from the same town, I pulled Ms. Bee back out and went over her with a fine tooth."

He learned from previous encounters with the doctor that he did not appreciate having his English corrected so he refrained from offering missing words such as *comb.*

"What in the hell could these numbers possibly mean?" Stan voiced one of the numerous questions roaming around in his head.

"How in hell should I know?" Doctor Mioaki replied, rapidly turning off the lights and rattling his keys, signaling their time was up. "That's your job."

⅄

Long drives always seem to go much faster when your mind is wrapped around multiple unsolved homicides he thought as he searched for possible connections between Irma and Wanda.

Both were born and raised in Chester and each had a connection to Huddelstone. Irma had been one of the homeowners and Wanda was the agent that sold the house. Tony, Irma Barrett's son, must have been the one to hire Wanda. Chester being the small town that it was only had room for one real estate office so Roseland Realty was the only choice. Knowing Wanda, she probably was at his front door before the thought of selling even occurred to him. It did not matter if the piece of property had a house that was about to collapse; she had to be the one to list it.

His deputies have yet to track down Anthony Barrett to notify him that his mother was found boxed up and stuffed in the cellar of his childhood home. When his real estate agent was discovered murdered, he became more than a person of interest.

It would save a little time if he had Kuster get a head start on some phone work but before he could retrieve his cell from his pants pocket, he felt it vibrate.

He didn't need the Caller ID to tell him it would be Kuster.

"I was just getting ready to call you."

"Really? What's up?"

Everyone liked Deputy Kuster which was strange because he wasn't even a local; he was imported all the way from Detroit. Upon introduction to the tall, lanky, and smiling officer, one cannot help but feel you have made a new best friend. He had a gift for putting folks at ease and Stan would swear, also somewhat telepathic.

"What happened over at the Berryman's last night?" Marc had called him while he was on the road to the morgue and he sent Kuster on over to have a look.

"Sounds like a peeping Tom through her bedroom window. She said a man called her on the phone, described the room she was sitting in and some rather intimate information about herself." He coughed slightly and Stan could tell his deputy was blushing. "It's all be in the report. Gave her a good scare anyway. Marc's fixing up her locks on her windows and doors today."

"I've never known too many Peeping Tom's to call on the phone and announce themselves." He didn't have this many open cases working homicide in New York. "I'll take a look at that report when I come in."

"You got it."

"Hey, can you run all the possible connections between Irma Barrett and Wanda Bee? I want everything; if they went to the same church, garden club, had mutual friends, what they collected and what their interests were." Chester was not that big of a town, they would have shopped at the same stores and visited the same places, but he was betting there had to be a closer tie.

"I can tell you one right now. Wanda use to date Tony Barrett until she dumped him for another guy. They were quite the item when they were teens and their breakup was pretty hard on Tony." Kuster paused for a second, as if thinking back in time.

"You're shitting me?" Tony was a skinny, squirrelly weirdo and Wanda was so big and bossy. He picked his brain to recall what Wanda was like when she was younger. Enormous boobs and poufy hair was all that came to mind.

"Wait a minute. How the hell do you know all this? You didn't even grow up here? What, do the good citizens of Chester simply walk up to you and tell you this shit?" It always amazes him how he knows everyone, where they are and where they are going.

"Well… yeah." Not the least bit offended. "I also use to spend some summers here as a young boy."

Chapter 26

"You what?" Stan barked into the phone. Had his deputy announced that he rollerbladed around town after dark dressed up as Superman he could not have been more stunned. He was positive this never came up in a prior conversation and he wanted to know why. He grew up in this town and personally interviewed Kuster for this job. How could he not know his right hand man used to spend his summers here?

"I was here for a few summers with my family. Rented one of those little cabins by the lake. I used to play chess with Tony."

Sure families would come and go during the summer, but as a kid he was everywhere and knew everyone. The cruiser's speedometer started to spin as fast as his thoughts and he eased off the gas pedal when it became obvious he was soaring past the stares of alarmed citizens.

"Why in the hell did you never mention this before? Because you sure as shit didn't."

"I did not mention it at the interview sir because I knew how you felt about summer people. Then, it simply never came up."

"Never came up? All of the times we drove by those cabins, you never thought to mention you used to stay there? When I told you to find Anthony Barrett, you didn't think to bring up that he was your old chess buddy? Meet me in the office; I'll be there in less than thirty minutes." He ended the call without waiting for a reply.

Then there was still Betty to deal with. *Shit.* Other than the steady stream of complaints he received about her, he lacked the solid proof needed to fire her. What he suspected and what he could prove where entirely different.

She had been with the department for over twenty years, hired by the last chief and had no plans on leaving.

At least not voluntarily.

Twenty five ticked off minutes later he stormed into the station and was treated to the demonstration of Betty devouring half a taco in a single bite.

"Good afternoon Betty. I'll be working with Kuster, so no calls for either one of us unless it is an *emergency.* That goes for any visitors on foot." One would think this was Mayberry with the amount of folks stopping by for a visit.

Betty nodded in a panic, searching for a napkin.

"And Betty, no more food at the front desk. You'll have to wait until lunch or for a break when another officer can fill in for you. It's unprofessional and I have found grease on some of our papers and files. Thanks." He left to find Kuster but not before witnessing a ghastly view of tossed Mexican from Betty's lower jaw.

Seeing Kuster drumming vigorously on the computer keys brightened his mood slightly.

"Hey there Chief. Just sit down and relax now, were going to figure this out." He turned and smiled.

He wondered if he overheard him reprimanding Betty.

Kuster shrugged his shoulders. "Something needed to be done about our dispatcher, she lacks guidance."

It was freaky the way his deputy could read his thoughts.

"The Medical Examiner gave me the results on those samples you took from the floor and that chest at Huddelstone. It came back as blood, most likely Irma's, only it had traces of formaldehyde and some other chemicals in it. The samples taken from inside the drain contain formaldehyde and a small amount of arsenic." Stan said as he sat dropped down in his chair.

"Huh." Kuster rubbed the palm of his hand back and forth vigorously over his balding head and sat back in his chair. "Well, you know women used to lighten their skin with a mixture of vinegar, chalk and arsenic."

"No Kuster, I didn't know that." He let out a long sigh. It was almost exasperating, the things that he knew and chose to share at the oddest times.

"Also, Huddelstone was once used as a funeral home for short period of time."

"For real?"

"Oh sure. Bodies were embalmed with arsenic before they started using formaldehyde and other chemicals. Embalming practices began during the Civil War out of necessity, not vanity, by a man named Dr. Thomas Holmes. He's considered the Father of Modern Embalming and his techniques certainly made things easier. It got awfully messy shipping back those bodies to their families so they could be identified and buried. Train workers would get upset when the bodies exploded all over and eventually the workers went on strike over it."

Stan gave a stunned nod to continue.

"Anyway, formaldehyde was used for a while but it isn't used much these days either. They use a mixture of chemicals now. So that could explain the traces of the arsenic and formaldehyde that were found there, unless it appears that they were used recently. Then someone's playing mortician."

Stan sat speechless, staring at his deputies shiny bald head. What he needed more than anything was a cold beer and a hot shower, in that order. To think he wanted to move back home because he wanted a simple life and an easy job. Nothing ever happened in Chester.

"Sheriff? You okay there?"

"How in the hell do you know all this Kuster?"

Kuster shrugged his shoulders slightly. "I'm a bit of a history enthusiast. If you want to know more about the actual house, I bet Athena Muncy would know. She knows about every old house in Chester and Huddelstone has always been a favorite of hers."

"It has?" He was trying to wrap his fatigued brain around Kuster sitting around gossiping with old ladies and why everyone was suddenly in love with a dilapidated ancient house that sat empty for five years.

"Sure, I know she would love to chat with you. Just give her a call. "

"I'll do that. In the meantime, I have some numbers I want you to run." He explained the series of numbers found clenched in Wanda's hand and carved in Irma's femur and handed over the lab photos.

"Wow." Kuster let out a low whistle. "You don't see something like that around here very often, that's for sure."

"Let's give it a go here first, see if we can't figure it out. It might be something relatively easy to crack. If not, then we will have to involve the feds."

"Well, I think I have the connection."

If only Kuster's psychic skills where that good. Then they could forget all about the work load piling up and throw a gone fishing sign on the front door.

"Huddelstone." Kuster offered as he rolled his chair back over to his own desk to face his monitor.

Huddelstone was nothing more than an old home in need of a lot of repair about the time of Irma's death. It was hard to visualize how anyone could be killed over it. Then again it was amazing to him that they actually found a buyer for it.

Kuster addressed his doubts before his boss spoke them. "It's who use to live in the house Chief."

"Anthony Barrett." Two simple words. He thought about the skinny teenager whose peers took pleasure in messing with him. He was not proud that he took a turn or two in his youth. "We still can't locate him?"

Kuster's fingers flew so freakishly fast over the keyboard it looked like he was typing in the air. "He left Chester when he was eighteen and then vanished. I know he would come home now and then over the years and check on his mother, but he kept to himself mostly. Then about five years ago or so, he moved her out to live with him and no one has heard a peep out of either one since." Kuster made conversation while he searched for the information he needed.

"You don't say?"

"Yup...here we go. Barrett's date of birth: July 18, 1968."

Stan gave a nod for him to continue.

"07181968." Kuster read it a little differently this time.

This time the light went on.

"Shit...really?" Stan jumped up and went over to Kuster's monitor to view the screen.

"Don't think I've ever heard of a murderer leaving their date of birth as a calling card before."

Kuster shrugged his shoulders. "First time for everything I guess."

"Did you ever see Barrett when he came home?"

"Nope. His mother would tell me when he stopped in. He never gave her any advance notice; he would just show up at night, visit a day or two and then leave."

"Did Irma call the station to tell you all this?" It was hardly a crime that your son was neglectful and weird.

"No..." Kuster's slight hesitation made Stan come to attention. Everything he learned about his deputy today was so out of character for his tall, good natured right hand man.

Maybe he never looked close enough.

"When did she tell you all this Kevin?" His voice was soft but not without authority.

"Over tea."

Chapter 27

Bretta tried without much success to redirect her thoughts to something else. From scouring cookbooks for a new gourmet recipe to reorganizing the already organized pantry, none of them brought her any closer to an answer or offered her relief.

It gnawed at her conscious the entire morning and by afternoon it consumed her every thought until she could not tolerate it for one more second. She needed answers.

Deputy Kuster had promised her he would call later that day and fill her in on what he had learned. He also told her not to go around asking questions on her own, she reminded herself as she glanced again at the kitchen wall clock. It was already going on three o'clock in the afternoon and there had not been a word from anyone.

The easiest thing to do would be to call the station, but that would mean having to speak to that nasty dispatcher again.

This was ridiculous. Alice Muncy was her friend and Bretta had run out of reasons why she could not simply walk across the street and ask her who the man was that nearly terrified her to death last night.

Her hand quickly snatched the small dying Jade off the coffee table before she had a chance to change her mind. She had been meaning to ask Alice about the wilted plant anyway.

The Muncy's black front door swung open before Bretta could raise her hand to knock.

"Hurry, hurry! I have everything ready so it will give us a chance to visit first." Alice hauled her through the doorway, barely allowing her to clear the entry before slamming the door closed.

Remembering the wilted Jade in her hand, she awkwardly offered it to Alice as if it were a hostess gift.

"Just put that over there for now dear." Alice waved her hand in the direction of sturdy cherry console table along the wall.

"Come on now; let's go have a seat."

Confused, Bretta followed her petite friend into the formal dining room and came to an abrupt halt at the entrance.

An embroidered ecru tablecloth with matching napkins that showed off a delicate cutwork design covered the table. Exquisite Petit Fours in a variety of shapes and colors were creatively stacked upon a three tier, cream colored cake plate with a gold trim. She was aware that Alice enjoyed baking, but she had to wonder if she was capable of creating such gorgeous works of art or if they came from a bakery.

Her eyes did not know where to look next. There were plates of finger sandwiches, roses carved in butter, assorted crackers, a large chocolate torte and a steaming pot of tea sat waiting in the middle of it all.

Her mind quickly raced through the week's calendar. Did she have a lunch date with Alice today and forgot? Maybe this was the reason she felt the strong urge to come over here this afternoon. It was hard to tell which one of them was supposed to be the crazy one when she was here with Alice in Wonderland.

As she placed her hand on the back of her chair, she noticed for the first time the table had been set for three. The air suddenly grew thick and uneasy as she gradually lowered herself into the seat and waited for her hostess to do the same.

"Alice, is someone joining us today?" Her voice came out just above a whisper.

Alice appeared puzzled and excited. "Why, yes dear. Did you forget?"

"I...uh." She was not exactly sure what she should say. She knew that if she were at all normal, she would simply inform her hostess that although her table was exceptionally lovely, she had indeed forgotten to mention having her over for lunch.

But these days she was just as unsure about herself as she was her neighbor so she sat in silence, trying to guess who the other guest might be.

Chapter 28

"Ok, tell me about your little tea parties." Stan said between clenched teeth. Kuster winced and made a face one usually makes when hearing nails dragged across a chalk board.

No matter what way he told it, he knew he would come across sounding like a fairy with a screw loose. But what could he say? He liked old ladies. He liked tea.

"I wouldn't call them parties, sir. I would visit now and then and Irma would make us tea."

"How often did you *visit?*"

Kuster shrugged his shoulders and pretended like he needed to give this some thought. "I'd say maybe once a month?"

"So, over tea, Irma would tell you all about her son. Then one day he showed up and moved her out. Did you see him when he came to town?"

"No, I received a note from Tony explaining Irma had a mild stroke and he felt it best to take her with him."

"Which was where?"

Kuster started to straighten up his already tidy desk. "I didn't ask that."

"Do you still have that note?"

"No..."

"Who else knows about your tea *visits?*"

Kuster cleared his throat and momentarily considered making up a story. However, he was not comfortable dealing in lies. He may not have always divulged all his secrets, but he was not a liar.

"Although I missed teatime with Irma when she moved away, I never mentioned my visits with Irma to another soul. Then one day out of the clear blue, Alice called me over to her house. When I arrived, expecting there to be some sort of trouble, I found the table set for tea. I didn't ask why or how she knew; I simply sat down at the table like I was expected to and poured the tea."

After that, it became a weekly event, which he wisely left out of the conversation.

His boss dropped back in his chair and finally unclenched the death grip that had clamped his mouth shut and now let his jaw drop open.

Kuster knew when to stop talking and wait it out.

Sure he could get tea anywhere, but Alice's tea was spiced and came with tiny sandwiches, cute little cakes with pink frosting, and intriguing tidbits of information that so effortlessly came from her mouth. She *knew* things.

He knew he had *the gift,* but the truth was Alice did too.

So the two mutually odd residents of the small town of Chester met for tea every Tuesday at approximately three thirty P.M. and over a steaming pot of tea would pour out the secrets, mysteries, and the mayhem of their community.

He had enrolled Alice in the *Tea of the Month club* for her last birthday and they now had the opportunity to sample teas from all over the world. Last week they sipped on Himalayan Majestic which was a divine black tea that originated from the pristine hills of Nepal and grew at the foot of the majestic Himalayan Mountains.

Alice would take great care to study, prepare, and present each new blend. It was remarkable how she could pull it all together considering half of the time at least one part of her outfit was missing, unbuttoned or her shoes forgotten, but like a proper gentleman he would pretend not to notice.

It was a closed, private gathering that no one knew existed.

Until today.

Kuster gave a glance at his watch then rapidly began putting his desk in order.

"What, do you have an appointment somewhere, Kuster?" Stan asked when he finally found his voice.

"Yes, sir." He stood up, finding it a bit difficult to look his boss in the eye. "I'm late for tea."

Chapter 29

The soft knock at the front door announced their awaited guest had arrived and her hostess sprung from her seat and bee lined it to the door. Bretta strained to make out the muffled voices drifting in from the entrance which soon were replaced with the clickity sound of ladies heals making their way down the hall.

"Bretta, dear, I believe you know Rose Delaney from our antique store in town?" Rose smiled warmly and somewhat sympathetically as she gently grasped Bretta's hand in her own. Though Bretta was baffled at her presence at this little gathering, she was genuinely happy to see the woman. She had met Rose on several occasions at Anderson's Antiques and enjoyed talking to her about the history of Huddelstone and of the town.

Rose apparently received her invite for the party because she arrived dressed for the occasion in a flowered dress similar to Alice's with old lady styled white gloves and purse that matched her outfit nicely.

"Why don't we all sit down now and I'll pour us some tea?" Alice was astonishing as she poured and served hot tea, passed out napkins, and gave everyone a petite four.

Bretta's mind flashed to the countless teas and lunches she had suffered through in the past with gossipy, cruel, and boring women that had too much time on their hands. At least these women were sympathetic and gentle, even if they were a bit unusual.

"It won't hurt to have just one while we talk. Now, Rose, tell us about what you found at the store."

Bretta was pleased Alice was getting right to the point, although she had a strange feeling she was not going to be particularly happy with the treasures Rose found in her antique store. She had no idea why, there could not have been anything in there that belonged to her.

"Oh, yes." The old women took great care to wipe a non-existent crumb off the corners of her mouth with the dainty lace napkin before continuing. "I was going through a box of treasures from the previous owners of Huddelstone and came across some items you will want back."

It took her more than a second to realize Rose was directing the comment to her and not Alice.

Slowly, Bretta lowered the fine bone tea cup back down in its saucer and folded her hands on her lap.

"I don't know what you mean Rose." She heard her own voice tremble slightly. "I would not have had anything at this house before we moved in." Technically now that was not true. It seems that one of her dresses found its way into a box of bones in her basement before she even arrived in town.

"Just a few things that I think best to put away for now." Rose continued on as if she had not spoken, Alice nodded her crazy head in agreement. "Alice can keep them here for you perhaps."

Maybe she had moved to Nutville like John had said or perhaps this was what it felt like to have a nervous breakdown. She was acutely aware that she was seated at the table, breathing, talking, and yet the air felt like it had changed to a thick sludge and the antique brooch she had so carefully selected this morning began to feel more like a noose rather than a statement of fashion.

As if on cue, Rose pointed to the cameo. "Ah, I see you found Irma's brooch! You know she looked for that darn thing for years. I think she would be glad that you finally found it for her."

Automatically her hand reached for her throat. "No...this was a gift from my husband. He gave it to me years ago." She shook her head to clear the profuse fog engulfing her brain. Things like this would happen all the time before with John. He would be talking and talking, and none of his words would make sense.

"What kind of things did you find that you think belong to me?" She kept her tone light and curious.

The ladies became silent until Alice gave silent nod.

"Patterns, fabric and sewing supplies in that lovely wicker basket. Your name is so beautifully embroidered on the lid; you must have done that yourself. Very talented you are Bretta." Reaching over she padded the younger women's hand lightly. "And the gun of course. I'm sure you will want that back, with that mean bastard of a husband you have, you may need it."

"What?" Bretta gasped loudly. Her mind raced in a million different directions. She certainly did not own a gun and she was sure that she never said much of anything about her husband. Or did she?

The doorbell chimed again and Bretta was not sure if she wanted to laugh or cry.

Alice jumped up eagerly and clapped her hands. "Oh good, now everyone's here. We can begin our party!" Alice turned to run for the door when suddenly she stopped and shrieked loudly. The loud noise caused Bretta to nearly spill her tea; Rose appeared not to have heard it at all. Again her mind drifted into the pages of *Alice in Wonderland*, Alice asking for advice on which way she ought to go and then telling the Cheshire Cat that she did not want to go among mad people.

"Oh, you can't help that," said the Cheshire Cat: "we're all mad here. I'm mad. You're mad."

"How do you know I'm mad?" said Alice in the book.

"You must be," said the Cat, "or you wouldn't have come here."

"I don't know where my mind is!" Her neighbor practically screamed out the words and brought Bretta back to the present. "I've only put out three settings! Rose, be a dear please and gather another setting from the hutch behind you." She left through the door and then quickly stuck her head back in. "We probably should not mention any of this to Kuster."

Kuster? She invited the deputy to a tea party?

She had no idea whose sewing basket Rose found, but it was not hers. She did have one as a young girl that sounded similar to the one Rose described, but she had not seen that in years and it definitely did not make the move to Chester.

Her basket would have her initials from her maiden name anyway. She knew these old ladies were a bit on the crazy side, but still she had to wonder why they were so positive the basket belonged to her. It was sweet of them to want to protect her, but if this little basket had a gun in it, they needed to give it to the police.

She did indeed feel like she fell through the rabbits hole and she took a moment to round up her thoughts when it occurred to her that it could not have been only the basket that convinced the ladies that the items belonged to her.

Rose had said she found fabric in the box. Her sense of bewilderment over their bizarre behavior was quickly being replaced with panic. It simply was not possible that the fabric she found was the same material Irma's dress was made out of.

Her eyes closed tight for a moment and then flew back open.

She had to ask before Kuster entered the room. "Rose…" the words died on her lips as their next guest made his entrance.

The tall, lanky deputy appeared in the doorway with a slight blush to his cheeks, filled with excitement. He turned to Bretta first. "Ms. Berryman, so good to see you again. Ms. Delaney, always a pleasure." He shook each woman's hand thoughtfully and gave them each a heartwarming smile.

"Alice, you've really outdone yourself this time!" His eyes immediately turned to the table. He took his time to appreciate the attractively set table and could do little do hide his own enthusiasm. "Did you make the petite fours yourself or did you order them from that catalog I sent you?"

Alice beamed under his praise. "I made them myself! I used fondant this time instead of making all that icing. It's just so much easier that way. You simply add a little food color to the fondant and roll it out! I'll have you over next time Kuster and you can help."

"Ok, great! I would love that!" His gigantic grin abruptly deflated when he noticed Bretta Berryman had been staring at him like he had arrived in a pink fluffy bridesmaids dress.

Kuster smiled warmly at Bretta. "Well, now my little secret is out. I enjoy having tea with Alice." He sighed. "And you might as well know I like to bake a little too." He glanced over to Alice and shrugged his shoulders. "Sheriff knows now too. Had to tell him." He took a sip of the tea Alice had put in front of him and smiled. "He knows about the tea parties, not the baking. We are each entitled to a few of our own secrets, aren't we ladies?" Kuster looked knowingly at each lady before locking eyes with Bretta's.

Bretta was more than ready to leave. She did not want to be rude, but this entire gathering was weird and if Kuster wanted to bake petite fours or host tea parties, he had her blessing. She only wished that was the craziest secret she was carrying around these days.

This obviously was not a good time to ask Rose about those items that she found so she would have to ask her later. She was about to start making her excuses when she noticed Kuster admiring her pin.

"That sure is a beautiful pin, Ms. Berryman." He stated simply.

"Thank you, Kuster. Well everyone, this has been lovely, but I must get back to check on the girls. Alice, thank you so much for inviting me."

Alice's wrinkled hand reached over and patted Bretta's. "I want you to know you can trust Rose. She can help you research the information you are looking for. It is hard when you forget things, this I know." She sighed sweetly.

Bretta did not think she was looking for information other than the history of Huddelstone; but now her mind was filled with unanswered questions. However she did remember the reason she came over here.

"Alice, who was that man that came to your door last night?"

Alice had a peculiar look on her face, different than usual confused look. "You must be mistaken dear. We had no visitors last night."

Chapter 30

Somewhere, buried in the stack of files he now had in his possession, Sheriff Stan Meyers knew he had the answers that would tie things together for him. Right now he was reading everything he could get his hands on about Anthony Barrett but it was all facts he already knew. Below average student, local trouble maker, loser.

Could Barrett really be that stupid as to leave his date of birth as a calling card with two victims that could be easily tied to him?

The deed on the Huddelstone house listed Anthony Barrett as the owner and another document showed he was the seller and Wanda Bee was the Real Estate agent handling the sale. The final check from the sale was found on Wanda's desk at the office still in the Huddelstone file, which he guessed meant she was either getting ready to mail it or did not know his current address either.

He thought about the skinny oddball that never did fit in. He was a loner most of the time, never getting into any serious trouble as a kid that he could recall. There was no record on him as an adult. How could he sneak back and forth into his town and he not know about it? His hand searched to find the Barrett file but instead stopped at John Berryman's. He might be a horse's ass, but that did not make him a murderer. The sheriff tapped his fingers on top of the file and opened it. He was up to something that was for sure. His eyes skimmed the report again for the third time, but this time he backed up and reread something.

John Berryman was a member of the chess club in college and won several matches. There was an article that quotes him as saying he learned to play when he was younger.

He knocked over a cup of pencils reaching for the phone and cursed as he punched in a number.

"Kuster" he ordered into the phone. "Can you get over here please?"

"I'm just pulling up to the station now. I'll be right in."

Stan pulled the phone back away from his head and stared at it with a puzzled look. "Ok, good."

He could hear Kuster's heavy gait work his way through the empty station.

"How was Alice today?"

"Just fine, thanks. She made Petite Fours from scratch." Kuster dropped down in the chair in front of Stan's desk. "So what did you find?"

"Tell me about your chess games with Barrett."

He hoped Kuster wasn't a poker player.

"You mean when I use to play chess with Tony?" He repeated as if he had not heard correctly. "When we were kids?"

"Yeah, yeah. Did you play a lot?"

"As a matter of fact we did. Almost every day. Why?"

Stan handed over the Berryman file. "It seems Mrs. Berryman's husband was quite the chess player back in his college days."

"You don't say?"

"Did you ever play with some of the kids that came just for the summer?"

"I believe we did."

"I ran out of time yesterday so I put the files on your desk, didn't you read them?"

"They weren't on my desk, chief." He glanced over at his neatly organized desk and then back down to the Berryman file. "Only five files on my desk and they are in alphabetical order on the right hand side of my desk, notes on the left."

Stan glanced over and knew that's exactly what he would find. The notoriously neat deputy arranged his desk like that every night before leaving. He never knew anyone to be so painstakingly tidy.

"I found these back on my desk when I returned from the morgue so I assumed you had read through them all." He stopped talking, his attention shifting to the front of the building where his noisy receptionist parked her chair all day.

"You're thinking Betty has been doing a little reading to pass the time?" Kuster said without looking up.

"I wouldn't put it past her. How well did she know Wanda Bee?"

Kuster shrugged his shoulders. "Both quirky, not extremely friendly. It could be possible that Betty formed some type of strange relationship with Wanda and fed her information." He commented but his eyes continued to scan the papers in front of him. "Looks like Berryman's more of a business man than a dentist. Made a real go of this Berrybrite Dental." Kuster remarked after a few more minute of reading. His eyes skimmed further down the sheet and let out a little chuckle. "Well, you certainly dug deep enough. I think you left out who his teacher was for kindergarten. Don't care much for the guy, do you?"

"Let's just say he doesn't make a first great impression and I wanted to know a little more about him."

"Like why the guy was going out of his way to make us believe his wife was so unstable?" Kuster spoke up, his eyes never leaving his file.

Stan froze. "You got that too?"

He answered with a slight nod. "He had done that before you know. Did you read this here about her being sick?"

"Done what before? How do you read so fast?" He stood up to stand over the deputy's shoulder so he could get a look at what he was reading.

"Tried to make her think she was sick. Looks like he made sure everyone else knew that too. More important, it appears he worked hard at making her think she was crazy." He pulled out a sheet of paper that was at the bottom of the file. "Look here, he tried to have her committed to a mental hospital a few years back. Her mother came to her rescue."

The sheriff looked dumbfounded. "Why? I mean, what purpose would this serve him?" He considered himself to be rather intelligent and thought he had seen just about every type of crime imaginable living in the big city, but this did not add up.

"Could be a power trip, maybe he wants her out of the picture. Maybe it's just because he can."

The sudden shrill coming from his cell phone broke their concentration. Irritated, Stan answered the call.

"Good evening, Sheriff Stan." He recognized the cheerful medical examiner right away. "You are well tonight?"

Some of his annoyance seeped away and was immediately replaced with curiosity. It was pretty late for Dr. Mioaki to calling. Maybe he was a workaholic and insomniac too.

"I call on your mobile so I don't have to speak with the vulture. The report came back on instruments used to cut up Irma Barrett. It's believed a Bone cutter and a Hand saw was used. Your people did not find tools?"

Bone cutter? "No, there was no tools on the scene…we sent everything."

"If we had the tools, we could tell more. No two tools are the same; they leave striations in the bone. The mark is matched with the blade."

Stan pulled the phone away from his ear and glared at it in disbelief. Did he seriously just get a forensics 101 lesson from Mioaki? "We didn't leave anything behind Dr. Mioaki, I assure you."

"Hmm…ok then. Well then, if the work was done there, then someone must carry their own set of tools around with them. You better get busy Sheriff." He advised before hanging up.

Chapter 31

"Look, all I want to know is if it is okay to go up into my attic now and start sorting through the stuff there. My workers are scheduled to arrive this morning and before I have them start hauling stuff downstairs, I want to be sure the officers don't have to come back and take pictures or something."

"I don't think you should go and mess with anything. I'll take a message and have someone call you back." Dispatcher Betty Grimes was in truth much more interested in finding that blasted bag of candy she hid away after the "no food" ban. She set the phone down so she could hunt through her desk and was past elbow deep in her left drawer when she cut her finger on something sharp. *Crap!* One of the idiots around here probably booby trapped her desk for fun. Speaking of idiots, she almost forgot she had the town fruitcake on the line, still chirping away. She stuck the phone back up to her ear and made some appropriate comments. She usually found it confining and irritating to use the headset for the handful of calls that trickled in to the station but now she began to think that freeing up her hands might be to her advantage.

"I already left a message the other day and no one called me back. We want to start clearing out the attic out today!"

"The Sheriff is *very* busy right now Mrs. Berryman, what with all the other activities going on here in Chester." She stressed the word *very* like she was addressing a room of silly preschoolers. "I'm sure he will get to you as soon as he can. Now don't go getting yourself all worked up over a bunch of old junk." Betty advised and then secretly snuck a butterscotch hard candy out of her drawer and popped it into her mouth.

"Listen, I don't want to destroy any evidence or anything, but we need to get started on that space today. Please have someone contact me as soon as possible or I will drive over there myself and ask."

Betty almost choked on her candy. "Is that a threat, Mrs. Berryman?"

"What?" Bretta stammered.

"Now just remain calm. There is no need to get hysterical or violent. Let me see if I can get someone on over there to help you."

"I assure you I am not violent or hysterical, simply extremely frustrated. "

"Perhaps I should call on over Doc Mueller to give you something to settle you down. You don't want to have a relapse."

"I beg your pardon?" Bretta gasped into the phone.

"Nothing, I just mean no sense getting all worked up over nothing."

"No, that's not what you said. You said you don't want to have a relapse, didn't you?"

"No, I did not!" Betty disputed loudly, trying to cover her mistake.

"I am reasonably sure that my personal and medical history would not pop up on your screen when I call in. Is that how you fill the time Ms. Grimes? Snooping through private files?" Betty quickly slammed the phone down and popped another candy in her mouth.

"What's got your tail in an up-roar so early in the morning, Betty?" Sally said as she slithered in front of her desk to fill her coffee cup. "Someone steal your Scooby-snacks again?"

Betty had the sudden and overwhelming urge to leap over the counter and punch Hiller in the mouth until her teeth fell out.

"Well if you must know, it's that psycho that moved into that dump over on Hollyhock Lane." She raised her voice so the rest of the station could hear her. "She threatened me!"

Kuster, who had been trying to avoid the cat fight altogether and sneak back to his desk unnoticed, stopped and came back. "What did you say there Betty?"

Betty adjusted her blouse and did a cleavage check for modesty. "Mrs. Berryman threatened me! She wanted someone to run right over and look around her attic and when I explained to her everyone was busy and she would have to leave a message, she started raving like a lunatic. Really! Things have just not been the same since she has moved to town."

"Well, what exactly *did* she say?" Kuster moved in closer and casually leaned against the counter.

"Oh, she babbled on about her dumb attic and that someone has to get there today or else she was going to march on in here and pay me a visit!" she rotated her bottom around on her chair several times before deciding on the right spot. "I mean honestly! She seems to think we are purposely ignoring her!"

"We all know how helpful and pleasant you are, Betty, so I am sure she must have misunderstood." Sally offered while blowing on a cup of hot coffee producing a noise that sounded like a hissing, angry cat.

Kuster stared long and hard at their receptionist. "*Has* she called before Betty?"

"She did and I have the messages right here. But they weren't exactly *911's* and since she has everyone tied up enough on other calls, I thought I would put them in order of importance." Her hand slapped the pile of papers next to her phone to make her point.

"Don't think, Betty. It weakens the team." Sally said, looking pleased with herself and ignoring Kuster's warning glance.

"We are to get *all* messages and calls, as they come in. It's not for you to say which ones are important or not."

Her face turned a shade of purple and she reluctantly agreed.

"Well that was fun." Sally chimed in as she made her way back to her desk.

"One of us will have to go and see her this morning, but I'll give her a call right now." He shook his head in disgust and went back to his desk and picked up his phone.

His call was answered on the first ring.

"Yes?" a heated woman shouted in his ear.

"It's Deputy Kuster, Mrs. Berryman. I apologize for your troubles with Ms. Grimes earlier. I promise, someone will be over this morning and then you'll be all set."

"That will be fine, Deputy, thank you."

"What was all that about?" Stan demanded as he stepped into the room with a fresh cup of coffee.

Kuster hung up the phone, finished jotting down some notes and took a second to make sure everything was in perfect order on his desk.

"You okay?" Kuster eyeballed the king size carry out coffee Stan had toted in with him and the nasty circles under his eyes.

"I'll feel better after I drink this." He said, holding up his coffee.

"I doubt it. It seems Betty here has been censoring our messages for us. Mrs. Berryman has been calling to see if we need to take another look around the attic before they start gutting it today and Betty has neglected to tell us. I promised her one of us would be over this morning."

"I'll go. I want to talk to Bill Harrison first though." Stan paused to take a sip of coffee and then made a face. "Get Bill on the phone; see if I can either swing by the funeral home or his house in five."

"You got it."

"Then as soon as we have some breathing room, we need to find a new receptionist out there before I wring her fat neck."

⅄

Stan pulled his cruiser into the empty parking lot of Harrison's Funeral Home and walked in the back door, the cloying scent of carnations greeting him straightaway.

Bill Harrison suddenly materialized to welcome him and requested that the sheriff follow him to his office that was located just down the hall.

As always Bill was impeccably dressed in a suit and tie with a starched white linen handkerchief peeking out of the breast pocket. He was a short man with a small build and wore his thinning grayish black hair parted far off to the side, exposing a bluish vein on his temple that pulsated when excited.

He walked fast, but took tiny steps, reminding Stan of a mouse scurrying down the hallway.

"Coffee, Sheriff? It's fresh and I would have to think far superior than what they offer at the station." He deeply inhaled the hot steam escaping from what looked to be a hand painted coffee mug and smiled. "It's a combination of several exquisite dark roasted beans from around the world. I order the beans online and do the blending myself." He announced proudly, as if he just baked a cake from scratch.

"Uh, yeah, sure. Thanks, Bill, I'll take a cup." He had to admit, it did smell better than the sludge he usually drank that by the time he got to the pot, was often burnt and smelled somewhat toxic.

"My pleasure." He beamed as he handed over a cup of black coffee.

"I was thinking of getting one of those machines for my office that you drop in a little prefilled pack of coffee and it makes a single cup."

"Those are garbage!" Bill looked horrified. "Get a French Press for one and an electric kettle to boil your water. Just as easy and it will taste so much better." He took a sip of his own coffee and savored the brew. "Now, what can I help you with?"

Bill Harrison spoke in his undertaker's tone which by now was probably the only way he remembered to talk. Today however, he had a slight dreamy look in his eyes as he sat in front of Sheriff Meyers.

"Well, for starters, what do you know about Huddelstone? More to the point, did you know that it was once a funeral home?"

"Oh, yes! Huddelstone. I'm so delighted to see it being brought back to its original brilliance." He sat down in the chair facing the sheriff, crossed his legs and sipped his coffee. Now he looked like a tea drinker. "And yes, I do recall that it was once a funeral home although I do not believe that it stayed in business very long. I'd have to look up that particular fact. I have some information pertaining to Huddelstone at home if you would like me to do a little research and get back to you."

"You have information on Huddelstone being a funeral home at your house?" Stan repeated, not sure if he had heard correctly. The Harrison's family home was located directly next door to the funeral home and was considered creepy by just about everyone. While the funeral home and its grounds were meticulously kept up, their personal residence appeared sad and run down.

Bill smiled. "Sort of a family hobby I'm afraid. We have history on all the funeral homes, cemeteries and crematories from this area going back about hundred years or so. I know I should probably transfer it all to my computer, but I prefer the old fashioned way of writing it all down by hand and storing it in files."

"Well, if you wouldn't mind then Bill, thanks. I'd appreciate that." He tried to conjure up a picture of Bill sitting around with his brother Bob and their eighty year old mother, all exchanging funeral trivia.

"There wasn't much need for funeral homes way back then you know Sheriff. Homes built back in the mid 1800's laid out their deceased in the parlor. Later the room was used for entertaining or for guests that came calling, but the original use was for a wake of a family member. Before Harrison Funeral Home opened their doors, Huddelstone operated as one of the town's first official funeral homes in a sense that they offered their parlor to those that perhaps had a very small home and would not be able to hold their own wake."

It was in a strange way refreshing to see someone so perfectly contented with their career choice, even if it was a morbid selection. Someone had to do it. He noticed the vein in Bill's forehead starting to dance wildly and wondered if he was in pain or simply excited.

Stan considered his history lesson and couldn't imagine what all this had to do with what was going on today, but he had to start somewhere. Perhaps he didn't need to go back so far, but something in his gut was gnawing at him since he found out about the whole funeral parlor business.

"A wake…" He thought out loud. "I suppose they had a different name for that back then?"

Bill shook his head. "No, actually they didn't. Stethoscopes were not invented until the mid-1800's and even then they weren't very strong. Unfortunately people were often buried alive when a pulse was not detected. To prevent this from happening, the departed would be laid out for three to four days to see if they would *wake* or start to decompose. So if the room started to smell, they would know for sure. That was of course the reason for all the flowers at funerals, to mask the smell of decaying bodies. Now it's simply a lovely tradition."

"So that was before embalming." Stan probed, recalling Kuster's history lesson.

"Precisely!" Bill appeared excited his student was contributing to the conversation. "Embalming was used primarily at first to preserve bodies before transporting them home to their families. We use slightly different techniques and chemicals today, but the idea is basically the same. When embalming was first invented, people actually thought it was a blessing mainly because they were so afraid of being buried alive." He grinned oddly. "They knew for sure that once embalmed, they would really be dead."

Stan was trying hard to hide his own odd look. He had never had this long of a conversation with Bill Harrison before and now he knew why. He could only assume the rest of the Harrison family was equally as weird.

"It was great fear back then you know, Sheriff Meyers." He had lowered his voice and allowed their eyes to connect. "To be buried alive."

There's a pleasant thought. "I can see how that would make people a bit nervous."

"More than nervous, people were terrified they would wake up in a sealed coffin. There was an actual device invented that was rigged from the ground to the coffin's surface with a long rope attached. One end would be tied to the deceased's finger in the casket and the other end would be fastened to a pole that held a bell. It was one of the caretaker's duties to watch over the grave site for a few days to be sure the device was not activated."

"You don't say." The part about the bell sounded familiar. He seemed to recall reading a mystery book about that very topic back when he was working midnights.

"Oh yes, in fact, before the corpse ever made it to the casket the morgue started tying a little bell to the deceased's toe. Mother said she would often hear the dinging of the little bell and would be sent to go and check it out."

"Really?" Stan questioned, trying to keep the skepticism out of his voice.

"Mother will be ninety-seven this fall, in case you are wondering." Bill volunteered, reading his mind.

"I was thank you. Did Huddelstone ever do embalming there?"

For the first time, the mortician appeared slightly uneasy. "If it did, it wouldn't have been for very long."

"Was it still in business when Harrison first opened?"

"No, it ceased to operate in that capacity several years before Harrison's was first established." Bill made a steeple with his two index fingers and pressed it firmly to his lips. "I want to say there was some type of scandal there, Sheriff, but I'd like to check on that first."

Chapter 33

"I just had the oddest conversation with Bill Harrison." Stan confessed into his cell.

"Well, he's an odd guy." Kuster replied back in a tone that suggested it's a matter of public record.

"What do you know about the guy?" Harrison did not seem the type to sit around sipping tea with Kuster and friends, but nothing much would surprise him after today.

"He hasn't been invited to join our little tea circle, if that's what you're thinking."

"Just wondering if you had any stories up your sleeve about him. You seem to know a little something about everyone."

"The family pretty much keeps to themselves. I've had a beer or two with The Buzzard before, but that's about it. He's not much of a talker."

Stan was lost. "The Buzzard?"

"Yeah, Bob, Bill's brother. His nickname's The Buzzard. You know, because he runs in and grabs the dead bodies and brings them to the funeral home."

"I knew he did that. I didn't know he had a special name."

"He's like stupid strong. He used to carry the dead bodies out in his arms like they weighed next to nothing and toss them into hearse until some family member freaked out and complained."

"I don't even know how to comment on that." He wondered again how he never noticed that half the town was certifiable.

"He just recently moved back to town. Is there anything you want me to ask him or should I bring him in?"

"No, nothing like that. Hey, see if Sally can meet me over at the Berryman's right away and help me go through that attic, will you? I don't want to keep Mrs. Berryman waiting, I'm sure she's pretty pissed already."

"Sure thing."

"I wonder if her husband is in town. I haven't seen him since that day in their barn."

"No, I heard he left right after that." Kuster offered with a sheepishly grin.

"Hear anything else that you'd care to share, Kuster?"

"No." He shook his head in response and quickly picked back up the file he had been reading. "That was it."

Twenty minutes later Stan pulled up the Berryman driveway and hit the brakes hard when someone suddenly appeared out of nowhere and jumped in front of his cruiser, scaring the crap out of him.

"Son of a bitch!" He swore under his breath before jumped out of the car to see what just happened.

"Sheriff!" Alice Muncy's spirited voice called out from under a gigantic straw hat adorned with dozens of real red roses poking out in various directions. She must have plucked the flowers from her garden recently as they still looked fresh. "I am so glad you have come back to help Ms. Berryman."

"That's a lovely hat you're wearing today Alice, is that one of your own creations?" He reached over to tilt the brim of her hat up, expanding her field of vision.

"Why yes it is! Did you know that courtships used to start with a meaningful bouquet and then change as the relationship evolved? It was a simply charming, unwritten way to communicate to your loved one, only you better hope they knew how to decode your message!" She let out a little giggle. "Some arrangements became quite complicated and complex as the color of the bloom changed along with the number of and mix of the colors." She allowed her lashes to open and close several times in appreciation and then cast a solemn glance to the front of Bretta's house.

"There used to be rows and rows of Marigolds planted all around the front of this house, years ago. They represent sorrow. And there was so much sorrow here." Alice exhaled sadly. "Flowers had great meaning during the Victorian times. Irma knew that. I wonder if that was why she planted all the darn Sweet Pea out back. Never made much sense to me at the time, but now I understand."

Stan stood patiently, waiting for her to continue.

"Understand what Alice?" He finally urged.

"Sweet Pea is a sign of departure of course. She must have known all along."

Lost in Alice's nonsense, he almost missed hearing Bretta approach. But he had a trained ear and a keen six sense himself, not the weird paranormal one that apparently plagued Kuster or whatever it was that had a hold of Alice.

He arrived back to his home town without the cumbersome baggage of a wife, children or even a pet. They would have still have gladly accepted him no matter what he dragged with him, but were incredibly grateful he came alone. This time the City Council wanted a sheriff that lived and breathed his job, but not drank it.

"Hello, Sheriff." Bretta smiled warmly. Maybe seeing Alice with a rose-bush on her head cheered her up and she temporally forgot that the Sheriff's department dispatcher had been snooping through her personal files. "Thanks for getting here so quickly. I am just putting breakfast on the table, please come join us for a quick bite. Alice, you come too."

Alice was already shaking her flowers no. "I want to go and take a look at your yard. You know there has never been a vegetable garden here for as long as I can remember. Only flowers. Flowers for this and flowers for that, but no vegetables." She looked agitated suddenly. "I think you should leave things as they were Bretta."

Stan and Bretta both exchanged a confused glance. "You don't think that planting a little vegetable garden would be a nice idea?" she questioned softly.

"No. Not here I don't." she replied firmly and then marched to the back yard leaving the two to just shrug their shoulders.

Stan followed Bretta into her warm, sunny kitchen and dillydallied in the doorway. He had a hundred and one things to do today and he knew it would be best to get right down to business, yet the aroma that filled the air pulled him in. He couldn't remember the last time he had a home cooked meal. The sultry sound of Norah Jones' Sunrise played softly in the background and he felt some of his tension drift away.

"Can you believe that?" Bretta stuck her hands on her hips but still had a smile on her lovely face. "The girls didn't wait for us!" she reached into one of the freshly painted cabinets and pulled down two plates. He noticed someone picked out pieces of ham out of whatever she was serving for breakfast and left it on the corner of their plate.

"Have a seat, everything is on the table and should still be somewhat hot. If not, then I can reheat it for you easily enough."

She turned to hand him a plate and he found himself only inches from her face. The crisp, light floral aura that surrounded her set off a punch gut reaction which totally took him by surprise. Something inside of him told him he should probably run out the front door, but his feet would not obey. "That's a nasty scar on your forehead." He commented as he gently swept a lock of hair off to the side.

"I was in a car accident when I was a teenager, it looks worse than it actually was Sherriff." She reached up to touch it self-consciously.

"If you're going to be feeding me breakfast, then you should at least call me Stan." It had nothing to do with breakfast. He wanted to hear her say his name.

"All right, Stan. Did you want coffee or orange juice?" her voice came out soft and a little breathy. Neither one backed up or made an effort to put a more appropriate distance between them.

This was ludicrous. He barely knew her. His inner voice was commanding him to take his butt and plate over to the table and sit down and eat, because he knew what he really wanted to do. He wrestled with the insane urge to set down his plate, grab a hold of the breathtaking creature standing barefoot in front of him and throw her down on the counter.

An irrational, he has been working way too hard, thought.

He noticed she made no attempt to move. Her eyes remained firmly locked with his, looking just as surprised by all of this as he felt.

Lightly he set his plate on the counter and let his hands come down to his sides. It had been a while since he bothered to go on a date but he still recalled that there was something that came before flinging a woman on a countertop and making love to her. A touch, an understanding, something, but for the life of him he couldn't remember what came next so he did what felt natural. His strong right arm went around her waist and he rested his large hand on the small of her back, gently pressing her towards him slightly, so their bodies were touching.

Shock registered on both their faces; still they did not speak, both afraid to break the spell. The attraction was so intense in a melting, urgent way; he found it difficult to breath.

The knock on the front door made them both jump apart and Stan's hand fell back to resting causally on the counter. Neither broke eye contact.

"Knock-knock. Hey Sheriff, you in there?" A loud female voice called out from the front of the house.

"That would be Sally, stopping by to help."

Bretta looked away as a blush crept up her neck. "I'll go and show her the way. Please, make yourself at home."

A thin, attractive blonde with a mass of blonde curls stood on the porch, peering through the screen door. "Mrs. Berryman? Officer Hiller from the Sheriff's department."

Bretta opened the door and stepped back so the officer could enter.

"Nice to meet you Officer Hiller, please come on in. We're back in the kitchen." Bretta led the way through the house, waving her hand for the officer to follow.

"You have done some amazing things with this house Mrs. Berryman. It's beautiful."

"Thank you and please, call me Bretta. It's still a work in progress, but it's coming along. Come have some breakfast with us."

Sally looked taken aback. "Well, thank you. That is very nice of you considering what a bitch Betty has been to you." When she saw Bretta was about to make light of her co-workers behavior, she shot her hand out to stop her. "I've worked with that beast for years; I know what she's capable of."

"Hey Sal." Stan called out from the table. "Thanks for getting here so quick."

Bretta passed her a plate. "Please, help yourself. It's an egg, ham, and spinach bake. One of the kid's favorites, so I hope that's ok. There is homemade cinnamon bread and fresh fruit over on there on the other counter too."

"That was delicious, Mrs. Berryman. Thank you kindly." Stan spoke up suddenly. He gathered his plate and glass and hurried it over to the sink. "I'm going to go upstairs and get started."

"Wow, you must be really something." Sally said after her boss left the room, right before cramming an enormous size of cinnamon bread in her mouth which she had to fold in thirds to get it to fit.

"I beg your pardon?" Bretta spoke up alarmed, wringing the dish towel in her hands. Even though nothing technically happened, it felt as if it had. Something electric and dangerous that gave her a fluttery feeling in her stomach.

"I said you must be some kind of cook to get the Sheriff to sit still long enough to eat." She shook her head in disgust. "The man never takes a break. I've never known him to sit and visit before on a call. He rarely sits when he eats. He'll pace around the room with a sandwich in his hand." Sally shook her head while shoveling a forkful of fruit in.

She didn't appear to swallow before taking another bite and Bretta worried the officer might choke. The thin but fit Officer Hiller certainly could eat. When she saw Bretta's jaw drop in astonishment, she laughed, spraying out a little food.

"Sorry about that. Since the Sheriff put a no food ban on in the station, thanks to Betty, I'm about ready to friggin starve to death." She swiped a napkin across her face. "That was amazing, really. Thank you. What, were you like a chef or something before moving here?"

She could eat faster than both her daughters and like Stan, gathered her plate and brought it to the sink.

"Thank you and no, I was a fashion designer." Bretta laughed, enjoying the unusual officer. "I plan on going back to work once my office upstairs is finished."

Sally's big blue eyes popped opened wide in astonishment and then traveled down over the petite brunette standing before her barefoot, dressed in ratty jean shorts and a slightly torn t-shirt. "Fashion designer...well, you don't say. Well, I guess you don't have to care much what you look like living out here, huh?" Instantly, her face reddened and she laughed out loud at her own bluntness. "I didn't mean it like that!" She was cracking herself up now. "I just would think you would dress up a bit. You know, show off your work."

Bretta held up her hands but was smiling. "It's fine officer. I guess I have let myself go a little." She glanced down at her outfit to see what she had even thrown on for the day. The truth was she always dressed for comfort, not style, especially when she worked out of the house. Today she was dressed for cleaning out the attic.

"Well, off to work I go." Sally slowed for an instant and yelled over her shoulder. "Hey, what times dinner?"

"Usually six, but it varies. You best call first officer." She was laughing, but was sincere. She was ready to do some entertaining and make new friends, especially with someone so amusing.

"Got it. Call me Sally please." She turned to find the attic entrance when Stan poked his head around the corner.

"Sally, can you please get Kuster over here with his kit and camera? And call up Bill Harrison for me and see if he can get over here to have a look at some things for us. Right now, if he is able."

"Sure thing boss." Sally walked out of the room while dialing on her cell.

"Mrs. Berryman, would you mind coming up to the attic with me please while we wait for Kuster? We can start going through the other items now."

"Sure. That would be fine. And please call me Bretta" It seemed pretty silly to keep calling her Mrs. Berryman after what happened between them in the kitchen. What almost happened. "Who's Bill Harrison?"

"He owns a funeral home in town."

Icy trepidation marched sharply down the back of her neck. "A funeral home?" She had a slight idea of what he found up in her attic, she had been expecting to find something like that herself. "Why?" she whispered.

He looked sorry to have to tell her this. "I found some things I need identified. There were some tools and other objects that I think might belong to a mortician."

Once upstairs, Stan carefully removed the dusty black lid to the box and they both leaned in to have a look.

"All these items were left behind so they do belong to you now. Once we are finished up here you can do with them whatever you wish. In fact, some of these things we can start going over right now. We can start over in this corner and work our way around the room. We will bag anything I think is important. What time is Marc due to arrive?"

She looked around the room. "We changed the time to this afternoon when I was having trouble getting someone to come out here."

"Hey, Sheriff?" Sally poked her head up the stairs. "I'll have to run over and pick up Mr. Harrison. They only have one vehicle and its out on a pick up right now. Kuster said he will swing by with his kit and tag everything himself. I can tell he really doesn't want me playing with his stuff. Boys and their toys." She rolled her eyes and then headed back down the stairs.

"Okay, thanks Sally."

Bretta found herself feeling a little awkward and shy, like she was on a first date. But she decided to stay focused on all the possible treasures the former owner left behind and soon she and the Sheriff were working side by side, sorting through the contents of the attic into piles of what she would keep and what would eventually be given away.

Thirty-five minutes later Sally delivered Bill Harrison, fresh from the funeral home and into the hot, dusty attic.

"What can I help you with Sheriff?" Bill inquired irritably, his hand patting a white hankie along his moist brow and then proceeded to smooth down his expensively tailored suit as if Sally had physically manhandled him on the drive over. "Your *girl* here was very mysterious."

Officer Hiller's temper was as quick as her right hand as it shot out and then came back to rest on her holster. Bretta noticed that her lovely blonde tresses had turned to a mass of frizz, reminding her of cotton candy from the summer fair and she wondered if she had cut the air on the ride over to further irritate Mr. Harrison.

"Believe it or not Mr. Harrison; I am not referred to as his *girl.* I am called an *officer,* and I carry a *gun.*"

Bretta had to question if Mr. Harrison was aggravated because he was dragged away from work and was kept in the dark or he disliked females in general.

"Thanks for helping us out here Bill." Stan interjected. "We came across a couple of things we were hoping you could identify."

"Certainly, always a pleasure to help the law when I can." His mood improved dramatically and he straightened up his spine, adding at least a half an inch on to his overall height.

"Kuster here yet with the kit?"

"No, I'll call him." Sally replied quickly.

"No need, I'm right here." Deputy Kuster bounced up the stairs, two legs at a time with his kit and camera in tow. "Hey, Bill, how's it going?" And then to Sally with a smile; "Nice hair."

"Wish I could say the same to you." She shot back and stuck out her tongue.

Although he looked awkward at all angles, his moves were fluid and fast, opening each case and container like he did this sort of maneuver ten times a day.

Kuster began with his camera, taking several shots of both the outside and the inside of the box until Bill Harrison walked over to observe and soon clutched his chest as if he was about to have a heart attack.

"What a find! Oh, wait until the society hears about this!" He moved in for a closer inspection, oblivious to the fact that all eyes were now watching him with concern.

"Uh, what *society* would that be?" Sally inquired and Stan shot her a warning glance.

"Bill, could you please identify each item if you are able?" Stan requested and Sally automatically retrieved a pen and paper from her uniform pocket.

Bill looked insulted. "Of course I know what each item is Sheriff. Let's see, this first one is an Aspirating Pump, probably from the early 1900's."

He belted out a screech of joy startling everyone and his hand automatically shot forward to touch, but Stan was faster and grabbed a hold of his dainty wrist before it made contact. Bill seemed unaware of the commotion he caused and continued on. "This is what was known as a Gravity Feed Container, you can see the enamel finish was baked on and I must comment on what superb condition these are in!"

Sally, who was note taking, interjected; "What would it have been used for?"

Harrison replied from his happy trance- like state. "Fluids were first placed into the container and then were fed into the body by a hose attached to the bottom here."

Sally's look was of total bewilderment. Even Kuster stopped snapping photos.

"What, this stuff was used to force feed people?" Officer Hiller finally spoke up when no one else did.

"Not exactly, *Officer*." His lips clamped together dramatically, showing his students how disappointed he was in Hiller's lack of intelligence. "These fine treasures are antiques and are exquisite examples of the various tools first used in embalming."

"Embalming?" Sally shouted loud enough for the house on either side to hear. "What in the world would Irma be doing with embalming tools?" She jammed her pencil behind her left ear and moved in for a better look.

"This was once a funeral home, though I must say I am surprised at the find. It was always my understanding that it was only open for a brief period and the morticians or directors at the time were not even trained in embalming. Embalming didn't catch on around here until the late 1800's and even then it wasn't always practiced everywhere."

"Why's that?" Stan prodded.

"Well, for starters, there weren't that many licensed morticians available and many families still preferred to keep with tradition and lay the body out themselves. Looks like they did a little of both, unless someone once liked to collect funeral memorabilia."

"What do you mean?"

"Well, we have the tools here for embalming. They would have needed embalming chemicals as well. Back then it would have come in glass bottles." He spun his head around the room as if such a bottle might miraculously appear. "But over there," he pointed to the far left corner. "We have a Cooling board. The women of the house would wash and dress the body and then it would be placed on a board like that, which sat on a block of ice."

All four left the tools and walked over to examine the strange looking board they had never heard of before today. Neglected and resting against the wall, it was coated in dust and cobwebs and resembled an old surf board.

With a carefully gloved hand, Stan turned the aged board over to find dark, blackish stains on the side.

"Sally, bag all the items Mr. Harrison is showing us." Stan said as he stared at the strange object in front of him.

The rapid fire shots of Kuster's camera was the rooms only sound until he stopped abruptly, put down his camera and got on his knees, his face pressing on the dirty floor boards. He twiddled with the zoom lens until what he needed to see came into focus and then took a few more pictures.

"You find something there, Kuster?" Stan finally asked.

Kuster stood up, tapped a few buttons on his camera and handed it over to his boss.

"Yeah, something you're gonna want to see."

Chapter 34

Once the Sheriff and his deputies were finished in the attic, Bretta's plan had been to pay Rose a visit at her antique store. She recalled her mentioning she still had a few things at her store that had once belonged to the Huddelstone Family and it suddenly became important that whatever the items were, they had to find their way back to the house.

Maybe the nervous anticipation she was experiencing was due to the fact the sheriff station was adjacent to Rose's store and she still needed time to process their earlier encounter. The very thought of him made the palms of her hands clammy and caused a funny, wavering sensation in her belly, further proof she has spent too much time alone in the country.

Ivy and Iris actually volunteered to accompany her today and she was enjoying spending time with them. It was a typical, hot end of summer day that felt even hotter now that they entered town.

"It smells like your old workshop in the city." Ivy said with a wrinkled up nose as they entered Anderson Antiques.

"It does?" Bretta took in a breath and shrugged her shoulders in a way that suggested she did not agree. Iris was already off admiring an antique doll and Ivy looked as if she had arrived to do their inventory.

"Hey Mom, doesn't this doll look like me?" Iris called out from across the room. She was standing in front of a porcelain doll in a white lace dress, captivated with its breathtaking features.

"Well, what a delightful surprise!" Rose greeted them as she walked out of the back room, her reading glasses dangling on a sparkly amethyst chain she wore around her neck. She was dressed elegantly today in a cream colored long sleeve silk blouse and charcoal pants, her grey hair arranged in a neat bob.

She ran over and hugged each of her visitors, starting with Iris. "I was getting ready to take a break from my bears and have some tea. Care to join me?"

"What bears?" Ivy tested, her voice filled with suspicion.

"Come on back and take a look." Rose led the way to the rear of the shop, stepping around rows of various chairs, tables and knickknacks that at one time most likely held a cherished spot in the home of a Chester family.

They followed her through a set of antique beveled glass doors trimmed in walnut and stepped into a workshop set to thrill any seamstress. Brilliant rays of sun streamed through the windows and illuminated a large wooden work table in the center of the room which displayed patterns, fabric, and Teddy Bears at different stages of completion. A long, wooden workbench had been built into the wall under the windows which held three sewing machines, one of which was clearly an antique and most likely not in working order.

"The old black sewing machine on the end is my favorite. I purchased it for five dollars at a flea market. Can you believe it still works? It doesn't have all the bells and whistles that the new ones have, but I still love using it from time to time." Rose offered when she saw Bretta admiring it.

"My mother actually has one very similar to that one at her main office." Bretta smiled at the happy memory. "It's where I first learned to sew."

"Oh, you make Teddy Bears!" Iris shrieked in delight and tucked a strand of silky, long black hair behind her ear as she bent forward to get a better view of the patterns laid out on the table.

Bretta noticed Ivy was observing Rose as if she discovered the older woman had secretly been practicing satanic rituals and sacrificing small children. Why did her daughter always have an issue with everything? She tried to make eye contact with her and warn her to behave.

Slowly Ivy circled the room, her eyes vigilantly inspecting the suspicious room until she made her way to a table in the back corner where she came to an abrupt halt and released an ear-piercing scream.

"Ivy! What is it?" Her mother shrieked rushing to her side, her eyes simultaneously scanning Ivy's body for signs of injury.

"What have you done to this poor animal?" A full length mink coat lie spread out on a table, several sections cut out and missing. "It's been butchered!"

Rose came over and put her arm around Ivy. "Oh, honey, this coat belonged to old lady Reinstein who passed away last fall. Gladys Reinstein. She wore this thing everywhere and I do mean everywhere! To the grocery store, over to Dottie's and church on Sunday…I bet she even slept in it."

"Why have you mutilated it? It's bad enough it had to be killed so some old bat could run around town in it but now you have hacked away at it."

"Ivy!" Bretta warned. "That's enough!" She was ready to clamp her hand over her daughter's mouth and drag her out, but Rose did not appear frazzled by her fervent hormonal teenager. She wondered if Rose had any children of her own.

"Dear, the family has requested that I use the coat to make memory bears for each of her three daughters since it would not be fair to leave the coat to just one of them. In truth, Gladys wanted to be buried in it, but her girls had a hard time sticking an heirloom mink in the ground, so this was the perfect solution." When she saw Ivy still eyeballing her like she was caught crawling down from a space ship, she offered a bit more of an explanation.

"Even though the store does well, I still had quite a bit of free time on my hands and decided I needed a hobby, so I created ***Rose-Beary Unique Bears & Gifts.*** The bears allow folks the opportunity to hold on to the memory of a family member who has passed or a special sentiment that you have attached to an article of clothing, like a baby blanket for instance."

"What a clever idea!" Bretta loved the scheme instantly and carefully examined one of the finished bears. It was utterly adorable and well-crafted with a bow tied artfully around its neck, a black button nose and lighter brown material for the pads of its feet. Gently resting around the little bear's neck was a small laminated white label that had a picture of an elderly woman in her long mink coat, almost smiling and under it read: *Dear mother.* Curious, Bretta opened the card to find the rest of the story. The inside cover gave her full name, Gladys May Reinstein, June 8th, 1920 – September 17th, 2014 and the inside page read; *close to our hearts, never far from our thoughts.* The back of the tag explained that this was a memory bear, created out of love and was not a toy.

Right away she considered how precious it would be to have Rose create bears out of the girl's baby blankets that she had stowed away before the move. Although she was an accomplished seamstress herself, her talent was fashion and she knew she could not even come close to creating a bear as exquisite as one of these even if she thought she had the patience for it.

"I have a whole showcase of bears and some other things that I've made at the front of the store if you want to take a look before you leave." She moved over to her steaming hot pot, assorted teas, and several cups and saucers that did not match. "What type of tea would you like, ladies?"

"I'll have whatever you are having Rose and I think the girls will pass," she could read their thoughts. "They want to go and explore your store."

Ivy and Iris, who were both eying the mammoth dollhouse across the room, smiled and took off to explore.

Bretta lowered her voice. "Rose, you mentioned at Alice's the other day about some sewing things and a gun that you thought belonged to me. Where did you get those things?"

"Oh, yes. A few years back when Irma moved away, I found a box on my back porch. I assumed it was from Irma's son who was moving her out and thought I would like these for my store as he would have no use for them. I like to keep possessions with the house they belong to if at all possible and was just waiting for the day a family would move in and take over Huddelstone. Then you and your family moved in!" Rose gave her arm a gentle squeeze before handing her a cup of tea.

"When I went through the box more thoroughly last week, I noticed that these things already belonged to you! I was a bit surprised, but then things often have a way of returning to their rightful owner. Who am I to question the ways of the universe?"

When she was at Alice's the other day, the thought came to her that the sewing basket they we're talking about must of contained the fabric that matched Irma's dress, and that was why they thought it belonged to her.

Now she could see Rose was much like Alice and she did not have a reason to worry.

"Why would you think the items belonged to me, Rose?" It was time to put an end to this nonsense.

"Well, there was a picture of you inside the basket of course."

Bretta's eyes grew wide in disbelief. "A picture of me? May I please see this basket Rose?" She was betting the picture bore nothing more than a slight resemblance if that, but she had to admit it had her curious.

"I gave everything to Alice for safe keeping dear." She said with a nod of her head. "Along with the gun."

Wonderful.

"I also recall you saying something about a few pieces of furniture that belonged to the original owners of Huddelstone. I would like to see those if you don't mind." She was already positive she would take them, but just in case some weren't in such great shape or totally useless items, she did not want to commit to anything.

"Oh!" Rose put her hand on her heart. "You're too late dear. I sold them just the other day."

Bretta was dumbfounded. "You sold them? To whom?"

"Some gentleman and his wife that were passing through town wanted them." Rose slipped on her glasses and stepped over to a Tomas Kinkade wall calendar held up by a single nail. "They came in last Tuesday. I remember this because I had a fabric order delivered that same day. They wanted whatever I had from that old house up on the hill. I thought perhaps you sent them in because they brought up your name."

Bretta shook her head in disappointment. "No, I haven't mentioned the items to anyone or sent anyone in." She couldn't even think of who knew about this place other than locals. "What was it that you had?"

"Oh, let's see, there was a silver tea strainer, a pair of Victorian wrought iron andirons and a striking 1892 Western Electric Folding Cabinet Desk Set that had an antique phone built in."

She most likely would have taken all of that, what rotten luck. Too bad she did not make it here last week. A female customer that had been browsing the fabric section stepped over to Rose to inquire about vintage lace and Bretta took the opportunity to stroll around the rest of the store. If she could not have an original piece to the house, she could at least find a couple of items from the same era.

A tall oak bookcase filled with teddy bears standing in the corner caught her eye and for some reason, made her happy. She must have one made for her mother. She knew how much she was missing her grandchildren and this would be so sweet.

She approached the display then stopped sharply, causing the timeworn wooden floor boards under her feet to groan boisterously.

A sense of foreboding rushed up her backbone to the very fine hairs at the base of her neck, causing them to rise on end and what little breath remained in her lungs rushed out in short, choppy blasts.

Sometimes things appear much different up close, she needed a better look.

Your eyes play tricks on you.

Sometimes, they even make things up to punish you.

Two more steps. Her heart banged fiercely inside her chest and the blood roaring in her ears sounded more like waves from the ocean crashing against the shore.

Rose's docile voice, which could be heard educating her customer on the various types of vintage lace and how to properly care for it, began to drift away.

She moved until she stood directly in front of the rustic wooden shelves and stared hard at the rows and rows of teddy bears, her mouth hanging open.

There, on the second shelf, sitting together side by side and practically holding hands were two bears made out of cloth, not fur.

One in an ivy material and the other in an iris.

Dear God, how can this be?

The exact material she had made dresses out of for her daughters so long ago. One of them in the same pattern that somehow found its way wrapped around Irma's bones.

The identical cloth she told the sheriff was not easily found and that she did not have any extra of.

The bears wore elegant, silky bows around their necks; each in a coordinating color and creatively tied. She stood fixated, unable to move even as she became aware of the girls calling her name from the other side of the store.

She knew she had to look. She was sure she was wrong, but there was no way she could leave this store without first checking. Her mind worked feverishly to process how a fabric she once found on accident years ago kept showing up.

Could she have purchased extra fabric and stashed it away somewhere? Was it possible that she made a bear like that and didn't remember?

Oh, God…what if John was right about her? That's why he was staying away. He knows she is crazy and doesn't know what to do with her.

Insanity has a calling card and it is called doubt.

One trembling hand covered her mouth while the other slowly extended out to touch the bears. Carefully she turned over their tiny ribbons to confirm what she already knew she would find.

There in bold, black letters were her daughter's names printed on the back side of each ribbon.

She backed up fast, crashing into Rose. "Is everything alright?"

"I have to go." Her eyes combed the store quickly for her daughters. "Girls?" In a tone that meant business, she headed for the door.

Rose lightly touched her arm. "Are you ill, Bretta?"

"No. Yes. I don't feel so good. I just want to get home. I'll be fine. Girls, let's go."

"I think you should sit down for a minute."

"Did you make these?" Bretta inquired, pointing to the cloth bears named after her daughters.

"Well, no I didn't. Now that you mention it, these were also in that box of stuff that was dropped off. I had forgotten all about these." Her face lit up. "Did you make these?"

Bretta began shaking her head. "No. No I don't believe so." Did she make them and forget?

"Mom, come here!" Iris called from the other side of the store as Ivy ran up and grabbed a hold of her arm.

"Mom, you have to come and take a look at this! You are never going to believe it." Ivy said, pulling her towards the side of the store to where her sister was busy playing with a dollhouse.

She did her best to force a normal expression on her face and went to check out whatever the girls were so excited about. From the way Rose was studying her, she knew she had better pull it together before she called 911 on her or worse, the Sheriff.

"Don't you see, Mom?" Ivy pulled her mother in the direction of the enormous wooden doll house that rested on someone's former kitchen table.

"It's Huddelstone! It's our house! It took us a minute too because its painted white and the front porch is not exactly the same, but Mr. Marc told me before some changes had been made to that area over the years." Ivy stood with her hands on her hips while she gave the house careful consideration.

Bretta took a step closer and tried her best to forget about the creepy hand holding bears across the room. Could this be her house? After circling the table twice, she had to admit the structure was essentially the same. On her third lap around, she took her time and began to peek inside every window.

The kitchen and two of the bedrooms had just enough natural light streaming through its windows to display an astonishing amount of detail from the striped red velvet wallpaper to a straight back chair with a needle-point seat cover and she could not help but wonder if this was how her house might have once looked. There was even a miniature green Tiffany lamp that, from what she could recall, looked very much like the one she had found in the attic.

"Where did this dollhouse come from, Rose? Did you make this?" Awestruck, she was unable to take her eyes off the smaller replica of her new home.

"Oh, heavens no! One day last year, a gentleman showed up with it. He said someday, someone was going to show great interest in this. I thought the workmanship was rather magnificent, so I took it." Rose tilted her head to the side. "To tell the truth, until today, you're the first to ever get that excited over it. I did not catch the resemblance to your home before, even though I have been to Huddelstone dozens of times, but it could be like what the girls said, the color threw me off."

Bretta was still poking her head into every window, taking in every detail. It really did appear to be Huddelstone.

"Here, let me show you something." Rose said kneeling down on the floor and facing the front of the house. "Over here, if you press this tiny button, the parlor lights up. Come on over and look inside."

An eerie glow of light streamed out of the parlor windows and casted out tiny shadows. Everyone picked a window to see what the Huddelstone sitting room might have once looked like.

Mother and daughters gasped loudly in unison. Ivy and Iris quickly jumped to their feet and stood a good three feet away while Bretta sat back on her ankles, trying to rationalize the situation.

Her system had enough shocks for the day and she tried to arrange a few words in her brain that did not come out sounding like panic. She knew she had to say something; she simply could not sit on her heels staring at a dollhouse.

"It's rather surprising, that's all. I mean I knew our house was once a funeral home, I just wouldn't expect to see this in a dollhouse."

"Yes, I did find that rather odd too. We've had several dollhouses brought in over the years and this is the first to have a coffin in the parlor."

Bretta leaned forward again, pressed the button for the light and looked through the window. "Does the inside parlor door open?" it appeared that there was a woman in the coffin, but she wanted to get a closer look from a different angle.

"I don't know, I never tried. Let's give it a go." Rose squatted down next to Bretta and gave the tiny door a tug and with little effort, it opened.

The view from this angle brought the tiny casket into focus and there was indeed a woman lying inside. There were wreaths, flowers, and a book inside with her, just what you might find at a real funeral today.

"Rose," Bretta suggested softly, her eyes fixated on the parlor. "Do you have a magnifying glass I could use?"

"Well, yes I do. I'll run and get it."

"What's wrong, mom?" Iris quizzed.

"Nothing honey, why don't you girls go and get an ice-cream?" Bretta offered but no one moved.

"Here you go, Bretta." Rose handed her the magnifying glass from off her work table.

Bretta put the glass up to her eye and gazed in one more time, this time able to make out every minute detail and read the inscriptions on every wreath.

No words left Bretta's mouth, only her hand opened and slowly, the magnifying glass she had gripped so tightly dropped to the floor. Two long seconds later, her body followed. The sickening sound of her head smacking against the hard floor made everyone scream.

Chapter 35

"She's coming to Sheriff…vitals are good." Dave the paramedic worked like he had two sets of hands but still he wasn't working fast enough for Stan who stood towering over him. Both men had already drilled Bretta's daughters on any possible health condition she could have: allergies, medication, or bumps on the head but came up empty. "Looks like she might have just fainted."

The paramedic's hands stilled briefly as he glanced up at the crowd gathering to gawk. "Ah, Sheriff…I think it's getting a bit crowded in here, sir."

Stan reluctantly dragged his eyes away from Bretta and for the first time took in the amount of people that crowded the small shop to stare at a woman sprawled out on the floor and her daughters crying. His temper quickly spiked several degrees.

"Everyone out!" He barked loudly, not noticing Dave's surprised glance. Kuster was suddenly by his side with a steady hand on his back.

His deputy spoke quietly in his bosses left ear. "I'll take it from here, boss."

Kuster smiled and opened his arms wide while walking towards the door. "Let's go on out to the front and give them some working room, shall we? Come on now, there's not enough air in there for all of us."

One by one the crowd made their way outside, many walking backwards, their eyes still fixated on Kuster's cheerful grin. He was almost out the door with the last of the gang when the slightest hum caught his attention from the rear of the store.

Rose stood by Bretta, her arms wrapped protectively around Ivy and Iris, seemingly unaware of the sound that grabbed Kuster's interest. The trio watched Kuster lock the storefront door behind him and cautiously make his way down the aisles of fragile knick knacks to the rear of the store and then pause for approximately three seconds before making his way over to the closet door and opening it.

The Nelson brothers appeared genuinely surprised to see an officer of the law standing in front of them. Exactly how long they thought they could hide out in a broom closet undiscovered was not clear, but after several seconds of staring wide-eyed at the Deputy, Kuster finally waved them out.

Both boys were notorious trouble makers, dumb as dirt, and honestly two of the ugliest teenagers in the county that were forever on the prowl for females. It didn't take special intuitive powers to know why these boys were sniffing around here.

"Hello, boys." Kuster laid a firm hand on each boys shoulder. "Make your way on out that front door now."

"We weren't doing nothing." One of the brothers moaned.

"This is a public store, you can't make us leave." The other one chimed in.

Stan saw Kuster take a step forward, probably trying to see which was the uglier out of the two so he could get their names straight.

"Well, Ederick, hiding out in a closet after I ordered everyone to clear out is a problem. Now you two were either getting ready to steal something or you were sniffing around after the girls over there."

Kuster was quiet as he listened to their nonsense. When he had heard enough, he increased the pressure on their shoulders.

"Now listen up boys. I don't have time for you two today, so I am going to let you walk out this front door and go home." The squeeze became painfully tighter. "You stay away from this store and those two girls. Tomorrow, I'll stop on in and pay a visit to your mother."

Durrel spoke up quickly. "Now, there's no need to do that Deputy. We'll get on home right now."

"I know you will." Kuster lifted his hands and smiled. "See you tomorrow."

At their dismissal the boys ran out the front door with Kuster trailing directly behind.

Stan was curious about the odd looking teenagers he saw his deputy ushering out the front door by their ears. He noticed them walking over by Harrison's the other day and made a mental note to ask Kuster about them later.

"Any idea why she fainted?" He was speaking to Rose but still staring at the woman who has suddenly been on his mind lately.

Rose took her arms off the girls and looked them directly in the eye. "Girls, your mother is going to be just fine now. I want you to go in the back room and sit down and relax. Go on now."

Bretta, now alert and talking softly to the paramedic, urged the girls as well. "Go on girls and have a snack. I am fine, really. I just feel silly."

Rose waited until the girls had made their way to the back of the store to speak again.

"Look at this Sheriff." Rose pulled him down the front of the dollhouse and pressed the tiny button, allowing the miniature parlor to once again fill with light.

For the first time since he had returned to his hometown, he started to sincerely regret his decision. He gave up a well-respected position to work in a town full of crazies. Maybe something was being dumped in the water supply. Although he felt a little foolish, he bent down and peaked inside the dollhouse as someone thrust a magnifying glass in his hand.

It only took a second to know something was not right. His eyes took it all in, every disturbing detail.

The tiny wooden casket, the heart shaped wreath made out of flowers with the pink sash that said ***mother*** all in a parlor that resembled Huddelstone. Bretta's new home.

Who in the hell puts a casket in a dollhouse?

Then he saw it.

The little heart pillow that lay tucked in the corner of the casket with the word clearly spelled out, *Bretta.*

Son of a bitch. There was no way this was some kind of weird coincidence. He let his finger slide off the light button and sat back on his heels, his hand automatically rubbing the knot on the back of his neck.

"Where did this house come from Rose?"

"As I explained to Bretta, a gentleman brought it here a couple of years ago and said someday, someone would show great interest in it. That's about all I know."

"Well he was right about that. Do you keep some type of sales receipt? Something that might have a name or contact information on it?"

"Yes, I take down their name and number when I purchase an item in case I have a question on the item later on. It will take me a day or so to go through my files, but I will find it and call right away."

"Dave, she okay to go home or do you have to run her in?"

"No, she can go home." He handed her a lists of precautions, just to be safe. "But she should take it easy tonight."

"Bretta, I am going to have Kuster drive you and the girls on home."

She shook her head no. "My car is here..."

"Don't worry about that, you'll get your car back tonight. I'll bring it to you myself."

⅄

If there was a legacy that Wanda Bee had left behind for her, Betty Grimes thought to herself, it would be to always have a plan B. It was not as if she thought there would be any trouble over that silly Berryman thing, it was her word against the town lunatic. After all, she did have over twenty years' experience backing her up in that department and Chester's newest resident had a file over two inches thick. If Berryman thinks anyone would take her seriously, then she certainly is certifiable.

However, a back-up plan was not only vital for job security; it was prudent for financial gain as well. A girls gotta eat.

Thank goodness she was not only intelligent, but also a far better detective than the amateurs she was forced to work with every day or she never would have put it all together.

Of course, she did have some good old fashion luck thrown her way. She had found him totally by accident. She had pulled up to the 7 Eleven to grab some donuts for her bi-weekly visit with her sister Ellie and there he was, walking to his fancy sports car carrying a newspaper and a bottle of something in a brown paper bag. She recognized him from his photo on file at the DMV. Again a credit to her superior detective work.

Imagine that, he had been living one town over all this time, right under their noses, and no one until now had been the wiser.

Not only did she know where he was living, but with whom because she forgot all about Ellie's stupid donuts that she hardly needed and followed him to his spectacular condo in a ritzy community by the water.

She had been back to the condo to spy four times now, taking notes and snapping several pictures of him and the little blonde bimbo that was always by his side and whom she immediately named Fifi.

Fifi was like the human version of a French poodle with her fuzzy blonde hair and the clickity click of her pointy shoes that sounded like doggie toenails scurrying across ceramic tile. Everywhere that the master went, Fifi was sure to follow.

From the numerous detective shows she watched, she knew she needed to establish a pattern of when he came and went and how long he was gone before she made her move to take a look-see inside.

So far, it appeared that he would stay for a couple days and then leave with a small black duffle bag again for about a week, sometimes longer. He left Fifi behind and Betty wondered what poodle lady did all day without her master.

Tonight, Betty promised herself as she entered her empty little bungalow she would not whittle away the evening hours playing Candy Crush on Facebook. Her time would be spent putting together a well thought out plan to get in and out of that condo without getting caught.

Wanda had been more of a mentor than a good friend she thought as she walked over to her kitchen junk drawer to search for a pad of paper and a pen. She dug her way through a stash of matches, over-due bills, chip clips, and dozens of salt and sugar packs and found what she needed plus three sugar packs. She was sure to scoop everything back off the counter and into the drawer in an effort to keep her house tidy.

She was not much of a house keeper. After all that cleaning she was forced to do at the office, how could she seriously have the energy to come home and clean?

She counted her lucky stars that Wanda had taught her all the tricks of the trade before she was killed. She successfully mastered lock picking, eaves dropping, and lip reading and after this mission was completed, she would advance herself to the more sophisticated tools now available that she had found online.

Grabbing a can of Mountain Dew from the fridge, two straws and her writing supplies, she set up shop on her mother's old Formica table and got down to work.

First she cracked open the Mountain Dew, dumped in the sugar packs, added two straws, and then paused to appreciate the fizzing and hissing. Better than a bottle of fine wine.

This was going to be planned out carefully because one thing for sure, she was not going to end up dead.

⅄

Back at the station, Stan sat back in his chair with his legs up on his desk, staring out the window that offered a perfect view of Main Street. A red Porsche zipped down the street looking extremely out of place even for tourist season. Who knows, maybe the town was starting to attract a different type of visitor these days.

Chester did look good. All the shops had recently been painted or spruced up in some way so that now it was a quaint little village instead of the tired old town he grew up in.

Moving back home was to be like a working retirement. He had witnessed man at their worse behavior working in the city and had seen it all. He met every low life there was on the streets and unfortunately a couple in his department.

When the City Council called him about the job opening, it seemed like the answer. Things were always peaceful and so quiet in Chester; it was like a more modern day Andy Griffith show.

But there was nothing serene about his hometown now and his mind naturally took a turn in the direction of Bretta.

Someone out there did not like her and this bothered him on a deeper level than it should have. Shoving his personal feelings aside, whatever they were, he needed to make some sense out of all this.

The most likely candidate behind all this would be John Berryman, since he apparently had done something like this before. But would he really be so stupid to try it again here? Unless he was under the impression that we would never find out his past.

And where in the hell is that bastard? He threw the pencil he was twirling across his desk when he thought about that day in the kitchen.

He gazed back out his window again and noticed for the first time that day that the sky was a spectacular clear blue and figured it was as good a day as any to take a walk.

"Hey Betty, I'm going out for a walk. Reach me on my cell if you need me." He called back, not bothering to slow down.

"A walk?" he could hear her shriek after him like he had announced he was going to trot naked down Main.

What's the point of living in a small town if you drive everywhere? It was one of those things he missed while he was away. He took a few steps out the door and it didn't take long to notice something felt odd.

Marv over at the corner store stopped sweeping, put his broom down, and kept his eyes firmly fixed on him. A young mother dragging her screaming kids into the barber quickly froze and stopped to stare. Even the old ladies in the hair salon had their faces plastered against the glass.

For Christ's sake, he was only taking a walk down Main Street. Kuster has tea and crumpets with a bunch of old bats and no one gives a hoot. Guess he had better venture out of the office on a regular basis and become a little more visible in Mayberry.

He gave a shout over to Marvin who enthusiastically waved back and appeared pleased to have been acknowledged by the new sheriff.

He happened to know that Athena would be working at the library today and thought it would be a good idea to find out what was so special about Huddelstone. He found her waiting for him at the top of the stairs as soon as he opened the library door.

"Heard you were out taking a walk today, Sheriff Meyers. Can I help you find something?' Athena offered.

Small towns. He had almost forgotten how fast they worked.

She was dressed in her librarian attire today which pretty much looked like how she dressed every day, only a bit more formal. Her shirt was white, button down, and starched so crisp, Stan thought it might slice her chin. Her pleated trousers were pressed and came with suspenders and black shiny penny loafers.

"Good afternoon, Athena. Actually, I stopped in to chat with you. You gotta minute?"

"Follow me." With a sharp nod to her head she marched down the hallway, past the young blonde librarian who whipped out a compact, lipstick, and brush faster than any outlaw in the Wild West when she saw Stan headed her way.

He was ushered into a small conference room and Athena closed the door behind her, pulled out a chair for Stan, then took one for herself.

"Athena, I am told that you are the authority on Huddelstone and I need to know, what's the deal with that house?" He caught a whiff of Old Spice and recalled his mother saying how she favored men's cologne.

Athena sat with her spine arched straight and her hands folded on the table in front of her, clear sign she was ready to get down to business. He always appreciated the fact that she never found it necessary to provide a lot of drama.

"I don't believe in venting one's spleen, Sheriff; we both know it serves no good to keep a story like this circulating. However, history sometimes has a way of making a nuisance out of itself. The legend has it that Mary-Louise Huddelstone held the first wake in that house for her husband five years after he built it for her. Held it right there in the front parlor."

The fine hairs on the back of Stan's head prickled sharply against his neck. "She held the wake in the parlor?" he said more to himself as he thought of the mini version of the parlor he saw earlier that day.

"She sure did! Made it big and grand, just like she did everything in life." Athena clucked her tongue and carried on as if she and Mary-Louise were once the best of friends. "She had to have the largest house, nicest clothes, most servants, and the very best of everything. Her hobby was filling the house with fine art, collectables, and beautiful furniture. She traveled to Europe several times and shipped back all kinds of treasures for her new mansion. Her husband was a hardworking farmer. Made a big success out of the specialty of raising onions and the project was quite a financial accomplishment so she had some change to play around with."

"People came from three towns over to pay their respects to the widow when he passed. Women sent food; neighbors took care of her children while she sat in mourning dressed in head to toe fashionable black. There was a new lawyer that moved to town a few months prior and had stopped in to pay his respects several times. It wasn't long before people started talking." She shook her head in disproval.

"On the second night of the wake, after all the visitors had gone home and she was alone with her husband, rumor has it that he woke up."

"Woke up?" He wasn't quite sure if he heard her correctly.

"This was pre-embalming days, so it happened from time to time." She waved her hand like she had seen this sort of thing herself and he recalled Kuster rambling on about something similar.

"Mary-Louise had gotten use to the idea of being the merry widow pretty darn fast and took a strong liking to that wealthy lawyer, so she was not too pleased to have to tell everyone that had come bearing gifts and had helped her that her husband was really alive. Plus, it was obvious to anyone with two eyes that she was romancing that lawyer."

"Did the husband find out about the lawyer then?"

"He never had the chance. She took a pillow and snuffed the life right out of him before anyone had a chance to say boo. Six months later she was remarried to the lawyer."

"How does anyone know she suffocated him? I am assuming she did not go to jail if she got married."

"One of the servant girls saw her do it. She went to the authorities, but Mary-Louise claimed the girl had been ill and delusional for some time. She died a few short months after that."

He rubbed the afternoon growth on his chin and wished he could call it a day. He could think a hell of a lot better with a cold one in his hand and the game on in the background.

"You wouldn't happen to know that servant's girl name and where she was buried do you?" He felt almost stupid asking the question from an event that happened so long ago and most likely did not matter. Even if he had it, he wasn't sure what he would do with the information.

Athena's hand shot out like a rocket and gave him a slip of paper. "Here it is. She's buried over in the Cannon Cemetery. I drew you a map of where you will find her."

Crap, she did all but exhume the body for him. "What do you think happened to her, Athena?" He had a pretty good idea himself, but she seemed to be about one step ahead of him.

She leaned forwarded and whispered. "I think she was poisoned, it wouldn't be too hard to do back then, now would it?"

He nodded while letting the idea toss around his head a moment longer.

"How exactly did her husband die anyway? I mean, before she held the pillow over his face?"

Her eyes grew wide and she looked like she was about to stand.

"Well, I'll be. She poisoned them both!" She quickly glanced down, scanned the table for the correct document and it handed over. "Here is where you will find Mr. Edward Huddelstone."

Somehow, he didn't think that digging up these remains was going to clear up anything for him today, but it was another piece.

He scooted his chair back and stood up. "Thanks for your help, Athena, I appreciate your time. Oh, one more thing, what was the name of the lawyer she married?"

"Theodore Barrett."

"Barrett? As in Irma?" How could he have grown up in this town the size of a shoe box and seriously not know a thing about it?

"Yep, that's the one. Theodore and Mary-Louise had a son together named Henry. Henry later married and had a son." She shrugged her shoulders. "The house always stayed in the family, one of the decedents married Irma and they had Anthony whom you know."

"Until now." He thought of Bretta and her daughters living in that old house.

"That must have Mary-Louise rolling in her grave. I remember reading somewhere she always swore that only a Huddelstone or one of her descendants would live there, after all the house was built for her."

"What happened to all her art and other valuables?"

"It stayed with the house. Irma was fairly plain and didn't care much for fancy things, but she put them out on display anyway to keep the old man happy. After he passed on I am sure she did not bother doing anything with them out of sheer laziness so everything remained right there in the house until she moved to be with her son. Then one day, about a year after Irma left Huddelstone, a moving truck backed into their driveway, two big thugs jumped out and off they went with Irma's antiques. "

"So Tony left most of his mother's belongings and now we know his mother as well, behind in his childhood home but came back with a U-Haul for the antiques?" It was a statement more than a question.

"I never said it was Anthony." She sat even straighter and waited.

"Well, Tony's hired movers."

Athena pursed her lips together tightly in disapproval, leaned in towards the Sherriff and whispered. "Assuming is sloppy detective work; you're much too good for that."

She was dead right. He felt like he had just been reprimanded by his second grade teacher.

"I remember your mother use to do some cooking for Irma and Anthony." She said suddenly, as if the thought just popped into to head. "Use to drop off vegetables for her too." She shook her head and laughed. "Irma could knit up a storm, but never would try her hand at a vegetable garden."

"That's right, I do remember that." The mention of his mother brought back a tidal wave of pleasant memories and a rush of guilt. He hardly saw her since he has been home.

At least he could count on his childhood home and his parents to remain unchanged. It felt like a good time to go home.

Chapter 36

Ten minutes later Stan rolled his police cruiser up his parent's driveway to find his mother outside watering her flowers. She smiled, shut off the hose and tossed it on the grass.

A surge of shame gave him a hard kick in the gut. He has been home for almost three months now and this is only the second time he stopped by the house. They spoke on the phone often and his mom stopped in the station every week, but that was it. In his effort to clean up the damage from the former Sheriff and deal with the town's recent wave of trouble, he has pretty much forgotten about his own family.

"Flowers look nice Mom." He was pleased to see that his mom kept so busy. She looked radiant. In fact, she seemed to look better each time he saw her. She wore blue jeans with a plaid work top and green garden shoes and her hair was longer these days, almost touching her shoulders and still not gray. Guess she could be coloring it; it was funny that he never really thought about that before. No one would ever take her for being in her sixties. "You look great too." He walked further down the end of the driveway and gave her a hug.

"Well thank you. Come on back for a glass of ice tea and tell me what's on your mind." Not waiting for him to bother denying he was chewing on a problem, he followed her to the yard, and then stopped in his tracks, his eyes fluttering several times before his lower jaw dropped.

The backyard that he grew up with was replaced with rows and rows of something green, thriving and springing out of the ground. This was not the little vegetable garden she kept while he was growing up. This resembled a farm.

Walking up closer for a better view, he saw a vast assortment of thriving plants. He ate vegetables now and then so he could identify a few of them by name. There had to be seventy rows of broccoli, lettuce, and tomatoes. How could his mom do all this and why would she? There was no way her and Dad could eat all that unless they expected him to start stopping in for dinner now that he was back in town.

"So, what do you think of our new business?' his mom said from behind him.

"Business?" he stood next to his mother and gave his old yard another look, this time taking in how careful each row was planted, labeled and how mother was glowing.

"Yes. We've added on to our little organic farm. Marc built us that portable stand over there. It has wheels on the bottom so we can move it to the front of the house for a roadside stand or put it in the truck and take it to the Farmers Market." There was no mistaking the pride and enthusiasm in her voice.

He was curious as to whom she would go into business with that would want to come over and farm her backyard. "Who is helping you with this?"

She looked surprised. "Why, your father of course. You didn't think I could do all this by myself did you?" she laughed.

His father was helping her do all this? His father hasn't lifted his ass off that living room couch for the last decade and now he is out working in the fields? He tried to hide the disbelief on his face.

"I never thought of Dad as being into gardening, that's all."

Her face became serious. "Oh, this is much more than planting a simple garden, Stan. This is organic gardening. It's near impossible to find good organic produce out here and this way we can eat everything we grow and sell the rest. Several of our neighbors help out here and it has been a wonderful experience. I wanted something for us to do together so we wouldn't sit like two old farts watching TV all day. I got the idea from an article in Readers Digest." She let out a long sigh. "I'll admit though, it took a bit to convince your father to give me a hand, but he is wonderful at it!"

"Really?" he was finding it difficult to wrap his brain around this one.

"Oh, yes! And now we eat so healthy, we both feel great and we are already making money. We spent a lot of time researching how to do this before we started, made a bunch of mistakes along the way, but that is how you learn you know."

Just then a man stepped out of the shed on the far end of the yard with a shovel in this hand. He was tall, lean and looked strong. It took a couple of long seconds for Stan to realize that was his own father. How could he have missed a change this big the last time he saw him? With long strides across the yard, he reached Stan in no time.

"Hi, son. Good to see you." He reached over and patted his son on the back and greeted him with a warm smile.

"You too, Dad." And he meant it. Not only was it good to see his Dad outside helping his Mom and looking so happy, but he looked younger too. The only one tired and worn out around here was himself.

"You know Mom, I'll take a cold beer if you have one instead of that ice tea." Something stronger might have been in order, but he still needed to go to Bretta's tonight and he didn't trust himself around her with whiskey in his veins.

She smiled in delight. "Can you stay for supper? I had a chicken and some veggies in the Crockpot, it's finished now."

It was the best offer he had all day.

"Yeah, thanks mom. That would be great."

His mom ran back out with two beers in brown glass bottles that she said were organic and ice cold. He took a long swallow and found it surprisingly good. While his Dad searched the radio stations for the baseball game, he glanced down at the beer label to be sure they hadn't started brewing their own beer.

He sunk back in the chair and enjoyed another long, slow sip of beer while both men stared out at the crop that somehow managed to grow despite the gardener's inexperience and remembered that this was one of the reasons he moved back to Chester. For these quiet, deathly silent moments he never thought he would miss when he fled for the big city as a young man and for the first time in a long time, he gave himself permission to relax.

His mom came back out and set a steaming plate of chicken smothered in a bunch of vegetables he did not recognize in front of him and a memory suddenly came to him of her cooking and packing up food.

"Mom, you use to cook for Irma Barrett sometimes?"

"Yes, I did." She sounded pleased that he would remember. "It was a little side job while you kids were little."

"You gave her vegetables from your garden too?"

She paused as she was setting the plate down in front of her husband while she thought. "Yes, I did. I would take her a few things. Many of us had little gardens back then, before stores carried a good selection of produce. Then folks stopped planting and went to the stores for all their shopping. It's funny, now gardening is popular again. Everything old is new again." She said with a smile.

"Irma didn't have a green thumb?" Stan repeated what he already heard.

His mother sat now with her plate. "No, that wasn't it. She planted all kinds of beautiful flowers, just nothing you would eat. Eventually she stopped that too. She was convinced the soil around her house was saturated with poison."

⅄

Rose Delaney decided she had seen enough excitement for one day. With flair she spun the sign in the front window from open to closed, locked up, and made her way to the back of the store.

She wanted to begin searching for that dollhouse receipt Sheriff Meyers needed anyway and she certainly did not want to be disturbed while doing it. Plus she loved to be alone with all her treasures. Each piece came with a story and every item held a memory.

Before she began the task of rummaging through receipts, there was something much more thrilling that she had been dying to get to.

Making her way to the windows, she pulled down the shades to ensure complete privacy and opened the door to the broom closet the Nelson brothers had been hiding in earlier.

She thought she might faint herself when they had dodged inside, but then she relaxed. Both boys were as dumb as they were unattractive, bless their hearts, and they wouldn't know what they were looking at if it bit them in those dreadful jeans they wore hanging off their boney butts.

But there it was, still covered up and tucked away in the dark corner where no one was the wiser. She brought the fur coat out into the light and placed it gently on the table so she could take her time examining it, appreciating the fine detail and workmanship.

She could never sell this one. Rose tilted her head to the side, her hands stroking the fur sleeves. She was going to have a hard time cutting this one up but she knew she eventually would. She didn't go through all that trouble of breaking in to steal it just to leave it in her closet, plus, she detested crowded closets. And it wasn't like she could wear the thing anywhere. Someone was bound to recognize she had on Irma's fur and then she would have to tell a lie.

No, she would stick to her original plan and make a couple of memory bears out of the coat. Maybe she would start on them tonight, after she located that receipt for the sheriff.

But before she cut up this beauty, she simply had to feel it on her body one last time. Quickly she exited out of her blouse so she could experience the silky, cool lining against her bare skin. The anticipation sent an icy, delightful prickle down her spine.

She took her time removing Irma Barrett's mink off the padded hanger and then wrapped herself up like a giant present.

She looked beautiful in fur. She always did.

Her late husband, Phil, had slaved away to buy her one of her own, but there never seemed to be enough money. She would always wave it off, pretending that it did not matter, that she did not care, when in fact she wanted to scratch the eyes out of every bitch at church that came to worship on Sunday draped in fur.

Heavily she sighed. Play time was over and she knew she needed to get back to work. She allowed the coat to slither off her arms all the while still studying her reflection in the full length mirror when a little detail in the inside lining caught her eye.

She knew of course that the older coats have splendid secret pockets built into the lining. However, in the excitement of stealing the coat and all that Huddelstone business, she simply forgot to check Irma's.

Now her hands raced to get at that pocket, shaking slightly in expectation. She knew it might be empty, but then it could have something for her. Some small trinket for her to hold on to.

This particular pocket had a snap sewn on the inside and she used prudence not to tear the fragile fabric as she opened it.

She was not disappointed. Rose's hand carefully and slowly removed a silver pill box, an aged business card from a Private Detective in Detroit, and some type of receipt. The small box was tarnished, but she could still make out the initials MM on the lid. The inside contained a powdery mess and a funky smell that made her nose wrinkle.

MM? Who in the world was MM? Maybe Irma found the case when she was out flaunting her coat at bingo and stuck in her pocket, but as soon as that idea popped in her head, she yanked the coat off completely and laid it out flat on the table.

Well, well, well! Someone didn't have their own mink coat after all. That hoodlum of a son of hers must of stole it or bought it used. Probably from a pawn shop or a second hand store she thought with disgust and shuddered.

When she takes a coat that is left behind and forgotten about by the family, she is holding on to a memory and keeping it alive by making beautiful bears out it. It is so upsetting when a family moves Grandma out and leaves her mink stole up in the attic for the moths to munch on.

Clearly Irma Barrett was not the original proud owner of this mink because the initials so elegantly embroidered on the lining read MM as well. How she missed seeing that before she did not know. She remembered when Irma first showed up wearing the fur, claiming it was a gift from her son Anthony, but how many years ago that was Rose could not recall. Her darling son either stole it or got it at a pawn shop.

She would need to wear this one more time before cutting it up, perhaps out to dinner in a nearby town. Oh, that would be fun. She could bring the pill box too.

Swiftly, she placed the coat back on the hanger and glided its handmade, black garment bag over the mink, tucking it away for the night.

The pill box and business card would be added to her special collections box that she kept locked up in her bedroom, which was conveniently located directly above the store. Her apartment suited her needs just fine even though she did secretly long for a little house with a yard and much more privacy than living in town can offer one.

A sharp wave of melancholy drifted through her soul and she made the choice not to spend the evening sad. Upstairs, safe in her room with her own cherished belongings she lit a few candles, put on some old, sultry jazz, and had a glass of sherry.

As she went to put the collections away, refusing to experience guilt, she took a look at the receipt from the coat pocket.

The sales receipt was from a motel at the edge of town, dated over twenty years ago.

"Irma, Irma." Her short bob swayed from side to side. "I knew that loser son of yours couldn't afford to buy you a fur, I only pray he didn't kill for it."

Sheriff Meyers should take a look at the receipt, but then that would mean she would have to offer an explanation as to how it came to be in her possession.

That was something she simply was not willing to do. All those years of pain and heartache were behind her. Her husband had a tender side, he was still a drunken cheat that made her life miserable, leaving her to scurry behind the scenes, trying to cover for him.

She promised herself the very second that bastard finally died that she would be good to herself, no matter what the cost.

Her only regret was waiting so long. If she would have had any idea of how easy of a job that turned out to be, she would have killed him years ago.

Chapter 37

Bretta found the art of list writing almost therapeutic, something she learned from her mother no doubt. She could purge everything that was clogging up her mind on one simple sheet of paper and not have to worry about forgetting something or sounding crazy.

Number one on the list for the following day was to call John and tell him it was time to talk. Second, plant a garden. She was just about to jot down a notation to call her mother and arrange for her to visit when she picked up the phone instead. This was something she could take care of right now. The house was ready enough and so was she.

Amazingly, Luisa Gerhard answered her personal line on the first ring.

"Hello darling, I was just thinking about you. Please say that your calling to inform me you are moving back home." Luisa Gerhard spoke quickly before her daughter had a chance to get a word in. It was no secret that her mother had not approved of her move.

Bretta smiled into the phone. "I *am* home mother and we would love for you to come and visit. We all miss you." It felt like forever since she had seen her mother and their separation was especially difficult since they used to work together and see each other every day.

"Ok then, I will arrive on Tuesday of next week; Darla will map out directions for me."

"Are you bringing Darla with you?"

"Heavens no! Someone has to stay behind and work. Plus, I want you all to myself. Is your husband there yet?"

Bretta paused for a second before replying. It was not like she could lie; her mother was bound to find out sooner or later.

"No, he's not here right now." She chose her words carefully.

"We can discuss that when I get there. Take care of yourself and I will see you next week."

With that being settled, she went to the fridge and pulled out the fixings to assemble her favorite; grilled chicken with a Spinach, Basil, and Pine Nut Pesto, an assortment of fresh vegetables and an exceptional bottle of Chardonnay she had been saving. Her experienced hands quickly whipped up the pesto as the kitchen filled with the deep aroma of fresh basil. She poured a nice big glass of wine in honor of her new list and went out to light the grill.

Wineglass in hand, she strolled around the backyard, mentally mapping out the perfect spot for her new plantings and for that pool. It was a lovely yard, full of old trees, lush plants, and rich history. Much of it had gone wild and suffered from neglect like the house, but in time she knew it would all be restored to its original grander or perhaps even better.

Call lawyer to inquire about divorce proceedings and stay away from Sheriff Meyers popped into her head. She should have brought along her list. Really what she needed was one of those mini tape recorders that she could carry everywhere with her, then she could even add to her list as she drove. She made a mental note to check that out later.

Scenes from earlier in the day attempted to play into her head but she firmly pushed them away. No sense thinking about any of that now, she was better off sticking with the present. Further back in the yard, past the sturdy old shed she hadn't yet bothered to do anything with other than use as a dumping post for interesting items she stumbled upon, grew a charming patch of wild flowers. Thinking they would dress up the picnic table she made her way through tall grass and longer weeds.

She was so far back in the yard that it occurred to her she might not be on her own property but since there was no one around to object it really didn't matter.

The flowers were truly breathtaking and as she bent over to begin picking, her eye caught a patch of dark gray cement peeking out from between the stems and weeds.

Kneeling down and with her free hand, she cleared away much of the overgrown grass and weeds to expose a long forgotten headstone of one of the Huddelstone family members, Mary Louise Huddelstone. A family burial plot was not mentioned in any of the research she had come across thus far and she wondered if Mary Louise was out here all by herself or if there were any other family members in her yard. Moving the grass around with her foot she uncovered another weathered grave marker, this one for Edward Huddelstone. For some reason, she found that the discovery of the original owners buried in her yard exciting, like a great find, yet at the same time chilling.

She gazed back at her new home as her body offered a harsh tremor. Death suddenly felt all around her. The realization that these bodies were most likely embalmed up in the house, mourned in her front parlor and then brought out to be buried in the back yard seemed cold and unpleasant, but she supposed it was quite natural at that time in history.

She was about to return to her barbequing when it came to her that something about the wild flowers was bothering her. Her head tilted to the side as she studied the flowers then moved in to get a closer view.

The fields did not grow randomly throughout her yard; their brilliance was concentrated in the area surrounding the graves. The planting was intentional and deliberate.

Almost lost amongst the array of wild flowers grew a patch of brightly colored tulips which was most peculiar. She was no expert on flowers, but she was sure that tulips bloom in the spring, not late summer, and these appeared so fresh and flawless.

When she came upon the tulips, she could see why. They were not planted in the ground, but bound together in a large, artful bouquet and stuck in the ground in one of those plastic cemetery vases. Who in the world would be mourning the Huddelstone family with fresh flowers? They weren't even placed near the headstones unless there was another grave way back here by itself. She squatted down in front of the flowers and pulled at the greenery rewarded with another marker.

Sleeping with the Angels was etched deeply in the smooth stone. No name or date. It appeared to have been in the ground a while, but nowhere near as long as the family markers.

She set her wineglass on the marker to free her hands and on instinct, began separating the weeds and grass again until she found another marker, this one read: *Forever in our Hearts.* Again, no name or date. Curious, she surveyed the earth under her brand new white Keds and began to shift the foliage to unveil two more nameless markers of the same type. Were they planning ahead or was there actually graves here?

Who would put nameless grave markers on private property? They didn't appear to be as old as the Huddelstone markers but did not seem like something the Barrett's would do either. She would have to ask the Muncy's about it next time she saw them.

It did not feel right to take flowers meant for someone else so she let them be and instead, took a moment to appreciate Huddelstone and her yard from a distance. The house and the grounds were coming along strikingly and she felt a jolt of excitement as she glanced over at each bedroom window and reflected on its transformation.

Suddenly, it occurred to her that there was one more window than there ought to be. She recounted out loud. Without doubt there was an extra window, one without a curtain or shade and for the life of her, she couldn't match the room to the window.

With her hands on her hips, she stood and faced the back of her new home and did a mental walk through, room by room.

The house has many rooms and little closets, she must have missed one. From the outside, she guessed the room should be right next to her bathroom. She tried to picture the hallway upstairs and could not recall seeing any other rooms other than hers and her daughters. Perhaps the handle came off the door and the wood blended right in to the wall; she probably walked by it every day. It would be something fun to check out on the way up to the attic after dinner.

"Hi Mom, what were you doing back there?" Ivy stood waiting by the barbeque.

"Just strolling around the property, waiting for the grill to get hot." Wisely leaving the cemetery find out of the conversation for another day.

Ivy arched her eyebrow to a sharp point, a trick she must have learned from Wanda Bee. "So you didn't see that cemetery back there by the wild flowers?"

For the first time that day, Bretta laughed and walked over to Ivy. "Yes, actually I did. I just didn't know if I should bring that up, given the day we have had."

"Iris and I am fine mother. In fact, we are all just *fine*." She gave her mother a hug.

There were so many things to love about summertime, but the extended hours of sunlight happened to be a real bonus for her lately. Since dinnertime in the Berryman household only lasted fifteen minutes on an average anyway, that gave her a couple of hours of daylight to appease her curiosity.

The second the dinner mess was cleared, she fled to the attic in search a couple of items she had recalled seeing in that dollhouse that looked strangely familiar.

She had forgotten that she was going to check out the mystery room on her way up to the attic. There could be treasures stored in there as well. Oh well. As soon as she finished up here, she would go and search for the door. She knew her girls would find that fun as well.

She had been right; the green Tiffany lamp did have an uncanny resemblance to the lamp in the dollhouse. It was in need of a dusting and polishing, but other than that would look smart in the parlor. She would take that downstairs with her for sure.

The peak of the attic was the perfect spot for her to set up her office space. It was small and cozy with three windows that would allow the southern sun to shine in. She dragged what might have been Irma Barrett's old dining room table over and climbed on top to get a better look at the lower ceiling beams, planning out shelf space.

As she was about to jump off, something on one of the beams caught her eye. She jumped down, dragged the table closer and reached on her tippy toes.

Someone had left behind a small box on one of the beams. Curious, she extended her right arm out as far as possible only to have her finger tips lightly graze the dusty box and launch it further out of reach. Mumbling a curse, she jumped off and grabbed the broom she had been cleaning with the other day and gave it another try, pushing it carefully closer so it would not crash to the floor. Who knows what was hidden away? Maybe money or valuables or perhaps just a few memories stashed away and forgotten.

One more tiny tap with the broom and she was rewarded with a dirty old shoe box with a tattered lid. She tried to guess its contents one more time by giving the box a slight shake, and then hearing what sounded like paper moving back and forth, lifted the lid.

Dozens of young, beautiful girls stared back at her as if they were waiting to be discovered.

Photograph after photograph of unsmiling teenagers dressed in seventies garb. Irma's son apparently liked the girls. She thought of the photo Marc found of her husband and dug through faster, hoping to find another glimpse into to her husband's secret past.

She could not help but to wonder what the story was behind each face and where they were now when abruptly the pictures began to look a little odd.

The lovely girls looked propped and unnatural.

Bretta stretched out her arm to see the photo from afar and then drew her arm in close, trying to figure out what was so peculiar about the picture. Two were lying down side by side on a bed, as if sleeping, each holding a long stem white Lily. Another was sitting in a chair, unsmiling with her eyes open but unfocused.

Maybe they were drugged and passed out but it was strange they all had their eyes open. The sun was setting; changing the attics already dim light and straining her eyes to see the image details. She was just getting ready to bring the box down to the kitchen when suddenly a gasp rushed out of her mouth in horror and her free hand retrieved the photo.

The photographs began to tremor in her hands as she stared at the same girls now stripped of their clothes and their dignity, lying in revealing poses. She thought of her own lovely daughters downstairs and shuttered.

Her first instinct was to burn them, to protect these poor girls, someone's daughters. But she knew she had to show the Sheriff.

She sensed someone behind her two seconds before she heard them. That prickly, uneasy sensation that tries to warn you, but unfortunately she did not acknowledge it until it was too late.

Her head snapped around as she quickly attempted to jump off the table, but before she could make contact with the ground, a figure sprung out of the shadows, lunging at her with full force.

Her attacker's hands put her airborne at a dangerous speed. The heavy oak table went with her, crashing down on her shin with a sick, disturbing sound.

As he stood over her motionless body, he shook his head and made that little tsk-tsk sound his mother always made when he was bad.

Well what did she expect? That he would stay silent forever while she destroyed his house and all his dreams?

Was it his fault that she could not take a fucking hint?

She did look lovely lying there though, unconscious and with blood on her forehead. If only he would have thought to bring his camera.

Time to wake sleeping beauty. He bent down and squeezed the flesh on her cheek tightly before giving it a sharp twist. He wanted to be sure she got a good look at him.

It was not fair to end someone's life if they didn't know who did it.

And unlike this little bitch, he did play by the rules.

Chapter 38

Betty Grimes checked her hair in the rearview mirror and then artfully applied a fresh coat of Drop Dead, high gloss red lipstick, snickering at the name.

He would drop dead all right if he did not live up to his end of the deal. No one would consider for a moment that she would be capable of killing but they would be wrong.

Dead wrong.

Earlier that same week, she slid a flat brown envelope under his front door and then ducked behind a row of hearty spruces to witness its retrieval.

It was comical, just like in the movies. He yanked the door open, whipping his important head back and forth like whomever delivered his little present was going to stand there in the rain like a fool and wait to be spotted.

Her note promised she would be back precisely at eight o'clock pm, Thursday August 15th and it clearly outlined what was expected of him.

Although she was not here to seduce him, it never hurt to look your best. She added a touch of a shimmery lip gloss to her bottom lip to give her that sexy, pouty look that all the models have. She read that tip in Glamour magazine.

Glancing at the car clock, she decided she would give it another three minutes before going up to the door. After all, she did not want to appear too eager.

Betty picked up her hefty, overstuffed briefcase and made her way to the front door. She had covered all her bases before this important date, gathered all her facts and it was doubtful even Wanda herself could have done a better job with the prep work.

Tonight she was loaded with dates, times, more photos than People Magazine and as a bonus, packed a .22 Semi-Automatic. The briefcase was a bitch to carry around, especially in these three and a half inch heels, but she felt confident she could pull it off.

All the extra attention to her appearance would be a serious distraction and guaranteed to throw the poor bastard off guard. She had spent hours preening for this evening from flossing and polishing to the careful wardrobe selection and she was rather delighted with the results. She walked with purpose and followed the path around back to his condo entrance, her heels tapping away noisily on the pavement as she realized she now sounded exactly like Fifi.

She could see why he chose this place; it offered exceptional privacy with its dense trees and shrubs and the resident's entrance tucked away in the back. No one would ever notice him coming or going unless of course they were set out to spy on him.

Directly in front of the entrance and down a slight hill was a good size lake with tall Weeping Willows outlining its shores, their long graceful branches dipping deep into the black water below.

Yes, she was very glad she made it part of their arrangement that she get to keep the condo. She was going to love living here.

She had worded her letter carefully to sound masculine so that he would be anticipating a male figure this evening, not a brunette bombshell to stroll up to the front door.

With her exposed cleavage, her short skirt hiked high, and a heavy blast of Elizabeth Taylor's Diamonds & Emeralds floating in the air, she knew she would have the upper hand.

That and of course she had the advantage of knowing every dirty detail about him.

Wanda would be so flipping proud.

She rang the doorbell and braced herself for the look on his face. Then, she waited. After a few long seconds crawled by, she pressed the doorbell again and did a quick glance at her watch.

What kind of idiot keeps someone waiting when they are being blackmailed? She double checked the address even though she knew she had the correct location, she had been here enough times before. Her feet did a slight dance as they began to throb and swell in protest to being stuffed in something so constricting and she briefly considered slipping off her shoes when she noticed she was standing on a large fancy area rug, like the kind you would find in a living room. Probably Fifi's brilliant idea of decorating.

She outstretched her hand and rapped on the door loud enough to raise the dead. If this didn't work she was seriously thinking of shooting it down. She didn't get all dressed up for nothing. Crap, she even shaved her legs.

"Good evening, Betty." A deep, male voice resonated from directly behind her.

In one fluid motion she spun around while simultaneously removing the gun from her case, aiming it directly at her callers head.

But sadly, given her marvelous performance, she was about two seconds too slow.

His shot rang out first, hushed by the silencer he thoughtfully attached ahead of time out of consideration for his new neighbors.

Wasting no time, he rolled her up tight in the antique Persian rug that he truly hated to part with, secured both ends tightly with rope and more around the middle for good measure and stuffed her through the front door that his girlfriend held open for him.

In the early hours of the morning, long before his neighbors even thought about rising to head off to work, he would bring her outside and send her and her briefcase to the bottom of the lake.

He gave the rug a little kick and smiled, knowing he just did the world one hell of a favor.

Casually he put his arm around his female accomplice as they both stared down at the floor.

"Look honey, it's a pig in a blanket!" He announced, laughing at his own joke.

"Calm down and only one of you talks at a time." Stan ordered through the phone. "Iris…tell me what happened." He was already in motion with lights and siren as he tried to figure out what in the hell Bretta's daughters were trying to tell him.

Iris's voice came out in broken hysterical sobs. "It's mom, up in the attic! Hurry, he's hurting her!"

"Who's hurting her?" He remained calm while his cruiser picked up speed.

"Some man! We just heard here fall and cry out. Ivy went to go get a knife and then we are going up there."

"No, get out of the house now! Do you hear me? Get outside and run to the Muncy's house. I am on my way now. I am going to hang up with you now and call for back up."

He disconnected the call and got Kuster on the phone. "We have a situation at the Berryman's. Get there right away and call in for back up."

He reached the house faster than he thought possible, sincerely regretting that the siren would alert the intruder, but understanding the necessity. He wanted to be the one to surprise the visitor so he could so he could skillfully and silently break his neck.

However every second that ticked by might mean her life. He would have to honor that need latter.

Bretta was alone in the attic when he arrived, the window was open and Stan knew the intruder was long gone. He radioed in a request for an ambulance while taking giant strides to get to her. Kneeling next to her, he searched for a pulse and slowly let out the breath he didn't know he was holding as Kuster bolted up the stairs, gun drawn.

"I got this." He barked and Kuster's eyes opened even wider. "He must have left down that window and is most likely on foot. Get some cars out here now to search the area and go then check on her daughters, I sent them to the Muncys."

Kuster immediately turned to head back down to clear the stairs for Dave the paramedic and his partner who were racing to get to their patient. As Stan moved aside to give them working room, he noticed a photograph sticking out from under Bretta's back. Using a tissue, he picked the photo up by the edges to get a better look. A young woman glared back at him, smiling and unfamiliar.

Dave gave him a questioning look when he recognized Bretta from the day's earlier run.

"I gotta take her in this time, Sheriff. They'll probably want a CT." He quickly accessed a vein in her arm for an IV and adjusted the drip, his partner checking all her vitals while trying to wake her.

Stan nodded. "I'll be by the hospital in a bit to talk to her. I need to finish up here."

"I have her info from earlier; do you want the hospital to call the spouse?"

Stan spoke without looking up from the picture he grasped in his hands. "No, I'll handle the husband."

Chapter 39

He sat quietly in the chair next to her bed and watched an ugly, purple bruise darken on her cheek while Bretta recalled the horror of waking to sharp pain everywhere and a man standing over her.

"Did you see all those pictures? Those poor girls. What do you think happened to them?"

It took Stan a second to make the connection. Retrieving the baggie from his shirt pocket he handed it over to her. "You mean this picture?"

Tentatively, she reached for the baggie, not quite sure she wanted to see them again. "Well, this looks like one of them, yes. Where's the others?"

"This was the only photograph at the scene. Do you know her?"

She shook her head, upset and attempted to sit up. "No, I don't know her. Where are all the other photos? They were in a shoebox. I dropped them when I fell."

"Easy there, lie back down. We didn't find any other photos or a shoebox. I'll have Kuster run back over and double check." He automatically rearranged the plain white hospital blanket around her without thinking. "Tell me about the photos."

"There was an old shoe box full of old snapshots of beautiful, young girls. They looked to have been taken in the 70's I remember thinking at the time. They were just odd at first, but then they turned alarming." She gave her head a shake to clear the fog that was engulfing her brain. The combination of exhaustion and pain medication made it difficult to match her words to the pictures in her head.

"Describe the ones you saw first."

"First the girls were posing for the camera, smiling and happy. Then they looked out of it…I remember thinking it looked like they had been drugged. They looked unnatural, in awkward positions." She hesitated before continuing. "Some looked like they were dead. Their eyes were open, but I remember thinking they looked dead."

"And how did the pictures change from there?"

When she did not respond, he tried again.

"Bretta, what made them alarming?"

"They were naked." She whispered and Stan leaned in closer. "And they were posing for the camera, it was disgusting, but they looked dead."

Sometime between jotting down his own notes and watching her sleep, he ended up dozing off in the chair alongside her bed. He had taken down all the pertinent information from her like he was supposed to when they slid into an easy conversation, talking until she eventually drifted off to sleep.

He had given John Berryman a courtesy call and found that he was not all that shook up to learn that his wife was in the hospital, but he did promise he would be around to check on her in a few days. What a thoughtful guy.

Then he sunk back in the chair next to her bed with the intent to leave after a few minutes and somehow managed to fall asleep right along with her until he felt his phone vibrate on his belt. Quietly he slipped out into the hall as a young orderly with a straggly goatee passed by him pushing an overly medicated man in a wheelchair. His patient's mouth hung open causing a stream of drool to travel down his face and neck.

"Hey, Kuster." Stan stood in the hospital corridor, rubbed his eyes and tried to work the kinks out of his neck and back. He was getting too old to sleep in a chair like that.

"How is she?"

Surprised, Stan quickly looked left to right, expecting to find Kuster walking down the hall.

"How did you know where I was?"

"Susan the Charge Nurse called me to say you stayed there all night."

Maybe Kuster should be the Sheriff. Everyone in Chester and in a ten mile surrounding radius seems to report to his deputy.

"She's all right. She has a concussion and a broken ankle."

"Did you find out what spooked her?"

Stan needed caffeine to shake the blanket of fuzz that was still wrapped tightly around his brain and peeked down the hospital hall to find it empty and silent. A good indicator it still must be early. There had to be a coffee machine around here somewhere. Hospitals and police stations always have coffee. He ducked his head into a room the size of a broom closet and found a mini kitchenette with an ice machine, small fridge and an empty coffee pot.

"You mean other than the man trying to kill her?"

Kuster hesitated briefly. "Sir…there was no ladder under that window. No footprints, and frankly, no way to get down from a window that high up unless the guy jumped. If he did jump, he would most likely have two busted ankles and not have gotten too far."

Stan's hand paused on the stack of coffee filters. "What the hell are you trying to say then Kuster? That she did this to herself? Christ, even the girls heard him!"

"What exactly did they hear?" He tested.

"They heard their mom screaming and a man yelling. I didn't have a chance to interview them yet, I thought I would do that today. But they heard their mother being attacked Kuster." He finished assembling the coffee and crossed his arms in front of his chest.

"I had a chance to speak with the girls when I went to check on them." He dragged out his pause before continuing. "They heard their mother screaming and thought their mother made reference to a man being up there with her, but they never actually heard him."

Stan felt his temper flair. "Well I don't give a shit if the girls heard him or not. He pushed her off the chair, tried to kill her and left with a shoebox full of pictures."

He could sense Kuster was treading carefully which pissed him off even further. "Pictures? What kind of pictures?"

"Shots of young, pretty women." He didn't feel like elaborating on the photos right now, he was too angry.

"So, this intruder beats up Bretta, snatches a box of pictures and then jumps out a three story window before we can get there?" Kuster was silent now, letting his question hang in the air.

The coffee finished brewing with a loud beep and Stan quickly poured a cup. "I would have to say it went exactly like that Kuster. How else would you explain it? Why in the hell would she make that up?"

"I don't know why, but I do know she's done something like this before. I spoke with her husband last night too…she called in a report very similar to this not quite two years ago. He let me speak to her doctor as well and he confirmed the story. That's why he sent her out here to live, for a rest. He thought she would be safer in the country."

"I don't believe she made this up."

"Sir, I am sure she doesn't even know she did." Kuster spoke carefully.

"That's a bunch of bullshit. This isn't my first time at the rodeo Kuster… "Stan stopped abruptly and observed a nurse entering a patient's room with a key card.

A sick sensation filled his gut as he slowly turned his head and scanned the long hall until he found the signs he was looking for but had failed to notice before.

The drugged out patient. The locked rooms.

"You put her in the fucking Psyche ward?" Stan yelled into the phone. Even though he was dead tired last night and severely preoccupied he wondered how in the hell he could have missed it.

The lifeless, desolate halls of the Psychiatric ward. Maybe it wasn't all that early. It was simply depressing as hell.

"It wasn't my call."

"Then whose call was it?" He lowered his voice and gave a friendly wave to the startled nurse that stuck her head out of a door to check on him.

"Her husband arranged it with her doctor. I heard about it from Susan, but I swear I had nothing to do with that."

He knew he needed to read those reports himself and find out what happened. In his years in law enforcement, he has met every kind of nut, liar, thief, and con artist that existed and Bretta simply did not fit in with them.

Perhaps he let his judgment become clouded with her and moving back to his small town lowered his defenses.

Either way, he knew he had the unpleasant task of telling Bretta where she was. He only hoped she would not think it was his idea.

"Oh and by the way, Betty never showed up for work this morning. She's not answering her phone either. I have a car on the way over to her house to check on her."

Stan leaned against the wall and closed her eyes. Betty was more bothersome than a swarm of hungry mosquitoes, but she was always on time for work. Her impeccable record was a matter of pride. He didn't need to call upon his vast law enforcement experience to know that something bad has happened to his dispatcher.

He drank down the bitter coffee in one angry gulp and went in to face Bretta.

Chapter 40

"Sorry, no more visitors for her today!" A big, burly nurse with her hair crammed into a messy ponytail barked at him when he entered Bretta's hospital room. She had the build of a linebacker and the mug of someone who had been stuck working the graveyard shift for the last decade.

He paused briefly at the sharpness of her tone, his own temperament on edge. "Why not?"

"Orders."

"Who's?"

She fiddled with the IV bag then tugged hard on the lines before writing something on Bretta's chart, making him wait. "Her husband's."

"Her husbands?" Stan shouted back in disbelief, trying to make sense of what was going on. From over on the bed, Bretta moaned softly. "He can't order anything. Christ, he hasn't even seen his wife in over a month." He recognized how stupid that sounded the minute he said it.

"Well, he *is* a doctor." With that she forcefully stuck a loud beeping device in Bretta's ear, making Stan wince.

"He's a *dentist*."

"Whatever. Dr. Berryman spoke with the doctor on staff here and that's what was decided." She roughly yanked Bretta's arm out of from under the blanket and wrapped a blood pressure cuff around it. Her brisk and forceful movements were making him angrier by the minute.

"I am the sheriff over in Chester and I am here on official business." He stepped a foot closer to the bed and glared closely while she took Bretta's blood pressure. Under his intense scrutiny, her hands eased up a bit but her eyes did not soften. "And I'm not leaving."

He has seen prisoners booked and processed gentler and so far, Bretta had only moaned. How in the world could she sleep through all that abuse?

"We'll just see about that." She huffed and started to gather up her equipment when she bumped into Bretta's arm that was hanging off the side of the bed. Annoyed, she picked it up and threw it across on the bed.

"Easy there Nurse Ratched!" Jesus, her patient was going to leave with more bruises than she came in with.

"It's Kremer, not Ratched, and don't worry, she can't feel a thing."

Obliviously not a *One Flew over the Cookoo's Nest* fan. Surely though he can't be the first to notice the resemblance.

"Did you put something in her IV?"

"Of course there is something in her IV. I would hardly hook up an empty bag."

His anger kicked up a notch while he tried to decide if she was a wicked bitch or just an idiot.

"Did you sedate her? You have been tossing her around like a rag doll for the last fifteen minutes and she hasn't moved a muscle."

Ratched shrugged her shoulders nonchalantly. "Something was ordered to settle her down."

"Settle her down from what? When I stepped out into the hall just a bit ago, she was still sleeping for Christ's sake!"

Again, the shrug but this time she added a smirk, enjoying his anger.

"Come to think of it, she *was* still napping when I stopped in. But when I whispered in her ear that her husband, *Dr. Berryman*, ordered she be thrown in with all the other crazies, she went wild." She exaggerated an innocent, apologetic look and abruptly her mood brightened.

He never struck a woman before, never actually wanted too, even though he has encountered some of the lowest individuals that society has to offer.

But at this moment, his right hand automatically opened and closed, his long fingers flexing as he fought the overwhelming urge to grab that stupid tail sticking out of her fat head and pull her out of the room.

Smugly she continued; "Her doctor ordered it after *I* explained how much trouble she was causing us down here. She's under my care now. I see she gets what she needs." With that she turned around to leave, stopping when her eyes picked up something on the bed and returned. Reaching over, she took Bretta's call button and placed it on the table, far out of her patient's reach.

Unexpectedly and with great force, the hospital room door shot open and bounced loudly against the wall.

"Get away from her this instant!" The visitor ordered with such authority, both Stan and the nurse jumped back from the bed.

A stylishly dressed woman in a designer suit glared hard at the both of them as if trying to decide whom she would kill first. She looked completely out of her element clad in her exquisitely tailored pale pink suit and a fancy black handbag.

"You," she pointed to the hideous nurse with the ratty pony. "Are dismissed from your duties. I have brought our own nurse." As if on cue, the nurse entered the room, giving Stan a shy smile when she noticed him staring with his mouth open. Straight away she opened her bag, took out some type of chart and went over to her new patient and began to speak softly to Bretta.

Without even hearing the other nurse's voice, Stan would clearly rather have this smiling, docile nurse but doubted very much Ratched was going to allow it.

"I don't know who you two are, but I do know you're both leaving." Ratched glanced furiously at both intruders. "My patient needs her rest."

Stan wanted all of them to leave or at the very least shut up. As much as he preferred any other caregiver over this beast, he was pretty sure these two ladies had escaped from one of the rooms down the hall and someone would be around to fetch them any minute.

"Ladies, I believe you have the wrong room. Perhaps the nurse here can help you find where it is you need to be." It was an order more than a request and Ratched raised her eyebrows, but did not comment.

The elegantly dressed woman stepped in front of Stan and examined him closely, her perfectly outlined lips pursed tightly. Her hands rested on her hips as she circled around him. "You're that Sheriff, aren't you?"

Stan was too experienced to let his surprise show. "Yes, I am. And you would be?"

"I am Luisa Gerhard, Bretta's mother. I have come to take care of my daughter." She spoke with authority, obviously accustomed to making decisions and issuing orders. Nurse Rat-tail might have met her match. "Now that we have the formalities out of the way, I would like to see about my daughter."

"Well you will have to see about her during visiting hours. Take your little candy striper back with you. Leave now or I will have you thrown out." Ratched reached out to grab Luisa's sleeve to show her she meant business.

"Do not make the mistake of touching me." Luisa Gerhard fiercely glared at the unkempt hand that was about to come in contact with her sleeve and watched it slowly retract. "I have informed this hospital that my daughter will have a private nurse, her own doctor is on his way and my lawyer has already drawn up the necessary papers. Step out of this room now and do not even think of injecting another drug into her veins or you will find yourself in the center of a serious lawsuit that will end your meaningless career and worse, you will have made me your enemy. Trust me when I say, either one of those alternatives will be devastating for you."

The room was silent while the nurse carefully weighed her options.

Nurse Kremer must have decided she wasn't paid enough for this kind of headache. Silently, she gathered her belongings and started to leave.

"Dr. Berryman will hear about this. Believe me; you do not want him for an enemy."

Luisa threw her handbag on the bed and put herself inches from the nurse's homely face. "I'm not afraid of that pompous asshole. You tell that bastard I am in town and I want to see him. I know he is here somewhere, hiding like a sissy while his family needs him." She pointed a long, painted red fingernail towards the door. "Now get out."

Surprisingly, she did just that, allowing the door to slam loudly behind her for effect. The second she left, the private duty nurse was at Luisa's side with Bretta's chart.

"Yes Samantha, how is she?"

"Her vitals are stable Ms. Gerhard and her injuries appear to be relatively minor. They are watching a concussion and she has a break to the left Tibia. I do not know what was administered to sedate her, it's not noted anywhere. Dr. Stanford sent me a text that he will be arriving within the next thirty minutes."

"Thank you Samantha. If you encounter any interference with the hospital staff here, please let me know and I will hire a guard to stand outside the door." Luisa's lips curved upward and she turned to look at Stan. "I am sure our Sheriff here will need to get back to work eventually."

He had been pretty much silent up until now as he was not exactly sure what he should say. There was no official police business left to cover; he had retrieved Bretta's full statement hours ago. He simply did not want to leave her side. Now that her mother was here, a private nurse, her own doctor, and her husband was being summoned, he had no role here at all.

He did however have a shitload of work waiting for him at the office. So why was he still planted in this hospital room?

Luisa dragged a chair over to her daughter's bed and Bretta turned her head towards the sound.

Stan studied the mother and daughter for some type of family resemblance, but from this angle he could not find even a trace. Maybe Bretta was adopted.

Both were beautiful in their own unique way, and although they looked nothing alike, there was no mistaking the older woman's distress over the health of her daughter.

"You seem very concerned about my daughter Sheriff." Luisa watched him with great interest.

"I am. She's had quite a bit of excitement lately." He shifted his weight from one foot to the other, both feet now wanting to make their way out the door.

"Protective too."

"I am protective of all the citizens of Chester. That's my job."

"Really? You stay all night in the hospital room every time a resident is hurt? You must be a busy man Sheriff."

"That was not my intention, I fell asleep." Ms. Gerhard must be friends with Kuster too; either that or she has spies on her payroll. He should have left with Ratched while he had the chance. A slight blush began to creep up his neck and he was grateful Bretta was still out cold.

"I see." She nodded and crossed her legs which he could not help but notice where long and shapely. "What I can't figure out is this, you seem to be there whenever she needs you. You sleep all night in a stiff chair watching over her and apparently you hate John as much as I do."

He couldn't deny any of that so he nodded for her to continue.

"Then why did you call the hospital and order her to be locked up in the mental ward?"

Chapter 41

Apparently he missed something while he was appreciating her legs.

"I beg your pardon?"

"You heard me correctly, Sheriff. It should be obvious to you by now that I have ways of finding out information. Did you sincerely think I would let my daughter move to this hick town without some way to check on her?"

"You think that I stuck her in this ward?" He glanced over at Bretta. "That I had *anything* to do with this?"

Luisa came to her feet, extending her hand out to silence him.

"I know the orders came directly from you. You insisted …"

His anger finally erupted and this time there was no one around to help keep it in check. He grabbed a firm hold on Luisa's hand and moved it out of his face and spoke between his teeth.

"I didn't even know we were in this God forsaken ward until this morning when I was out hunting for coffee. I happen to be the only one around here that does believe her story. Why don't we start with you telling me everything you know right now?" Slowly, his fingers softened their grip when he saw the surprise in her eyes.

Luisa Gerhard was silent a few long seconds; the wheels could almost be heard whirling in her brilliant mind. He did not need Kuster's special talents to know she was a very smart lady.

"I underestimated you Sheriff. That doesn't happen often." She smiled at him, like she had just been let in on a great secret. "You're in love with my daughter!"

Fascinated now with the man in front of her, she started her examination at his big feet and worked her way up to his handsome face. Her hand shot out fast in front of her to stop the denial that was forming on his tongue and waved the air. "Oh, please! Don't bother to deny it. No one has been around the block more times than me."

"Ms. Gerhard, I assure you our relationship is strictly professional."

She continued as if he hadn't spoken. "Well, John is a prick and will give you trouble. You can count on that. He doesn't want her, but he sure as shit does not want anyone else to have her either. You best be fully prepared for him Sheriff. He is as smart as he is evil and he will show no sign of remorse." Her face turned solemn and pale.

Stan looked doubtful. "Why would Bretta stay with someone like that?"

"For a long time, I was the only one that could see how malicious he really was. I think he was doing something to make her sanity start to slip, slowly trying to drive her insane. It was like one of those old movies. Of course I could never prove any of that and by me accusing him only made me sound crazy too."

He had to agree with her on that. The second he laid eyes on Berryman he had an instant dislike for the man, however that didn't mean he was lurking in the shadows trying to drive his wife insane.

"I have had someone following him, watching his every move to finally get the evidence needed to put him away. I have a file two inches thick that so far, only proves how shrewd he is. But one day his luck will run out." She shook her head slowly. "He has been a very bad boy Sheriff."

"Listen, if you know something…"

"No, you listen here Sheriff. I tried that before. I went to the police with what I knew to be true and he got off. And you know what that arrogant ass did? He came right up to my face and mocked me. He threatened me in a way that would hurt me most. He said he would kill my daughter in a slow and agonizing death while my granddaughters watched and there wasn't a single thing I could do about it." Her warm hazel eyes darkened. "The next night I saw him at a black tie fundraiser, sitting at the head table with the mayor, police chief, and other important city officials. He was quite entertained by the fact I was watching him. His hand made a gun gesture to me and then winked." She showed him with her own hand. "I carry a Glock 26 tucked away nicely in my purse and I almost smiled back and shot the bastard between the eyes." She exhaled dramatically before continuing. "But, it wouldn't do any good to my daughter or my grandchildren if I am the one who ends up behind bars."

"I assume you have a permit to carry that thing around?"

"I do and I am prepared to use it."

What in the hell happened to the small town of Chester? So much for long lazy lunches and sneaking out early to go fishing. He massaged the back of his neck and tried to squeeze out some of his frustration.

"What did you mean that by for a long time, you were the only one that that could see what John was doing? Who else knows?"

She looked surprised. "Well, Bretta knows for one. Since moving here she has found that things have become clearer. Perhaps the time apart, the fresh air, I'm not sure. But suddenly she has come to see her spouse in a different light. I have to say, I suspected that you were on John's payroll since your department ordered her here."

He shook his head to disagree. "It wasn't me. But I'll find out who did, that's for sure."

⅄

He did not want his hunch to be right. In fact, he prayed he was dead wrong. Having to start over from scratch would be better.

Back at the station, Stan stepped over to the desk adjacent from his and allowed his eyes to search the files neatly stacked in alphabetical order, stopping when he found the one he needed.

Warily, he opened the file labeled Bretta Berryman as if he was looking at it for the first time. He read rapidly over the details of her life prior to moving to his childhood town. Nothing of real interest stood out until he came across an interview between the detective that handled her complaints and her doctor. Several references had been made to Bretta's bouts of illness, both mental and physical, however there was no real diagnosis listed. The former detective on the case had grilled the doctor and husband regarding Bretta's care. Stan turned the page over to see what his final report had been and found nothing. The report simply stopped.

Quickly he flipped through page after page of the report to see if the missing page was stuck someplace else. Not likely since Kuster was the last one with the file. If the page had been there it would have been in the right order.

There was only one for sure way to find out. He picked up the phone and punched in the number to the former detective's office that had handled the case.

"Detective Scalabrina, please." He said to the female voice that had answered the phone.

"Who's calling please?" The desk sergeant was polite but guarded.

He plucked a pencil out off a cup on Kuster's desk, observing that each pencil tip was sharpened to the exact same length. "This is Sheriff Stan Meyers calling from Chester, MI. I'm working on one of his old cases."

"Sheriff? May I get your number please? He'll call you right back."

While waiting for the call back, he continued on through the report when he picked up something that he either missed the other day or it wasn't there. Two phone numbers written lightly in pencil on the top of the first page of the report. He was getting ready to call one of them when his phone rang.

"Hello Sheriff, this is Detective Troszak. What can I help you with?" A deep, gravelly voice spoke in his ear.

"Thanks for getting back with me. I was hoping to chat with the detective that handled a case I am working on. By chance is Detective Scalabrina around?"

"What case are you working on?"

Stan hesitated briefly before replying. "A female by the name of Bretta Berryman, her husband John Berryman is a dentist. Detective Scalabrina was investigating a complaint Mrs. Berryman made against her husband a couple of years back. "

"I am sorry to have to inform you that Detective Frank Scalabrina is deceased, and unfortunately, I'm not familiar with that case. I can look it up and get back with you if you like."

Stan was caught off guard, but cops die just like everyone else.

"I am sorry to hear that."

"It was a great loss, both personally and professionally. He was a great guy..." an awkward silence filled the line and Stan waited patiently. "Scalabrina was murdered in his own home about a year and a half ago. We are still in shock over it. His partner up and retired after that then moved out of state."

Slowly he gripped the pencil tighter and reached in the drawer for a legal pad, knowing Kuster always kept fresh pads of paper in the top right drawer. An uneasy sensation filled his gut.

"May I inquire, was the murder solved?" Having a fellow officer that you work with and see every day killed is a very close and personal thing. Even as a law enforcement official himself he had to be careful how he asked.

Troszak exhaled roughly. "No. No it's not been solved. The investigation is still ongoing. Oddest damn case too. No sign of forced entry, nothing stolen. It was almost as if he opened the door and invited his killer in for a visit. Shot once in the head."

Murder always reminds you of murder. Immediately he thought of Wanda, sitting in the kitchen chair with her briefcase spread open, as if she had been in the middle of closing a sale.

"Not a single piece of evidence to go by or even a case he was working on to link it to."

"That's rough. I'm sorry." Truly he was. He knew what it was like to lose a colleague.

"Only thing we found at the scene is a scrap of paper clutched in his hand with a bunch of numbers on it. And I'll be damned if I can figure out what in the hell they mean."

Chapter 42

Waves of excitement, the bad kind, rippled through him as Detective Troszak read off the now familiar series of numbers. He sat in stunned silence for a few seconds before thanking the detective and ending his call.

What kind of connection could Barrett have to Detective Scalabrina? And how stupid would he have to be to leave his personal calling card all over? His large hand tightly squeezed the back of his neck which now felt like it was clamped in a metal vice. He was about to hunt for the Motrin stashed in his desk when he noticed the phone numbers again, handwritten lightly in pencil and standing alone at the top of the paper in Kuster's neat penmanship.

Something written so lightly could be easily erased.

On a whim, he quickly picked up the phone, punched in *67 and then the number.

It was answered on the third ring. "Admitting." A polite, female voice greeted him.

"Hey, is Sammy there?"

"I'm sorry sir; you've got the wrong number. This is admitting over at Mercy."

"Ok, thanks."

Now he knew who arranged for Bretta to be put in the ward, but what he didn't understand was why.

Next he tried the second phone number his deputy and friend left behind and clamped his eyes tight when the Voicemail picked up and Dr. John Berryman's arrogant voice announced to callers he was unavailable. *Shit Kuster.*

The phone felt heavy and awkward in his hand as he prepared to make his last call. Listening to an inner hunch born out of twenty years of law enforcement, he slowly dialed the number he had called earlier and asked for Detective Troszak.

"Hey, how would I go about tracking down Scalabrina's former partner?" Stan inquired after thanking the detective for taking his call.

"Ya know I'm not entirely sure where he ended up. He calls now and then. Wasn't with us for very long." He paused briefly. "Hang on. My partner just walked in. Got a memory like an elephant, let me see if he remembers."

"Thanks." Stan gripped the phone even tighter as he sensed the calamity coming his way.

"Hey Smithers, you got a phone number or something for Kevin Kuster, Scalabrina's last partner?"

⅄

Bretta attempted to force her eyelids apart but they refused to obey and remain open. A strange beeping noise seeped into her slumber along with a soft clicking sound. She did her best to concentrate on their gentle, familiar rhythm, positive she has heard them both before, but quickly grew tired of the battle and drifted back to sleep.

"Bretta?" The tender voice called out again, the clicking and the beeping still serenading her softly in the background. "Bretta honey, can you open your eyes for me? Jesus Christ, what the hell did they give her?" The recognizable voice was now angry and she knew she must comply.

"What?" Her mouth felt like it had been packed with cotton and her voice sounded like a ball or two was still lodged at the back of her throat.

Finally she pried her lids apart, continuing to blink several times to clear away the haze.

She allowed her gaze to travel around the room until it came to a rest on an identifiable face. Her mother, looking stylish and worried, stood at her bedside. A nurse that she was positive she has met before sat in the corner knitting, the long needles tapping lightly together. She held up her own hand to observe the clamp pinching down tightly on her finger, streaming her vitals into the noisy machine at her bed side. At least now she has deciphered the sounds.

"Bretta, listen to me now." Luisa Gerhard waited impatiently for her daughter's eyes to fall back to her face before continuing. "You were attacked in your home. Your girls are safe. Your leg is broke, but healing nicely and... it was ordered that you be put back in the ward, but I don't want you to panic. I will get you out of here."

Too late. Bretta grabbed at the hospital gown that had worked its way up around her neck and yanked it away.

How could this be happening again?

"I have Dr. Stanford on his way and your own private nurse is back. You remember Samantha?" Luisa waved her hand in the direction of the nurse who gave a warm, genuine smile to Bretta.

Her mother's words made her sober up fast and she remembered exactly what happened, the callous nurse taking care of her and the hours spent alone with the Sheriff.

She had held one of his big, powerful hands while she lay on the bed last night and slowly her fears melted away. They talked about everything from childhood, heart aches to her horrible marriage.

"How did I end up here?" Memories of the last time she was in the psychiatric ward flooded her intellect and she felt a sharp bolt of nausea.

"I'm not sure dear." Luisa turned her gaze away from her daughters and focused on her bed sheets.

Bretta gasped. Her mother was lying to her?

She had worked by her mother's side for over twenty five years and it was unbelievable that she would even attempt to be dishonest.

"Mother?" This time, Bretta's voice was demanding with a no nonsense tone of her own.

Luisa exhaled and sat on the edge of the bed.

"The orders came from the Sheriff's department Bretta."

Chapter 43

Bretta threw the covers back and grimaced loudly as she attempted to swing her bad leg over the side of the bed. The sudden movement caused her head to sway.

"Mother, get Doctor Stanford on the phone and have him discharge me right now." There was no way in hell that she would go through this again. She was not the same person, no longer that week, timid young woman who was going to sit by and let her husband tell the world she was insane. Today, she was giving the orders. "Then help me get out of here."

"Bretta, your leg!" Luisa hurried to her daughter's side as Samantha threw her knitting aside.

"Really Mrs. Berryman, you need to rest."

Rest? She recalled the last time John said that word to her she had to fight the urge to bury an ax in his head.

"I don't need to *rest,* thank you Samantha." She said through clenched teeth. Maybe she was on John's payroll too along with the Sheriff. She pushed away thoughts of how good Stan smelled and how his massive hand covered hers, allowing her feel safe and protected.

"Dr. Standford is on his way here now Bretta. You need to take it easy now until he gets here."

"What I need is to get out of this place before they lock me away for good." Something felt final about her hospital stay this time because John would not make the same mistake twice. He was not going to let her go free.

She turned to her mother and fired off instructions. "Please step out into the hall and find a wheelchair Mother. Samantha, make up some type of order that shows you were told to switch my room."

Luisa Gerhard, much more familiar with issuing the commands than receiving them, hesitated briefly until she saw the fiery look in her daughter's eye. She considered her daughters words and then agreed; it would be best to get out of this hospital and away from the clutches of John Berryman.

"Samantha," The name came out of Bretta's lips like a puff of air as the two other women helped her in the chair. "Now is the time to make yourself invaluable to me. If anyone should try to stop us, you say you are following Dr. Stanford's orders. Please call him and tell him he is not needed here and that we will check in with him later."

The nurse looked worried and unsure, but gave her word she would cooperate.

They made it all the way to the elevators before a loud voice bellowed stop.

Nurse Ratched was on their heels. She wore her favorite scowl and a dollop of mayonnaise on the corner of her mouth signifying her lunch had been interrupted. "Just where do you think you are taking her?"

Now fully awake and angry, Bretta was more than ready to take on her warden.

Samantha took her hands off the back of the wheelchair and turned to face the other nurse. "I have orders to take her to a different floor. *This* floor is not good for her health. If you have a problem with this, you may call Dr. Jacob Stanford and take it up with him." She shoved a piece of paper at her. "Now please excuse us, my patient needs to get settled in her new room." Just then the elevator doors dinged opened and the three women moved swiftly inside, leaving Ratched staring at her slip of paper. There was little doubt she would run and call Dr. Stanford and have security waiting by the time they reached the parking lot if they did not hurry.

"I have the car waiting for us out the side door that we used to come in. I left a message for Doctor Sanford telling him that we have left and I am finding a place for us to stay."

She knew her mother would not tolerate being bossed around for long, she was too accustomed to being in charge and truthfully, she was relieved. The pain in her leg was intensifying and just about every inch of her body was throbbing.

She let her eyelids close and scootched down low, allowing her head to rest on the back on the chair. Samantha's' soft voice assured her that she would give her something for her discomfort once they were in the car.

"Oh, I almost forgot! I have a present for you." Luisa spoke up loudly once they were all seated in the car and began to rattle a cluster of shopping bags that were nestled at her feet. Eventually the irritating commotion stopped and Bretta felt something being placed on her lap. Reluctantly she forced her lids apart to find a large box magnificently gift wrapped in front of her.

She let her head roll sleepily to the side and forced herself to give her mother a smile. It didn't feel like it was the time or the place to be passing out presents, but she knew her mother lived by own agenda. "Thank you mother, that was sweet of you."

"Here, let me open it for you."

Luisa took her time pulling apart the enormous burgundy silk ribbon and carefully lifted the lid off the silver box, as if the gift was for her and separated the coordinating tissue paper.

"Perhaps if things get straightened out with that hunk of a sheriff, you might want to call him over wearing this little number and not those God awful t-shirts you seem to favor."

It took her a second or two to process that her mother was talking about Stan and her eyes flew open.

A long, ivory satin nightgown with the smallest amount of black lace was draped over her mother's arm.

"Mother!" She didn't know which of the comments to address first. "I *am* still married."

"That predicament can be fixed Bretta; it is not a fate you are stuck with for the rest of your life." She thrashed her hand up lighting quick to silence her daughter, her signature trademark to ensure she would get the last word.

"We can get into that later dear, when you are stronger, but just know that I have been working on this. As far as your sheriff goes, don't write him off yet. He's not the only one that works in that office that could have made that call you know."

"My judgment is off and honestly, I am simply too tired to think of any this now Mother. I want to take a nap while I can."

When she opened her eyes again, they were pulling up in front of the Muncy sister's house. Alice, Athena and her daughters were running out to the car to great them.

Relief at seeing her girls safe filled her entire being and warm tears flooded her eyes that she quickly blinked away. Ivy and Iris climbed into the backseat with her and she gave them each a big, reassuring hug.

Their joyful reunion was suddenly interrupted by a loud pounding on the car window.

Alice stood in the street next to the car, her outfit much more subdued than normal. Today's dress was black with tiny coral flowers instead of the normal loud patterns she usually favored.

Bretta rolled down the window to thank her friend for watching the girls, but Alice surprised her by reaching in the car and firmly grabbing her arm before she could speak.

"Do you like my dress today Bretta?" Alice asked. There was an anxious, almost desperate quality to her voice. Perhaps her friend had been spending too much time in the garden.

"Why yes, I do Alice. It's lovely." She was more than familiar with her neighbor's off the wall questions, though she was generally not this somber.

"This is the outfit I want to be buried in." Her eyes locked firmly with Bretta's, pleading to be understood. From the corner of her eye, she could see an angry Athena marching towards the car. "And I want the choir to sing *In the Garden.* It's an old church hymn but I still love it. Very fitting for me, don't you think?" Alice's grip on her arm tightened painfully as she continued on quickly before her sibling could stop her.

"You should get your affairs in order too." She leaned forward and spoke directly in Bretta's ear, her warm breath buzzing softly on the side of her face. "You don't have much longer." Alice paused briefly, as if to catch a thought before it slipped away. "It's a shame about the dying really…they never quite ready to let go."

Bretta gasped loudly and spun her head towards her friend who was being dragged away from the car.

"Alice! Get your dingbat head out of that car so they can leave!" Athena yanked her sister back roughly, nodded to Bretta and banged twice on the trunk of the black Lincoln, signaling the driver to leave. The two sisters stood side by side in silence and watched the shiny black car speed away down Hollyhock Lane.

⅄

"What the hell do you mean she's not there? She's a patient at that hell hole! Now please get someone on the phone who can give you an update on her status. And don't get that nurse Ratched bitch on the phone either." Stan dropped in his office chair and stared down at the growing stack of evidence building against his deputy and friend.

A wide-eyed Sally stood in front of her boss and appeared to weigh her words carefully.

"What I mean sir, is that she has left the hospital without being discharged and was last seen being wheeled out by her nurse and her mother."

"Well get a car out to the Muncy sisters right away. I'm sure she'll head out there next and pick up her girls."

"I already did that sir. She's been there, picked up her daughters and then left. The sisters do not know what Mrs. Berryman's plans were. I have a scout car out now looking for them now."

Stan's silence dragged on until Sally finally gave her throat a little clear.

"Sally, sit at Kuster's desk and start with John Berryman's file. I want to know everything there is about that man. Likes, dislikes, family, work, what kind of trouble did he get in. Don't leave anything out. Make it fast, but make it thorough."

"Ah...what do I do when Kuster comes in and sees me at his desk?" As fun as it was to mess with Kuster, he could get pretty darn cranky when it came to his personal possessions.

Stan picked up the desk phone and started punching in numbers. "I wouldn't worry about that. It doesn't look like he's coming back."

⅄

Forty-five fast working minutes later, Sally hung up the phone, did a full swing around in her co-workers chair and let out a little cheer. She had just enough time to compile all her facts into a semi-legible report before Stan returned from a call.

It only took five minutes into her report before she confidently declared John Berryman a full-fledged asshole. How in the world did Bretta end up with such a bozo?

After that the data took on a startling new change that took him from idiot to dark and disturbing, but what was more alarming was why hadn't Deputy Kevin Kuster uncovered this?

Kevin is a dot every i and cross every t kinda of guy. If he overlooked this, he did it on purpose which was almost impossible to comprehend. Kuster was as honest as the day was long.

As she did every day when she was alone in the office, she took her time to read the contents of Kuster's inbox, outbox, and garbage can before taking her daily peek at his emails. Other than his girly tea parties with his geriatric pals, he led a rather quiet life.

Snooping was out of necessity when Eb Perkins was Sheriff. The male chauvinist pig went way out of his way to be sure she never knew what was going on and set her up to look like a fool when she first started with the department. Now she did it just for fun.

With her report finished, she did what she thought was a sufficient job of putting Kuster's desk back together again in case he should return. He could always tell if you so much as borrowed a staple. She liked Kuster in that brotherly, rearrange a few things on his desk and see if he notices kind of way.

She was in the process of banging the files loudly on the desk top in an attempt to align the stack into what she considered a neat pile when she noticed one of Kuster's "To Do" lists fly out into the air and land right in front of her.

The list was numbered one through ten and all but number four was checked off. A neat, perfect checkmark sat before each assignment, signifying its completion. Number four on the list reminds him to ask Rose about a receipt for a dollhouse. It didn't sound all that earth shattering, but she definitely would run it by the Sheriff when he returned.

A peculiar sensation began to bristle up the back of her neck with sharp needle like pulsations. Over time she had developed her own six sense through experience and hours of pouring over books that promised one could develop their own intuition if they really tried hard enough.

She thought of Wanda Bee and Betty Grimes who were both meddlesome, brash, and most likely discovered this same information on John Berryman.

Now they were dead. Murdered in this small town where nothing bad ever happens.

Slowly she sank back down into Kuster's chair and stared at the tidy desk in front of her in an entirely new light. She began her search over again, this time to see what he might be hiding, instead of what he neglected to share.

The deafening silence of the empty office began to give her an edgy feeling, the one that usually comes right before trouble. Her fingers lightly swept across her reliable Glock for comfort, relaxing slightly from the familiar reassurance.

Now that she was finished here, Dottie's Diner seemed a much better place to wait for her boss. Famished as usual, she had heard in town earlier that Dottie was making her renowned strawberry rhubarb pie for tonight and she had been fantasizing about it all day. Taking everything she deemed important, she jammed it all into the frayed briefcase she found next to his desk in a manner that she knew would make Kuster ill and stood to leave.

"You weren't going to wait for me?" A masculine voice spoke directly behind her taking her by surprise in such a way that a small sound escaped her lips. Her hands, now busy holding a weighty briefcase, stumbled to reach for her gun as she felt something firm and hard press against her back.

Chapter 44

"You will feel better darling once we get you settled in my apartment." Luisa said confidently as she tugged her elegant black leather planner out of her purse along with a sleek gold pen. Bretta observed that her mother had another new ink pen, knowing that she prefers the feel of traditional writing methods over the modern gadgets that everyone is constantly toying with.

"We are not going to the city mother, we are staying right here. I need some time to think." She rested her head back on the seat and allowed her eyelids to fall shut.

"You are medicated and under a great deal of stress. Let me handle everything and don't worry."

Bretta shook her head no. "I no longer need people to handle things for me." She said a bit sharper than she intended to. This wasn't her mother's fault. "We are going to stay here until I can figure out what is going on."

Her mother appeared confused and chose her words carefully. "Dear, you do know what is going on." She lowered her voice in an effort to protect her grandchildren who were straining their ears to hear. "No amount of counseling will fix this and the best thing for you would be to get out of this God forsaken town!"

"I have to know why. Why he is doing this? What purpose could it possibly serve him? And I need to know why someone wants me out of that house. *My* house." Of course there were other things she needed answers too as well, but could not put a voice to her fears. There were so many unanswered questions, like how her sewing basket arrived to town before she did or the mystery behind the beautiful music that plays only for her.

Because if John was not responsible for all those stunts, then that could mean only one thing.

She turned her head to gaze out the car window, her own pale reflection staring back at her.

She was indeed insane.

⅄

"Son of a bitch!" Officer Sally Hiller shrieked loudly. "You scared the crap out of me. I almost shot you dead!"

There are a handful of officers that probably shouldn't carry a loaded gun on a day to day basis Stan thought. Hiller was one of them, but he needed her and she was good at her job.

Sally's face turned three different colors before it settled on a vibrant red as the realization set in that she just swore at her boss.

"Sorry Sal, I thought you could use some coffee." He pushed the cardboard tray towards her.

"I'm sorry sir, you scared me a bit." An obvious understatement since she was still shaking. "I was just headed out to Dottie's for a piece of pie. I'm starving."

He remembered his no food ban in the office and noticed she seemed a bit thinner than usual. He often forgot to eat but he knew food was a big thing with her. "Sounds like a good idea, I'll go with you. And I think it is safe to allow food in the break room."

"Oh, thank God!"

A few minutes later they were comfortably seated in a booth at Dottie's Diner which was a cross between retro and just plain old. Dottie purchased the small café over thirty-seven years ago "as is" and rolled with that theory ever since and changed only the diner's name. She decided she liked seeing her name in neon lights.

Dottie insists that her black and white checkered floors be kept shiny clean and stares down anyone that dare enter with muddy boots. The original red ruffled curtains still adorn each window and add a bit of nostalgia for the old timers that have memories of tasting their first soda up at the counter. Each table has its own little jukebox which unfortunately for some has not seen updated titles since 1975.

Dottie's dinner menu changes almost daily, giving patron's only two entrees to pick from. They are handwritten in cursive on a large chalkboard easel that greets you as enter the front door. If you don't like what is offered, you are free to dine someplace else.

Dottie rarely speaks and chooses to grunt and point as opposed to carrying on a real conversation. Tonight she dumps a large, steaming plate of something that looks like beef stroganoff in front of Sally and stares impatiently at the Sheriff until he finally announces he will take the same.

He sat back and watched in amazement as Sally devoured half of her meal in a few record breaking minutes, apparently not bothered by the fact that it was served blazing hot. Abruptly she stops, wipes her mouth on her napkin and noisily slurps down her entire ice tea before picking up her notes.

"John Berryman has been a very naughty boy." She manages to get out right before a loud belch.

Bretta's mother had conveyed a similar warning. It was a simple statement, but the tone in which Sally delivered it left Stan uncomfortable and he nodded for her to continue.

"Bretta had been sick for over a year and doctors were unable to give an exact diagnosis. After about a year of this, John Berryman got a doctor to write that she was creating all the drama for attention, that she was psychosomatic. Apparently, incredibly creative people often suffer from this. He went on a campaign to convince the courts that she was in danger to herself and her children."

"Was she put in a mental hospital?"

"Yes, for almost a month. But I could not find if she was cured, or even if she improved."

"Why not?" Thinking she simply did not dig deep enough.

She paused briefly when Dottie stopped by the table to deposit a plate in front of Stan and refill their drinks.

"I think because a bigger story came up. Someone blew the whistle on the good doctor. Seems a few of his female patients came forward saying they had memories of being fondled while under the gas."

This should have come up before. "I never found a record on him."

"That's because the women never pressed charges."

"He bought them off?"

Sally shrugged her shoulders. "He might have; I found each one dropped the charges. Two of them eventually died. One a hit and run, the other fell off her balcony."

"Really?"

"Yep." She nodded then took a sip of her ice tea. "And you know who knew about this?"

"You mean besides Kuster?"

Her eyes opened wide in surprise. "You knew Kuster was keeping something from you?"

"I just recently discovered that." Now he needed to find out what other secrets his deputy was keeping. "Wanda Bee must have known too. I found a couple of things in her notes that would indicate she knew all about the Berryman family. Strange though, some of the news clippings are quite old. I wonder where she would have gotten them from. It's not like she would have started collecting dirt on this guy before he even moved here."

"Any thoughts on why he would go through all this trouble to have his wife declared crazy? Wouldn't it have been easier to just divorce her?" Sally cross-examined as she lowered her face to her plate and was about to lick it before apparently remembering she was in public.

"Yes. But then he wouldn't be able to get at her money. He had signed a pre-nup so he would walk away with exactly what he brought into the marriage and have to give her half of what his dental businesses was worth. In the event of her death, her money goes into a trust fund set aside strictly for the children."

"What money?"

"Luisa Gerhard's money. Her mother's loaded. Owner and CEO of an exceptionally successful fashion design company. Bretta was content designing and living a simple life, but her husband had a burning desire for more. He wanted her to step up and take over the business. When she wouldn't, I think he simply wanted her out of the way."

"So now he is back trying to make her think she's crazy. He's going to try again to have her locked up."

He nodded his head in agreement. "He wants her out of the way, that's for sure."

Chapter 45

"Well, isn't this quaint?" Luisa Gerhard said in a lack luster tone and forced her lips to curve into a semi-smile. "Honey, I do think we would all be more comfortable in the place that I have arranged for us."

Meaning she would be more comfortable. "No mom, I want to stay here." Bretta swung her bad leg out of the car and tried to use her crutches to stand. "Samantha, I think I need some help."

"I'll help you, mom. Give me the crutches and put your arm over my shoulder." Within a second, Iris had her out of the car and leaning on her crutches. Bretta chose for now to ignore Ivy's inquisitive stare that she held since the minute they picked her up from the Muncy's. She truly did not have the strength for all the questions she knew would be coming.

"Are there enough beds?" Luisa requested nicely but most likely prayed that there were not. She was tip toeing up the path hoping to prevent her pointy heels from sinking into the earth, her arms stretched out on either side of her as if walking a tight rope.

"You don't have to stay with us Mother. We'll be fine."

"Don't be ridiculous! I am not leaving you alone out here in Uncle Tom's Cabin to wobble around and fend for yourself."

"I'm hardly alone. I'll be fine here." The last thing she needed was to have to worry about was her mother's comfort.

Her thoughts were interrupted by Luisa's loud screech. She turned back to see her mother running back to the car on her tippy toes. She knew country life would be too much for her.

"Do not set those on the ground!" Luisa yanked her Louis Vuitton luggage out of the driver's hand. "That is a Louis Vuitton Keepall 60! We don't rest that on dirt!"

A deep red worked its way up the driver's neck and spread out to his checks and he muttered an apology as he finished unloading the trunk.

This was the perfect place to stay. Her mother might not think so, but it truly did fit their needs.

She grinned at her own cleverness.

Blending in with the summer people in one of the Wickedwinds cabins by the lake was not only particularly sly, it was poetic.

Now it was her turn to play games.

Sometimes the best place to hide was right out in the open.

Besides, he would never think to look for her here, especially since her mother was with them. This was not exactly the type of place that Luisa Gerhard was accustomed to.

"Mom, this is so awesome!" Ivy yelled and Iris agreed. "A real cabin! This is so cool."

"Can we get our bikes here, Mom?" Iris pleaded excitedly.

They were supposed to be in hiding. The girls can't suddenly appear riding their bikes through town, but it wasn't fair to keep them cooped up in the cabin all day either. "I guess it would be okay if you rode them out here only, around the cabin."

"Thanks mom." Iris said. "Hey, can you have Marc look at my bike? My kick stand is broken."

It would have been nice if she had mentioned that to Marc on one of the fifty or more times he was at the house. "We'll get him to look at it later. Just be careful with it in the meantime."

Both ran to investigate their new sleeping quarters. At least they were happy. She heard them laughing and one of them called out their chosen bed.

The furnished cabin had two bedrooms, a loft, and one small bathroom with a decent size kitchen that flowed into the living room. A large cobble stone fireplace was the focal point of the living room which offered a cozy, rustic feel. It was clean and tastefully decorated in carefully chosen knick-knacks she guessed were from the local flea market.

Cabin number nine was hidden in a thick patch of pine trees. Because there was no easy water access and this wasn't a hopping vacation town, the cabin was not usually requested by the summer people.

They would be perhaps a bit crowded, but perhaps she could convince her mother to send Samantha back with the driver. She hardly needed a private nurse. She did however, need to lie down and noticed her mother watching her with concern.

"Simply because I did not want my thousand dollar Louie ruined, doesn't mean I'm going to act like a spoiled, pampered princess." Luisa retrieved a note pad from her purse and started writing. "I'm making a list of things we shall need." She began walking around the cottage with her nose scrunched tightly, peeking her head into every room, inspecting closets and cupboards. "I will need all new bedding and towels too." She handed the list over to the driver who looked surprised at the long list.

"Maybe you should go to the store, Mom." Her mother was not afraid to ask for what she wanted, that was for sure.

"No, no. Chuck is more than competent. He may be new, but he comes highly recommended. Be sure to pick out sheets that are...just purchase the most expensive sheets you can find for a double bed please." She overlooked her daughter's embarrassment and continued with her inspection.

"Please be sure to drive to the next town over before you start shopping, Chuck."

"Yes, of course Ms. Berryman."

By nightfall they were all reasonably settled into their own rooms, the cottage quiet. Bretta had managed to convince Samantha to leave with Chuck. There was no need for a nurse, she could swallow a pain pill on her own and what she desperately needed was time to think.

Chuck had done an amazing job purchasing the supplies and had returned with groceries, new bedding for all the beds, and swung by her house and grabbed the kid's bikes.

What she did need to do was make a list, a habit she must have inherited from her mother. She had several calls she needed to make tomorrow as well as arrange for a rental car to be delivered. It wasn't the best of ideas to be isolated out here without a vehicle.

She wobbled into the kitchen and noticed the light that shone from under her mother's bedroom door; she was probably still inspecting her room for bugs.

She'd try a cup of the tea she used for insomnia before popping another pill. She had been delighted if not somewhat surprised to see that Chuck had purchased the exact brand of her nighttime tea without her even asking. She had been out of it since right before the move and could not find it in any of the stores since moving here.

Standing at the kitchen counter she allowed a moment to enjoy the hot, sweet-smelling steam before taking a sip. It was a special blend to induce sleep and was the only time she ever drank tea. Just the familiarity of the taste and smell was enough to calm her down.

Alice's haunting words played out in her head. She did not know what to make out of her neighbors cautionary advice. Did she need to get her affairs in order?

Alice was a delightful blend of eccentric and early dementia, however there was no denying she was somewhat clairvoyant. Simply the fact that Alice was able to pluck part of John's warning out of the air took her breath away.

The moon shone full and brilliant through the backdoor window, illuminating the perimeter of the cabin. Slowly Bretta maneuvered her crutches towards the radiance and rested her head upon the glass pane, watching the trees dance silently in the wind. The backs of two white Adirondack chairs faced the cabin and she decided that would be the perfect convalescing spot for her tomorrow.

Only then would she allow herself to think about Stan and his calming presence or exactly how long her husband had employed him.

Suddenly her stomached rolled.

It was that old, familiar nausea that was her constant companion last year. Panic ripped through her body until finally her grip around her crutches became so tight, her fingers turned numb.

All the stress and drama that she had been through would make anyone want to throw up. But the feeling was so terrifyingly recognizable that it made her feel worse.

Beads of sweat formed on her head and under her arms. Her head began to pound, her knees ready to buckle. She thought about calling her mother, but hesitated. As sick as she was, she still had her common sense. How would she explain the return of these mysterious symptoms, the ones that doctors could never explain nor cure? Her mother and daughters would never say it, but she knew what they were thinking.

No, the best thing to do was get back to bed and pray she felt better in the morning. Carefully she manipulated her crutches back in the direction of her bedroom, stopping abruptly when a flicker of movement appeared out of the corner of her eye. Probably just a tree branch, dancing in the wind.

Ever so slowly, she turned her head back in the direction of the patio.

The yard was empty, exactly as she thought it would be. No boogie man waiting to jump out and scream surprise. She officially declared it past her bedtime when suddenly, she knew she had to check one more time.

The wind had kicked up, shifting leaves around and distorting her field of vision. It took her eyes a few seconds to narrow in on the object that did not fit in with the charming landscape.

He stepped out from behind the trees and started walking away. She blinked hard to sharpen her focus and clear the blur but the apparition kept moving.

Undoubtedly she was hallucinating again. It happened before when she had been unwell. Objects were rearranged, music played, appointments were switched.

John had been right. All the signs were there but she had refused to see them.

She watched the figure stroll away and then sharply stop, as if he knew he was being watched. He blended in adequately with the darkness but she could still make out his features as his head turned towards her and offered half a smile, as if he could see her clearly through the night.

Unhurried, his right arm lifted and he pointed his forefinger finger straight at her. Quickly she stumbled to the door to check the lock when her crutch slipped out from beneath her and crashed loudly on floor.

He then transformed his hand into the shape of a gun by lifting up his thumb. She could see him laugh, his features turning demonic under the moon's intense glow.

"Bretta, everything okay?" With great relief she heard her mother's bedroom door open. "Did you drop something?" Luisa ran out of her room, belting her long ivory silk robe around her tiny waist.

"My crutch just slipped, that's all. Scared me a bit." She had to say something; she was practically shaking like a wet dog. Nonchalantly she took another look out the kitchen window to find her visitor gone, like she knew he would be.

Back in her room she began to make plans. First she would retrieve her little sewing basket back from Rose.

The one that now apparently contained a gun.

She may be sick. She may be delusional. But there was one thing she knew for sure.

Her caller would return eventually and next time she would be ready.

Chapter 46

It was a perfect summer evening to take a run outside. Not too hot with a mild breeze rustling through the trees. He knew the fresh air would help untangle his crowded mind; however it would be guaranteed to invite too many interruptions. Porch sitting was considered something of a sport in this town and folks can last for hours just waiting for someone to walk by so they can strike up a conversation.

Upon moving back home he had immediately converted his basement into a gym and tonight it seemed like a good spot to hang out.

The mile marker on his treadmill hit five and so far he hadn't come up with anything other than a slight headache. Kuster had become his sounding board since moving home. Stan glanced down at his phone, half expecting his deputy to call in at any second and still undecided if he should be worried instead of pissed.

He exhaled a long string of curses when his cell phone went off for the twentieth time and it still wasn't Kuster, but his mood lightened slightly when he saw it was Marc.

"How's it going?" He hit the down arrow to allow the machine to slow down to a fast walk.

"Nothing on my end. Heard you've been busy though. How's Bretta?"

"She discharged herself from the hospital and went into hiding, that's how she is." Marc paused a second, the way he often did when contemplating a situation. "Do you think she went back to the city?"

"It is hard to say where she went. Maybe she left the country because she sure as hell didn't feel safe anywhere around here."

"She could have gone to see her husband. I know the kids missed him, she might have too. She seemed pretty messed up about him."

"What do you mean messed up?" He didn't picture Bretta pining away for her absentee spouse, unless he simply had not wanted to see it.

"When the husband finally came to see his new house, she got all worked up that he was going to take the girls. He was starting a campaign to convince Bretta she was a crazy, unfit mother and he was planning on taking custody of the girls. Really shook her up. You know how some women are, they get under a guy's spell and it's all over."

He read enough in the files to know Berryman had unsavory intentions towards his wife; he hadn't heard a thing about him threatening her. It made him sick inside to think she still had any feelings for the guy and he was not sure if it was out of compassion or jealousy.

"I heard Betty's missing too."

"Did you call just to cheer me up?" He barked back.

"Sorry… just joining the grapevine."

"Yeah, I know." Not much point taking his frustrations out on his friend even if yelling made him feel slightly better. "Betty never showed up to work and hasn't been back to her house now in couple of days. Very unlike her, she never even takes a vacation."

"Hey, I'll tell you what else was very unlike her. I saw her leaving a 7 Eleven just outside of Chester dressed like she was going out hooking for the night."

"What, you mean like a prostitute?" He stopped the treadmill and jumped off. He had to admit Betty sometimes had a flare for dressing odd, but he would never mistake her for a hooker.

"Had on heels so high that she could barely walk in them, short skirt, bright red lipstick." He swore he could hear Marc shudder over the phone as he recalled the unpleasant image.

"You sure it was Betty?"

"Oh, yeah, it was her all right. I saw her get into her car and drive away."

"Maybe she had a date or something."

"Or something."

"Did you ever hear of her dating anyone?"

"I never heard a thing about Betty other than vicious complaints."

"Yeah, me neither. We've already checked in with her sister who told us that she missed their weekly visit, but she wasn't too worried about it."

"Did she call in and report her missing?" Marc asked.

People never ceased to amaze him. "No, she's still pissed at Betty because she didn't bring her donuts or something on her last visit."

"That sounds like someone that would be related to Betty."

The sad fact was, no one gave a rat's ass what happened to Betty, but she still deserved to be treated like any other citizen.

"I'll send Sally over there tomorrow to have a chat with the sister. See if she has any idea what Betty has been up to." Stan took a quick gulp of water but was thinking about a beer. "Hey, when we gonna sneak away for a little fishing?"

"You tell me." Marc let out a laugh. "You're pretty busy these days."

"You got that right. Lots of pumping up tires and putting out fires."

"Funny, Chester didn't have all that many fires until you moved back home."

⅄

Deep into the dark, damp night, the clear, distinct popping sound of a gun ran out. It jolted him a tad and then made him grin. Perhaps an unfortunate stranger wondered on someone's property or a lone hunter captured its prey.

The shot was too far away to have been meant for him. Not that it would have scared him away. He was not afraid to die.

Death was all too familiar to him.

He has seen death. He has felt death and he certainly has caused death.

Right now he was simply passing through time, taking pleasure in each moment.

He moved through the night like an experienced outdoorsman. A hunter.

A man's man.

If his father could only see him now, what a man he turned out to be. Unlike his girly brother who was always sipping on fancy coffees and loved to play in the kitchen. He walked methodically, taking care not to crack a branch that might draw attention to his whereabouts. He knew how to be quiet and merge with the night.

He had conquered the house on the hill and now it belonged to him. It was exactly as he envisioned and as a bonus, it was restored to its former grandeur.

Only it felt empty without her. She made the house a home.

Dreams often went like that. You work so hard to get something and then when it's finally yours it's nothing how you imagined. He had become so used to seeing her in the house that she became part of the dream.

He exhaled with disgust and wished this little epiphany would have happened sooner. It would have saved him a lot of time and effort. Now after successfully chasing her out, he will have to go fetch her and bring her back.

He had found her easy enough, tucked away in the tiny cabin in the woods and had been back several times to watch her. He wasn't sure why, but he had become fascinated with the ridiculous way she wasted time. No matter if she was at the old house or hiding at the cabin, he would always find her engaged in a pointless activity; digging in the earth with her tiny shovel, sitting on the swing staring into space or talking to that screwy old lady.

Tonight as he made his way back to the cottage, he considered how he would extract her and bring her back to Huddelstone.

It was when he started to make his way back down the trail towards home that he saw it. Quickly he approached, no longer distressing that cracking a large branch with his heavy gait would wake her.

There it was, carelessly thrown on the ground like a piece of trash. Those little spoiled brats; he never should have shown such mercy that day by the lake. Too angry to play rhyming games today, he would simply have to punish them.

That was how he had learned.

He yanked the bike off the ground and swung his foot out to extend the kickstand, the blood pounding ferociously to his head. Rage surged through his veins and the bike felt weightless in his heated hands. He missed the stand twice and swore out loud when suddenly he began to see the problem.

Something did not seem right with the bike.

Meticulously he tested the bike and found it was in need of repair. His eyes scanned the property to seek out the other bike and found it not far from the cabin, propped up properly.

Well now, that was different. It was broken and of course, girls being girls, they were too stupid to know how to fix it.

He was not without heart. He was even a Boy Scout for a time until the other parents complained, forcing him to quit. Without much thought he removed the pocket knife out of his pants and went to work, repairing the bike.

There, he just did one of those pass it on bullshit good deeds the liberals were always chirping about, but this was it. The next time he found those bikes being mistreated in any way he would simply take over ownership.

Amusement escaped his lips when he envisioned himself peddling down Main Street on a little girl's pink bike.

Enough fantasy, it was time to head back in for the night and make plans for his new companion.

Chapter 47

The next morning, Deputy Sally Hiller peeled out of town via Main Street to have a *friendly* chat with Ellie Johnson, Betty Grimes one and only sibling.

The early air of dawn had a sweet, flowery smell that always put her in a good mood. It reminded her of her childhood which unlike everyone else she knew, was a happy one. The windows of her cruiser were cranked all the way down allowing a surge of warm wind to noisily toss the multitude of candy wrappers and empty chip bags around her back seat. Another simple pleasure she enjoyed.

To save time and effort, she had attempted the conversation thing earlier with a polite phone call to the charming Ms. Johnson. Three long and agonizing minutes later, it became crystal clear that Ellie wasn't in the talking mood. Not without donuts.

Ellie was a bitch. Just like her sister.

Now she would have to drive her already overworked and underpaid butt out to Ellie Johnson's dwelling and have a visit. Normally she would have done that to begin with but she knew in truth, with her case load recently tripled and Betty being one of her least favorite people on the planet, she tried the easy way first.

She just about cleared the outskirts of town when she hit the brakes hard and spun her police cruiser back around, causing several early birds out walking their pooches to startle. She might have to drag her fanny all around town but she didn't have to starve herself doing it. Plus, she was much too cranky, therefore trigger happy, on an empty stomach.

Within minutes she was happily seated in her favorite booth at Dottie's and began flipping through the old jukebox as if she didn't already know which song she would play first. She was probably the only patron that actually enjoyed the sorry selections the little mechanism offered.

Dottie's service is often faster than fast food and a heck of a lot better. Her husband Bruno is the cook and prefers to stay behind the scenes. He is a big, beefy man with a brush cut and a permanent scowl who will grant you a nod from behind the lunch counter if he likes you.

Together Dottie and Bruno run a good business even if the pair looks like they are filming a commercial for anti-depressants.

"*Billy, don't be a hero*" busted out of the little box as her breakfast plate magically appeared before her. It was different every morning which she secretly found thrilling. Today it was some kind of cholesterol enriched special that included an oversized cheesy omelet, a side plate piled high with bacon, sausage patties, and two links, a glass of mystery juice, and whole wheat toast. They only served whole wheat. Perhaps Bruno considered himself a health nut of sorts. With a mouthful of food she muttered a thanks before Dottie sped off to her next table.

If she felt any more contented she would begin to purr.

She was so engrossed in her meal, she almost missed that Dottie was still standing in front of her. She must have been eating with her eyes closed again.

"Uh, everything is real good Dottie. Thanks."

Dottie nodded, but didn't rush off to the next customer.

Sally glanced around the table and did a quick assessment. Salt, pepper, ketchup, napkins, food, and utensils. Everything seemed to be in order. Unsure of what to make of Dottie's unusual behavior, she lowered her fork back down to the table and waited patiently.

Dottie stood before her and stared hard, arms folded across her massive chest. Sally found her actions uncharacteristic and somewhat concerning considering she eats here ten times a week and Dottie can barely slow down at her table long enough to drop off the food. Curious, Sally set her fork down on her plate and reached for a napkin.

"Something on your mind, Dottie?"

"I don't like talking much." Dottie irritably spat out the understatement.

"That's ok. I do enough talking for the both of us." Sally eased back in the booth, smiled and tried to make her feel comfortable, warning her eyes not to look down at the breakfast that was now growing cold. Whatever it was must be good. Chances were Dottie wasn't going to inquire about her nonexistent love life or share some scandalous gossip.

"People are idiots." She finally declared to Deputy Hiller who happened to agree. "They think that because I don't talk, I can't hear." She shrugged her shoulders all the way up to her ears. "I learned long ago to shut up and mind my own business. No one ever takes my advice anyway. If they are going to screw up their lives, let them. Sometimes I want to take Bruno's iron skillet and crack them over the head with it, but I hold back."

Sally pursed her lips together and nodded. "I'm glad to hear that Dottie." This time her left eye shot a quick look at her bacon. She'd give her three more minutes and then she was cleaning her plate.

"The Harrison boys come in on Sundays with the old lady, always talking death and other weird shit. They're like the damn Adams Family. Anyway, they've been messing with that new owner of Huddelstone and once they finish with her, the Buzzard's going run in and snatch her up."

With her civic duty completed and her conscience clear, Dottie marched off to her next table.

Chapter 48

Getting comfortable and settled in the Adirondack chair out back took a little creativity and a lot of hard work.

Ironically for all her mothers' insistence that she stay to help, she was never actually around when she needed her. She ran out the door earlier that morning bearing a close resemblance to Greta Garbo, sporting enormous sunglasses and a tightly wrapped scarf around her head and hollered back something about redecorating the cabin to something at least shabby chic.

Bretta loudly exhaled an exhausted puff of air as she finally managed to prop a beach towel under her leg to help bring down some of the swelling. A pillow would have been a better choice but she didn't relish the thought of hobbling all the way to one of the bedrooms and back again when a towel was right next to her.

Her daughter's voices started to drift out softly from the thick woods in front of her and became louder until they soon materialized on the path.

"Oh, hi Mom. It's good to see you relaxing." Iris called out.

Bretta had to laugh at her daughter's take on the situation, like this was a trip to a day spa. There was no point in terrifying them, not yet anyway.

"Were going in to get a snack, do you need anything?" Iris kneeled next to her, concerned.

"No, I'm fine girls. Go on in and get yourself something to eat."

She could feel Ivy staring at her and knew she might as well get it over with. Questions have been mounting in her daughters head since she picked her up from the Muncy's house.

"Yes Ivy?"

"When can we tell Dad we are here?"

"I'm not sure." That much was true. "Let's wait and get settled in a little first."

"You don't think he had anything to do with that break in, do you?"

"I will let your father know we are all okay."

Ivy rolled her eyes. "Well, that's not exactly answering my question. I get that he is not like other fathers and that you cover for him." Her hand went up to stop her mother from interrupting, a trick she must have picked up from her grandmother. "I understand much more than you think. Oh, and thanks for having Chuck get my bike. He is awesome; no wonder why dad likes him."

"What?" Bretta called after her daughter who was almost in the cabin. "What do you mean Dad likes him? Dad doesn't know Chuck."

Ivy gave her a weird look as she paused at the door. "Yes, he does. Chuck works for Dad, I saw him before at his office. He even fixed my bike, unless you had Mr. Marc do it."

Ivy disappeared into the cabin and let the screen door slam loudly behind her and Bretta immediately dialed her mother's number.

"Chuck used to work for John?" The words rushed out of her mouth the instant her mother's voice come on the line.

"Chuck?"

"The driver that drove us here to the cabin?" She reminded Luisa.

"Oh, that Chuck. Not that I'm aware of. Why do you ask?"

"Ivy told me. She saw him at John's office."

"It could be a coincidence." Luisa suggested calmly but without conviction.

"You don't believe that any more than I do."

After hanging up with her mother she examined the bikes. Ivy had been right, her bike had been repaired. Her phone rang and she answered automatically, assuming it was her mother calling back.

"Bretta," Stan's relief was genuine. "Are you ok?"

She hadn't thought she wanted to talk to him but there he was and she found herself happy to hear his voice.

"I'm fine." *Fine* might have been pushing it a bit, but she felt safe and reasonably content.

"Where are you, Bretta?"

"No, really I'm fine." To her disgust her voice cracked slightly.

"Tell me where you are, I'll be right there. I can help you."

"Yeah, I saw how you helped me."

"I had nothing to do with putting you there, I swear." He hesitated slightly. "It was Kuster."

"Kuster! Are you kidding me? What, is that some kind of joke? I'd trust my life to him."

"Well you'd be sorry if you did. You can't keep running."

"I'm sure going to give it my best." She glanced around the yard like she was considering giving it a try right now.

"Why not just stay put for a while? Let me help you."

Suddenly she felt chilled and exposed out in the open. "It's not safe here." She whispered. As soon as she said the words out loud, she knew them to be true.

"Why isn't it safe Bretta?"

"He already knows we are here. He even fixed Ivy's bike. We have to get out of here. I'm not feeling good." No good-byes, she simply ended the call and closed her eyes to stop the spinning.

⅄

Pacing was sometimes helpful so Stan gave it a try by wearing out a path around the perimeter of his desk and tried to guess who Bretta had been talking about. He assumed her husband. He picked up his empty mug, made his way over to the coffee pot and grabbed the can of crummy ground coffee the department punished them with. Maybe he could get Harrison to run him over some of his special blend. When the water started to gurgle down through the machine, something occurred to him.

The bike.

Bretta had said Ivy's bike was fixed, but he saw that the girl's bikes had been left behind at Huddelstone. He had gone through every inch of that house for some hint of where they might have gone and he remembered seeing the bikes.

The report was somewhere on his desk and started digging through endless files and papers. Why in the hell did Kuster have to be the bad guy? He's come to rely on his handy organizational skills. He finally found what he needed buried in a stack of reports that needed to be entered into computer.

He quickly devoured the report.

Two girl's bikes in yard. Neither had looked broken, but then he didn't take them out for a spin.

So if Bretta had them with her now, then she must have come back for them which means she couldn't be that far away.

He tried her number again and found it turned off.

There were not too many places to hide in a town this size. If the townsfolk get a whiff the law is looking for her there won't be a corner small enough for them to hide in. The Berryman's are still newcomers who always seem to be surrounded with suspicion and trouble.

His cell phone wrecked his train of thinking and he grabbed for it fast, not bothering with the caller ID.

"Yeah, Sheriff Meyers here."

"Good morning, Sheriff, Dr. Berryman here."

He stopped reading and sat on the edge of the desk, a bit stunned at the coincidence. "Yes, Mr. Berryman. What can I do for you?" It was childish of him he knew, to withhold the Doctor title just to piss the man off.

"I was rather hoping that you found my wife and children."

"I was not aware they were lost, Mr. Berryman."

"You know very well that Bretta took the girls and is hiding somewhere. She is not a stable woman, you need to capture her and bring me the kids before she hurts them."

"Capture her? She's not a fugitive, Mr. Berryman, and I don't believe your children are in harm's way. Most likely she is recovering somewhere, perhaps went to visit some family."

He let out an extended dramatic sigh. "I didn't want it to come to this, but I am afraid you leave me little choice. I will have to bring in outside help. I am well connected in Detroit and New York."

"I am sure you are doing what you feel is best."

"You are in way over your head you know; you have no idea how to handle a woman like Bretta."

He wondered if the doctor was speaking figuratively or if he was trying to be clever and this was his way of saying he knew there was something going on.

"She is delusional, a hypochondriac, and a threat to society."

"I'll keep all that in mind."

"Please forgive me for being so frank, but I hardly doubt that a small town Sheriff is qualified in a situation like this. You'll waste hours of your understaffed department's time chasing after phantom burglars or her peeping Tom's, not seeing the quandary that is right in front of your eyes."

"And what is that?"

"That my wife is not right. I know it, her family knows it and deep down, she knows it. Don't underestimate her Sheriff; she needs to be brought in before someone gets hurt. You're simply a bunch of Keystone cops running around like a pack of fools; I would allow the experts in to help you if I were you."

"Hey, thanks for the recommendations. Coming from such an important, well connected doctor, that means a lot."

"I can see you're not taking me serious."

"No really, I am. Jotted it all down here on paper." He tapped his pencil on the pad loudly. He wanted to be sure he had every word right. It was dated and timed along with where the call took place; he was funny about keeping track of little details like that.

"Well then, Sheriff," his tone suddenly turned dark. "We'll just see who finds her first."

Chapter 49

Her cheesy eggs lost some of their appeal when they turned cold, but there was no way in hell she was going to waste it. Her mother taught her to always clean her plate and by golly, she always did just that.

She couldn't wait to rat out Harrison, the asshole, and his squirrelly family and the very second she was back in her car she went for her phone. It would have been so much more fun to detour over to Harrison's and have a chat with Billy boy herself, but she was already running late for her appointment and besides, his uptight disposition always managed to bring out the worst in her.

Stan barked out a hello on the second ring, sounding like he had rusty nails for breakfast.

"Good morning...did you need me to bring you some coffee?"

He looked across the room at the full pot he had forgotten about. "No, I made some, I just haven't any yet. I was busy on the phone with a concerned citizen." He said somewhat sarcastically.

"Musta had a lot of concerns to put you in this foul of a mood."

"Mr. Berryman called to tell us his wife is crazy and dangerous and we are too busy running around with our heads up our keesters to notice. He's going to send someone in to help us, since our lack of expertise is showing."

"Well, that was mighty thoughtful of him."

"I thought so. You talk to Ellie Johnson yet?"

"On my way right now. I stopped for a quick breakfast first and had an interesting talk with Dottie."

"With who?"

"Dottie, you know the owner of the diner."

"Oh." He paused briefly. "I've never known her to talk much."

"Well, apparently today she had something to say." She filled him in on Harrison and their odd dining conversation.

"Hmm." He sniffed the burnt substance in the pot that closely resembled the muck at the bottom of the pond he likes to fish in and clicked off the machine. "Maybe I'll drop by and see Harrison. Let me handle this Sally. Last thing I need is for you to is get pissed off and shoot him."

⅄

Betty Grime's sister resided in Regency Hills, one of the finer mobile home parks of her town. Sally allowed her cruiser to roll slowly on through the small community and noticed that only about three quarters of the homes had an address visibly posted. The rest apparently tried hard to discourage folks from dropping by unannounced. Overall the homes gave the impression that they received a decent amount of attention and thus far, no one gave her an unwelcoming hand gesture which she took to be a good sign. As she made her way further down the main road she came across about four or five residents standing outside their trailers enjoying the lovely summer morning that upon seeing a police cruiser, suddenly decided to slip quietly away.

Ms. Grimes had proudly mentioned over the phone that her domain was a double-wide, making it standout somewhat from the other single wide mobile homes and Sally noted unkindly to herself the same could be said about her rear end when she answered the door.

"Ellie Johnson?" Deputy Hiller asked politely though there was no doubt this was Betty's sister, the resemblance was unnerving. Their faces were almost identical and each had the same dark black hair only Ellie's appeared to have been recently chopped off with garden sheers.

"I'm Deputy Hiller, we spoke on the phone. May I come in?" She lifted the large cardboard box in her hand to show her offering which produced a happier grunt from Ellie.

"I sure hope those aren't store bought and you at least took the time to stop at a bakery." Ellie was eyeballing the box like she skipped her last two meals and Sally had a feeling she would have eaten week old donuts from the thrift store, box and all, if that was what she brought.

"Only the finest for Betty's sister. These were made fresh at Dottie's Diner this morning."

"Well, I should hope so." She snatched the carton out of the Deputy's hand and turned away from the door. "Might as well come in."

Ellie wasn't much of a house keeper; either that or a tornado had recently ripped through her double-wide.

"I've been too distraught to clean lately, with my sister missing and all." She pointed to the sofa that was piled high with clothing, magazines, and other unidentifiable debris. There was a strong smell of old bacon grease and cat pee. "You can just throw that stuff on the floor or we can sit at the kitchen table."

Sally opted for the plastic kitchen chair, thinking somehow it might be cleaner. She never met anyone messier than she was and it gave her the sudden urge to run home and scrub her house down, a feeling she was sure would pass once she got back home.

"You have a cat?" Sally asked, looking around the cluttered kitchen as if a feline might suddenly appear and jump on her lap.

"No, why'd you ask?"

"No reason in particular." Sally replied with a pleasant smile but not totally convinced there wasn't some kind of animal living under all this mess.

Ellie plunked down at the table in front of her with a loud exhalation.

Not knowing Ellie's preferences, she picked out two of everything Dottie had and so far she seemed pleased with the selection. She allowed Ellie some time with her snack while she sat back patiently and admired the stunning ceramic pig collection that took up every available counter and shelving space.

"When was the last time you heard from Betty, Ellie?"

She licked her fingers and gave it some thought. "Well, about two weeks ago when she was coming for a visit and she was supposed to bring me donuts."

"She never made it?"

"She made it, *finally*, but she never brought the damn donuts or anything else for that matter! I waited until almost ten o'clock for her."

"What happened to her?"

Betty's sister picked through the donut box like it was a Whitman Sampler and did not bother to look up. "Hell, I don't know. She was off playing amateur detective while I sat here worried sick about her. You know how it is when you have a taste for something and you wait all night for it, and then you don't get it? "

"Sure, I can relate to that." Food was pretty much always on her own mind so she wasn't about to judge. "Could you elaborate on how she was playing detective?"

"Huh?"

"How was she playing detective, Ellie?"

"Oh. When she stopped at the 7 Eleven, she saw him come out of the store and followed him all over town, forgetting all about her sister that was waiting for her." She shook her head in disgust. "I didn't know why she would give a shit."

"Who did she follow?"

"I don't know and frankly, I don't care. Some hot shit in a sports car. Had a little bimbo he took along on car rides like a prized poodle, just the sight of her ticked off Betty something awful."

"Can you tell me anything about the man? Like where she knew him from? Did she describe him to you?"

"No. He didn't live around here, I can tell you that. She said he was a stuck up fancy dresser. But that's all I know. I didn't ask more about it because I was too irritated with her."

"And she just followed him that one time, from the 7 Eleven?"

"Hell no! She acted like some kind of stupid Nancy fucking Drew! Hiding out in trees, spying on him. She was pretending she was Wanda, but she wasn't nearly as good. I knew she was planning on setting up a meeting with him." She shook her shaggy hair and powdered sugar went flying. "Dumbest idea I ever heard of. I am sure she met up with him and he killed her."

"So you don't know if the two ever actually met."

"I just said I was sure she did. Don't you pay attention?" Her eyes narrowed to two tiny slots. "You're staring pretty hard at my donut, Deputy. I know you people like these things. You want one?"

"No, I'm good. Thanks."

Ellie looked relieved and helped herself to another.

"So after the episode about two weeks ago where your sister kept you waiting, when did you talk to her last?"

"About a few days after that I think. She called me up to brag that she would be able to retire soon."

"Really? Do you know what she planned on doing?"

"No, she didn't say and I didn't ask."

"What about the girl he was with? What else can you tell me about her?"

"I don't know about her either. But I'll tell ya what, if you see a fancy pants driving around town in a red sports car with a bitch in heat named Fifi, then you got your man!"

Chapter 50

Stan knocked softly on the back entrance on Harrison's Funeral Home and let himself in. No one rushed to greet him today.

The usual smothering silence that he had come to expect had been replaced with Mother Harrison's scratchy and somewhat shaky voice belting out off- key church hymns on an old organ.

Wandering down the hall he could make out muffled, angry male voices battling to be heard over the dreadful music.

One of the voices he knew belonged to Bill. He had a distinct way of speaking, even in a heated discussion, which came across like he was scolding you for having lint balls on your suit. Stan leaned against the wall and stood silently when another voice spoke up loudly.

"*We've wasted enough time already*! *I'll do what needs to be done. God knows you're not man enough to handle it!*"

He assumed that was Bill's brother, Bob. Aka, the Buzzard as Kuster had referred to him.

Abruptly the music stopped and was replaced by a coughing jag that sounded almost as bad as the music.

"*You don't get to make decisions, I do. Keep your mouth shut and stay out of trouble.*" Bill's growing impatience demonstrated in his voice. "*Now get back to work, you have a pick up.*"

"You're not in charge of anything Bill. Not a damn thing. Not of me, this business, Huddelstone or what went on there. It's best you remember that or I'll be putting you in a box next."

Stan gave it a couple of seconds for the dust to settle before giving a light rap on the office door. After a brief moment of silence, Bill cracked open the door slightly and recovered nicely when he saw the Sheriff standing in his hallway.

"Sheriff, what a nice surprise." He straightened his tie and brushed off his jacket as if he had been rolling around his office floor with his brother. "Come in, Bob was just leaving."

"Bob," Stan gave a friendly nod. "How's it going?"

"Just fine." His pale blue watery eyes shot an angry look at his brother. "I'll talk to you later. I need to get back to work." He replied with a forced politeness before turning around and quickly exiting the room.

No one would ever guess the two men were brothers. Bob looked like a creepy version of the Brawny Man stuffed unhappily into a business suit and towered over his petite brother.

"Sheriff, how about a cup of coffee? I can make us a fresh pot." He waved his hands over his table of coffee paraphernalia like he was about to perform a magic trick.

"I was hoping you would offer. The coffee around the station just doesn't taste the same since I tried yours."

Bill let out a little laugh. "I'm afraid I've spoiled it for you, Sheriff. Once you have sampled the finer things in life, it is hard to go back to mediocrity. It holds true with fine wines, dining, and flying first class. I think I'll make us a French Press today." He stood facing his table of coffee gadgets and looked animated over all the choices. He began measuring, boiling water, and arranging cups with enormous concentration while Stan took the opportunity to stroll around his office.

Stan stuck his hands in his pocket while he looked at the photos on the wall. "So, do you consider Dottie's Diner fine dining?"

Bill looked aghast at the suggestion. "I should say not! We stop in occasionally on Sundays, a treat for mother. Chester is in dire need of an upscale restaurant; however it would be wasted on these hillbillies. I attended a French Culinary school in New York and prepare most of our meals at home you know."

"No, I didn't know that. Your mother must appreciate that."

"No, she complains all the time. She would be happier eating the slop over at the diner seven days a week." He returned his focus back to his coffee concoction while Stan ventured around the office.

He noticed for the first time that Bill's office furniture looked like it came from Rose's store. The desk was old but in excellent condition. Possibly an antique, well cared for and most likely expensive. He was no expert in that area, but he worked a case before involving stolen antiques and picked up a thing or two. It was easy to picture Bill out antiquing on Sundays with a cup of his specially blended coffee in hand, hunting for the perfect armoire.

"What's your fascination with that Huddelstone house, Bill?" The words came out rather softly and not as an accusation, but none the less; a flicker of apprehension shone in Bills eyes.

His delicate, manicured hands paused briefly before pouring the boiling water into the glass carafe.

"It's true; I am completely riveted with that old mansion, Sheriff. Its nostalgia and architectural particulars have always captivated me." He stopped his coffee busywork and his face took on a dreamy faraway look. "We would stay for hours in that house, playing and hiding."

"Hiding?"

"Hide and seek. Kids' stuff, you know that kind of thing."

"I wasn't aware that you were friends with Anthony Barrett."

"We weren't exactly friends. This town did not offer much for kicks back then, not that it does now, but kids have those little games now days you see them walking around with and five hundred channels to choose from on TV. We threw rocks in the pond and watched grass grow. I don't have to tell you this, Sheriff, you grew up here. Anyway, when mother would let us out, sometimes we hung out over at Huddelstone."

"Let you out?"

He smiled nervously. "We were hard workers, we didn't get out as much as we would have liked."

Stan gratefully accepted the coffee and studied Harrison who was acting weirder than normal. "You must have known Mrs. Barrett pretty well then if you were there so much."

Harrison quickly brought his coffee to his lips and took a sip, a nice trick that allowed him to stall long enough to compose his careful reply.

"I knew her of course, but she really wasn't around when we would stop over. She was always busy with something."

Stan set down his coffee and shook his head. "Boy, someone sure didn't like her to mutilate her body up like that. Did you ever hear of her having enemies?"

"No." He answered too quickly. "She seemed nice enough."

"You're a bit older than Anthony, aren't you?" About ten years if his math was right, a considerable difference when you are that age.

He shrugged his shoulders as if the thought never occurred to him. "I guess so."

"So you knew Kuster then?"

His eyes grew wide, an automatic reflex in which he quickly recovered and replaced the look with one of confusion.

"Kuster isn't a local."

"That's right, he's not." Bill's obvious panic rolled into the room like an early morning fog as Stan crossed his arms, staying silent.

"I know who Kuster is, if that is what you're asking."

"No, I'm asking if you met him when you were hiding out in Huddelstone. He use to come here as a kid. One of those summer people."

"Sorry, I can't say that I would have met him back then."

Stan gave a slight nonchalant nod and walked around the room, curious to get a better look at the framed pictures on the wall. Slowly moving by each print until he comprehended they were telling a story.

One he had recently heard before.

A man in a tattered suit stood over a soldier on a table in a makeshift hospital tent. "That's a soldier being embalmed during the Civil War." Bill declared proudly. Another photo contained various glass bottles and unusual looking tools.

The next photo was of a lady sitting in a chair, sewing. Something grabbed at his attention as he took in the details, but he was unsure what it was. Finally, he got it.

The desk behind the woman. Slowly he took his eyes off the desk from the photo and moved them across the room to Bills antique desk.

It was the same. He glanced around at the other furnishings, not caring that Bill was fidgeting.

"This furniture all from Huddelstone?"

"I wish!" His hand flew to his heart like he had a case of the flutters. "I'm in love with the era and the pieces but sadly these are mere replicas." Bill ran a hand lightly over the back of his chair and then lowered his voice. "You should see my bedroom, Sheriff."

"I'll have to pass on that, Bill."

He turned away from the funeral director and continued exploring the grouping of photos, aware of Harrison's penetrating gaze on his back.

These pieces weren't copies; he was pretty sure about that. Rose should be able to find out how in the hell Harrison ended up with a house full of Huddelstone furnishings. He wanted to see that dollhouse receipt anyway.

He scanned the room again, slower this time. How could he have dismissed him that easily?

Suddenly the Harrisons were so much more than just an odd family. Right under their noses and living three doors down from the station was Chester's most bizarre citizens.

Until Deputy Kevin Kuster came along.

Chapter 51

The night was getting warmer and she knew muggier, even though the cabins air conditioner was cranked on high at her mother's insistence. The small unit did not kick out enough cold air to in fact reach her room or even begin to remove the humidity that was fast filling her bedroom like smog, causing her hair to form soft curls around her face.

The nightgown her mother had given her still sat unused in its pretty box and now rested on the white wicker chair in the corner of her room. She had meant to put it into one of the drawers earlier and had gotten sidetracked. The cool, silky fabric was so different from what she normally wore to bed, she decided to strip off her shorts and t-shirt and slid it over her head.

Ivy and Iris would have plenty to say when they see this she thought with a smile. They were bound to come in her room after their game of Monopoly with Grandma was over. It had certainly been awhile since she had worn something so elegant. Her thoughts drifted over to the Sheriff and she felt a warm blush darken her cheeks and travel down to her belly.

It wasn't as if there was anything wrong with the gown. In fact, it was quite exquisite. She made her way to the oval, full length on the back of the closet door to have a better look and let out a little gasp at her reflection.

The delicate shoulder straps showed off her toned and lightly tanned arms. The front of the gown plunged to a deep V, presenting an impressive amount of cleavage. Soft waves of curls lightened slightly by the sun almost touched her shoulders and she realized her hair must have grown over the summer.

She looked good. Too good and too young to spend every night home alone while her husband was off *working*.

Bretta froze in the mirror and held her own gaze, realizing the excuse she gave everyone else about her husband's extensive absence she now just gave to herself. *He was off working?* How about he was an abusive, arrogant, self-involved man that does not love you?

Suspicion started to creep in a few years back that she had been nothing more to him than a stepping stone to success, and then suddenly, everything changed. The doubting, confusion, and sickness started.

Taking a look around the charming little cabin, she accepted that this had not been one of her brighter ideas. It felt so ingenious and poetic at first, visiting John's former stomping grounds, but now she was not so sure.

A strong wind began to howl and lash in through the cottage's tiny cracks and crevices, generating an eerie sound that made her shudder. The thin, wooden walls vibrated from the heavy rain and as she glanced around she thought how easy it would be for someone to put an axe through the wall if they wanted too.

They would be much safer back at Huddelstone.

She could get an alarm system installed; new windows; maybe a dog and apparently she already owned a gun. Suddenly it seemed like the best idea she has had in a long time.

With her mind made up, she began packing. They could leave first thing in the morning.

"Mom, can you come in here please?" She called out, trying her best to sound normal.

"Everything ok?" Her mother's head popped up from the game board, her hand about to throw the dice.

"Oh, yes. I just need a little help with something."

Luisa entered her daughter's room and closed the door, a trace of Chanel Number 5 trailing lightly behind her.

Her mother looked suspicious. "What's wrong?"

"Mom, I've started to have some problems again lately, like before." No sense dancing around the subject, she could be honest with her mother.

"I see. And how have you felt? Physically that is?"

"Fine, up until last night that is. Then I felt sick again. But that could be from the pain medications and exhaustion."

"Explain to me what kind of problems you have been having. By the way, that nightgown looks stunning on you." Luisa helped her daughter sit on the edge of the bed and then did the same, crossing her legs like she was conducting a board meeting.

"Thank you, mother." She replied before filling her in on the sewing basket, the music that played for her, the bears outfitted in fabric exclusively for Ivy and Iris's and the man she saw out back.

"Go on." Of course her mother knew there was more.

"I found out that John used to spend his summers here in Chester as a young boy. He had told me that he randomly picked this spot for us to start over and to heal the family. One of the workers discovered a picture of him as a child, taken with Anthony Barrett who grew up in my new house." She ran her hands through her hair, disturbing the curls. "When I confronted him about all this, he said I was delusional and threatened to take the girls away from me."

"Bretta, John is a sick and cruel fuck. I've known this for a long time. It is only a matter of time before he finds us here." She pulled her little gun out of her pocket and pointed it to her suitcase. "Now pack up your things, we are getting out of here."

"Mother!" Bretta shrieked. She didn't know what she was most stunned at; her mother's bad language or the gun.

"Honey, he's been Gaslighting you for a long time now. I just couldn't prove it." She leaned against the doorway, choosing her words carefully. "Now he's going to kill you."

Chapter 52

Anderson Antiques apparently was set to thrive in any economy and Rose Delany enjoyed being the proprietress of such a prosperous establishment. She had a distinctive knack for sifting through discarded junk and recycling it into valuable antiques that always sold.

The memory bear business that started as a mere hobby to help chase away the blues now took on a flourishing life of its own and gifted her with a pleasurable sense of self satisfaction.

Life was good and if she blocked out her own painful past and all the dirt she was not supposed to know, she was indeed happy.

Rose bent under the counter and grabbed a few cleaning supplies. It was past closing time and generally that meant business would be slow to dead. Folks tended to settle down early in Chester.

Gently she swept the special lint free dust cloth over her prized nineteenth century Ladies French Writing Desk, a personal favorite of hers, and recalled the torrid love letters she found secured to the bottom of the drawer, expertly hidden. The heartbroken author had poured out her love and anguish to a man she could never have. Rose had discovered much about the woman that for a brief time in history had sat at this gorgeous desk and confessed her adoration for her best friend's husband.

She understood of course the devastation of having a secret so precious and dear to your heart you simply could not let it go, even though it would most likely destroy you.

Often it was difficult to look a neighbor in the eye knowing the forbidden love they once had or a shameful truth they carried with them. Oh the secrets she has accidently uncovered. They needn't worry; their indiscretions were safe with her.

The pewter bells clanked together boisterously at the front door indicating her time was no longer her own and she glanced over to welcome the Sheriff into her store. It did not matter how old she got, that man always took her breath away.

Sheriff Stan Meyers was the very thing that romance novels were made out of. Tall, masculine, strong, and incredibly gorgeous all in an unassuming way. His confident, street smart personality only added to his charisma and she found it charming that he did not realize that half of the women and even a couple of the men in this town were madly in love with him.

"What a pleasant surprise, Sheriff."

"Good evening Rose. Open kinda late tonight aren't you?" He smiled easily and let his eyes drift from one table to the next.

She gave her shoulders a slight shrug "I wasn't in a hurry to close up. Are you looking for something special today?"

"Actually, I was curious to see if you came across that receipt for the dollhouse."

"As a matter of fact, I did last night. Let me get it for you." She wished she would have lit her cinnamon strudel candle earlier today. A room full of antiques can smell rather musty. "I am afraid it won't be of much help. There's only a number on the receipt, no name. I tried calling several times and it only rings. No voicemail." She said as she handed over a white envelope.

He took the receipt and read it for himself.

"Thanks Rose. Hey, what do you know about the furniture Bill Harrison has? He said his office is full of reproductions from Huddelstone."

Her demeanor instantly darkened. "He's a weirdo and a thief. Several pieces I had my eye on from that house were mysteriously missing by the time the house went on the market and I was allowed in to look around. Poor Irma. I doubt she can rest in peace after being chopped up and then ripped off! She wanted me to have those pieces…I should've had her write out a will." Her index finger rested on her lips and her brows knit together tightly as she considered her mistake.

"Irma didn't care for Bill? I know he hung out over there for a while as a child."

"Hung out? He was hiding out! It was the perfect spot with all those secret rooms and tunnels, nice little break from that domineering, overbearing mother of his!" The words flew out of her mouth along with a spray of spit, noticeably still fuming about the furniture.

"Huddelstone has secret rooms?"

"Well of course it does! It was part of that Underground Railroad thing. They all spent quite a bit of time over there. "

"They?"

"Bill and I think his brother and of course Anthony, he lived there." She thought for a second and then appeared disgusted. "Wanda too. She was always hovering around, shoving those vast breasts of hers in everyone's face."

"Did you ever see Kuster around?"

"Kuster?" She asked, hoping she had heard him wrong. She along with the entire town had been hoping their new Sheriff would be a major improvement over that drunken bozo that held the position before, but now she was having some serious doubts. She'd never known anyone to possess true beauty and brains other than herself and sadly her attractiveness is not what it once was.

"Sheriff, Kuster didn't grow up in Chester." Her head gave a little shake. "Maybe if he did, those boys might have been steered in a different direction instead of getting away with murder."

"What exactly did they get away with?" It was difficult to picture Harrison being a hellion now or then.

She put her hands on her hips and her lower jaw dropped down in disbelief.

"Well you know, Sheriff; they got away with killing all those young girls. They never did find the bodies but I bet if you look hard enough you will find them in one of those hidden rooms at Huddelstone."

Chapter 53

He thought about Rose's off the wall accusation as he stepped up to Wanda Bee's front door and worked on removing the yellow crime scene tape that encircled the tiny bungalow that she and her aunt had called home for so many years.

More out of curiosity than any actual concern, he had been about to ask what she meant about the young girls but his cell rang and he took the call and waved good-bye to Rose instead. He sensed she was eager to close up shop for the night anyway.

What was with the women in this town? Had they always been this nuts or was he just now noticing? He considered his own mother and all those darn vegetables and wondered if he had stayed away too long or not long enough.

He had never heard anything growing up about Harrison harming young girls and frankly, he couldn't see him ever being interested in the opposite sex but if something did go on, he was positive Wanda knew all about it.

There was no way something that significant could slide under her radar.

He would run it through the computer later but a rumor of teenage boys murdering girls would have run wild through a town this size.

He sure as shit missed working with Kuster. His anger was slowly turning to concern the deeper he dug. He wasn't returning phone calls nor had he been back to his own house in almost a week. It didn't feel right.

Technically Wanda's house was not a crime scene; no murder had been committed within these walls but the bright yellow tape offered him the time he needed to go through Wanda's possessions at his own pace.

For someone that sold houses for a living he found it surprising at first she chose to never move out of her childhood home. But after his initial visit to the house he had decided it wasn't out of nostalgia or sentiment that kept her from moving on, but more out of sheer laziness.

Heavy, humid air mingled with the sporadic soft thud of thunder off in the distance promised a late night storm. He unlocked the door and used his flashlight to find the light switch on the wall to his right.

The inside was hot and stale with that peculiar odor that pairs with a house that's been closed up for too long. She had a lot of furniture stuffed into her small living room and he took his time to maneuver around a sofa, loveseat, Lazy-boy, and a fifty-two inch flat screen which looked to be her only recent purchase in the last two decades and was outlandish in a room that size. She probably had to sit out on the driveway and look through the window to watch it comfortably.

The smell of decay intensified as he made his way towards the kitchen, the source most likely rotting food in the refrigerator or pantry. The room itself was old and outdated and he couldn't help but think of Bretta's warm and inviting home. He recalled those new, shiny Granite counters he had wanted to throw her down on and felt his mood shift from crabby to downright pissy. He gave himself another lecture on how irrational and unprofessional it was to be fantasizing about this particular married citizen, but it did not seem to matter.

The ladies from the Christian Service group over at the church were scheduled to come in at the end of the week to clean and pack up Wanda's belongings. He was pretty sure most of the gossipy old bats used the pretense of performing a good deed to find out what dirt Wanda Bee had stashed away on their neighbors or perhaps even themselves.

He and his men had already been through the house and had conducted a methodical and prudent search, but before he invited the ladies in he needed to be confident himself that nothing significant had been left behind.

A home takes on a different feel when you are the sole guest. Surrounded by vacant house sounds he was not aware of on his last visit; the hum of the refrigerator, the clock on the wall and the occasional drip from the faucet, he found it filled him with a heavy, disheartened awareness.

He sifted through the stack of mail on the counter without much interest. They had been through this before and it wasn't as if anything new had been added to the pile. All Wanda's mail had been redirected to the station since she had no family.

The putrid stench that was now permeating the air became distracting and he brought his arm up to use his elbow as a mask. He was already testy enough without having to deal with a restricted air flow. Leaning over the kitchen sink he pulled hard and lifted the window.

He'd have to warn the ladies about that fridge when they came to clean. Bravely he opened it to see if there was something that could be removed easily enough and help clear the air. But surprisingly it was essentially empty with the exception of a few jars of pickles, some homemade strawberry preserves, and two bottles of cheap white wine. He went over to the cabinets, opened one and found basically the same thing; empty except for a few cans of tomato soup and one can of tuna fish.

It was doubtful she forgot about a roast in the oven; cooking didn't appear to be one of her passions. Cleaning didn't either. He noticed a dust bunny the size of a soccer ball wedged between the refrigerator and the stove. As he passed by the appliances he causally pulled down the oven door anyway and the stench immediately assaulted him.

"What the hell?" He swiped a towel off the counter and removed an old tin pie pan from the oven, careful not to breathe in the rancid air.

He let the tray slide out of his hands and onto the stove top and back, turning his head to the side to get his nose as far away as possible while he examined his findings.

A dead, decaying rat lay stretched out in the pan. Directly under the rat was a small white strip of paper with black typing. It reminded him of a high school science project at first glance until he read the note.

"I thought I smelled a rat."

This little offering could not have been overlooked the first time around. Wanda's house had been searched the day after she was found murdered. It took two days for her office to report her missing, her body discovered in the house she was showing on the third. Stan knew that by the third day after being in a house during the middle of summer, the rat would have made its presence known.

It had been about two weeks now since the house was last searched, so that meant that during that time someone carefully broke in, leaving no sign of forced entry other than a dead rat.

Was it possible that the intruder was unaware of Wanda's death or was the rat meant for him, knowing perhaps something was missed the first time and would be back?

He stepped over to the sink and gave his hands a good scrubbing before calling an officer to come to the house to bag it.

Next he snapped on a pair of latex gloves and cautiously made his way down the narrow, steep steps, thinking about the dead rat with its note and tried to conjure up who Wanda had pissed off enough to send a calling card.

He once worked a case in which a former Mafia family member had reluctantly turned into an FBI informant. The individual was later found dead in his apartment with a pigeon crammed so far up his ass, only its tail was visible. After the medical examiner finished up with him he called to say the bird had a 14 karate gold ID bracelet on its left foot that read *Stool Pigeon*.

The lower level of Wanda Bee's home did not look like an area she visited often except for the occasional load of laundry. It had a musty smell like one of the summer cottages by the lake. The washer, dryer, and wash tubs were located directly to the right of the stairs and in front of them stood an ironing board with an old, outdated iron parked on top. A clothesline ran the length of the basement, naked with the exception of a rather large white stretchy looking contraption draped over it that he guessed was a girdle.

On the other side of the basement stood a tall metal shelving unit which housed an odd assortment of can goods, a few rolls of paper towel, and several cardboard boxes.

She was not much of a saver. The upstairs of the house was untidy and leaned towards filthy, but apparently the only thing she horded was dirt on other people.

One of the boxes was marked "Aunt Maddie" which seemed to be all that was left of the only family member he ever recalled her having. Wanda apparently suffered a brief sentimental breakdown and threw together a random collection of items that must have triggered some emotion. An old ladies hat, a well-worn Bible which he had to assume did not belong to Wanda, and several dozen hankies. The box had been taped shut and stored away in the corner next to the furnace.

The other boxes held labeled manila files on just about every important citizen in Chester he could think of and some minor players that she had taken an interest in. She was organized in her efforts, each file was in alphabetical order and rather tidy. If she had another file on him other than the malicious one he found earlier in her briefcase it was missing.

Stan shone his flashlight up on the beams in the ceiling, behind the furnace, and even in the box of laundry detergent. It wouldn't be the first time he found an odd white powder stashed away in the soap box although drugs did not appear to be her thing.

Directly above his head was a laundry chute that connected to the upstairs bathroom. Why they ever stopped making houses with them was a mystery to him. He loved the idea of simply opening a little door, dropping in the days dirty clothes and sending them off to the basement. It was better yet when someone else did your laundry for you and it magically appeared washed, folded, and back in your drawers the next day. He seemed to recall seeing a hamper in Wanda's bedroom and on the floor in front of the washer was a basket of dirty clothes. Emptying out a hamper and dragging a basket down a flight of stairs seemed way too much work for Wanda. She insisted on driving her car through the annual town parade instead of hoofing it like everyone else.

He shifted his gaze up again to the small trap door, reached up, and tried to open it. When it wouldn't give, he grabbed a screwdriver from a nearby shelf and pried it loose.

He dodged to avoid the thick, yellowed envelope that came torpedoing down at his head.

Opening it carefully with his still gloved hands, he allowed the contents to gently spill out on top of the dryer. Several aging newspaper clippings, a hand written note, and a necklace with the letter *C* dangling from it.

He chose the letter first.

March 12th, 2010

To whom this will Concern,

"I know where I'm headed and I'm certain that it's only a matter of time before the others will be frying right alongside me. But until that day, I won't have them living in the peace and freedom that I was never allowed.

I must confess, my reasons for always being so cruel to the residents of Chester were not only monetary as you may think, but merely for the simple delight of observing their misery. I dangled their secrets around like carrots, threatening to tell thus ruining their meaningless lives. I kicked my Aunt Maddie down the basement stairs when I decided she had lived long enough, stole from all my neighbors and even set Mayor Milburn's house on fire but I'm still not as evil as those boys.

Of course now the boys are all grown up and went on to live their lives in separate directions and no one is the wiser. No more time for games.

I'll assume that it is you, Stan that found this note, just as Alice predicted you would. God knows good old Eb Perkins couldn't find his asshole with a flashlight and a GPS unless he thought a bottle of whiskey was hidden up there.

They let me live so long because they knew I would never tell. If I couldn't blackmail them, I had to leave them alone. Plus, I wanted to live. Even my shitty ass existence here in this God forsaken town was better than none at all.

Somehow though, the ends once thought to be tightly bound have begun to unravel and the culprits have found their way home.

All those young girls…that useless fool never put two and two together.

Let's see if you're a little smarter.

Wanda Bee

His hands froze on the letter and at the moment he felt none too superior to his predecessor. Murder, larceny, and arson had gone down all around him and he hadn't a clue. Some cop.

Heavy footsteps moved swiftly overhead and stopped near the foot of the stairs. The comfortable silence that had fenced him in shattered abruptly when a female voice belted out a terrifying scream which was quickly followed by an angry stream of profanities crass enough to make a sailor blush. He braced himself as heavy footsteps pounded down the basements stairs.

"Oh good, you're here." Stan said calmly as he put down the letter and picked up the necklace.

"You might have warned me, Sir."

He didn't bother to hide a grin. "And ruin the surprise?"

Sally looked wound up. "I hate rats. Rats and bats."

"I'll keep that in mind."

"Fitting though, that someone should have left Wanda a *rat*."

"I thought the same thing."

"What do you have there?" She noticed the necklace in Stan's gloved hand, fast forgetting about the disgusting rodent upstairs with its cryptic message for Wanda.

"A little something Wanda left behind."

Sally made a face as she promptly donned a pair of gloves. "I can't believe she wouldn't have found a way to take it all with her."

"This she wanted me to find." He handed over the letter for her to read.

She let out a loud whistle when she finished. "I'm sure she's right about the burning in hell part. Kicking her own aunt down the stairs and Mayor Milburn's house…you know his wife Mable died in that fire?"

Stan gave a nod. "I remember hearing something about a fire now that you mention it…I don't recall hearing about Mrs. Milburn."

"You see when this letter was dated? It's from 2013, a year before you even interviewed for the job." She let a little laugh out. "Not surprising Alice knew you would be moving on back before you did."

"She couldn't of." He took the letter back. "Hell, I didn't even begin to think about moving back here until a few weeks after the interview."

"Well, she's got the gift like Kuster. Everyone around here knows it…" She hesitated briefly. "You never noticed that, being that you grew up here and all?"

He recalled Kuster telling him that now but at the time he dismissed it along with a pile of other strange oddities his deputy rambled on about. "I guess I must have missed that."

He picked the necklace back up again, examined it, and passed it to her.

"What's the significance in the necklace?"

He could see her excitement intensify with each new object he presented. It felt a lot like show and tell in Mrs. Clark's fourth grade class.

"It was with Wanda's letter. I found that along with the old newspaper articles in an envelope stuffed up in her laundry chute." He went back to the aging article.

"According to this article from August 8th, 1975, sixteen year old Carrie Hines had already been missing for two months by the time this was written." He skimmed through the article, pulling out the pertinent facts. "Carrie Hines was reported missing from Lake Love Summer Camp after failing to return from a late afternoon walk. Last seen wearing cut off blue denim shorts, a red halter top, and a 14 karat gold chain with a small letter "C" suspended from the chain."

"This is Carrie Hines in this photo." He pointed to the young girl's throat in the photo. "Wanda's way of saying she knew what happened to the girl."

"We're gonna need to track down her family." She picked up another one of the old clippings and began reading. "Hey, did you read this one? Eighteen year old Katherine Mallard of Grand Rapids, Michigan, was reported missing by her family when they could not reach her at Lake Love and she did not return home that fall. Katherine was hired as a camp counselor for the summer and then agreed to stay on into fall to help with some of the adult retreat programs that were offered. Her mother, Madalene Mallard, left their hometown to look for her daughter herself and was never heard from again. At least she was still missing at the time of the article, it's dated October 26, 1978. Maybe she resurfaced since."

"There's another missing teen from Lake Love." He added and quickly picked up the rest of the articles and started skimming through them.

"What the hell's Lake Love anyway?" Sally asked.

"It was a Christian summer camp about twenty miles from here. I think it's a Boy Scout Camp now."

"You're thinking these missing girls are the girls Wanda is talking about?" It was more of a statement than a question. "We need to run this through the computer." She spoke out loud, but he knew her mind was working fast to put the pieces in order.

"Apparently not all of the girls were from the camp." He held up another article. "This one was a runaway. Doesn't mention the camp, although there could be some connection. Let's head back to the station and take a look at some things. I want to see if these girls are still listed as missing."

"You got it."

Stan's hand shot back out and grabbed the clipping he had just set down. "Well look at that."

Hiller stood next to him on her tippy toes to see the article. "What?"

"Look who wrote the article." His hands shifted quickly through the rest of the aging newspapers. "All the articles as a matter of fact."

"Wanda Bee was a reporter way back then?" Deputy Hiller counted on her fingers to help her along with the math. "What, she would have been about eighteen? What paper hires eighteen year old reporters?"

Stan re-read the articles again, this time more vigilantly. "Nineteen, but going on thirty. She had a unique style; bold, brassy, and smart, not to mention she had a keen sense of uncovering gossip. These are all small, local papers, not the New York Times. Shit, she's telling us she knows exactly what became of these missing girls, but she isn't going to share. We have to figure it out ourselves. She really was a heartless bitch. "

"Hmm…so Wanda confesses to killing her own aunt, tormenting her neighbors and arson yet she thinks she is not as evil as those boys. I wonder what boys she's referring to." She read the letter again.

"Anthony Barrett, Bill and Bob Harrison, and possibly a fouth guy that came for the summers I believe, but I need to check that out when I go back and talk to Rose."

"Harrison?" The word spat out of her mouth like she was trying to get rid of a bad taste. "You know I hate the weasel and would love to find him guilty of just about anything, but I find that hard to believe." She was thoughtful for a second. "He doesn't even swing that way you know."

He was pretty sure about that too but that didn't give him a free pass. "Doesn't have to be about sex. We don't have a single body so we don't even know what we are dealing with." He reminded her of the inconceivable acts of cruelty inflicted on another human that had nothing to do with sex.

"And are you referring to the Rose from the antique store? I'm not sure if we should consider her a reliable source, her and Alice are an awful lot alike, and not in the fortune telling way." Sally pointed out.

"Rose complained to me earlier that all those boys had gotten away with murder and that I'd probably find their bodies in the secret rooms at Huddelstone."

"That just sounds like another of her random, off the wall comments."

"True, but you know my feeling on coincidences."

"So who do you think is the fourth guy that came for the summer?"

"John Berryman."

"As in Bretta Berryman's husband?"

He answered by a nod.

"Really?" She looked doubtful for a moment and then perked up. "Hey, I forgot to fill you in on my conversation with Betty's sister, Ellie. She said Betty had been playing amateur detective and started tailing some guy in a fancy sports car. According to Ellie, Betty had become obsessed with him and had planned on meeting him. It sounded like blackmail although I have no idea what she held over him."

"Hmm..." He thought for a second. "Did she happen to say what color the car was?"

"Uh...yeah, red. I remember because I started singing Little Red Corvette in my head, although Betty never told Ellie what kind of car it was."

"John Berryman drives a red Porsche. He had it at Bretta's once and I saw him whip through town before."

"This all gets weirder by the minute. So Betty uncovered some dirt on Berryman which wouldn't be hard to do, possibly that he was involved with these girls' disappearance. But if that was the case, I wonder why she didn't go after Harrison or Barrett. "

"She might have. It's not like either one would file a complaint against her."

She went back to the old Polaroid again and studied the photo in her hand. "So this photo was in the envelope too?"

"No, it's from Bretta's attic."

"Ok…" Obviously not following.

"The night she was assaulted, Bretta found a shoebox full of disturbing photos of young women. The assailant fled with the photos, this was left behind. Didn't you read the report, Hiller?"

"There was nothing about a shoebox full of anything in that report. I read it twice."

His frustration flared again with Kuster for deliberately leaving the box of photos out of his report. Was it that he didn't believe there were photos to begin with or was it that he knew something about those photos he didn't want to share?

"Any word on Kuster?" He asked even though she surely would have brought up anything she learned on her own.

"No. This is so out of character for him…I don't know if I should be pissed off or worried."

"I'm moving towards worried." They had an officer working full time on Kuster's disappearance who so far has come up with nothing.

"If the girls in these clippings are still missing, what…are we thinking Harrison, Barrett, and maybe Berryman had something to do with it? And possibly Wanda?" Sally confirmed out loud, probably to reiterate how out-landish it all sounded that no one would have put it together until now.

"I know it sounds pretty far-fetched, but what I thought was another off handed comment from Rose mirrors what Wanda refers to in her letters. If there is any truth in this, I'm having a hard time believing that this has never been made public before. You know I'm going to give Perkins a call and see if he ever heard anything about this."

"I doubt that you'll find him sober enough to be of much help."

"Well, it's worth a try. I'm also going to stop by Huddelstone to see if we missed any other photos. It's pretty unlikely, the room was searched thoroughly but who knows?" He let out a heavy sigh. "Hey, did you ever hear about any secret rooms over there?" He started assembling the papers into one stack, not nearly as well-ordered as Kuster would do but it did the job.

"You mean like the Underground Railroad? That kind of thing?"

"Yeah."

"Oh sure, the local historian at the library said that Huddelstone had at least two rooms." Excitement filled her eyes. "Hey, I just recalled something weird. There was a Dr. Thomas Holmes that was like America's first embalmer and then we found embalming equipment. Then there was a guy named Henry Howard Holmes that was America's first serial killer. He had a mansion full of secret rooms and passages, now we're talking about Huddelstone's secret rooms…strange coincidence."

Stan frowned. "What, are you some kind of history buff too? Whatever happened to the normal hobbies this town once offered like fishing or bowling?"

"Nah, not really." Her eyes landed on Wanda's big ass TV as they walked in the living room. "I happened to come across it on Kuster's desk." Then she looked down at her shoes. "Accidently."

Chapter 54

"I'm not so sure about this now." Bretta whispered into the dark, turning to face her mother's silhouette. The air inside the vehicle smelled like dirty gym sneakers, wet hair, and a lingering trace of Luisa's expensive perfume. Rain continued to dance rapidly on the rooftop, reminding them the storm had not yet passed while the wiper blades cleared their path at a rapid, anxious pace.

"You mean going back to Huddelstone?" Luisa kept her eyes on the road, her voice low. Even in a sweat suit her mother was stunning with exquisite taste. A sort of a blonde version of Jackie O. Bretta reached up and self-consciously touched her own hair trying to recall when the last time she bothered to run a brush through it.

Ivy and Iris sat in the backseat connected to their iPads, the music so loud it escaped past the ear pieces, filling in the gaps of silence.

"I mean showing up at night, in the dark. What if someone is there?"

"Who would be there? John? No one knows we are coming back tonight. We will lock up tight and don't forget I do have a gun. I also think we should tell the sheriff we are back."

"I suppose you are right." She hesitated briefly. She might as well be honest. "Sometimes, it felt like I wasn't alone. I would get a feeling that someone had been in the house when I was not there and sometimes even when I was."

"You always were a little *sensitive* to things like that." Luisa exhaled softly, keeping her voice low. "You're a little like my mother...wonder why that skipped me?" She paused for a second, thinking. "She *knew* things. There wasn't much I could get away with growing up."

"Well, I don't know about that but I might as well tell you everything. I've been hearing music."

"Music? Like from the radio?"

"No, not exactly. I can never find where it is playing from. It's lovely and so familiar and plays only for me."

"Have you told the Sheriff that?"

"What, and sound like a lunatic? There's no doubt he is questioning my mental stability already."

Luisa pulled the car up to the end of Huddelstone's long, expansive driveway and Bretta was taken by surprise to be overcome with the comforting sensation of being home.

"Did you leave a light on?" A soft glow of light radiated out of the parlor window, reminding her of the old dollhouse at Rose's antique store.

"The kids probably did. I left by ambulance..." her words drifted off as she tried to block out the memory of being attacked.

Ivy and Iris were already jumping out of the car and running towards the house.

"Just a minute girls!" Their grandmother called after them. "Please come back and unload the car. I want to help your mother in first." Luisa stepped out of the car and went around the front of the car to open the passenger door.

Making her way to the side door to avoid the front porch steps was awkward and painful. The rain kicked up a notch, drenching them in heavy droplets of water while an occasional beat of thunder sounded off in the distance.

It would have been nice if someone left a kitchen light on too Bretta thought as she tried to navigate the key into the lock. After two attempts, it finally clicked open and her mother held the door for her to get through.

Stepping into her kitchen she felt how much she missed her new home. It's now familiar smell, the mixture of old and new furniture along with all the changes she had installed reminded her that every inch of this old mansion now belonged to her and this was where she needed to be.

Her daughters dumped a pile of their belongings on the floor behind her, clearly glad to be back.

"We'll go back out to the car and get the rest of the stuff. Why don't you sit down, Bretta, I'll get you a dry nightgown when I come back in." The screen door banged behind them as they hurried back out into the rain.

Glancing down she noticed for the first time her gown was soaked. She could get dry clothes herself; her mother did not need to wait on her. The hallway leading out of the kitchen was dimly lit and she leaned on her crutches for a moment as she tried to recall where to find the nearest light switch when suddenly her heart started to race.

She sensed a presence about five seconds before she heard it.

Too late to run or hide or to release the terror that quickly became lodged in her throat. Heavy footsteps were attempting to step softly at the end of the corridor, making their way towards her.

The image of her daughters running into the house and into the intruder almost collapsed her in fear; the urge to protect them became overwhelming. Hastily she spun around to go and warn them, tripping on one of the crutches.

Her fall to the ground was hard and painful, but the shriek that came out was to save her daughters.

"Get out of the house girls! Mother…run!" She tried to scramble to her feet as she heard the figure moving closer. She was not sure if the girls were back in the house, if they even heard her.

"Bretta?" A deep and concerned voice startled her and a flashlight shown in her face. "Hang on, let me find a light." She heard commotion by the couch and then the click of the lamp.

Her brain took a few seconds to match the voice to the man and when it finally did, she almost started to cry out of relief just as the room lit up.

"Shit." Was all he could think to say when he saw her collapsed on the floor and ran over to help her, tucking away his gun. "It's ok now. Let me..." He stopped mid-sentence and froze, his eyes fixated on her and his lower jaw dropped slightly.

"I'm alright. You nearly frightened me to death, that's all." She did a quick inventory of all her body parts and nothing new appeared to be broken, cut or bleeding. Only an excruciating jab of pain began to radiate up her leg. Clearly she scared him too. Either that or she must really look injured because he was staring oddly at her.

"Really, I'm fine." She reassured him again and then followed his fierce gaze that left her face and was now locked on her body. Maybe she had a gaping hole in her head and was now bleeding on her pretty nightgown and didn't know it.

The realization then hit her, along with a warm, tingly glow that journeyed up her body and tinted her face.

The beautiful nightgown that her mother had given her was slightly sheer and very wet. The strap on her left shoulder had slid off, exposing a good part of her breast.

Her face heated but her body appeared unable to move.

She saw his mouth open and then close, but no words came out.

Finally he found his voice. "I'll grab you a blanket."

"Over on the chair in the parlor there is a throw."

He was back in two seconds as the back door banging loudly announcing her family entering the house.

"Mom, are you ok?" Iris's voice shouted from the kitchen and then proceeded through the house to find her.

"Well, isn't this a nice surprise." Luisa glanced at the two of them, ignoring the awkward tension that hung in the air. "How thoughtful of you to welcome us home, Sheriff." She cast him a wicked smile and then asked her granddaughters to take their things to their room.

Ivy was not convinced. "Mom, are you ok?" She gave the Sheriff the evil eye and waited for her mother to explain why she was sprawled out on the floor.

"I am fine honey. I just tripped. Go ahead and get settled in now."

Her daughter tilted her head to the side and pursed her lips tightly before finally agreeing.

"I think I'll go and do the same, Bretta. Give a shout if you need something, like a dry nightgown." She left the room without waiting for a reply.

Once alone again, Stan tried to help her to her feet, avoiding her eyes.

"It will be easier if I carry you." His sturdy arms quickly swept her legs out from under her, ignoring her protests and effortlessly deposited her on the couch. The very scent of him made her stomach flip flop and she wondered what was wrong with her.

"Why are you here anyway?" Her question came out more like an accusation than she had intended, but the strange attraction she felt mounting towards him was irritating.

"I wanted to go up to the attic and see if I can find any more of those photos like the one I found and just take a look around." He sat down next to her and took out his little notebook.

"Take a look around?" Her voice rose slightly but her thoughts were centered more on the fact that their bodies were touching ever so slightly and she was practically naked. "At night in the dark and without my permission?"

He wavered for a second and then must have decided honesty would be his best option. "Well, mainly I came to see if I could find any hidden rooms. And I would have asked your permission if you would have answered your phone."

"Hidden rooms? Seriously?" She sat a bit straighter now, trying to decide if he was telling her the truth.

"I heard around town that this house had secret rooms and I wanted to come and look for myself."

"So you had to run right over here at the midnight hour to check out an urban legend? She looked doubtful. "What are you looking for?"

"Just checking something out. It's come up in a couple of conversations recently, some of the local kids use to hang out here years ago. So I take it you haven't come across any?"

"No, but I hadn't really looked either." It was something she had intended on doing, but never got around to it. Then it hit her.

"You know, I did see something odd last week. I was out back in the yard when I discovered a small cemetery. On my way back up to the house

I noticed a window without a curtain or a shade that I couldn't recall seeing before. It's between my bathroom and my bedroom. I remember I was going to check it out on my way up to the attic, but I forgot all about it until I was already up there."

"I'll go and take a look then." He responded softly and then hesitated. "If you don't mind me asking, where's your husband?"

"John?" The question caught her off guard although she knew it wasn't an unreasonable thing to want to know. Her forever absent spouse had to be a hot topic in this small town. "He hasn't moved here yet." A small voice in her head warned her to stop at that but she already knew she would not pay attention. "I'm not sure I want him too either."

"You don't?" His pen froze in his hand and he looked up to meet her eyes. Suddenly the atmosphere shifted. There was no mistaking the sexual tension that swiftly filled the space between them. Like a match to dry kindling, a flame ignited quickly shocking them both.

She became intensely aware of the flimsy, wet negligée clinging to her body and even though his eyes were still locked with hers she felt her face flush from a warmth that traveled up from a place long forgotten. There was no more denying that there was a powerful attraction between them.

"No...I'm going to ask for a divorce." Her breathless declaration was the permission he needed. The forgotten pen dropped from his hand and he grabbed the back of her neck, bringing her head firmly towards his own. His kiss was deep and demanding as his strong hands tenderly explored everywhere at once and all she knew was she didn't ever want it to stop. She could not recall ever experiencing such an urgent and intense passion. She felt the heat from his fingers linger as he began reaching for places on her neglected body that she no longer thought about. Until now that is. She released a pleading whimper into his mouth that caused him to groan loudly and in one swift movement he yanked the lamp cord from the wall, covering them in a blanket of darkness. Carefully he swung her legs up on the couch and laid her head down on the pillow before climbing on top of her, his elbow bearing his weight. His kiss deepened and rushed down her slender body. His free hand tugged at the hem of her gown, releasing the silky fabric tangled around her legs and brought it up to her midsection, exposing her bottom half.

Her pelvis rose to meet him and the electrifying sensation was shocking to them both. She was semi aware of her lace panties being removed and started to offer assistance when he stopped abruptly, letting his forehead come to a rest on her flat stomach and let out a curse. Then he brought his lips to her ear, breathing heavily.

"I want this more than you can imagine." His speech was horse, his breath warm. "But I want to do this the right way."

His voice of reason in her ear snapped her out of the dense fog of passion clouding her judgment. Was she really about to have sex in her living room with a man she hardly knew? With her daughters and mother only a few rooms away?

Yes, dear God, she was. Thank goodness one of them had some self-control and common sense.

"I don't know what came over me." She was grateful for the darkness that hid her emotions which she knew had to be evident on her burning face. Embarrassment, astonishment, and what was worse, she was left with an unfamiliar emptiness.

He kissed her forehead and then her lips before slowly lifting himself off of her to a seated position, tenderly adjusting her nightie so she was not exposed.

"I thoroughly enjoyed whatever it was that came over you." He picked up her hand and lightly caressed her fingers. "Do you have plans Saturday?"

"No, nothing in particular." What did she even do on Saturdays now? Work on her garden and mosey around the house.

"Good. We'll go on a picnic. I have the perfect spot." He went over to the wall and plugged in the light. "Now if it's okay with you, I'll go on up and take a look around."

"I'm coming too." She sat up and grabbed her crutches off the floor. He was about to suggest she wait on the couch until he noticed the look of determination in her eyes.

"Come on then."

She hesitated at the foot of the stairs and wondered calmly how in the world one maneuvered the stairs with crutches when in one swift swoop he had her in his arms and marched up the stairs.

She shot him a sharp look of irritation for his chivalry but she had to admit it would have been a real pain in the ass doing it herself. There was no place to put her head comfortably so she let it rest on his shoulders, inhaling his scent which was now becoming familiar and did funny things to her stomach.

Once she was deposited on her own two feet, she steadied herself on a crutch and stretched her arm out awkwardly to flick on the light switch. The upstairs was notably quiet considering her mother and daughters were awake and in their rooms, her mother no doubt had her ear pressed against the door.

"I was thinking it should be right around here." She said as she inspected the dark paneled wall for some type of indication of a hidden room. "I should have asked John about the hiding spots in this house since he used to hang out here when he was a kid. Boys always find secret rooms and hiding spots, don't they?"

He looked surprised. "So you know then that John spent some time here when he was a teenager? Marc mentioned that you said your husband picked Chester randomly and sent you here house hunting."

"Yes, I recently discovered this. I have confronted him about it but he denies it of course."

"Any idea why he'd lie about that?"

"No, I don't know what he is up to. He was insistent about moving here, yet we have only seen him once. He said he has never been to this house prior to us moving here, yet Marc found a picture of him as a young boy that was taken in front of this house." Not that she was complaining about that part.

The hallway walls were laden with elaborate walnut moldings and she watched his curious brown eyes follow the line of trim, silently absorbing every detail. The scent of Murphy's oil soap with a trace of lemon furniture polish filled the air and reminded her of her childhood when she would return from school after their apartment had been cleaned.

"Where does that door lead to?" He pointed to the door with the shiny crystal door knob adjacent to the bathroom, carefully avoiding brushing up against her.

"That's a linen closet."

He quietly surveyed the rows of shelves with neatly folded towels and bed sheets before pulling out a cardboard box that was under the last row and set it off to the side.

"That's just a box of dust rags."

He got on his hands and knees and went for his flashlight. With his knuckles, he rapped first on the side walls and then the far back. Patiently he felt around until he found what he was searching for.

Bretta lowered herself to the ground in time to see the barrier at the bottom half of the closet give away, a shot of anticipation rippled through her as she leaned in closer for a better look.

Hot, disagreeable air rushed through the dark opening.

Stan's automatic reflexes were lighting fast as he blocked her from sticking her face in any further.

"I hardly think anyone's still hiding in the underground would be a threat to us now." She let out a little laugh.

"Most likely not, but I make it my policy to never go crawling face first into a dark hole."

He hesitated a moment and considered his options.

"I'll come back tomorrow with Sally to have a look around. We have some work to do first at the office so I'll call first before coming over." Stan proceeded to walk to the top of the stairs, avoiding eye contact. "I can see myself out so you don't have to do the stairs again."

"Thank you. I'll see you tomorrow." He turned around to face her and after several quiet seconds, reached out his hand and lightly caressed her cheek.

He pounded down the stairs and gave a shout up over his shoulder. "I'll lock up."

Upon hearing the click of the lock, she went to her bedroom and let her body cautiously fall on top a heavenly, feather filled comforter she had recently purchased online. It had promised to be cool in the summer and warm in the winter and right now it felt like a giant fluffy cloud under her bruised and tender body. She was going to rest her mind and body and the best thing for her she knew, was to not think. Nor replay what had just happened downstairs. She knew she needed to get her life in order before she started a new relationship with any man but the mere thought of Stan filled her stomach with the nervous fluttering of butterflies.

The decorative Euro pillows that artfully adorned her bed felt remarkably comfortable and a peculiar contentment washed over her. Dreamily she gazed up at the ceiling and watched the moon cast out curious shadows onto the ceiling while the fragrant, evening breeze played with the bedroom curtains, sending them dancing into the room. She focused her awareness on their gentle swaying movements along with the rich resonance of the wind chimes that radiated up the house from somewhere in the yard and floated into her room. The combination manufactured a swift lullaby and within minutes she began to drift to sleep.

Suddenly her eyes flew open wide with a question, her heart pounding almost painfully.

How was she hearing wind chimes?

Certainly it was possible that one of the neighbors recently added them to their outside décor but it was extremely unlikely. The houses on either side of her happen to belong to elderly, widowed gentleman who rarely ventured outside let alone would start ornamenting their property with garden gnomes and chimes.

She bolted upright in bed and tried to recall what she saw the last time she was in the yard. There definitely were not chimes out in her yard or anywhere else within hearing distance or she would have noticed.

She made her way to stand in front of the open window just as a strong, balmy breeze burst through the screen, sending her hair and gown to flow freely behind her.

The garage light had been left on, illuminating a good portion of her property and there, under one of the elm trees were indeed wind chimes.

Long tubes of shiny aluminum that closely resembled the Corinthian Wind Chimes she had considered buying but never got around to doing so, glistened brightly under the glow of the moonlight.

There was nothing scary or forbidding about having wind chimes in your yard. In fact she had always cherished the tranquility from perfectly pitched chimes and had even checked out a few online sites a few weeks ago, searching for the perfect sound. She had found a site that allowed you to listen to each pair, however she could not narrow down her favorite melody so she decided to come back to the site another day.

But what she was starting to find frightening was for the life of her she could not recall purchasing them and had no idea how what appeared to be the exact pair she had considered buying ended up hanging from a tree in her backyard.

"Dear God," Her trembling hands covered her face as she struggled to come to terms with what was now beginning to look like her reality.

"John was right. I am losing my mind." The agonizing words escaped past her lips, her hands staying in place as if they cover up the ugly truth.

"I'm pleased you've finally come to accept that, Bretta." A deep, malevolent voice floated out from one of the rooms murky four corners, catching her off-guard. "You need help. I'm going to see that you get it."

"Shh." He cautioned when she was about to scream. "You don't want to wake the girls with all you're blubbering. You've already generated enough anguish in their lives, don't you think?"

"John! What the hell are you doing here?" She demanded, trying to hold her fury.

"What am *I* doing here? Oh that's rich!" He feebly attempted to suppress a laugh. "I have been coming to this house long before you even knew it existed. This house *belongs* to me, but then I thought you already discovered that with all your digging and prying."

"I knew it was you!" The disquieting image of the unsmiling little boy in the photo came to mind and she wondered if he would again try and deny it.

"Keep your voice down." He warned even though she had not yelled. "I know the bitch in law is staying with you." He lowered his own pitch to a whisper as his eyes took an unhurried trip down her body. "I don't recall you dressing like that for me."

"My mother gave it to me." Although her answer was true, it bothered her that she felt the need to give him any response.

"You know, the best summers of my life were spent in this old house." He looked around the room wistfully.

"I thought you stayed at the little cabin by the lake." Her reaction was instantaneous, pretending it did not sting that his happiest memories were not of her and the kids and she caught the quick flicker of amusement in his eyes.

"You found my little calling card then. I wondered what sent you running back so fast." He appeared pleased and then took a step closer. "I know every creak and crevasse, every hiding spot of this old mansion." He paused, perhaps to decide what to do with her. "Careful, Bretta, you're not smart enough to play this game."

"And what game is that?" She asked coolly, deciding to skip the inquisition, for now anyway, into his previous lie of never having stepped foot into the town of Chester.

"This house comes with many mysteries, most of which you will never know or could possibly understand." He offered her a big, toothy sneer and she couldn't help but notice he bleached his teeth again to an absurd shade of white. He looked like a ghoul standing there in the dark.

"I see you took the keystone cop on a little tour tonight. That was awfully gutsy of you."

She gasped loudly, not bothering to hide her shock. "You've been spying on me?"

He threw his head back and laughed. "Spying on you? I've practically been living with you! For God's sake, Bretta! Snap out of it! I've been tip toeing around you for three months now and you seriously never noticed?"

"What do you mean living here with me?" A disquieting sensation filled her, forcing her body to shutter.

"Someone had to watch out for you. Make sure the girls were safe or that you didn't burn the house down."

Her head was shaking no but her gut whispered something different.

"So you have been here this whole time? Where....hiding out in the walls?"

"I've been here with you most of the time, but I have my own place right outside of town. I needed a real bed, shower, and clothes; I mean I'm not the crazy one here." He started laughing, as if she made an amusing joke. "I couldn't just live inside your walls."

His own place? Was he kidding? His daughters have been missing him and waiting for their father to finally show up and all the while he has divided his time between the crawlspaces of her home and living like a bachelor the next town over? What in God's name was wrong with him?

She pulled at her brain for a memory or a sound of him moving through the house. There *were* times she felt she was not alone, that she was being watched, but that could not have been John. Surely she would have felt a certain familiarity to his presence.

"You insist that your family pack up and move to a town that no one has ever heard of and we agree only because you have totally humiliated us back home. But instead of moving in with us, you play a game of hide and seek? That's crazy! Why wouldn't you simply live here with us for God's sake? You're my husband!"

"Your husband, huh? You weren't thinking about me tonight when you were bumping and grinding against the sheriff. No, this way proved much more enlightening." His eyes locked intently with hers and he stayed silent, as she tried to process what he was telling her.

"I'm sure you thought you were quite the genius." He continued. "After all, the decedents of the house are either dead or have moved on. Your little history books you so diligently devoured night after night never once mentioned hidden rooms or passageways so you thought your secret was safe." He released an odd, abrupt laugh, causing her to startle. "I have to admit though, you surprised the hell out of me, first that you even found it and second that you'd stuff that gangly goofball in there. I didn't think you had it in you." He tore his gaze away and took it around the room. "It must be something about this house; it does tend to bring out the worst in people."

"What are you talking about?" She was growing weary trying to make sense of his gibberish.

"The sheriff's right hand man?" He offered as a way of explaining.

"Kuster? What does he have to do with anything?"

"I must thank you, that stunt was way better than anything I could have cooked up for you…you're going to spend the rest of your days locked up."

"What stunt? What are you talking about John?" If his plan was to totally confuse her, it was working.

"Curiosity is getting the best of me though. Why'd you do it? I mean, did he catch on you were nuts? Come across another skeleton garbed in one of your hideous frocks? I don't care either way, but I find I must know."

"Why would I be locked up? I haven't done anything!" Poker hot frustration surged down her body like an electrical current and her foot responded by pulsating in pain. The combination of his sparkly fangs and penetrating gaze picked away at her nerves and she wondered for the hundredth time what she ever saw in him.

"You really don't know, do you?" He asked finally after an exaggerated span of silence.

"No, John, I really don't know what you are talking about. Why don't you just tell me so you can leave and I can go to bed?" She cursed her bad luck that he would chose tonight of all nights to resurface.

"You're so fucking crazy; you don't even know what you've done." His taunting tone turned to one of astonishment and he stared at her in awe.

She was about to yell back at him that she hasn't done anything but marry an asshole but his new demeanor became unsettling.

"I think you've spent a lot of time making it look like I was not right so people wouldn't look too closely at you."

"But you're not right, dear wife. Your creativity is being choked out by your paranoia. You can't work so you play dress up with skeletons. You make up stories to the police, invent stalkers, and now you've killed the deputy."

"*What*?" No one would ever say that John had a sense of humor, but this was bad even for him. "Why would you say something so preposterous?"

He was silent now and she knew from years of attempting to read him, quite serious.

"You think I've killed the deputy…you mean Kuster? Seriously?"

"Really Bretta." He tested, watching closely.

"Really Bretta *what*?" She swallowed a frustrated scream and felt the overwhelming urge to run, as if she could.

"I happened to stumble upon his corpse today. He's starting to smell you know. You should have buried him out back with the others."

She shook her head hard to clear it. "What are you talking about? You're not making sense!"

He smoothed the sides of his hair down with perfectly manicured hands that she noted looked far better than her own.

"The deputy's body that you shot all to hell is decomposing. Even if I don't turn you in, which I will by the way, the odor is going to give it away. Didn't I hear lover boy is returning in the morning to look around? He's bound to recognize the stench of rotting flesh."

"You're lying." She whispered. "I don't understand why or what you thought you'd accomplish, but I'm exhausted and going to bed. Go back to your bachelor pad, you can come back and see the kids in the morning if you wish."

"Let's go have a look then, shall we? He's right where you left him."

Christ he was exasperating! If she did own a gun, now would be the time she would use it.

"Fine! Lead the way." She thrust the crutches back under her already tender pits and followed the man she once knew as her husband silently down the hall, careful not to wake the household.

Prickly hot anticipation skipped down her spine as they approached the closet door. They weren't going to find a body, but his determination and demeanor had her edgy.

All sorts of unscrupulous thoughts crowded her head and she knew it probably wasn't a good idea to go anywhere with him. She was about to turn around and hobble away when she became aware that he had walked right past the linen closet- secret entrance that Stan had found and entered the bathroom. Curious now, she stumbled in his shadow until he stopped and faced the wall to the left of the sink. Before she could ask him what he was doing, he slid the wall effortlessly, unveiling a large black hole just wide enough to allow an adult to pass through if they went in sideways.

A pungent bouquet of decay swept past the opening, igniting in her a primitive and almost forgotten instinct to pray, to plead for some type of assistance although she was uncertain as to why.

Vaguely she became aware of John retrieving an object off the floor and soon a ray of light whirled around the room, finally coming to rest upon a ghastly image. One would think her first response would be to scream and then to get away as fast as possible. But her legs suddenly felt stiff and awkward, making them impossible to escape on even if both limbs were functioning properly and her scream it occurred to her, was drowned out in a title wave of vomit.

He was still quite recognizable with his long limbs and sullied uniform even though he lay broken and rotting on her attic floorboards, patiently waiting to be found.

"Oh my God!"

"God can't help you now, Bretta." He reeled the flashlight around the room, probing in and around the shadowy corners before coming back to shine on a bulky object on the floor.

Rancid air rapidly filled her lungs although she could not recall having inhaled.

"What have you done, John?" She gasped in disbelief. It felt surreal, to be standing in the darkness with the man she once loved and trusted and a dead, decaying corpse.

"Save your performance for the jury." He kicked a small woven basket that she hadn't noticed before towards her. "The police will call this evidence."

A sewing basket, very much like the one Rose had entrusted to Alice for safekeeping, mockingly stared up at her. She was confident it could not be the same basket the ladies had been so fascinated with that day at lunch. Alice had promised to hide that one away along with the gun they had mistakenly believed belonged to her.

"This is simply old junk you found in my attic, it doesn't even belong to me." Bravely she locked eyes with her soon to be ex but with a fierce sense of foreboding and without glancing down, her injured foot gave the basket a slight nudge to gage its weight.

"Yes." He whispered softly, as if someone might overhear. "It's still in there."

"What?" She replied back almost as quietly, her heart skipping over a beat before she came to her senses. Surely he could not know about an ancient wicker carrier two eccentric old ladies were convinced belonged to her.

"The gun you used to kill Barney Fife over there. It's still in your little sewing kit."

A peculiar sound startled her, causing her to sway back on her crutches.

"No...you know I didn't do this." Her words were barely audible and the bizarre noise she now understood had somehow come from her own throat.

He smiled brightly with his hands deep in his pockets, no doubt thinking about her long upcoming incarceration. The maddening noise of the coins jingling in his trousers filled the quiet space.

"There is no way out of this, you realize that don't you? I almost feel sorry for you. Well, I'll be back in the morning with the authorities. Won't your new boyfriend be surprised? You'll want to say good-bye to your mother and the kids before I return. Wake them early to talk to them. I'm being exceptionally kind you know. I could simply call them now and have you dragged out in handcuffs in the middle of the night."

"John, be reasonable! You know I couldn't have done this."

"I'll move in here with the girls, but tell your mother to pack it up. We hate each other. I'll get live-in help, someone young and fresh with perky breasts...the girls will adjust faster than you think." His outrageous enthusiasm was intensifying. "Yes, this will all work out just fine."

Either one of them has totally lost their mind or she was dreaming. But with the roughness of the crutches under her arms, the throbbing pain in her leg and the putrid aroma that filled the air, she began to believe this nightmare was real.

"No one is going to believe that I did this."

"We'll see." He said over his shoulder.

And with that he vanished, escaping from the same hidden portal from which they had just entered, leaving her alone with Kuster.

The space felt quickly different without John; fear, death, and an overwhelming sadness infused the atmosphere along with an insufferable odor. How was it she did not detect it before? Panic began to lock her limbs and a multitude of thoughts flooded her brain at once, but one thing she knew for sure. She couldn't squander her remaining free time.

He would return as promised and take from her the new life she has prudently crafted and come to love.

She should have killed him and let him rot alongside Kuster.

Chapter 55

Stan awoke long before the sunrise without the help of an alarm, quickly showered, dressed, and jumped in his car and made it to the station in ten minutes.

He started with an internet search and just as he suspected, none of the missing girls in the articles were ever found. Neither was Katherine Mallard or her mother Madalene that had come looking for her.

He sure missed Kuster's organizational skills and as exasperating as Betty was, her absence had begun to be noticeable in the day to day running of the department. He lifted a stack of files and papers off the corner of his desk to make room when a little pink message slip caught his attention. Dated almost a week and a half ago and scrawled out in Betty's barely legible handwriting was a call from a police department in Detroit saying that Anthony Barrett's body had been found in a warehouse. Since it was too early to return the call, he went online to find out the rest. Anthony Barrett, age 35 died of blunt force trauma to the head, his dead body rolled in leftover carpet and dumped in an abandoned building. His badly decomposed body was discovered by a real estate agent who was there to survey the property before listing it.

He heard the front door open and seconds later looked up to find Sally walking in with two cups of coffee on cardboard tray and jiggling a white bag of something from the bakery.

"Cinnamon glaze donuts, made fresh this morning." She announced proudly and deposited both a coffee and a donut in front of him before setting up shop on her own desk.

"Sally, you are a life saver. Thank you." He pulled the lid off his coffee and took a quick sip. "Hey, Anthony Barrett was murdered." He rolled his chair to the side so she could get a better look at the monitor. "They found him in a warehouse in Detroit."

"Well that explains why I couldn't find him." She crammed almost an entire donut in her mouth and attempted to wash it down with a gulp of steaming hot coffee. Watching her eat was like having front row seats to a freak show. "So we got Irma, Wanda, and now Anthony all murdered and Betty and Kuster missing, everyone's connected to Huddelstone in one way or another." She shoved the remainder bit of donut in her mouth causing the last few words to come out a little muffled.

"Yep, that about sums it up."

"We have Bill Harrison and Berryman. Both on the suspect list mainly because they are so weird."

"Don't forget about the Buzzard." He said, remembering the nickname Kuster told him about. "He is up to something with his brother."

"The Buzzard…I did forget about him for a minute. I never see him around and he's hard to miss. The guy is huge. Hey, I like that Mrs. Wills you hired to fill in for Betty. She brought in some plants and homemade cookies."

"I didn't see any cookies."

"Well this was the other day. We probably ate them all while you were out."

"*We* ate them all?"

"Hey, I brought the plate back here for everyone." She took another bite of donut. "If there was anything incriminating or suspicious left in Huddelstone, I'm sure Mrs. Berryman would have come across it by now, don't you think? I mean she's torn that place apart."

"I did find the access door to what I believe is a hidden room when I went over there last night. Too dark to see anything though so I'm going to head back there this morning and take a look."

"Really?" Her face lit up. "I want to go with you."

"I think if we look hard enough and in the right spots, we will find some type of evidence. But that's not why these men want that house. I think they are a group of sick men and living there again would bring them back to a happy time in their lives when they could act out their fantasies."

The donut in her hand paused about an inch from her face. "What are you talking about? What kind of evidence?"

"I think we're going to find some traces of the missing girls and that girl's mother in that house."

"You mean the missing women from the newspaper articles Wanda had?"

"Yes."

"Hmm…that's an interesting theory." She put down her second donut and took a swig of coffee. "And how exactly did you come up with that?"

"Some of the comments from Wanda and Rose and the things we found in Bretta's attic."

"You know, I was thinking on the way here how we haven't heard from Alice. I mean, you'd think she would be calling to check on Kuster by now." Sally licked her fingers and then reached for a napkin. "You know how close those two are, with their little tea parties and all."

"You'd think. We'll drop in and see her before we go check out that room." He glanced at his watch. "My grandma once told me that all old people always wake up long before the sun rises. Let's head there now."

⅄

The stranger began to feel exhaustion seep in his bones but the thrill of the hunt kept him going. He yearned to step out of his hiding spot and stretch his massive limbs but even in the predawn light it was too risky. A stake out was a lot harder than it looked on television but at least it was proving to be fruitful. If he would not have been planted out here all night he would have missed the show.

Just as he was getting ready to call it quits, his eyes opened wide in astonishment as a male figure slipped out of the trap door with ease.

He hadn't seen or heard a thing about him in over twenty years but he would recognize that arrogant ass anywhere. Even from a distance the guy still had that know it all smugness that made him want to stomp on his face. It was hard to believe that there was a time a time in his youth they had called each other friends.

After the initial surge of shock wore off it was quickly replaced with rage. He's got some balls to come back to this house like he owns the place he thought as he watched the ghost from his past vanish into the night. Quietly he made his way over to the secret door and let himself in. Heaven...or hell won't be able to help him if he messed with his handiwork.

Chapter 56

"Mother! Wake up!" Bretta spoke in a panic through darkness into what she hoped was her mother's ear. "I need your help…John was here." She tried again, shaking her shoulder firmly this time.

"Bretta? What's wrong dear?" Her mother asked calmly, as if Bretta had simply awoken her to say she had trouble sleeping or a bad dream. But that was Luisa for you; she never displayed fits of hysteria or suffered from raging hormones like every other normal woman in America. Bretta heard a click sound and the little lamp on the nightstand lit up the room.

"Mother, it's John, he was in my bedroom tonight! He's killed that deputy and now he is going to tell the police I did it. He's coming back in a few hours with the sheriff and he is taking the girls…he's got it all figured out. What am I going to do?" Her wide, panic stricken eyes locked with her mother's and she allowed the gravidity of her words to sink in, assured that her mother would spring to life with a plan.

"John was here tonight?" She asked in an astonished tone.

"Yes! He's been here all along; he told me he has been living in our walls, spying on me. Now he's killed Kuster and framed me so I will be locked away."

"Just take a deep breath and lie down here on the bed Bretta. I'll be right back." She pushed her daughter gently down on the bed and gave her back a reassuring pat.

"I have to show you where he is...you won't be able to find it on your own."

"Don't worry about that right now; I'm just going to get you a little something to help you relax."

"You don't believe me?" This was almost as shocking as finding a dead body in her attic. Her mother was the one person she could always count on.

"Honey, you've just had a bad dream, that's all. You can sleep in here with me tonight."

"Follow me." She grabbed her crutches back and got back up.

"Let's do that in the morning, after you've rested." She called out after her. "And we can see."

When it was obvious that her daughter was not going to listen, Luisa sighed deeply and trailed behind.

⅄

Bill Harrison took enormous pleasure in rising before the sun did. There was something magical about that first cup of coffee in the pre-dawn hours. First cup always tasted the best. Some said the same about cigarettes, but he found the vile little sticks to be quite distasteful.

He went to work in the kitchen measuring, boiling water, and scooping coffee into the glass carafe all the while humming an old show tune. Another perk to being the first and only one up was that he could begin his day his own way. Breakfast was always thoughtfully planned out the night before, giving him something to look forward to when he awoke. Today's menu was simple, yet elegant. The burgundy silk robe was a good choice he thought as he approached the ancient radio in the far corner and flipped on the switch, filling the room with the tantalizing notes of classical music.

Feeling relaxed, he removed a bowl of raspberries from the refrigerator, peeled off the plastic film and poured heavy cream into a small crystal creamer. He sliced a plain bagel in half and put it in the toaster oven with the timer set for precisely four minutes on light and then began assembling the cream cheese, salmon, and cappers in strategic stations on the counter. Bagels and lox were more of a Sunday morning treat, but today felt special.

The dream he has passionately clung to for more years than he could recall was at last about to come to fruition. He would be moving out of this old, disheartening house and into the manor that he believed was made just for him, bringing along all the original furniture and treasures he has been holding in his careful possession. He had not been in favor of that woman making changes to his house but he had to agree, some were rather extraordinary and saved him time, effort, and a great deal of expense. Restoring all the fireplaces to working order delighted him. He envisioned himself reading in an elegant high back chair in front of a roaring fire with a glass of excellent Merlot. The kitchen however was a hideous mistake. Too bright and cheery, like something out of one of those old Doris Day movies mother forced him to watch.

A slight, unidentifiable noise caught his attention. The butter knife froze in his hand as he tilted his head towards the sound and waited. No one ever stirred at this hour, not in his house or the neighborhood. Deciding it was nothing, he went back to the busy work of spreading an even layer of cream crease to each bagel half when a high pitched squeak came from the direction of the yard caused him to pause again. It sounded like the side door to the garage had opened. It always stuck in the summer months.

Crime was rare around here. Most folks did not bother to lock their doors at night but he guessed it was possible that someone might be breaking into the garage. Boy, would they be wasting their time he thought as he turned off the kitchen light and went to the window. There was nothing in there but old, useless crap.

He waited a full minute staring out into the yard before deciding it was not worth ruining his breakfast over. If someone did want to steal their garbage they were welcome to it. He wasn't about to go running outside in his robe or spoil his morning. Besides, his coffee was ready. He started to turn away when the door he had been watching began to slowly open and a man stepped out.

The sky begun to brighten ever so slightly and while he could not make out a face, he could recognize that shape anywhere. His first reaction was anger. Why in the hell was he up this early? Well forget it. Whatever the idiot was up to didn't affect him so he would simply have to ignore him and pray he did not wonder into the kitchen expecting to be fed. He was about to turn the lights back on when something about his brother's behavior caused him to pause. Bob was up to no good, he could feel it.

"Dammit to hell!" Bill said out loud, fast forgetting about his peaceful morning ritual. He stared out the window in open mouth disbelief as his brother lifted a body out of his trunk and carried it effortlessly through the garage side door. He had a good idea as to the identity of the corpse. "That stupid moron!" He muttered under his breath as he stormed out of the house to follow his brother.

Bill stood in the entranceway for a second and observed in silent shock. He hadn't been out here in well over a year but his brother certainly had. Newspaper now served as privacy curtains and covered both windows, the place had been cleaned up and there were chairs and a table that he did not recognize. Tools he knew they did not own before hung neatly on the wall and on the long workbench lay the corpse. The air was thick with a lingering aroma of death that announced this was not the first victim the Buzzard had delivered here.

"What in God's name is wrong with you?" Bill asked between clenched teeth, regretting the day his brother moved home and back in his life.

"He was in the way." Bob said calmly without turning around. After a few moments of consideration he selected two different saws and stepped back over to the body.

"What in the hell do you think you're doing?"

"Don't worry. I'm not about to chop him up here. I was going to sneak him in the lab tonight when you were sleeping, but now there's no need." He turned and attempted to smile.

He could see why people were afraid of his brother. He had a chilly, disturbing smile that made one want to take a step back.

"You have killed an officer of the law!" He kept his voice low and controlled but there was no mistaking his fury. "Not to mention I'm sure you left a mess in my trunk." His hands clenched into fists at this side. "This isn't one of those little runaway whores that no one gives a shit about! They're already looking for him!"

Bob smiled and laughed. "Well, they should have looked a little harder. I found him fairly easily. He was poking around the hideout. I wanted to just bury him in the usual spot with the others, but that bitch and her kids are always around. Plus I saw her out there the other day snooping around. She'd probably notice if the earth was disturbed."

"Well that was commendable of you." He replied sarcastically. "The sheriff has already been here twice asking questions. You need to get that body out of here now." Bill massaged the throbbing vein on his temple while he thought. "You should have simply left the body where it was. Thanks to Betty, the entire town already knows Mrs. Berryman has some psychological issues. The body was in her house after all, they would have assumed she did it."

"I didn't want the police there tearing up the place or looking too hard for evidence. Who knows what they'd find…and that would open a whole new can of worms."

His brother was finally right about something. "How did you plan on disposing of him then?"

"I'm going to get him on the table and drain him a bit. It won't be so messy this way." He nodded towards the house. "Then I'm going to get my saw out and go to work, toss the pieces in a box and take a drive up north."

"Your saw?" An uneasy awareness hit him as he quickly connected the dots. "You killed Mrs. Barrett! Don't deny it!"

"I won't. She was in my way." He put a tarp over the body and then scooped it back into his arms. "Hey, get the door will you?"

"I just assumed Tony did it." He stood in unmoving shock. "You didn't have to kill her; she was always kind to us."

"Oh, *now* you're getting sentimental? She was old and useless and I wanted her out of that house, plus she knew too much. Now get the door!"

"Well if she hadn't said a word in all these years, I doubt she was going to start talking now!" Bill yelled as he held open the door and reluctantly trailed behind his brother across the yard to the back entrance of their funeral home.

"She was getting senile like all old people do. Who knows what would have come out of her mouth. When things settle down we need to start thinking about mother, she's another blabbermouth. Now please shut up about it."

"Really Bob?" He always knew his brother was not wired properly, but he did not think he had it in him to kill his own mother. "The residents of Chester start getting murdered or disappearing and you think no one is going to look into it?" If anyone needed to be taken out of the picture it was his brother and if his real reason for getting rid of Irma was so that he could live in Huddelstone, he was seriously mistaken. "I don't have my key on me you know." Bill said once they approached the door.

"I've already unlocked it." Sure enough Bill tried the handle and it opened with ease.

"Barrett's house always did bring me peace." Bill heard his brother say. He was probably the only person around Chester that did not refer to it as Huddelstone. "I like to sit up in the attic…it calms me down. Plus, I miss the game."

"Please do not mention the game!" Panic quickly grabbed ahold of Bill's gut, causing him to tremble. "Do not tell me your plan was to take over Huddelstone so that you could revive that sick and twisted game?" He began to shake his head no. "We have put all that behind us. Buried it and moved on and I have spent a life time looking over my shoulder, ever so grateful that the Sheriff we had was a drunken, clueless loser but that is not the case now! You go kidnapping and killing young women again Bob and you will get caught." His voice crackled with fear and he knew he sounded like he did when he was thirteen, striving to reach puberty and caught his brother arch his eyebrows in surprise and disgust.

"Don't get your pantyhose all in a wad there Billy Boy. I said I sure missed the game, I didn't say I was going to do anything about it. Gee…you're such a girly girl sometimes."

Bill's insides turned to mush. There was no way in hell his brother would be joining him when he made the move. Their original plan had been to get the new homeowner out so that they could turn it into a new funeral home, but that was not actually ever going to happen. Once Mrs. Berryman was out of the way, he would be moving in by himself. His mother would not be around much longer to deal with and he would give his brother this house. His plan had been in the works for far too long and his deranged brother was not going to ruin it. The man seriously needed to be locked up again but since that never seems to last, perhaps he should consider removing him permanently.

"Hey, you'll never guess who I saw sneaking in and out of the trap?" Bob asked, changing the conversation without a care and then pausing to wait for his brother to catch up.

"Who?" Bill finally snapped irritably when it became clear his sibling was never going to tell him otherwise.

"Johnny." The word tumbled out of him breathlessly as he dumped the body onto the shiny, stainless steel table.

One simple word that grabbed ahold of his attention. "Johnny Adams?" He asked but already knew the answer. There was only one Johnny.

"Yep, Johnny Adams. Surprised the shit out of me to see him sniffing around there."

"Hmm...Johnny hasn't been around here in over twenty five years. He comes back, doesn't get in touch with any of us and then shows up at Huddelstone?" He said more to himself as he considered the implications. Bill then wrinkled his nose, making a face. "Honestly, Bob, why'd you wait so long to do something about him?" He took a step back from the corpse. "He's really stinking up the place."

"Christ Bill, you do this shit for a living. You'd think you'd get used to it. Anyway, it's only been a couple of days, but you know how hot it is up there." With practiced skill he went to the lower right side of the neck and made a small incision at the carotid artery and at the jugular vein and inserted the tubes. "Yeah, this is much easier this way, with the proper equipment."

Bill gasped. "You attempted some primitive form of embalming on Irma, didn't you?" He thought about the pristine Gravity Feeder he had drooled over in the Huddelstone attic and a particular conversation with the Sherriff. "Where in the world did you ever find those antiques?" He asked curiously, putting his outrage forgotten for the moment. "They were in superior condition."

"They were in storage over there at the house. I came across them years ago and always thought it would be cool to try them, like going back in time. It was actually a pain in the ass."

"Wait, I have a better idea." Bill grabbed his brother's arm to stop him. *Any* idea would be better than this half-baked plan. "Mr. Jamerson is being buried today directly after the 9:00 A.M. prayer service. It's a closed casket, no church service. We'll place Mr. Kuster at the bottom, under the lining and Mr. Jamerson on top and they can be buried together this morning." Bill switched hats easily from angry older brother to Mr. Funeral Director. "No one will open the casket but as a precaution, I'll lock it before I take it out."

"You've been watching too many of those stupid movies with mother." Bob gave his brother an exasperated look. "That's never going to work."

"Well if you've watched any of those TV forensic shows, you'd know that doing it your way is going to leave a measurable trail of DNA! And most likely a hiker or hunter is going to find those chopped up limbs and call the authorities." He squeezed his eyes shut tight for several seconds to control his exasperation. "Even if you bury them, an animal will surely dig it up."

He could see his brother mulling it over in his gargantuan head and for the hundredth time in his life, wondered if he had been adopted or switched at birth. He bore zero resemblance to his mother or brother. His father has been gone for so long it was hard to recall what he actually looked like, but from what he could tell from the two pictures his mother had, he did not take after him either.

"Alright." Bob agreed unhappily. He yanked out one of the tubes when he noticed his brother was already standing by to stitch up the incision. He stewed in silence as his brother took his time to meticulously pull each stich. "We're not performing plastic surgery here, just hurry the hell up and close the damn hole so he doesn't leak all over the place."

Bill gave a snooty look. "I am a perfectionist and take pride in my work."

"You piss away way too much time on details that don't matter and that no one will ever see. Hey, you know, I thought about Johnny the other day."

He commented as he pulled out the second tube. "I was sitting in my car over on Hollyhock and I saw this guy come out of that house wearing a business suit and for some reason I remember thinking of Johnny."

Bill stopped stitching and looked up, deciding to not get in to the fact that his brother did not own a car. "Really, why?"

"I don't know. At the time I didn't think too much about it, but as I look back, I think he resembled Johnny." He began to clean up the equipment and table, something he wouldn't bother to do if he wasn't under the tidy, watchful eye of his brother. "But now that I just saw Johnny, I think it was the same guy. He definitely came out the front door and I know the family was home."

"Maybe Johnny knows that new family..." Bill's voice trailed off and his eyes grew cold. "I heard the Sherriff talk about the new family and he said the husband's name was John. John Berryman." He shook his head. "No, it can't be one and the same. That's too far-fetched."

"What's too far-fetched?" Bob said, quickly putting together the pieces. "That he would move back here to Chester and change his last name? He was always weird as hell, nothing would surprise me."

"Rose had mentioned that Mrs. Berryman came here alone and has been restoring Huddelstone and that her husband would be joining them soon. He was a dentist and busy opening up a new office."

"Well that's fitting. Johnny loved to pull teeth out with pliers. Remember?"

"Yes, I remember." Bill made a face of disgust which then turned quickly into anger. "If it is Johnny, then that means that bastard got my house!"

"Your house?" He asked with ice in his voice. "What the hell do you mean by that?"

"I guess it doesn't matter now. I've been making plans to move there live by myself. The new furniture in my bedroom and office actually came from Huddelstone. I decided to keep the business right where it is and you can have this house all to yourself."

"You decided all this did you? Well, I have news for you; I want to live in Huddelstone too." Bob said angrily.

He sighed. "Well now neither one of us will be moving. Wanda had promised me that house. I can't believe she sold it to Johnny. He messed with her heart one summer and she never forgave him, but I guess she'd overlook a lot of things for money."

"Maybe she didn't know it was him. I mean, if he hasn't been to town much, she could have sold the house to the wife and not even known."

He pursed his lips together, surprised at his brother's insight. "Yes, that is a possibility. He certainly has kept a low profile until now."

"He's probably the one that killed Wanda and you know blabber-mouth Betty vanished, bet he got rid of her too. I wonder how Anthony is faring."

Bill released another dramatic sigh. "You know I would love to simply hand this over to the Sheriff and let him look into this, but if it is Johnny and they get enough evidence on him to convict him, he won't stay quiet."

Bob nodded. "I'll take care of Johnny. Then the only one left to talk to is Toni. I'll see if I can find him."

"Do what needs to be done then." Bill replied but his brother was wrong. After his brother took care of Johnny, both his brother Bob and Anthony were left and they both had to go.

⅄

"What do we do if we don't see any lights on when we pull up to the Muncy's?" Sally asked her boss, breaking through the veil of silence that held each captive in their own respective thoughts.

"Knowing Alice, she'll be expecting us."

Both took care to close their car door quietly but by the time they made it to the porch steps, the door opened wide.

Alice greeted them with a weak smile and dressed in somber black. She nodded and held the door open for them to enter.

"I didn't tell Athena you would be stopping by this morning. It's better to have her out of the way. Let's sit in the parlor."

Sally and Stan exchanged a look and followed Alice down the hall. This was a different side of Alice, one he had never witnessed before. Serious with a take charge attitude that was totally out of character, at least from what he knew about her. Maybe this was what she was like when Kuster came for tea. The coffee table he noticed was bare except for one lit candle in the center. No fancy cookies or pretty little plates of enticing desserts waited for them.

"I'm a tea drinker. Athena is the only one around here that would know how to make coffee and I wasn't in the mood to have a tea party today. I'm sorry Sheriff." Alice acknowledged his unspoken thoughts, another reminder of Kuster.

"That's fine Alice. May we sit down?"

"Please do." She sat down herself and waited for them to do the same.

"Alice, why didn't you tell me about Wanda's letter?" Stan asked, getting right to the point.

"You needed to discover that on your own. I knew you would eventually." She smiled sadly.

"How did you find out about the letter? I can't see you being tight with Wanda."

"No, Wanda did not have friends. Not in the true sense of the word. But as we get older and for some of us, wiser, we tend to think about our sins and what consequences they might bring."

"She wanted to know if she was headed to hell, is that it?" Stan asked.

Alice nodded.

"And what did you tell her?"

"I told her that I was sorry, but I did see her in a place that definitely was not heaven." Alice's face took on a look of pain, as if she was witnessing Wanda's destiny.

"No advice for her on changing her life or repenting before it was too late?"

"There was nothing I could do for her, she felt no remorse. Some people are born evil."

"What boys was she referring to?" This he believed he already knew, but he wanted to hear what she thought.

"Sheriff, you already know all the answers to your questions. Everything you thought is true. You need to trust that inner voice, stop dismissing it. Just because you don't like the answers that come to you doesn't mean they are not true."

What he thought really did not matter if he couldn't prove it. He put together the pieces from reading Wanda's files, but that wasn't going to hold up in court.

"Where are those missing girls?"

"I don't know. But I feel they are not far from here."

"They're all dead?" It seemed a stupid question, after all this time someone would have resurfaced by now.

"Yes, they are all dead. But their energy is still around this area."

He noticed Sally had stopped writing and with narrowed eyes, was gazing around the room and up at the ceiling.

"Why didn't Wanda tell me any of this? Was she involved too and did not want to be implicated?"

"She was involved to the extent that she knew what was happening but did nothing. She was there for it, but really did not get involved only because it didn't interest her. She wasn't looking to have the boys punished for their sins, but for ruining her life. And she felt that anything she had ever achieved only came to her with great effort on her part, so even though she wanted you to know, she wasn't going to make it easy."

"Why didn't you ever tell me any of this, Alice?" His voice remained calm, not reflecting his inner feelings.

"You never asked."

"Did Eb?" He asked, referring to the former Sheriff.

"No, but I did go and see him after the visions started. I could never find him clear-headed enough to engage in a real conversation but I told him anyway." She made a sad face. "He told me to go away, that he didn't want to hear any more of my nonsense." She paused briefly and then continued. "I told Athena too. I told her everything I suspected. She told me to keep my mouth shut because if anyone in this town knew how crazy I really was, I would be locked up forever."

Sadly, Athena was probably right. The former sheriff was not capable of dealing with any of this and the story itself, what he understood about it anyway, was so farfetched that if it came from Alice's mouth no one would have believed it. In small towns there is not much tolerance for eccentric let alone insane.

"Tell me about the visions."

"That was a long time ago Sheriff, most of the images have faded."

"Just give me an impression of what you can recall."

"I remember terrified girls; I could feel their fear and pain. I saw death. The visions always got stronger when I went over to see Irma. Eventually, I stopped going into the house. Until recently that is."

"What about Irma? Did she know what was going on under her roof?"

"I don't think she knew all the details, but she was aware of the fact that whatever they were doing was very wrong. But Anthony was her only child. He was all the family she had left in the world so she pretended everything was perfect. She took precautions and eventually I think she believed her own lies."

"What do you mean by precautions? Was she afraid they would hurt her?"

"Not directly, but she stayed out of the way, cleaned up after them, and stopped growing vegetables in her garden, that sort of thing."

He looked to Sally as if she could shed some light on Alice's comment but she appeared just as confused as he was. "Stopped growing vegetables?"

Alice shook her head yes. "Yes, she did not want to risk getting sick. She threw her passion into flowers and plants after that. Irma was a master gardener you know."

"She did not want to risk getting sick?" He repeated and suddenly recalled what his mother had told him. "Irma was worried the soil was contaminated with arsenic." He asked Alice.

"Arsenic?" Sally repeated as if she had not heard correctly. "Why would there be Arsenic?"

"Legend has it that Mary-Louise Huddelstone poisoned her husband." Alice answered quietly. "One of her maids witnessed Mary-Louise dumping the remaining poison out the pantry window and into the yard. Once, when I was chatting about gardening with Irma, I brought it up again about planting vegetables. I thought that after all these years it would be safe. It was then that she confessed that she caught one of those Harrison boys emptying a bucket out back of what she suspected was dangerous chemicals. All her flowers and plants at that spot shriveled up and died and after that she declared her property unsafe for anything other than flowers and plants." She shook her head. "She didn't want to say it out loud, but we both knew what they were up too."

"What?" Sally asked swiveling her head from Alice to her boss and then back again. "What were they up to?"

"Alice, you should tell us everything you know."

The room was silent for several long seconds.

"I have. I've told you all I know for sure. You've come about Kuster though." Alice stated despondently.

"Yes, we have." He cleared his throat and continued. "He's been missing as I'm sure you're aware of and I know you two are good friends. We haven't heard much from you and wondered what your thoughts were."

"He's dead now." She stated matter- of -factly but he did not miss the flash of pain in her eyes. "I did try to warn him, but it happened anyway."

His gut had already prepared him for this news days ago, but to hear it verbalized was a jolting shock.

"How did you warn him?"

"I read his leaves one day over a cup of Oolong. It was very upsetting. I did my best to caution him but there was not much I could say. His fate was stitched in his soul."

"Can you tell us anything that might help us locate him?" Stan asked when he could finally find his voice.

"No...he's not there anymore. He was moved."

"The killer moved his body? Do you know where?" He stole a quick look at Sally, noting her rare silence and the sickly pallor of her skin.

Alice answered by shaking her head no and they both stared at her, waiting as she began to twist the fabric of her skirt in her hands.

"Alice, do you know where his body was moved from?"

"When Kuster would stop by for a visit, we always sat in this room. We would talk and talk, he was very intelligent you know."

Stan nodded in agreement. "Yes indeed." He could not speak in past tense. Not yet. Not until he saw with his own two eyes but finally he had to ask. "Alice, do you have any idea where Kuster was killed?"

"Oh, yes, across the street, at Bretta's. He waited in the darkness for days, but he's not there anymore."

Chapter 56

"Early risers in this neighborhood." Sally commented as they crossed the street over to the Berryman's house and noticed Bretta's mother standing on her daughter's front porch, as if waiting for them. "Either that or no one sleeps." She was giving it her best hard and seasoned act, but Stan could tell she was swallowing her emotions.

"Good morning, officers, please come in." She held open the door and waved them in.

Luisa led them into the parlor and Stan pushed away that now familiar sensation in his gut when he saw Bretta sitting on the couch, still in that silky nightgown. Unlike her mother, she looked surprised to see him. When their eyes connected he reminded himself of why he was here. She had her cell-phone in her hand as if she were about to make a call.

"I was just about to call you." Bretta held up the phone and he could see she was shaking.

"You were?" Stan asked with concern.

"Bretta's had a nightmare and I have been trying to convince her to go back to bed." Bretta's mother nervously interjected. "But she insisted on speaking to you."

Stan kept his eyes locked with Bretta. "Why don't you tell me about it, Bretta?"

Luisa spoke up quick. "Sherriff, my daughter is overly tired and on pain medication. Why don't you come back tomorrow?"

"I don't even know how to tell you this." Bretta interrupted her mother and her eyes pooled with tears.

"Just tell me." Stan said, not wanting to drag it out longer than necessary.

"John's been here...he said he has been here all along, hiding in the house." She ignored the strange look he shared with Sally and continued. "He was in my bedroom last night after you left, waiting for me. He said Kuster had been killed. I didn't believe him, but he led me to Kuster's body and I saw it for myself, I swear I did."

"Take me to the spot."

"He's not there anymore. When I took my mother there to show her, he was gone and so was my basket. I know this doesn't sound believable, but it happened."

"I need to see where you found him."

"John thinks I did it and he is returning this morning and bringing you... to arrest me."

"Well I'm already here. Do I have your permission to search the house?"

"Yes, of course." She looked anxious, but took care getting to her feet and led the way and for the second time in less than six hours, he helped her up the stairs by scooping her up in his arms. He didn't think about it until he saw the stunned look on Sally's face when he turned back to make sure she was following.

"I'll wait down here." Her mother called up.

"They're going to take my girls away from me and John's going to raise them." She spoke into his neck and he squeezed her tightly to his chest.

"I doubt that very much." He said as he deposited her lightly at the foot of the stairs. "Is it the spot we were at last night?" He asked glancing down the hall towards the linen closet.

"They connect I believe, but John had an easier way in." She led them to the bathroom and the slide out wall was still open, exposing a black hole. "We stepped in here a few feet and then he shinned a light back there so I could see." As if on cue, Sally switched on her flashlight and directed the beam into the darkness.

"What's in all these boxes?" Stan asked as he shone the light on a stack of cardboard boxes and a couple of crates.

"I don't know. They're not mine. I think some of these have been moved, I don't remember seeing them all together like that."

Sally stepped closer and carefully moved the boxes around with her foot. "We've got something here…we need to call the techs." She stepped back around the room, checking the dark corners with her light.

"Bretta, why don't you go on down with Sally and wait." Stan suggested. "We're going to be here awhile."

⅄

The stranger waited patiently for over three hours in a cramped, unwelcoming position. He could wait much longer if he needed to. It was all so captivating, watching the police and the techy people in their pristine white suits come and go. He laughed quietly.

They weren't going to find anything. Contrary to what his brother thought, he did know a thing or two about cleaning up a crime scene. After all, he has been doing it for years.

Chapter 57

After five long, exhausting hours, everyone was gone.

Bretta brought her mother and daughters over to the Muncy's to wait while sci- fi type looking individuals dressed in something that looked like bee suits invaded her property and once the officials gave the okay for them to go back home, Luisa announced she was taking the girls out to breakfast and insisted her daughter go back home for a nap.

She had made it up the stairs on her fanny, scooting one step at a time and once she made it to the top what she needed most she thought, was a bath. The opening had been closed back up and they had to all promise not to move the wall or explore any of the hidden spaces until their investigation was completed which sounded like a bad joke to her. She did not think she would ever want to step foot in there again.

She filled the tub with the hottest water she thought she could tolerate, dumping in a generous scoop of lavender and rosemary bath salts and then one extra scoop to mask the lingering smell of death that was still stuck in her nose. The label promised to transport her to a place of tranquility and bliss however sitting in a tub of seriously hot water always reminded her of cooking live lobsters.

Even though she was alone in the house, she locked the door and removed the key, carefully setting it down on the side of the sink. She took her time undressing before lowering her bottom cautiously into the water, keeping the injured leg as high in the air as possible and then allowing it to rest perched on the edge of the tub.

The hot water felt ridiculously good and it began to work its magic instantly. Anxiety oozed out of her pores. She opted to forgo the jets today and instead treasured the silence. The giant knot at the base of her neck began to soften and she decided she would allow her eyelids to rest, just for a moment.

The house sung shyly with its familiar, soothing sounds. The rhythmic ticking of the Grandfather clock from out in the hall along with all the other creaks and groans blended nicely with the gentle hum of the neighbor's lawn mower producing a reassuring melody that soon made her feel drowsy.

Her head jerked back violently, an unconscious reflex she knew to falling asleep and awaking too fast. The water was still reasonably hot, a good indication that she had not been asleep for long. Not the best place to take a nap she thought as she scooted herself up in a position that wasn't quite so comfy to help resist the temptation of snoozing again when a noise that didn't belong forced her to pause.

Holding her breath, she tried to determine if it was a sound that had awoken her or her own bodies warning mechanism. Her eyes fixated on the locked door, realizing it offered little in the way of a barrier if an intruder was indeed in the house and out to harm her. Suddenly she felt foolish. Of course being all alone in an old house after just finding a body in the next room over was bound to kick up her imagination.

The noise came again and this time it was unmistakable. A slight but real sound that did not go with the house brought her to attention and delivered a warning.

Music began to play from somewhere in the house and familiar notes that she knew well but now found unnerving drifted in from underneath the bathroom door as an uninvited guest.

"*Con te partiro.*" She whispered the title, her hand moving through the cooling water. Yes, it is *Time to Say Goodbye.*

Nothing as vulnerable as a naked, injured woman sitting in a bath tub she thought as she considered her options. She had neglected to bring in the phone. She could not run.

No one would even hear her scream.

The house released a loud, angry creak and she strained her eyes to determine if the thin, dark line that ran the length of the wall was truly separating or only a trick of her panicky mind. Her eyes began to water from her intent gaze and her heart pounded so loud it echoed in her head. She was ready to look away when finally she saw it. The small space was slowly becoming a black gaping hole right before her eyes until it was large enough for her to walk through.

It occurred to her that she ought to do something other than simply stare ahead in frozen disbelief, but not a single sane idea came to her that would be of any use.

"Hello Mrs. Berryman." The voice sprung forth from the other side.

"Hello." She replied with false bravado and moved her good leg leisurely through the water.

"You don't appear too surprised to see me."

"I've been waiting actually."

"You're making this far too easy for me." He said stepping in the room, visibly pleased with her helpless state.

"Haven't I always?"

"Then I guess I should thank you." He replied his face bright with a genuine smile and she watched curiously as he slipped his hands into a pair of black leather gloves.

"You've got this all planned out do you?" She asked, her voice composed and blasé.

"The police will find that you slipped and fell back in the tub, noting of course that you would be unsure footed due to your injury." He replied as an answer. "This will cause you to hit your head, knocking you unconscious and you shall die by drowning."

"You think I didn't know, John?" She asked curiously, not bothering to cover the exposed parts of her body that once upon a time she had offered willingly.

"What is it you think you know?" He had a mildly curious look on his face.

"That you manipulated my mind, slept with my friends, and poisoned my tea."

He raised an eyebrow and waited a few seconds before replying. "Well, kudos to you. You're not as dumb as we all thought."

"The music was a nice touch."

"Music?" He let out an unpleasant chortle. "If you heard music then it must have come from your own crazy head."

"You needed me to buy this house so you could slip back to this town unnoticed." She continued on. "You were confident this would be one of the houses Wanda Bee would show me and that I would fall in love with it. Well you were right about that part. I took one look at this house and had to have it."

"I don't need to waste my breath denying anything now. I grew up envying Tony. He had this beautiful, grand mansion that he never appreciated and while we went from one rented crappy apartment to another." He glanced around the bathroom. "I always said that one day this would all be mine."

"There's one thing about the house I neglected to mention." She stated calmly, as if she were about to confess they were still having issues with the plumbing or the ancient furnace would need to be replaced before winter.

"There's nothing you can tell me about this house that I'm not intimately aware of." He laughed at her. "I have more of a connection to this house than you will ever have."

"Not anymore." A chill slipped through her from the cooling water. "I fell in love with this house so much so that I wanted it all for myself. I purchased it with my own money. Your name is not on it anywhere on the title and when I die it will go to the girls." Now it was her turn to smile. "So your elaborate scheme was nothing more than a big waste of time for you but it did get me a fresh start."

He wasn't amused now and his ugly smile vanished as he glared at her with the hatred she always suspected he felt.

"You're a miserable bitch. I won't feel guilty about killing you. I thought there might be a chance, since you're the mother of my children, but now I know the only emotion I will only experience is euphoria. Well, the joke's on you. After I got rid of Wanda, I left with her briefcase. She didn't rush to file all the paperwork on the sale; I have the deed and the title. You won't be able to *will* something you don't own."

He released a short, angry laugh. "So don't drown yourself patting your own back and deny me that honor. In the end, the house will belong to me and I will have you permanently out of my life."

"Looks to me like you'll still have some competition for this house." She smiled.

"I doubt that."

"You can't actually believe that I killed that Deputy, left him to rot in my attic and then came back and moved his body?" She nodded her head towards her wounded leg. "Even if I wasn't already in this incapacitated state it would be physically impossible."

A veil of pure abhorrence distorted his features while he measured her words. "It had to be one of the others." He said more to himself as he reflected on the implications.

"The others?" She wondered if at last he would tell her. "You mean one of your former playmates?"

He watched her guardedly but said nothing.

"I know about the game." She didn't add that she only knew fragments of it, suspicions that have only recently been confirmed. Evidences she accidently stumbled upon in the attic along with a cryptic message from one of Irma's old journals. It was surprising that the old woman was allowed to live so long.

"The game?" He was testing.

"The game where you kidnapped young innocent girls and held them in the attic, performing unspeakable acts of torture upon them before murdering them." She was wondering which one was the photographer when the next part of the enigma came unexpectedly. It was all so obvious. How could she have not put it all together before? For that matter, how could anyone in this strange town not have put it together? "And then buried them in the little cemetery out back."

He stared into space quietly for a moment while his left hand automatically went to his trouser pocket in search of the ever present coin collection. He looked temporarily dumbfounded to discover his hand was gloved. That could be her next mystery to work on. How in the world did her husband always have a fist full of spare change on his person when he never carried cash? Change is the direct result of using paper currency to pay for your purchases and never in all their years together did she ever see him bother with cash. He insisted on using a credit card to pay for everything, most likely racking up bonus flyer miles to surprise his bimbos with exotic vacations.

"Not that it matters what you think of me, but I didn't have anything to do with the kidnapping or the murdering. That was all Bill's psycho brother."

"So that makes you less guilty?"

"Those girls were going to be killed whether I was there or not, I simply took advantage of an opportunity to further my education. By the time I entered dental school, I was an expert at extractions." He laughed loudly. "Nothing would make me happier than to have you suffer the same fate as the other whores, but your absence would cause too much of a stir. We'll have to stick to my original plan." He nodded confidently as if to solidify his decision and took a giant step to the edge of the tub.

"Around three hundred people die every year by drowning in a bathtub." He announced as he snagged a bottle of her favorite Jo Malone bath oil from the shelf and dumped a generous but not ridiculous amount into her bathwater. "With the slick tub and your incapacitated condition, it will be declared an accidental drowning." Roughly he took ahold of her wounded leg and with a sharp jerk and a twist, lifted it excruciatingly high into the air, forcing her upper body and then her head to slip underwater.

The pain was so shocking at first that her mouth remained open in surprise. Used bathwater rushed to the back of her throat and she instantly clamped it shut. Holding the mouthful of water and her breath, she thrashed about violently to get to the surface when suddenly the grip on her foot relaxed, freeing her to lift her head and sit up on her elbows.

She was neither so strong or so ingenious that she was able to catch this break. His intentions then became transparent; her death would not be swift, painless or easy. He was going to drag it out and enjoy watching her suffer.

"You know what, John?" She sputtered and tried to cough up the bit of water that had still managed find its way to her air passageways despite her attempts. She was proud of her voice that remained uncannily calm. "You were right."

She knew he would allow her to continue. His ego would insist upon hearing any sort of praise or accolade. In a leisurely manner, she scooted her bottom to the back of the tub and used her hands to grip its sides, as if she were attempting to help herself sit upright.

"I do need help. Thank you for making me see that." She coughed again and blinked several times to dry her eyes before reaching to the stack of folded towels on the table next to her to mop her face. "I shouldn't have fought so hard against you. You were only doing what you thought was best for me and the girls." His eyebrows lifted as if to say he knew he was being fed a line of bull.

"I've known for some time now that I am not right. But what is worse, what is so terrifying is that I can't even remember doing some of the things I've done. I realize that it had to have been me that made that dress for that old woman that use to live here and outfitted those little bears. That was indeed my old sewing basket that has resurfaced with a gun in it. I have had to have been to this town before but I can't even say for sure."

She went to mop her forehead when the towel fell from her hand. "Oops." She said simply and then reached for another. "I've been ignoring the obvious for far too long. I am psychotic. I am unwell and possibly insane as you always said."

But instead of grabbing another fluffy white towel, her hand slipped quickly underneath the pile and came back out with a gun. She smiled brightly as she took aim at his face. "But I'm not stupid."

It took a second longer than she thought necessary for him to catch on but once he did, the astonishment that registered on his face was priceless. It was an irrational notion given the severity of the situation, but none the less she couldn't help but think how amusing it would have been to catch this little encounter on film. One of those Vines the kids are always watching on their phones that devoured their data plan. Of course she was probably the only one that would see the humor in this because she was the only one who fully understood the evil he was capable of.

She was certain it had never occurred to him, not even for a moment, that the day's mission would not go precisely as he had orchestrated. If they had more time she would like to hear what he had to say now. Would he beg for his life or say how sorry he was for ruining hers?

"Bretta, surely you don't think I was really going to…" He chuckled out loud as if this had all been one big prank.

"What hurt me? Kill me?"

"I admit I was a bit rough, but you can't think I was serious. I was only trying to scare you."

"I'm too crazy to be scared, remember?"

"Okay, I confess, I toyed with you for so long it became a habit. But we both know there has never been anything wrong with you mentally. You had to have known it was me. I mean seriously…How else would old lady Barrett get one of your old dresses? I was just having fun. I've been at it for years but you are right, it has gone on long enough."

"Let's not forget the cryptic dollhouse."

A wicked smirk illuminated his face. "I thought that was a nice touch." He paused briefly. "Listen, I'm going to turn around and walk out the door." He turned around slowly and faced the opposite wall, his hands held high in the air so she could see them. "I promise you'll never be bothered by me again. You can file for a divorce and live happily ever after with your policeman if you wish. Besides, we both know you won't be able to live with yourself if you kill me."

"Thanks to you, pleading insanity will not be a problem. You made sure everyone knows I am insane and you've had it well documented."

"Bretta, think about this." He started to sound a little apprehensive now. "If you kill me, you will still be put away and not here to raise our beautiful girls. Who will take care of them? Your mother?"

He was right there. Not being here to raise her daughters would kill her and she could hardly shoot him in the back and call it self-defense.

"You know me too well." She sighed, defeated. Although she could not see his face, she was sure it radiated self-satisfaction. "You know I could never pull the trigger. I'll let you leave, but I have a couple of conditions."

"Such as?" He turned only his head in her direction and kept his hands held high.

"I want full custody of the girls. You will not receive a penny of alimony from me, so don't even try. Oh, and I will keep this house. You can have Berrybright Dental for yourself; in fact I want my name off it. That's your fiscal mess and you can deal with it." She did not bother to add that she was well aware that the business was experiencing financial trouble. She suspected he had been using company funds for a kept mistress or blackmail. She did not need to see his expression to recognize his fury. A heated rage seeped from his pores and filled the room like hot steam.

He turned fast, his face red. "You little…" He caught himself when he saw her raise the gun slightly and forced a smile.

"You agree then?"

"Yes, I agree. Come downstairs when you're all dressed and I will sign whatever papers you wish." She watched his eyes relax when she slid the gun back under the towel.

She smiled with satisfaction. "I'm glad we could come to an understanding, I really didn't want to have to kill the father of my children." She began to position herself to get out of the tub. "Now please give me a hand and help me out."

"Fine." He moved forward extending his hand and before she could react, his strong hands were on the top of her head, pushing it forcefully down beneath the water. She had never understood the depths of his hatred until this precise moment and it stunned that his actions felt so personal. She would have thought that her only consideration in a situation such as this would be survival and not this wounded sensation that burrowed deep in her gut.

"You stupid, miserable bitch!" His muffled voice cut through the water. "There wasn't a chance in hell I was going to let you live."

Sparks of white light erupted behind her eyelids and she fought to hold her breath, her lungs screaming in agony.

The brightness faded as she spiraled down a dark tunnel, her thrashing and fighting efforts finally came to a rest and when her body agreed to surrender, his hold slightly relaxed.

From underwater the gunshot blast was deafening and much louder than she had expected.

He was also substantially heavier than she had estimated. It took all her strength to wiggle her left hand out from underneath him and search blindly from below the neatly folded stack of towels until she found her newly acquired mini recorder and turned it to off.

"You made that far too easy for me, Mr. Berryman." Bretta sputtered as she wrestled to maneuver herself to an upright position and heaved her husband's lifeless body off of her.

"I guess I should thank you."

⅄

The silence was unnatural. Normally any amount of time spent with Officer Sally Hiller was filled with chatter, sounds of chewing and a flurry of activity mostly all on her end.

However the drive back to the station had her uncharacteristically quiet and Stan knew why.

"I haven't crossed the line." He spoke up softly to ease into the conversation but even as he said the words he knew that was one big fat lie. He stepped over that line when he stood in Bretta's kitchen and so desperately wanted to kiss her and again, mere hours ago as he lay on top of her, seconds away from entering her.

"I didn't say anything."

"It's you not saying anything that says it all."

She shrugged her shoulders. "Not my business."

He chose for now to leave it alone. What could he say anyway? Don't worry, I came to my senses in the nick of time and climbed off of her.

"Let's drop by the Harrison's. I think we can get Bill to talk now that we have some of the pieces."

The news of a possible Harrison interrogation seemed to cheer her up. Grinning, a bag of salty nuts suddenly appeared in her hands and she began crunching loudly.

"You want me to call him, tell him were on our way?" She asked optimistically, a fine spray of ground chips and spit misted the air.

"Nah, let's keep it informal."

They parked a couple of houses down the street and cut through the Harrison's back yard instead of showing up at his front door. Sally nudged him with her elbow and pointed to the open door on the garage.

"Bill?" Stan gave a light rap on the side door announcing their presence. Everyone was so testy and armed these days. "It's Sheriff Myers, can I come in?" He glanced at Sally who gave him a face for not announcing her presence as well, but she knew the response would be more favorable without her.

He pushed the door open wider which offered a clear view of the covered windows, tools and saws. No Harrison.

"You smell that?" Sally asked, wrinkling her nose.

"Yeah." He replied unhappily and began to search the garage, opening a large cabinet in the corner and lifting up a tarp that was on the ground. When his exploration came up empty, he started out the door leaving Sally to follow.

"Don't you want to go to the house to see Harrison?" Sally called out after her boss.

"Let's check the funeral home first. When we finish up, get the crime scene techs out here. Have them start in the garage."

"Ok. You know it's kinda early…they're probably not open yet." She said referring to the funeral home as she jogged to keep up with him.

Stan approached the side entrance of the funeral home first and tried the door, this time without knocking and let himself in. Down the hall and on the right, a light shone out from an open door and sounds of movement wafted out.

Bill Harrison stood over a casket with his back towards the door, fussing with the final resting position of an elderly gentleman.

"Hey Bill, guess you didn't hear us knocking out there." Stan finally said after a few seconds of observing and watched him visibly startle.

Bill jumped in the air and spun around in genuine shock and put his hand on his heart dramatically. "Sheriff! You scared the living daylights out of me!"

"Sorry about that Bill. We were out and about and thought we'd stop by to ask you a few questions."

"Rather early isn't it?" He quickly closed the casket and stepped over to his visitors.

Stan gave a nonchalant shrug of his shoulders. He must be rattled by their visit; he didn't seem annoyed by Sally's presence. "We start work pretty early these days." He paused briefly before continuing. "Looks like you do too." Stan's eyes shot down the funeral directors petite frame.

Harrison's eyes widened, his face quickly turning crimson to match his fancy bathrobe when he remembered that he showed up for work today in his smoking robe.

"Well, yes. I had a few last minute details to attend to for Mr. Jamerson. In fact I do not have much time; he has family coming this morning to pay their final respects."

"This won't take long." Sally said, speaking up for the first time directly to Harrison who was discharging weird, guilty vibrations into the atmosphere.

"Well, let's step in my office then." He quickly moved away from the casket and waved them both out the door. "It's across the hall, second door." He announced a little too loudly as he closed the door behind him.

Once in his office, he went directly over to his coffee station and clicked on the electric tea kettle and began his fussing with his coffee gadgets.

"Do you recall that back in the late seventies, several young girls were reported missing?" Stan paused and watched Bill's hand freeze in midair. "They were last seen not far from here."

"Really? No, I don't recall hearing about that." He went back to his coffee making sideshow and Stan watched the ugly vein on the mortician's temple began to agitate.

"We know about the game, Bill."

"The game?" He attempted to look confused but panic swept across his face and the previous flush of color swiftly drained.

"The sick and twisted game that you, John Berryman or Johnny Adams as he was known back then, and Anthony Barrett made up so you could each act out your demented fantasies. The one where you kidnapped at least three young women tortured and eventually killed them in the attic at Huddelstone." From behind Bill's back Sally gave a surprised look.

"I don't know what you are talking about…"

Stan interrupted him. "Certain types of men don't fare well in prison. They get passed around roughly, it becomes a game. Bob's going to be able to take care of himself but you…" He stopped and shook his head in repulsion. "You won't stand a chance." He stopped talking and let the silence drag out.

"I'm sure I have no idea of what you are talking about." Bill struggled to get the words out.

"Wanda left a letter, did you know that? It was just discovered late yesterday."

"Wanda was a greedy, lying bitch and everyone knows that! Even if any of this nonsense had the slightest bit of truth to it, you have to realize by now that I have no interest in females." His eyes bore into the man in front of him.

"I think each participant had their own reason."

"Where's your brother?" Sally asked.

"My brother?" The question appeared to have caught him off guard. "I assume he's in his room sleeping, he's not an early riser."

"Let's go have a chat with him. Is your mother up?" Stan held the door open for Bill and he reluctantly stepped into the hall and walked towards the exit.

"Mother stays up watching old movies, pops an Ambien and then sleeps till noon." He said bitterly.

All three had reached the exit door when Stan abruptly stopped, turned around and headed hurriedly back down the hall to the room Bill had been working in when they first arrived.

"Sherriff! Whatever are you doing?" Bill shrieked.

By the time Bill and Sally caught up with him, Stan had the lid lifted on the casket and was frantically pulling at the lining.

Bill lurched forward but Sally was quicker, firmly reaching for his arm and holding him in place. "Please remain where you are, Mr. Harrison."

"Jesus Christ!" Stan shouted and jumped back. Slowly, he turned back around and the murderous look in his eyes made Sally tighten her grip painfully.

"Please, I didn't do it." Bill began to whimper.

"Get him out of here." Stan yelled over his shoulder to Sally. "I'm going to look for Bob."

"I swear it was all Bob." Bill sobbed. "He's the one that killed your Deputy and poor Mrs. Barrett."

"Cuff him, read him his rights before he says anything else and throw him in the back of the car."

"Stan…" Something in Sally's voice made him stop and turn back. "We just got a call. You need to get over to the Berryman's, I'll take over here."

Chapter 58

"Bretta?" She could hear Stan's authoritative voice shouting out her name from somewhere in the house and then her mother directing him to the bathroom. Knowing that Stan had arrived calmed her. He could take over now. Her mother could help her dress and clean all the ugliness out of the room and at last, she would be free.

His eyes scanned the room swiftly and she caught his visible relief at finding her to be unharmed. He drew his gaze away from hers and took it around the room to put the pieces of the puzzle together.

"I shot him." Her voice was unrecognizable to her own ears and came out thick and mumbled. She wondered if he even understood what she had said. "He was trying to kill me."

"Don't say anything until your lawyer gets here." Stan warned.

"I think this will say it all." Bretta said as she offered the recorder to Stan.

"When you have eliminated the impossible, whatever remains, however improbable, must be the truth."

-Arthur Conan Doyle, 1859-1930

Epilogue

"And he walks *with me, and he talks with me and he tells me I am his own…*" Alice had a lovely singing voice and her sweet song drifted about the yard like a gentle breeze.

"Alice…what are you doing?" Bretta asked affectionately as she approached the old cemetery behind her house to find her friend kneeling in the grass, a tiny trowel in her hand. She did not know what was more surprising to her, the fact that her neighbor was digging around in the graveyard behind her house or that today she was wearing denim overalls instead of one of the unusual and somewhat peculiar dresses she favored.

"Planting lavender. I wanted to do it last year, but it was too late in the season." She answered without turning around and reached for another plant. "Lavender represents harmony, love, and joy and these poor souls deserve to finally be at rest. Their remains may have been taken away but their spirit will stay on. Plus, I'll be buried here next and I've always been partial to Lavender." Her head spun around quickly so that Bretta could see her noticeably distraught face. "You will permit me to be buried here, won't you? Irma always said I could."

"It's fine by me, but I'll speak with Athena and make sure whatever documents needed are in place." In truth, she had no idea if someone could still be buried in this cemetery, but she certainly would look into it as promised.

Satisfied, Alice went back to work and she watched wordlessly as the small but sturdy shovel broke through the soil again to make ready for the next plant.

"And the Daisies?" Bretta quizzed with a lazy smile and dropped down to the ground next to her friend. "What's their meaning?"

Alice stopped digging and turned to face her, looking oddly solemn.

"Daisies are for keeping secrets."

"You have one of their secrets, Alice?" Bretta asked curiously as she gave a nod towards the grave markers that were only yesterday put properly back in place and now included the names of all four victims as a special memorial.

"No dear." Alice grabbed a fist full of dirt and clasped it tightly in her hand. "I hold one of yours." She admitted, smiling sweetly.

"What?" Bretta gasped, unsure if she had heard correctly.

"I've always loved a good mystery. I used to be an avid reader in my youth; I still am during the long winter months when I can't get to my garden." Her hand opened and she allowed the soil to slip through her fingers. "Even though I figure out the ending before I get through the second chapter."

A shiver skidded down her spine when Alice hesitated and she began to anticipate her next words.

"I guessed the ending here too, not long after you moved in." She stopped talking and plucked a single Daisy, bringing it to her nose.

"What secret, Alice?" Bretta tested.

"They call that pre-meditated murder, when you plan out a murder in advance. I read all about it in an Agatha Christie novel years ago." Alice said proudly and rested her dirty hands on her lap.

She sat in stunned silence and stared at her friend.

"You did what had to be done. Your husband was an evil man." Alice kept her voice reassuring while she went back to precisely tucking each plant in its new bed.

"Alice..."

"Now don't you worry, I'm not going to breathe a word of this to another living soul. Not even Athena." She shook her head rapidly back and forth, reminding Bretta of her daughter Ivy when she was little and said no to everything. "Especially Athena; she thinks it's her born duty to keep every citizen in town well informed." She deliberately changed the topic. "Sherriff Stan is about to pull up in front of the house any second. I know you're sweet on him and I'm glad, he's a fine man, but you can't let this eat at you. Chances are he's got it all figured anyway. If you go and confess, he'll have to do something about it."

"I suppose so."

There was nothing more to say on the subject and she agreed with her friend. It was time to move on. Almost all of the bizarre mysteries that plagued Chester have been unraveled minus a few unexplained events. Betty the dispatcher's body had been discovered in the lake behind John's condo and Bill Harrison confessed that all the killings, except for Deputy Kuster, had actually been committed in the barn. As soon as she received the go ahead, she had the outbuilding torn down and the hidden room connected to her bathroom permanently sealed off.

She left Alice and made her way to the front of the house in time to see Stan climbing out of his vehicle. He looked rugged but still incredibly handsome in his khaki cargo shorts and an army green t-shirt that she saw did marvelous things to his eyes.

"You ready?" He asked with a smile, visibly happy to see her and produced a bouquet of yellow and white daisies from behind his back. "From my mother's garden."

"Thank you! They are lovely." She quickly tried to cover her shock over his flower choice. "Yes, I'm ready." She returned the smile easily and felt that familiar flutter in her stomach. "Let me grab a light jacket, just in case. Are you sure I can't pack up something for us?"

"I have everything we'll need, two picnic baskets full as a matter of fact."

That surprised her. "Two? Wow, I'm impressed and thankful because I'm starving." She wasn't exaggerating; she had been running around all morning and skipped breakfast.

"Well don't be too impressed, my mother helped me." He confessed with a sheepish grin. "She wants to meet you by the way."

"That would be nice. I would like that. So, where are we going?" She inquired as he opened the passenger door for her and she paused in front of him, inches from his freshly shaven face. He smelled really good and she was overcome with a strong urge to reach out and lightly caress his cheek. He stood still in front of her with their eyes locking and she felt a fire in her belly light so fast it took her breath away.

"I thought we'd head on over to one of my favorite hang outs." He finally responded, a bit breathlessly as he pointed to the fishing boat attached to his car as if to explain his companion's presence. "Drift around awhile and then stop when we find a spot for a picnic."

"That sounds delightful." It was a perfect late spring day with a vivid blue, cloudless sky and the heat from the sun quickly swept away any lingering chill in the air. She felt a flash of guilt at how much she had been looking forward to their first official date. They stayed clear of each other all last fall and during the long, brutal winter while all of John's dirty secrets, including the fact that he had a mistress were made public knowledge. When they did meet, they had kept things strictly professional. But today all that was behind them and she could clearly feel the difference. Today was a date and she had wondered if the heat they had once felt would take a bit of effort to reignite or if there had been anything real there at all. She could see now that she had nothing to worry about.

As if he was reading her thoughts, he put his hand behind her head and brought her face towards his. His kiss was deep, urgent and wonderful. She had never been left with such wanting from a kiss before, not that she could recall, not one that mattered.

He reluctantly moved his lips to the side of her head, his hot breath buzzing delightfully in her ear. "Let's get out of here." He gently bit her lobe. "Before I do something scandalous to you right here on the front lawn."

With his hand pressing on the small of her back, he ushered her into the car and within seconds they were on their way.

"I swear if everyone in town didn't recognize my car, I would park it right behind those trees over there." He pointed to a wooded area as they drove quickly away from her neighborhood.

He did not need to say what was on his mind, his intentions were completely clear. She felt a reckless rush of desire and was about to suggest that they go directly to his house when she realized they had already exited the town and were turning down a dirt road.

"I feel like a teenager." He said once he found the perfect spot near the lake, swung his car and trailer around and backed up expertly. "I want to tear your clothes off your body right here and now. I want it so bad, my hands are shaking. But I have something more romantic in mind." He opened the car door and she followed him out, watching in awe as he skillfully unhitched the boat and got it into the water in what she thought was record breaking time. His lips grazed her cheek softly as he helped her into the boat and before she knew it, they were drifting about the lake. A bottle of wine magically appeared and as she made herself comfortable on the cushioned seat she felt her body relax.

"I know I have a wine opener in here somewhere." She heard Stan say and she opened her eyes to observe him digging in one of the baskets. It was then that she noticed there was a third basket behind the other two. She had not exaggerated earlier when she said she was hungry but seriously, how much food could two people eat?

"Is that dessert in that little basket?" She inquired playfully.

"No, it's not." He admitted. "I stumbled upon this one at Alice's house." He stretched forward to retrieve the basket and then placed it on her lap. "She asked that I return it to you."

It took only an instant to identify the familiar relic from her past and she wondered how in the world it ended up back in Alice's possession. Calmly she lifted the lid and a strong sense of nostalgia caught her breath. The ruby red pin cushion, the small pair of rusty scissors, and the cloth measuring tape had all helped shape her future profession. Carefully, she picked up each item and held it in her hand to examine it before noticing a photograph near the bottom.

Her heart began to strike fiercely within her chest as her shaky hand pulled out the photo. She studied the unrecognizable image of a much younger version of herself and tried to recall when it was taken or who the girl in the photo standing next to her was. She estimated it had to have been in her teens but the way too short of a dress she was wearing and even her hairstyle did not look at all familiar.

"Bretta." Stan spoke her name tenderly and took a hold of her trembling hand. "Take a look at the house you are standing in front of."

She looked past her image at the large house when suddenly it came to her. "No…that can't be possible." Her stomach reeled and she felt the urge to run. Maybe that was why Stan waited until they were in the boat to show her this.

"You're standing in front of Huddelstone." He waited for the words to sink in and perhaps even, trigger a memory.

"No, that can't be Huddelstone…or it was photoshopped. I had never even stepped foot into this town before last year when I came house hunting." Surely she would remember visiting this strange town and when she glanced up at Stan it became clear that he knew something that she did not.

"When you were a teenager, your mom sent you to a Christian summer camp called Lake Love." He paused to see her reaction. "Do you remember that?"

"No." She denied, shaking her head no but a flash of a memory came to her anyway and then quickly fled. "Believe me, my mother was not the sort to send me to bible camp."

"She did Bretta, I spoke with her." He was using his soothing, police tone with her which today she did not find reassuring. "You met a friend there named Carrie Hines. The two of you went on an afternoon walk and never returned back to camp."

"I've never been to camp before and I don't know anyone by the name of Carrie Hines." None of this made sense. She wanted to yell at him that he had this all wrong but she knew Stan was the type that would have checked out all his facts before making such a statement.

"You and Carrie met up with a group of teenage boys and they brought you to town. She never returned but you managed to escape on foot where you were eventually picked up along the side of the highway by an older couple."

"If this were true, I would have some memory of this. My mother would have told me."

"You had a head injury and once you recovered, you did not remember anything that happened. Your mother wanted to protect you so she kept quiet about it and the two of you went on as if it never happened. But in the long run, that never works out because your subconscious knows the truth."

As if her subconscious wanted to prove a point, her head began to throb and her hand automatically went to the scar and in that instant, she knew what he was saying was true. She looked down at the photo again, this time carefully studying each face.

"That is Carrie Hines standing beside you." Stan offered.

"John was one of those teenage boys, wasn't he?" She asked.

"Yes."

"No, none of this makes sense." She wasn't willing to accept all of this yet. "My mother would never allow me to marry John if she knew this."

"We only just discovered who the boys were through Bill Harrison's confession; your mother had no way of knowing. I believe John came looking for you because you were a loose end, but once he met you he realized you were not a threat. You were however a way to fund his ambitions. You paid for his dental school and financed his franchises. It was the perfect solution for him; he had access to all your money while monitoring you up close in case you remembered anything. I think when you would start to recall something; he would drug you and tell you that you had mental issues. And by declaring to everyone he could that you were mentally unstable, it made anything you said doubtful."

"I…I don't know what to say." She stammered.

"You're not crazy." He affirmed with a smile, pulling her into his arms. "You never were."

Crazy as a fox maybe she thought slyly to herself.

It had taken her some time, longer than it probably should have given the fact that her brain had been cleared from the drugs and the brainwashing. It wasn't until that day up in the attic when she discovered the box of photos, including one of herself, that the gates of hell were opened.

In that one moment she remembered John.

It was astonishing the way the human mind worked. How it could manipulate thoughts and memories if it was influenced to do so.

Briefly she had toyed with the idea of turning John in right then and there, however her allegations were outlandish and had lacked facts. Plus, it was extremely likely that she would only sound even crazier and he would slip away unscathed.

In the end she did have enough evidence on her little recorder to send him away for a very long time but she felt that way would be harder on her girls.

Planning out his murder turned out to be great therapy. She felt fantastic.

She did feel guilty for not being truthful with Stan but perhaps Alice was right; he might have already figured it all out on his own. He seemed like the type that would be good at keeping secrets too.

That was probably why he brought her the daisies.

66118086R00196

Made in the USA
Columbia, SC
20 July 2019